Real Vampires Don't Diet

GERRY BARTLETT

B

BERKLEY BOOKS, NEW YORK

THE BERKLEY PUBLISHING GROUP
Published by the Penguin Group
Penguin Group (USA) Inc.
375 Hudson Street, New York, New York 10014, USA
Penguin Group (Canada), 90 Eglinton Avenue East, Suite 700, Toronto, Ontario M4P 2Y3, Canada
(a division of Pearson Penguin Canada Inc.)
Penguin Books Ltd., 80 Strand, London WC2R 0RL, England
Penguin Group Ireland, 25 St. Stephen's Green, Dublin 2, Ireland (a division of Penguin Books Ltd.)
Penguin Group (Australia), 250 Camberwell Road, Camberwell, Victoria 3124, Australia
(a division of Pearson Australia Group Pty. Ltd.)
Penguin Books India Pvt. Ltd., 11 Community Centre, Panchsheel Park, New Delhi—110 017, India
Penguin Group (NZ), 67 Apollo Drive, Rosedale, North Shore 0632, New Zealand
(a division of Pearson New Zealand Ltd.)
Penguin Books (South Africa) (Pty.) Ltd., 24 Sturdee Avenue, Rosebank, Johannesburg 2196,
South Africa

Penguin Books Ltd., Registered Offices: 80 Strand, London WC2R 0RL, England

This is an original publication of The Berkley Publishing Group.

This is a work of fiction. Names, characters, places, and incidents either are the product of the author's imagination or are used fictitiously, and any resemblance to actual persons, living or dead, business establishments, events, or locales is entirely coincidental. The publisher does not have any control over and does not assume any responsibility for author or third-party websites or their content.

First edition: January 2009

Library of Congress Cataloging-in-Publication Data

Bartlett, Gerry
    Real vampires don't diet / Gerry Bartlett.—1st ed.
        p. cm.
    ISBN 978-0-425-22564-6
    1. Saint Clair, Glory (Fictitious character)—Fiction.   2. Vampires—Fiction.   3. Rock musicians—
Fiction.   4. New Year—Fiction.   5. Parties—Fiction.   I. Title.   II. Title: Real vampires do not diet.

PS3602.A83945R423 2009
813'.6—dc22   2008043276

PRINTED IN THE UNITED STATES OF AMERICA

10   9   8   7   6   5   4   3   2   1

6/09

Real Vampires Live Large

"The return of ancient vampiress Glory surviving in a modern world is fun to follow as she struggles with her lover, a wannabe lover, vampire killers and Energy Vampires; all want a piece of her in differing ways. Fans of lighthearted paranormal romps will enjoy Gerry Bartlett's fun tale starring a heroine who has never forgiven Blade for biting her when she was bloated." —*Midwest Book Review*

"Outstanding . . . equal parts humor and spice, with mystery and adventure tossed into the mix. Glory's world is a place I look forward to visiting again, the sooner the better." —*Fresh Fiction*

"Gerry Bartlett has created a laugh-out-loud book that I couldn't put down. *Real Vampires Live Large* is a winner." —*The Romance Readers Connection*

"Glory gives girl power a whole new meaning, especially in the undead way. What a fun read!" —*All About Romance*

Real Vampires Have Curves

"A sharp, sassy, sexy read. Gerry Bartlett creates a vampire to die for in this sizzling new series." —Kimberly Raye, *USA Today* bestselling author of *Just One Bite*

"Hot and hilarious. Glory is Everywoman with fangs." —Nina Bangs, *New York Times* bestselling author of *Wicked Fantasy*

"Full-figured vampire Glory bursts from the page in this lively, fun and engaging spin on the vampire mythology." —Julie Kenner, *USA Today* bestselling author of *Deja Demon*

continued . . .

For my mother,
Willys McKay,
always my main cheerleader and role model.
Thanks, Mama,
for always being there.

One

"Of course I understand. No problem. Have a nice trip." I snapped the phone closed and thought about throwing it against the wall. But at that moment, I loved my state-of-the-art cell a lot more than I loved Angus Jeremiah Campbell III, who in recent centuries has called himself Jeremy Blade. The phone rang. I knew who it was, and if I didn't answer, he'd just keep trying.

"Yes?"

"Are you angry? You hung up on me."

"Oh? Ya think? I guess I missed the part where you invited me to come along." I glanced at the three dresses I'd laid out trying to decide what to wear tonight. New Year's Eve. Yep, he'd broken our date for New Year's frickin' Eve. No biggie.

"I just assumed—"

"Of course. I have a business to run. End-of-year inventory. You name it. Can't get away right now. But, hey, telling you that would have involved a discussion. We don't have those." Why in the hell did I ever think I wanted the strong, silent type?

"Gloriana, calm down. I'll be shifting. You know you don't want to—"

"Right. You're in a tearing hurry. Not that I need to know why of course. Just be careful and don't let a hunter shoot you down." My boyfriend shape-shifts into a hawk to do his traveling. Dangerous. And, even mad, I felt my stomach turn just thinking about Jerry flying alone across an ocean. Damned impossible man. Me, I prefer something with a seat belt and air bags.

"You're mad. But I promise I'll make it up to you when I get back. Drive the Mercedes while I'm gone. I left it in the alley for you."

Okay, that was a nice peace offering. My own car was currently DOA. "Do you have any idea when you'll be back?"

"No. Lily could be anywhere. Mara called and said our daughter's running with a pack of dangerous radicals. Her boyfriend's set himself up as leader of the group. I've got to find Lily before she gets herself staked. My first stop will be Paris to see if Mara has found out a more specific location."

Mara. Of course. That's where Jerry's sudden rush to take flight had come from. Mara had been married to Jerry's best friend. But recently, since Mac's death, she'd "confessed" that her daughter Lily was really Jerry's child. Personally I think it's a hoax created by a woman hot to have Jerry for herself.

He'll do the DNA thing, but just hearing the way he'd said "*our* daughter" made it clear Jerry was deep into protective father mode. Typical. He'd made me vampire back in the day, the early 1600s actually, and has been protecting me, not to mention playing the passionate lover whenever I let him, ever since.

"All right. Go. And happy birthday. I'll give you your present when you get back." I blinked back sudden tears. I do love Jerry, and I hated the fact that he was going to have to cross the Atlantic and land in the middle of a bunch of vampires who thought stirring up mortals against us was good, clean fun. I hoped this "daughter" was worth it.

"You got me a present?"

I didn't blame Jerry for sounding skeptical. My funds

were always pretty limited. But I'd had a fairly decent Christmas season in my shop, Vintage Vamp's Emporium.

"Yes. And not just me naked on satin sheets either." Though he never seemed to mind that gift.

Jerry groaned. "Now you're making me want to come over there and—"

"If you're going to beat the sun, you'd better hit the skies, Jerry." I sighed and looked down as I felt a warm, furry body press against my legs—my dog and bodyguard, Valdez, a shape-shifter with a little something extra. "Take care. Seriously. Call me every night."

"I will. I love you, Gloriana."

Now how could I stay mad when a reticent Scotsman busts out a declaration like that? "I love you too, Jerry. Happy New Year." This time I closed the phone gently. I looked down at Valdez. "What? No snort? We were getting pretty mushy there."

"Sounded right to me. Blade's your guy and don't you forget it, no matter who else makes a move on you while he's gone." Valdez trotted into the living room. *"Since we're obviously staying in tonight, how about a movie? Something with action."*

"Might as well. That's obviously all the action either of us is going to get." I scooped up the dresses, the best my vintage-clothing shop had had to offer in a size twelve, and hung them back in the closet. I took a moment to rub my cheek on the midnight blue velvet, which matched my eyes. Nice low-cut bodice. I figured Jerry would have had it off me long before midnight. The red was made for dancing: swingy skirt, another low neckline. I've got the goods and know how to use them. As for the black . . . I liked the way it slimmed my hips, enough said.

Action. I thought about putting on my flannel jammies and really vegging out, but my roommate might drop in. Not that she was really living here anymore, but she and her new—I couldn't believe it—husband still had a closetful of shoes to collect. I was sorting through my DVD collection and threatening Valdez with *The Devil Wears Prada* when the phone rang.

"Hello." I hadn't even glanced at the caller ID. That's how depressed I was.

"Glory, I think you need to get over here. Right now."

"Brittany?" I felt Valdez practically hanging over my shoulder. He had a thing for the shape-shifter who served as bodyguard for another vamp in Austin, a rock star who was turned recently in a pretty nasty trick. I'd taken on the role of mentor because I'd felt kind of responsible for his condition. Long story. "What's going on?"

"A party. Typical rock-star blowout apparently. And guess who's getting drunk off his ass?"

"Will?" This could be a problem. Will Kilpatrick is a vamp I'd recommended to serve as another bodyguard for Israel Caine. Caine is routinely hounded by paparazzi and girl groupies. Yeah, tough life.

"Of course Will, but worse than that. Ray's drinking too."

"God, no." Ray—Israel's nickname—is a made vampire. Like me. Turned by another vampire. We can't eat or drink anything but blood. Alcohol can make us really, really sick. After the fact. Not during. So Ray could be knocking back shots and think he was okay for a while. But later . . .

"He went on a rant about how he was tired of watching everyone else have a good time and how it was New Year's Eve, then he started hitting the Jack Daniel's. The mortals thought he was just falling off the wagon." Brittany sighed and I could hear yelling in the background. "Now they're all drunk and talking about going out on the lake."

"Do whatever you can to keep them there in the house. Valdez and I will be right over." I turned off the phone and jumped up. Mercedes keys. I kept my spare set in a kitchen drawer. Valdez already had his leash in his mouth and was sitting by the door when I grabbed my coat and purse.

I wished I could change clothes. Put on one of those sexy dresses. But my snug black jeans and the low-cut blue sweater that matched my eyes weren't too bad. Not exactly New Year's Eve glitz, but when I threw a sparkly silver knit scarf around my throat, I felt slightly less pathetic. Besides, I was on a mission here.

"This is bad, Valdez. That idiot could actually succeed in killing himself, and he's supposed to be immortal." For the second time that night, I felt tears fill my eyes. For a badass vampire, I was turning into a real wuss.

"Aw, Ray'll be all right, Blondie. Probably have the mother of all hangovers; that's all. Let's go. This will be a hell of a lot better than spending New Year's Eve watching one of your chick-flick DVDs."

"You would say that. You'll get to be with your honey." I opened the door, and we headed down the stairs. As usual, Valdez checked out the alley before we ran to the car and jumped in. I felt a real urgency. I liked Ray and hated to think he'd end up breaking his damned neck on the lake. Vampires can heal from a lot of things, but a broken neck . . . ? Not sure. I'd hate to put it to the test.

I drove through the Austin hills to the area where Ray rented a house on top of a cliff, complete with elevator down to a boat dock. I pulled up to a circular driveway filled with cars. Bad sign. Since Ray didn't hang out with other vampires, this meant he was surrounded by his band buddies, rockers who were used to his hard drinking.

Brittany met us at the door. "I kept them here, but it wasn't easy. I hid the boat keys, but—wouldn't you know?—mind-reading Ray just found them. Hurry. They're in the den, downstairs."

The den was a massive room down a curved staircase. A two-story wall of windows framed a view of Lake Travis, the twinkling lights of houses outlining the water. The men and women lounging on the leather furniture scattered around the room didn't spare the breathtaking view a glance. Music pounded from large speakers, and a drummer used his sticks on a black lacquered coffee table. Three couples danced across the tile floor until one of them broke off and headed for the stairs, brushing past me with barely a nod. They were clearly into each other and looking for a bedroom.

I turned to say something to Valdez, but he and Brittany were still by the front door, whispering. Well, hell. I guess I was on my own. I spotted Ray standing on the balcony. I took a moment to just look at him. The sexy heartthrob whose poster had stopped me dead in the middle of an Austin mall one night was not a happy camper if the way he was tossing back the Jack straight from the bottle was any indication.

I stepped off the stairs and headed for him when a hand shot out and grabbed me around the waist.

"Dance with me, darlin'." Will swung me around. He was clearly drunk.

Damn born vampire. He wouldn't even have a hangover. "Out of my way, Kilpatrick." I pushed him and he staggered. "Fine bodyguard you are. Ray's out there on the balcony presenting a target for whoever feels like taking a shot, and you're in here getting drunk off your ass." I gave him another shove, and he landed on a couch.

"My night off, sugar. Tell it to Brittany." The idiot grinned and grabbed the woman sitting next to him. She didn't seem to mind, and I turned on my heel in disgust.

I dropped my coat and purse on a chair, then stepped out into the cold night air. I closed the French door and stood beside Ray.

"Rough night?"

"Not at all." He smiled his famous guaranteed-to-seduce-you smile and winked. "In fact, it just got even better. Looking good, Glory." He took another swig from the bottle. "You here to kiss me at midnight?"

Would you believe it? I felt myself flush like a grade-school groupie. "No, I'm here to keep you from doing something stupid." I gestured at the bottle. "That working for you, Ray?"

"Hell, no." He held up the bottle. "It tastes the same, but I'm not even feeling a buzz. What's that about?"

Ray might not be feeling a buzz, but I sure was. Inside, someone had put on one of his love songs. There were some groans, but then the lights dimmed and I could see people pairing off, slow dancing to the seductive tune. Good distraction from talk of midnight boat rides. While Ray sang with the kind of passion that made a woman turn to liquid right where it counts, the men obviously figured it was time for some indoor sport.

The last time we'd been alone together, Ray had even made some moves toward me. If I weren't involved with Jerry . . . Well, Israel Caine was and *is* temptation wrapped in a delicious package.

I deliberately blocked out all sexy sounds—thoughts, whatever—and focused on the problem at hand. Ray was still making serious inroads on that bottle. He was my responsibility.

"Listen, Ray. You want a buzz?" I glanced over my shoulder, but with the glass doors closed and a general lack of attention from inside, I was sure no one could hear me. "Bite one of your mortal buds in there." That got Ray's attention. I make no secret of the fact that I'm strictly a synthetic-blood drinker. No biting mortals for me.

"What the hell?"

"I mean it. You'll get the buzz. But I have to warn you: If you suck down enough blood from a drunk, you'll have a hell of a hangover later. Booze is like poison to you now. And that really wicked hangover will last days, maybe weeks. You've got obligations after the first of the year, don't you? Can you afford to feel like death warmed over for that long?"

Ray looked away from me to stare at the water again. "Yeah, obligations. Always. People depending on me. Fans wanting a piece of me. And now that I'm a freakin' vampire, I have to do it all at night." He barked out a laugh. "Man, welcome to my piss-poor pity party, Gloriana St. Clair."

"You're entitled. Lucky played a damned dirty trick on you." Lucky. A vampire who'd turned Ray in her own little revenge drama, then dumped him on me. I looked at Ray's perfect profile. At the long, dark hair that drifted over his shoulders. His white silk shirt blew in the slight wind off the lake and showed off his buff bod. He was tall and lean in worn jeans, his feet bare. Long, narrow feet. My heart thumped, and I reminded myself I was supposed to be immune. Because of Jerry. Of course I was.

"You know, I always denied I had a drinking problem, but I was really thinking about checking myself into rehab before this happened." Ray set the bottle on the wooden rail, grimaced, then tipped it over. We both watched it tumble down until it hit the rocks below and shattered into dozens of pieces.

"I'm sorry, Ray." And not a bit surprised. I devoured anything the tabloids printed about Ray. His drinking had been a hot topic. "Didn't you promise me a boat ride once?" Yeah, I was a sucker for a sob story. Besides, Ray *wasn't* drunk. And I figured it wouldn't hurt to offer him a distraction.

"You want to go? Seriously?" He smiled, suddenly looking alive again, as if the pity party had never happened.

"If you meant it when you said you weren't even feeling the buzz."

"Yeah. Let me prove it. Believe me, I've been through the drill dozens of times. You can ask my lawyer." Ray walked a straight line, then did the fingers to the nose thing. "Want me to count too?"

"No, I believe you. Valdez says you have an elevator down to the boat dock."

"It's right over here. Let's ditch the bodyguards. Just you and me. Are you up for it? Or don't you think we'll be safe?" He grinned, probably expecting me to be my usual cautious self.

"I can swim, sort of. You can swim." I'd seen the butt shot of him skinny-dipping in *Star Snoops*. "What kind of trouble can we get into out in the middle of a lake late at night?" Would you like a list? Sometimes I can be such an idiot.

Two

"Nice boat, Ray," I shouted as we roared across the lake. Leave it to rock star Israel Caine to have one of those lethal-looking speedboats. It was a sexy red with white leather seats and noisy as hell. Bet his neighbors loved his late-night rides. Me, not so much.

"Not cold, are you?" Ray grinned and turned the wheel so we were heading away from the lights of several houses clustered along the shore.

"What do you take me for? A wimp? Or do you just want me to come closer?" Vampires don't get cold. A nice perk along with immortality, something to do with our metabolism. I watched the wind press Ray's silk shirt against him, a good distraction from the way the boat was hitting the water. I gripped the chrome rail to prevent being tossed overboard. "My hair's going to be wild."

"Watch it, Wonder Woman, you're bending the handrail." Ray throttled back the engine until we were practically coasting in the darkness. "Closer is good. And I like my women wild." He reached over and brushed some curls from my face. "But I think you know that."

"Yeah. I read the fanzines and the blogs." I tried for a

careless shrug. Tough when his fingers lingered near my left ear. "Since we've become an item, I can't seem to help myself." Long story. Pretending to be Ray's flavor of the month had explained my involvement in his life while I tried to teach him what he needed to know as a new vampire.

Since I could stand to lose a few pounds, especially in the hip area, I'm a novelty in rock-star world. The tabloids had started a "Glory watch" and chubby women everywhere had clasped me to their well-endowed bosoms. Several blogs were dedicated to me too. Yeah, to not-so-little old me. Cool, huh?

"They'll move on as soon as another drunk star plows a Bentley into a tree. Don't get too hung up on the hype." Ray's hand slid off my cheek and he peered into the darkness. "Did you hear something?"

Besides the pounding of my heart and my inner slut screaming at me to jump Ray's way too sexy bones? I shook my head. Damn. He'd decided to hold on to the chrome steering wheel instead of me.

"Listen, Glory. I think someone's calling for help." He pointed in front of us. "What the hell's that?"

I jerked my brain into drive and looked around. A strange light shimmered and floated a few feet above the water just yards away. I'm not easily spooked and unless the mother ship appeared in front of us, I was more interested in Ray right now than fog and reflections.

"Spirits maybe. I've heard there are sacred Indian burial grounds on the shore of Lake Travis." I'm down with spirits. Two ghosts call my shop home. "Hippie Hollow's along here too. Customers say it was a popular area for skinny-dipping back in the sixties." Was I hinting? Hmm. When Ray didn't ask for directions, I shut up and listened. I'll be damned. I did hear a faint plaintive cry for help.

"Cut the engine, Ray. You're right. I do hear someone."

Ray turned off the engine and we both listened intently. Except for the slap of the water against the hull, it was eerily silent.

"He . . . lp. Pleeeease help meee." The voice was high-pitched and singsongy.

I slapped my hands over my bleeding ears, then sucked it up and looked around the lake, trying to pinpoint the direction the voice had originated from. It seemed to have no relation to the floating light that had drifted away like a phosphorescent cloud. I glanced at Ray.

"Can you tell where it's coming from?" I whispered, in case the person called out again. How creepy to be stranded in this vast lake. In case you haven't figured it out yet, I'm strictly a land lover. Water just isn't my element. I can swim enough to stay afloat, barely. But Lake Travis is *huge*, miles across and filled with all sorts of wiggly, slimy, creepy, well, *things* that a vampire should just shrug off, but I never could. What can I say? Inside I'm still a girly girl who jumps on chairs when a cockroach scurries across the kitchen floor. Go figure.

"Not a clue. See anything?" Ray leaned forward when the voice sang out again, louder this time.

"Heeelp. What are you waiting for? An engraved invitation?" This last was a screech.

Ray and I winced and both pointed at the same time. The voice was definitely coming from our right. But if this person was in the water and in real trouble, she was in need of an attitude adjustment. The screech had been female and in bitch mode. I should know. I've come up against more than a few bitches in my four hundred plus years and could give this one a run for her money if it came to a bitch-off. Yeah, I'm a girly girl with attitude when it's called for.

"Hold on, honey. We're on our way." Ray cranked the engine and turned the wheel toward the voice. We chugged slowly through the water. He had a searchlight on the bow and nodded to me to aim it ahead of us.

I figured we'd see someone in a lifejacket, or maybe in a boat with engine trouble. I was hoping for the boat. The water was really cold, though for New Year's Eve, Austin was almost balmy at forty degrees. Got to love Texas winters. A mortal wouldn't, though. Not tonight. They'd be in serious danger of hypothermia.

I scanned the water ahead of us with the searchlight. What Ray and I saw floating in front of us made us both gasp. When the engine went dead, we couldn't even speak. Because we were paralyzed. Yep. Frozen stiff. And not from the cold. Talk about a freak-out. I couldn't move so much as my little finger. And, believe me, I concentrated until I thought my brain would burst.

"God, what a night. A twofer." The creature climbed into the boat, making it rock and sloshing us both with cold water. Not that we could complain. We were statues. Oh God. Oh God. Oh God.

"Sorry I had to trick you like that, sweeties, but that's what I do. I'm a Siren. You know, the kind that makes ships wreck, makes sailors steer into the rocks, like that." The beast actually giggled.

I'm not being mean calling it a creature and a beast, though I sure as hell had a right to be mean. I couldn't *move*. You know how horrible that is? Never again will I laugh at those scenes on TV or in movies where the guy has both arms and legs in casts and can't scratch his nose. I can so relate.

But back to the *thing*. It would definitely come in a distant second to the Loch Ness Monster in a beauty contest. Imagine scales, green, slimy with tufts of seaweed and barnacles clinging to it like it hadn't bothered with a shower in a few millennia. Its eyes were red and uneven, but had long beautiful lashes. A good thing, since its teeth were too gross to stare at for more than a second. That explained the miasma that gusted from its pursed leathery lips.

"Now, darling, you can just quit judging me. Under this disguise I'm as cute as a button. Wear size-four jeans." She flicked my size-twelve (okay, fourteen without Lycra) butt with a slimy finger. "But I'm cursed. Because I screwed up. So I'm stuck here in Lake freakin' Travis in Austin freakin' Texas until I can bring the goddess who cursed me three vampires." She grinned and blasted me with some of that breath.

I would have gagged if I could have moved. I had just discovered hell on earth. Yep. If I could, I'd fall on a stake right now rather than spend one more minute so *helpless*.

"I've been stuck on the rocks over there for a month. Waiting. I've sensed humans, shifters, even a damned witch and her coven out for a joyride in a stolen cabin cruiser. But not one vampire." She sloshed to Ray's side.

"So you see why I'm so thrilled to get two in one boat." The moon came out from behind a cloud and she got a good look at Ray. "Oh. My. Goddess." The man always has that effect on women.

I felt a surge of hope. Ray's not shy. Maybe he could bargain his body for our freedom. Of course his standards would have to take a nosedive. I struggled to find a shred of optimism. Ray would have to be struck deaf, dumb, blind and wear a clothespin on his nose to hook up with the big ugly here. We were *doomed*.

"Honey, no way am I turning you over to any other woman until I have a sample first." She waved a scaly hand and Ray suddenly fell to the deck. "Speak to me, baby."

Ray rubbed his face, blinked, looked at me standing there in concrete mode and managed to show me horror, sympathy and resignation before he faced the creature without flinching. If we got out of this, I was calling his agent. He definitely had a future in Hollywood.

"Someone cursed you too? Sorry to hear it." He smiled and I saw the woman inside the Siren melt like all women do for Ray.

"Too? Oh, honey. You mean someone did you dirty?" She squished across the deck and collapsed on the white bench seat that ran across the back of the boat.

"I'm Ray. What should I call you?" Ray actually had the stones to hold out his hand. God, I couldn't believe it. I tried to move, but only my eyeballs were operative and I'm sure they were bugging out of my head.

"Aglaophonos. It's a mouthful, honey. Just call me Aggie." She frowned down at her scaly appendage, then placed her fingertips gently in his hand. "Sorry about the way I look. If I ever get this curse lifted . . . Well, the only way to do *that*, though, is to deliver three vampires to Circe. You and the chubby one there are my first two catches. One more and I'm good to go." She sighed.

"What'd you do to this Circe? Seems the punishment is a little harsh. What kind of goddess is she?" Ray managed to slip his hand from hers and actually refrained from wiping it on his jeans. I couldn't believe him. I was falling in love where I stood. Too bad I'd never live to do anything about it. Somehow I figured a delivery to Circe didn't allow for returns.

"Circe is the goddess of the night. She's got some serious skills. You don't want to cross her. On top of that, she's a bitch."

The boat suddenly rocked, thunder cracked and Aggie's scales turned bright red. My vision of hell just got worse. I could be pitched overboard while paralyzed. Fishy crawly things could have their way with me while I sank to the bottom unable to move. Ray grabbed me just before I toppled over the side and righted me, setting me closer to the steering wheel and slapping a bungee cord around my arm to secure me there. Have I mentioned how much I love him?

"Holy shit, Circe! You trying to burn me alive? Sorry, oh wondrous one! Do you see me working here? I've got two vampires for you. Let me do my job, okay? I'll cut out the trash talk. I promise." Aggie was shaking but seemed to have calmed her goddess down. The boat settled and her scales went back to pea green.

"She took my singing voice too." Aggie said this in a quiet voice and a pink tear dripped off the end of her snout. "That's my pride and joy. When I'm in top form I can bring a whole ship to a standstill. Every man in the crew falls in love with my voice and will do anything I ask." She reached up in what looked like an automatic gesture, as if to fluff her hair, then frowned. "I'm a shape-shifter. She took all my forms too and stuck me in *this* thing. When I'm on my game, I can be a mermaid or look human, a beautiful woman with long golden hair." She sighed. "But it's my voice I miss most. There's nothing I love more than a fantastic singing voice."

"For true?" Ray smiled. Vampires don't really need to breathe. Ray's a really new vampire, but I guess he'd figured that out because he couldn't be taking in her nasty fumes and still look so cheerful.

The only cheerful thought I could come up with was how it would feel to rip open Aggie's throat, tear her hideous body to pieces and turn her into fish bait. Even an immortal would have a tough time snapping back from that. Ray moved in on Aggie. I hoped he tossed her overboard.

"You ever hear of Israel Caine in whatever land you're from?"

"I move around. But sure. Who hasn't? I could listen to his CDs forever." Aggie straightened and peered at Ray. "Holy goddess of the night. I don't see so well in this scaly outfit, but are you, I mean, could you possibly be . . . ?"

"I am. Would you like for me to sing to you?"

"Are you kidding? After a month with a rock up my butt and only a few bats for company? Hell, I'd do anything to hear some decent music."

I wanted to scream. Ray was going to *serenade* this monster slash woman? While I stood here helpless with, damn it, a hair in my mouth that was driving me certifiable?

"All right then." Ray became my hero when he reached over and pulled the hair from my lips. Thank God I'd taught him to read minds. "I'll sing for you if you'll do me a few favors."

"I can't let you go. I've got to satisfy Circe. And get my voice and my form back." Aggie actually looked a little desperate, but not so much that she didn't take a second to grab Ray's hand and pull him closer. She stroked his face with a claw that had certainly never had a manicure. "Israel Caine. Wow. I didn't know you were a vampire."

"It's a new development." Ray gestured at me. "Come on, Aggie. At least let my lady relax. Like you did me. She's going crazy being stuck like that. You can see her eyes moving."

"Yeah, it's hysterical." Aggie laughed, a horsy bray. "Might as well. You guys may think you're badass vampires, but I can freeze you again with a look if you come at me with a fang or try to shape-shift out of here. So don't even think of making a break for it." She waved a finger and I flopped to the deck, the bungee cord jerking me back up like a yo-yo.

"Thank God! I *was* going crazy." I was shaking as Ray unwrapped the cord, lifted me to my feet and wrapped his arms around me. I hugged him tight. No matter what Aggie said, we were getting the hell out of here. I hate to shape-shift, but right now I'd even risk doing the bat thing to win my freedom.

Aggie gave me a sharp look. "Don't even think about it, vampire. You're not the only one who can read minds and if you so much as shift a toenail I'll freeze you permanently and hold your head under water until you wish you *could* die."

"Ease up, Aggie. Glory's not going to try anything. Are you, sweetness?"

"Who me?" My voice was a few octaves higher than usual and I decided that burying my face in Ray's shirt was the best way to filter Aggie's odor and comfort myself in what was clearly a lose-lose situation.

"Let her go and sing something for me, Israel Caine. Man, I think my luck is finally turning." Aggie leaned back in the seat with what probably passed for a smile on her gruesome face.

"One song. Then I want to discuss a deal." Ray settled me in the driver's seat with a comforting pat on the shoulder. I hoped to God he had a plan because my mind was as blank as . . . crap, I couldn't even think of a clever metaphor, I was so strung out.

"What kind of deal?"

"There are some vampires in town we wouldn't mind getting rid of. What if Glory and I brought you three *primo* vampires? You could wait here for months before another vamp came by, if ever. You want to take that chance?" He moved close to the creature again.

"Maybe your vamp friends will send a search party for you when you don't come back from your boat ride." Aggie looked at her nails, then snorted in disgust and shook her head.

"And what makes you think we told anyone where we were going?" Ray smiled at me. "It's New Year's Eve. We were having a private celebration." Then he turned his back on me and got down to business. "Come on, Aggie. Think about it. Three male vampires who could make Circe happy. You'd get your curse lifted and I could keep singing. Maybe write a special song just for you." Ray sat on the bench seat next to Aggie. "Make a video. Put you in it. I have a thing for beautiful blondes."

He turned to wink at me, like I was one of them. And, even in the middle of a major freak-out, I felt my hormones happy dance. Stupid. I should be all about survival. I wondered if I could block my thoughts from Aggie like I could from other mind readers. I put up a shield.

"I don't know if I should deal with you." Aggie fluttered her lashes. "Why should I trust you? Your friend over there is doing her best to block her thoughts." She gave me an evil grin. "Not working, hon. And you're not helping Israel's cause either."

"Glory's upset. Ignore her." Ray put his hand over his heart. "I swear it, Aggie. I don't know what the situation is with Sirens, but I don't make promises I can't keep."

"Sirens have their own code. Which I'm accused of, ahem, bending. Strictly speaking, Achelous, the Storm God, is my boss, not Circe, but she found out about my transgressions and is blackmailing me."

Cue the thunder and boat tossing. At least this time I could hold on to something, though Ray's railing was getting bent all to hell and back.

"Well, sorry, sister Circe, but that's what it is. Calm yourself. I'm playing by your rules. I know you're listening. The guy's offering to serve up some vampire men." Aggie looked at me. "Are they hot? Circe really likes to roast and toast hot guys."

I thought about the one I really hated. Ugly as sin, but he could make himself look like anyone's dream guy, one of his more useful talents. Some of his evil minions were actually good-looking.

"Yes. We can come up with three hot vampires for Circe." I breathed a sigh of relief when the boat quit rocking and the wind calmed.

"There you go, then. Let me finish negotiations, your goddessness." Aggie sighed. "Touchy, touchy. But powerful. You don't want to get crossways with any of the hierarchy. Trust me on that."

"So do we have a deal?" Ray's smile was looking a little strained.

"Not necessarily. What if I want more than just a video with you?" Aggie scooted closer to him, until her scales were making his jeans wet. Ugh.

Ray shook his head. "We'd have to play it by ear. See how things go."

Aggie nodded at me. "What about her?"

Her, me, *I* just stood there, visions of Ray hooking up with this swamp thing making my skin crawl, no matter what form she ended up in. I knew what he was doing, trying to talk our way out of this. And clearly Aggie had no interest in hearing from me so I kept my trap shut.

"Glory and I are just friends. She's teaching me about being a vampire. Like a mentor. I've only been this way for a few weeks. The tabloids made us a couple, but it's all an act. We sneaked out on the boat so Glory could teach me more about being a vamp, that's all."

Gee. Would it have killed him to pretend we were lovers? Not that I should care. Ray was only telling the truth. I had Jerry, a boyfriend who said he loved me even if he did stand me up on the most important date night of the year. Yeah, and look where that had landed me. Hostage to the swamp thing here. Jerry was so going to pay for this. The thought of retribution almost made me smile.

Aggie smirked. "Wait'll you see me in my regular form. I'm much more your type than this . . . oversize vampire." She flung out a hand, seaweed trailing from her fingertips.

"I'm sure you're beautiful, but then so is Glory." Ray turned to smile at me. "I'd appreciate it if you didn't disrespect her. I owe her my life."

Wow. Now how was that for a feel-good moment? I smiled back and waited for Aggie to throw a thunderbolt at me or something.

"Huh. Whatever. Maybe I'll think about your 'deal' while you sing." Aggie laid that icky hand on Ray's thigh.

I gritted my teeth but kept quiet. Ray began to sing. It was a new song. About finding out who you are when you've lost your way. Good choice. I'd like to get lost right now. Ray was getting to Aggie, I could tell. Her eyes closed and she swayed with the music. By the time he came to the end, she was humming the chorus, but Circe had clearly taken her voice because even that was painful to listen to.

"Oh, Ray. Did you write that song?" You knew I couldn't stay quiet forever.

"Yep. Just yesterday. Seems the vamp gig hasn't dried up my creative juices. For a while I was afraid they'd gone along with my ability to chow down on a steak and fries." Ray's grin was full of relief.

So he really had been worried. I wanted to reach out to him but Aggie stopped me with a hard look.

"Nope. You've still got it, handsome." Aggie grabbed Ray's hand and pulled it to what passed for a scaly bosom. "Great song. You and me, Ray. I'm thinkin' we could have made beautiful music together if I didn't have to give you to Circe."

"Guess we'll never know." Ray shrugged. "What'll Circe do to us if you give Glory and me to her?"

Aggie winced. "She hates the night. So vampires are a boil on her backside. She'll torture you until she decides to put you in the sun to die. Or maybe she'll stake you. No, probably not. Too quick." She gave me a narrow-eyed look. "She really really hates men. I don't think Glory there would do it for her. Oh, she'd take you out, hon. But I'd probably be sent back to get another vamp anyway. A hot guy or at least a good-looking one."

"Well, then. I should just get the hell out of here." I felt queasy and my knees were weak—talk of stakes and death by sunlight did that to me. "But I'm taking Ray with me. Come on, Aggie. You know you can't send Israel Caine to a certain and ugly death. Did you hear him just now? Could you really silence that voice? Destroy that talent?" I got up, ready to wrench Ray out of her slimy grasp. I'd taken one step when I was frozen again.

"Aggie, let her go. You just said Glory is a nonstarter. Let her swim to shore. I'll sing another song." Ray scooted closer and put his arm around Aggie. "One last song before I die."

"Aw, you've got me. Glory's right, Israel. I can't let Circe destroy you. You sing like an angel. I really respect a voice like that." Aggie slumped. "But I've got to get out of this nasty body. If I agree to this deal, you've got to come across with those three male vamps. And soon."

"I will. You've got my word on it."

"More than that. I've got you both on a leash." Aggie grinned. Oh, those teeth.

"What do you mean a leash?" Ray said what I was thinking. Oh, God, I hated not being able to move so much as an eyelash. I couldn't even swallow spit.

"Now that I've got your scent, I can call you to me at any time. Both of you. No matter where you are, you won't be able to run away, far enough or fast enough. I can *make* you come to me. Like a compulsion. Just hope there's a boat nearby or you'll be swimming for your life. Never doubt it. That's the power of a Siren. Even one who's cursed." She waved a finger and I was limp again.

I took a moment to swallow, blink and generally celebrate being able to move. Then I stood up and faced her.

"Gee, you're just full of power, then, aren't you? But if we bring you three other male vampires, you'll leave us alone? That'll be the end of our 'relationship'?" I was really sick of this "now you're frozen, now you're not" crap. And really eager to never see this creature again.

"Right. Bring them to the lake. And fast." Aggie looked up at the sky. "By the next full moon. That's three weeks away. That's my deadline. So it's yours too. If I have to, I'll take you two. I figure Israel Caine is a big enough catch to satisfy Big Mama." There was a clap of thunder. "Well, if I can't find three men anyway." Aggie scratched at some red patches on her scales. "I've got about five minutes before I have to get back in the water. Sing me my favorite song, Ray. 'My One True Love.'" Aggie grinned. "And sing it to *me*. Then I want a big juicy kiss to seal our deal." She turned to me, her crooked eyes narrowing. "Start swimming, vampire. We want to be alone."

Then she tossed me overboard.

Three

The water was damned cold. I'd been swimming for *hours*. I sure wished I could touch bottom. Something brushed my arm and I shrieked.

"Glory?"

I heard the chug of a boat engine and saw the sweep of a searchlight.

"Over here." I waved an arm. Stupid move. I sank like a stone. I came up sputtering just as a life ring hit a few feet away.

"Grab the ring, and I'll haul you aboard." Ray sounded hoarse.

I threw my arm over it and hung on, too tired to do more than grunt as he reached for me and dragged me into the cockpit. I was shivering in earnest now, wet from my ruined suede Marc Jacobs boots to my dripping cashmere sweater that would probably shrink once it dried. Damn. The icy wind kicked up. Double damn.

"Get out of those wet clothes. Here's a blanket you can wrap around you. I'll get us back to the house." Ray went to the wheel, pushed the throttle and the boat rocketed forward.

I decided against an undignified struggle to peel off

tight jeans while a boat tossed me like a silver ball in a roulette wheel (old gambling problem—don't ask). I staggered to the bench seat that looked surprisingly slime free and sank down, pulling the blanket over my shoulders.

A few minutes later the night sky lit up and sounds like gunshots made me drop to the deck and cover my head. Ray shut off the engine and we coasted across the water.

"What?" I figured I looked little better than Aggie as I swiped strings of wet hair out of my eyes. Hey, bullets couldn't kill me, but I'd had a rough night, okay?

"Relax, Glory. Fireworks. It's midnight." Ray helped me up to the seat again. He used the corner of the blanket to wipe my cheeks. "You all right?"

"Not really. God, I think there's something crawling in my bra." I stretched out my sweater and tried to see.

"Want me to check?" Ray grinned when I pulled a string of some kind of plant from my cleavage and tossed it overboard.

"Just get me back to dry land. What's the holdup?"

Ray glanced at the sky, then at the Rolex on his wrist. "In a minute. Like I said, it's midnight. Happy New Year."

"Tell me you're not expecting a kiss." I stared at his lips, which were firm, sexy and, I knew firsthand, extremely talented. "Did you have to kiss Aggie?"

Ray grinned. "I never kiss and tell. Come on, it's tradition." He leaned toward me, eyes closing.

I put my hand in the middle of his chest. I'm strong, vamp strong. I could hold him off all night if I really wanted to. "Ray, I'm not kidding here. Swamp thing *kissed* you? Then it's going to take some serious dental hygiene before—"

He was obviously pretty strong himself because his mouth was suddenly on mine and his lips didn't taste a bit nasty. His tongue was clever and not slimy at all.

He pulled back and smiled at me. "Happy New Year, Glory."

"Happy New Year, Ray." How can you stay mad at a man who is so damned gorgeous?

He reached for the bottom of my sweater. "There might be

all kinds of things hiding under here. You've got to get out of this." With the moves of a man who's had way too much practice, he ripped it off over my head and tossed it aside. It landed on the deck with a noisy splat.

"That's as far as this goes, Ray. I'm pretty sure I got rid of anything that doesn't belong." I grinned, glad I'd worn my new black cami with the slimming control midriff and the built-in underwire bra. It had a cute bit of red lace trim at the plunging vee. My hair might be wet, my makeup history, but clinging lace made up for a lot. Hmm. Ray was looking *really* interested in that clinging and the effect of cold water . . .

"You sure? I always try to start my New Year with a"— he traced the edge of the lace bra with a fingertip—"bang."

"And I thought *I* was the ancient one here." I grinned and lifted his finger off my chest just as it headed for a nipple. "You really need a new line, Ray. Now start the *boat's* engine and get us back to the house. If these wet jeans shrink on me, we may have to cut them off." They hadn't been that easy to get on in the first place. I have the fantasy that tight makes me look smaller. Yeah, right. What I'm afraid they actually do is give me a muffin top. Which is why the camisole has industrial strength spandex. Now the jeans were going from tight to vise. My thong would probably have to be surgically removed.

"Be a shame to cut off jeans that look that good on you. Maybe we can work them off together. With our vamp strength and all." Ray dropped a kiss on the swell of each breast, then pulled the blanket closed. He got up and headed for the steering wheel then stopped with his hand on the key. He turned and looked at me.

"Oh, Glory."

"Hmm?" I was heavily involved in a blow-by-blow mental replay of that kiss, comparing it to one of Jerry's. Not better, no way. Just . . . different.

"I did have to kiss Aggie. Teeth, tongues, slime and all."

My stomach heaved and Jerry's kisses won, no contest.

• • •

"*Where* the hell have you been? I've been freakin' out here."
Valdez paced the dock. "*And you're soaked. He's dry. Did he
make a pass and you had to swim for it? You must have been desperate to get away from him 'cause I know how you hate the water.
Son of a bitch! I'm so gonna rip him a new one. And where's your
sweater? The boss is gonna fire my ass for this.*"

"Take a breath, then shut up, Valdez." I took Ray's hand
and stepped carefully onto the dock. I'd left the wet lump of
wool that used to be a sweater on the boat. "Ray didn't do anything. I'm okay. I'll tell you what happened on the lake later."

"*Later?*" Valdez snarled as Ray brushed past him, but a
stern look from me convinced him that I meant what I said.

The house was still lit from top to bottom and loud music boomed from the upper level where the doors to the
wooden deck obviously stood open. Several people were outside smoking what smelled like illegal substances. I knew
Ray banned any kind of smoking inside his house. Bad for
his voice. Or at least it had been for mortal Ray.

Glass crunched under my boots and I remembered Ray
was barefoot. "Careful, Ray. Watch where you step."

"Too late." Ray held up his foot. It had been sliced open
by a piece of broken bottle. Blood, a beautiful bright red,
welled from what looked to be a pretty serious cut.

"That looks bad." Really bad, though I couldn't deny it
stirred my vampire senses. First a kiss, now blood. Was Ray
trying to *seduce* me?

"Well, shit. That's what I get for making a grand gesture." He hissed between his teeth. "Damn, that hurts like a
son of a bitch."

"I'm sorry, Ray." I reached down and picked up a piece of
glass with the label still attached. His favorite brand.

"Yep, it's the bottle you tossed over the edge." I was trying
to distract myself. Because my fangs had descended with the
first whiff.

"Valdez, take a hike. Glory wants me." Ray grinned,
reached down to smear blood on his finger and then waved his
hand under my nose. "We need some privacy."

"Well, we sure can't join your mortal friends upstairs until I get myself under control." Which wouldn't be anytime soon. I looked down at the widening pool of blood under Ray's foot.

"Why hasn't it stopped bleeding, Glory? Where's my vamp power?" Ray limped around the deck.

"Good question. Maybe Jack Daniel's has the answer. Come here and let me look at your foot." I squatted and waited for him to come close. As usual, he came too close, but I ignored his zipper practically pressed against my cheek as I used a corner of the blanket to wipe away blood. Yep, there was a piece of glass embedded in his foot. Ray's hand tangled in my wet hair and he leaned against me. I tried to pull out the glass.

"Hey, that hurts!" Ray jerked and almost pulled out a hank of hair.

"Sorry. Don't snatch me bald, you big baby." I stood suddenly and almost knocked him over. "Obviously this isn't the place to deal with your foot."

"Looks serious, Blondie. And, yeah, it must hurt like hell." Valdez looked up at Ray. *"Is that why you're still bleeding? You drink all of that booze?"*

"Most of it. But that was hours ago." Ray gripped my shoulder this time. "Seriously, Glory, you think the alcohol screwed with my healing ability?"

"Don't ask *me*. I avoid the stuff. Wait until tomorrow night. Then you'll know why." When he woke up with the mother of all hangovers. "Let's go inside. Where we've got better light and I can get that glass out." I looked at Ray's hand on me. "Can you walk on your own? Get in the elevator."

"You'll have to help me. And you know that elevator opens right at the deck area." Ray looked around. "You shouldn't have to carry me. Valdez, where are *my* bodyguards? Seems like I have five of them around here. Two of them paranormals."

"Your mortal bodyguards, Sam and Buster, caught two teenage girls trying to climb the rocks to get inside. Last I heard, they were

hustling them toward town. One of the kids was crying 'cause she scraped her knee and threatened to sue." Valdez gave a doggy laugh. *"Sam straightened her out about* that. *Then Brittany had to whammy a couple of paparazzi who tried to crash the party and caught Will with his fangs down. It's his night off so he's drunk off his ass and hit on one of your bandmate's girlfriends."* Valdez chuffed. *"Yeah, Glory.* Some *bodyguards actually get time off."*

"Can we not do this now?" I realized Ray's foot was *still* bleeding. *Had* the alcohol he'd drunk earlier hurt his ability to heal?

Ray was pale and fell against me. "Seriously, Glory. I'm messed up here. I really need to lie down." He tried to unbutton his shirt, then just ripped it off. "Here, wrap this around my foot and let's go. When we come out of the elevator, play along with whatever I say or do. Your fangs are still out there, darlin'." He slung his arm over my shoulders. "Sexy as hell. Maybe later you can—"

"I think you've lost enough blood, Ray." I don't take orders well. But Ray was obviously in no shape to slap down, so I just dragged him into the elevator. Valdez crowded in with us. I tied the silk shirt around Ray's foot, then pushed the button to take us up. "Just do whatever you can to get us past your friends upstairs without causing a 'Look there's a vampire!' riot."

"Whatever I can. All right then." Ray's grin was weak, but still full of the Devil as he leaned heavily on me. "Better hurry, I'm fadin' fast." He looked down at his foot; the blood had already soaked through his shirt. "Stupid."

"Valdez, since we seem to be under siege, you stay with Brittany and help with security. I'll take care of Ray." I was desperately willing my fangs to retreat before we hit the top deck. I hoped the sight of Ray's foot would draw all eyes, and my fangs would go unnoticed. Yeah, right.

"Relax, Glory. The guys are all drunk, stoned or both. Like I said, let me handle it." Ray grabbed the blanket that I still clutched. "Won't be needing this."

The elevator doors opened. "Showtime." Ray reached for

the hooks on the front of my cami. I held his hand. "Part of the show," he whispered, "Trust me."

"Like hell." I pulled him out of the elevator. He was clearly too weak to make it on his own.

Valdez growled and dragged the blanket out of the elevator with his teeth.

"Hey, Ray. What the hell happened?"

He grinned and held up his foot with the blood-soaked shirt dangling from it. "Ran out of Jack. Got pissed. Broke the bottle and, like a fool, stepped on it. My baby's takin' me upstairs for some first *aid*." He buried his head between my breasts.

Shouts and whistles accompanied that announcement. And when Ray leaned back and showed he'd managed to unhook my bra with his teeth . . . the men laughed, hooted and stomped their feet until the deck shook. Ray captured the cami before it hit the ground, twirled it over his head, then pitched it over the railing onto the rocks below.

"All right, men. I challenge you. Ladies topless. Make it happen."

Squeals, giggles and general chaos. As a distraction, it worked like a charm. Obviously no one was looking at my *fangs*. I dragged Ray upstairs and to the room he pointed to weakly as the master bedroom.

"You are so dead." I dropped him on his bed.

"Don't you mean undead?" Ray's last words just before he passed out.

I locked the bedroom door, then put towels under Ray's foot. I plucked out glass until I was satisfied that I'd got it all, even prodded it with some tweezers I found in a bathroom drawer. And, yeah, I snooped through all the drawers. Usual guy stuff, including an assortment of condoms, gels and lubricants that made my imagination do backflips. Hmm.

Too bad Ray stayed unconscious while I worked on his foot. He'd earned some serious pain and suffering for that stunt downstairs. At least he'd finally quit bleeding, but he was very pale under his forever tan. I picked up a piece of glass and ran it across my wrist. Ow. When blood welled up, I pressed the cut to his lips.

"Drink, Ray. Come on. You can't start the New Year in a coma." I rubbed my wrist between his lips. His lashes fluttered, then I felt the pierce of his fangs. Despite the mad I still felt simmering inside me, the pull as he drew on me was unbelievably erotic. Yeah, believe it. And I was foolishly sitting here still topless. Both of us were. That just added to the sexy situation.

I grabbed a pillow and stuck it in front of me. A little late for modesty. The entire crew downstairs had seen my boobs, including Valdez. He'd been beyond furious with Ray. Only the rock star's deteriorating physical condition and our audience had saved Ray from being torn apart by my doggie protector. As it was, I'd staggered up the stairs with Ray clutched to my chest like we'd already started getting busy. Good thing I was strong because I'd been carrying him before we'd reached the third step.

Ray's eyes opened and he reached up to touch my cheek.

"Guess you'll live. I think you can let go now." I nodded at my wrist.

Ray pulled away, carefully licking the punctures closed before he smiled up at me.

"Thanks, Glory. You saved me. Again."

"Waste of time since now I'm going to kill you." I slammed the pillow onto his grinning face and held it down. "Since when does stripping me become the only way to distract that crowd?"

"Worked, didn't it? You have beautiful breasts. Made to distract any man who's into women. Wish I had X-ray vision. I'd distract myself right now." His voice was muffled. "Are you trying to suffocate me? Won't work."

"I know that." I put the pillow back over my "beautiful" breasts. What can I say? I'm a sucker for a compliment. "You tossed my bra over the railing. You're going to buy me *the* most expensive bustier I can find. No, make that a whole new wardrobe of bras, lacy under things, the best Victoria's Secret has to offer."

"You're right." Ray grinned. "There's a little shop on Rodeo Drive that you'd love. I'm seeing you in red lace. How about a garter belt?" His blue eyes were gleaming as he ran his hand down my bare arm.

I shivered. "Garter belts are pretty retro. You have no idea how I celebrated when panty hose were invented." I used one hand to lift Ray's hand off me and smiled. "Garter belts are sexy, though. *Jerry* loves them. This little shop have a Web site?" Wet jeans, bare breasts and Ray half-naked on the bed. No wonder I had a sudden vision of strutting out of a dressing room wearing expensive and very skimpy lace and satin for Ray's approval. Crazy. I should be doing that for Jerry, who was . . . somewhere far away.

"Forget the Internet. I'll charter a jet. We can be there in a few hours. Spend the day holed up at my favorite hotel, then you can pick out whatever you want. The manager will stay open late for us."

"Know her well, do you?" Of course he did. Israel Caine probably bought sexy lingerie for his bimbos by the gross. Good reality check. "Much as a trip out to La-La Land sounds like fun, I have a business to run. It's year-end sale time. And I need to take inventory." Wow. Even *I* was surprised by how businesslike I sounded. "Bet they do have a Web site. Even my little shop has one. I just hope their undies are very expensive."

"Of course they are. Nothing but the best for my ladies."

"Which is a cast of thousands. I get that." What was I doing still sitting here? I stood, wincing as I straightened and my jeans discovered a new crevice to torture. "I need something else to wear. These jeans feel shrink-wrapped. I may be permanently, uh, damaged."

Ray laughed, a happy relieved sound that, damn it, charmed me. "One night's healing sleep, and you'll be good to go again, Glory. We both will."

"You hope. Sorry, but that booze is still in your system.

You have no idea what's coming." I staggered to the enormous walk-in closet next to a master bath that was calling my name. After our encounter with the slime sister and my dunk in the lake, I wanted a hot shower and a shampoo in the worst way. I grabbed a black cotton T-shirt and some khaki cargo shorts I hoped I could squeeze my butt into.

"You keep saying that, but I feel fine. Want a shower? Go ahead. Help yourself. There's shampoo, whatever you need, in the bathroom." Ray came up behind me. "I'm reading your mind, just like you taught me."

I turned and looked at him. "I also taught you not to read *my* mind without permission. So cut it out. But I will take that shower. Thanks. I bet you feel slimy too. There must be six other bathrooms in this place. Go brush your teeth. Gargle with paint thinner. God, how could you kiss that, that *thing?*"

"I didn't have much choice. It was kiss her willingly or she'd have made me a statue and done whatever she wanted to me." We both shuddered.

"Yeah, I guess a kiss was the way to go."

Ray nodded. "And I knew you were out on the lake somewhere. I just wanted to get it over with. So I could find you. I knew you were probably freaking out."

"Hey, thanks. Yeah, I was." Every time I decided Ray was a shallow jerk, he managed to surprise me again.

Ray leaned down to study his healing foot. Nothing like a little of my ancient blood to do the trick. "You know why I was so hoarse?"

"No." I resisted the craving to touch his silky hair, to invite him into the shower with me. I'd shared my blood with him. That's an intimacy that makes vampires feel very . . . close. And he'd sacrificed himself for me. Well, sort of. I blocked my thoughts before Ray read the invitation and tried to take me up on it.

Ray looked up and shook his head. "She jumped back into the water, then ordered me to sing just about every love song I know. I tried to take off, but she's right. She has us on a leash. I got about ten feet away, then was compelled to go right back to her. It was the damnedest thing. Then I had to hear her sad story."

"What was it?" Must be pretty bad to leave her wearing the worst outfit to ever come out of the dark side. And that's saying something. I've seen some pretty creepy creatures in my day.

"She has, had, a lover. Guy named Charlie. Circe had him marked for extinction and Aggie wouldn't give him up. You see who lost *that* battle. Aggie's not supposed to be involved with the goddess. We should google Aggie. See what we can find out about her boss. Maybe we can get this Storm God to get Aggie out of here."

"Good idea. Just our luck she picked this lake to stake out." I headed for the bathroom.

"Circe picked it. I should have asked Aggie if she knew why." Ray limped after me.

"I'm sorry about her lover, but Aggie's problem shouldn't have to be *our* problem."

Ray pulled a leaf out of my hair. "But it is. I don't see any way out of it."

"Neither do I." I sighed. "I'm hitting the shower now."

"Knock yourself out." Ray twirled the leaf then turned his back on me.

What? No pass? Not even a *little* attempt to jump my bones? Yeah, yeah, so I was all primed to reject him, but, come on now. He'd seen my *breasts*. I may have some excess junk in my trunk, but I was twenty-two when I was turned vampire. My perky double Ds are awesome if I do say so myself. I'm sure all the guys downstairs had thought so too. Right. I should be furious with Ray, not wishing he'd make some kind of move on me.

Ray sank down on the bed again. Okay so he was probably still suffering from blood loss. He lay back and closed his eyes. I took a moment to enjoy the view of his bare chest and low riding jeans that made it obvious Ray hadn't bothered with underwear.

I sighed then stomped into the bathroom, shut the door, then dropped the pillow and sat on the tiled bench seat built into the shower to peel off my boots. Thank God they had zippers. I was afraid they were ruined, but I set them carefully aside in case they could be salvaged.

Next I tackled the jeans. Unsnapping them and unzipping the short zipper gave me some relief from the pressure of the low-rise waist, but when I stood and tried to work them down? No go. Oh, I almost got them over my butt, but no way were they moving past my thighs. Damn it. I sat on the bench again and tried to pull from the bottom of the legs. Hopeless.

This was ridiculous. I had vamp strength. I stood again and jerked at the waistband on both sides. All I got for my trouble was a broken nail.

"Damn it to hell."

The bathroom door swung open. "Seems a shame, but I've got scissors." Ray grinned and strolled in.

"Get out." I grabbed a towel and held it over my breasts.

"What about the jeans?" Ray walked around and eyed my backside. "Red thong? Cute. But obviously you haven't made much progress here."

I felt cold metal slide between my butt cheeks and shivered. "What the hell do you think you're doing?"

"They've got to come off, so here goes." His hand landed on my shoulder. "Don't budge now, I've got to get the blade in a little lower. Wouldn't want to hurt you."

I stood rooted to the floor. Oh. My. God. How perverted was it to be totally turned on by the chill of a metal blade easing lower? I felt Ray's breath against my back. I didn't need to look to know his lips were inches from that "cute" red thong.

"Don't move, I said." He slid a finger beside the scissor blade and wiggled it.

"I didn't—" Not move? I braced both hands on the granite countertop in front of me before my knees buckled, my towel dropping to the floor.

"Yes, you did. And these damned jeans . . . Wet denim. I can't seem to cut through it. I'm feeling weak. Maybe I need to feed from you again. The neck this time. Or Will told me there's a spot on the inner thigh"—I jerked and the point grazed me—"but we'd have to get these off first."

"Ow! Watch it back there." I just bet Ray was grinning. "I think you're plenty strong enough to handle cutting a lit-tle cloth if you just concentrate, Ray." There's nothing a new vamp likes more than feeding from an ancient one. And, while I'm a lot younger than some vamps I know, to Ray my blood is an aged vintage.

"Oh, man, I think I cut you." Another finger joined the first and I closed my eyes. "Oh, yes, you're definitely bleed-ing."

God in heaven, was that his tongue? "Ray?"

"You're okay, I healed you." Every word was another puff of warm air on my backside. "I'm sorry, Glory. I promise to be more careful."

"You—you do that." I have absolutely no willpower when it comes to resisting men with clever hands or . . . tongues. A flush heated my cheeks. I wet my lips and bit back a moan. Oh, God. At least I couldn't see my reflection in the double mirrors over the twin sinks. Glory the slut would be staring back at me.

"I think the material's about to give."

Give. Oh, yes. Come on, Ray, give me . . . Then I heard the snap of the scissors. Cool air on my butt. Ray peeled the wet fabric down my thighs then eased it off first one foot, then the other. Sanity finally arrived when I realized he was getting the full back-door view.

I grabbed the towel, wrapped it around me and kicked the jeans away. "Thanks, Ray. Couldn't have done it without you." I took the scissors and laid them on the counter. "You don't need to feed again so soon, just rest while I take my shower. I won't be long."

"Seems like I earned a reward for rescuing you from lower body strangulation." Ray grinned and moved closer. He ran a finger down one of my thighs. "Look at these terrible red marks. You were suffering. I've got lots of jets in the shower. Let me show you how they work and soothe your hurts."

I put my hand on his bare chest to give myself some space. Enough of this. I blamed all of these restless urges Ray had stirred up on Jerry. *He* should be here helping me see in the New Year properly. Then I never would have been out on the lake, met Aggie, been in this horrible . . . Oh, hell.

"I'm fine, Ray. But speaking of suffering, go lie down. That alcohol you drank is bound to kick in soon and you're going to wish you were really dead. Trust me on this."

"You can trust *me*, Glory. Your boyfriend stood you up on New Year's Eve. Will told me he took off for Europe tonight when he could've waited one more night."

"He had something important—"

"More important than *you*?" Ray shook his head, obviously mind reading big-time. "That's just wrong. You going to let him get away with that? Come on. Let's shower together. See where it goes. There's plenty of room and look what you've done to me." He pulled me against him.

Oh, yes, I'd definitely found myself a butt man. But bringing up my boyfriend had been stupid. I do love Jerry, and sex to get even with someone isn't my style, though it probably was pretty common in Ray's world.

All in all, Ray making a move was a nice ego boost. I have a healthy libido and I was definitely attracted, but I also have a little loyalty-to-Jerry thing going too.

I smiled and shook my head. "Sorry, Ray, but it's not happening." I gave him a gentle shove. "Now go rest while I shower."

"I won't beg." Ray held up his hands and backed up. "I'm not feeling so great, to tell you the truth."

Once under the hot shower, I ignored those sexy shower heads, shampooed my hair and took stock. Tonight I'd been abandoned by my lover, collected a one-way ticket to hell and taken care of a wounded rock star. Did Glory St. Clair know how to ring in the New Year or what?

Four

"How is he? Valdez said Ray's not feeling so great."

"Begging me to stake him and put him out of his misery." It had been tough not saying "I told you so." But seeing Ray laid low had killed any desire I had to gloat. "He's in bad shape, Nate."

"I thought the vampire healing sleep was supposed to cure everything for you guys." Nathan Burke, Ray's best friend and manager, had arrived during the day.

"Normally, it does." I'd decided to sleep over, to be here when Ray woke up. Strictly in my capacity as mentor, of course. Good thing, since he was in agony. And I hadn't shared everything with Nate yet.

"So what's the deal here?" Nate paced around Ray's king-size bed. "I don't care if his head's about to explode. Give him an aspirin or the whole damned bottle. Get up, Ray. We've got to go over your schedule. This is important."

"Alcohol screws up our systems. Ray drank a boatload of it before I got here and stopped him." I shut the hall door. There were shouts downstairs where a football game played on the big-screen TV. Delicious smells came from the kitchen. Will was cooking chili for the crowd that apparently figured a

New Year's Eve party included the day and night after. "I haven't told you the worst of it."

"What?" Nate sat on the edge of the bed. "Ray? Come on, bud. It's not like you to wimp out on me." He tried to pull the sheet down but Ray held on to it and a mortal was no match for a vampire, even one in subpar condition. "Sienna's going to be here tomorrow. You still want her to stay here? Or should we arrange a hotel suite?"

No response other than a weak foot jiggle.

"He can't say anything, Nate. His voice is gone."

"What?" Nate jumped like he'd been goosed by a hot poker. "No. Can't be. That was the single most positive thing to come out of this vampire crap. That his voice would be golden forever." He ran his hand through his close-cropped black hair. "Sorry, Glory, but you know blood sucking has complicated the hell out of Ray's life. Then we thought, okay, at least he doesn't have to baby his voice. Watch his throat, like that." Nate grabbed my arm. "This is temporary, right?"

"Should be. Give it a day, a week at most."

"No, no, no. Not a week. Sienna Star is here to rehearse. For their big number at the Grammys. On TV. Their duet is nominated. This is huge." Nathan jerked the sheet off Ray. Apparently stress had given him superpowers. "Look at him. He should at least be wearing a T-shirt."

I looked at Ray all right. He'd come out of the shower in a towel, then dropped it to root around in a drawer for about an hour looking for a pair of blue silk boxers. That apparently took the last of his energy and he'd collapsed on the bed, unconscious again. It had been near dawn by then and I'd had a quick conference with Valdez, issued orders and crawled into bed with Ray. We slept like the dead, anyway.

When he woke up this evening, Ray had felt the effects of his binge drinking the night before. His whole body had been shaking, his head splitting and he'd been violently sick and throwing up. Fortunately, he'd managed to stagger into the bathroom before *that* happened. When he'd finally collapsed on the tile floor, I'd washed his face, helped him rinse out his mouth, and then carried him back to bed. Yeah, we'd had loads of fun.

In a note, because he really couldn't squawk a single syllable, Ray had admitted he'd already polished off one whole bottle of Jack Daniel's and was on his second when Valdez and I had arrived. No wonder he was in such a bad way.

"Ray, roll over." Nate had found a black sweatshirt and tugged it over Ray's head. "I'm going to the drugstore. I'll get some throat lozenges, cough syrup. First I'll call Dr. Calvin and get a prescription. You know he'll take care of it for you, even on a holiday."

"Forget it, Nathan." I put a hand on his arm. "Mortal medicine won't help Ray now."

"Then what the hell will?" Nathan was desperate. "This is critical, Glory. The label execs set this up. Sienna's young, appeals to a different demographic than Ray." We both saw Ray fall back on the bed again. His eyes had never opened. "Not that you're old, buddy. Thirty-seven? Hell, we're both in our prime. Hah. Hah." Nate grabbed my arm and pulled me out to the hall.

"What can we do, Glory? This Grammy thing . . . You read the tabloids. Ray's sales are still strong. Of course they are, but the duet with Sienna put us right back up where we belong. Ray has to do this gig and be great. Keep the ball rolling while we record his new album. He and Sienna need the rehearsal time. Work some of your vampire magic here. Surely there's something you can do."

"I'm not sure. I avoid alcohol for this very reason. I'm not into pain and suffering."

"*Unless it's for Cheetos.*" Valdez was parked near the bedroom door and had come in with Nate.

Nathan looked from me to Valdez. "I don't get it. Will's a vampire and Valdez said he was drunk last night. Now he's downstairs cooking, business as usual. Hell, he's got a Scotch next to him right now. Why isn't he laid out, begging for a stake through the heart? Is it because Ray's new at this game?"

Valdez didn't wait for me to answer Nathan. *"Will's a different kind of vampire from your buddy Ray. He was born from another vamp, not made like Ray and Glory were. Will can eat, drink and be merry in ways 'made' vamps can't. Ask Glory about those Cheetos sometime."*

"He's right." I gave Valdez an evil smile and a mental promise to boycott Cheetos, which were also one of *his* favorite snacks. Oh, and forget Twinkies too. He slumped to the floor, his tail down. I'm sure if I bothered to read his mind, I'd get called a few names I'd rather not hear. Tough.

"Well, hell." Nate walked back into the bedroom and pulled the covers up to Ray's chin again. "Now what?"

"I'm thinking." I sat on the foot of the bed. "There might be something another vampire could do for Ray, to dilute the effects of the alcohol. Unfortunately, if Will's still drinking, then I guess it's on me."

"So how *do* you help Ray?" Nathan had almost shredded the list in his hand. I hope he had another copy. "He's got to be able to sing by tomorrow morning. Oh, shit, I mean night. We'll have to come up with reasons why he can only rehearse at night. Maybe we'll tell Sienna the truth. She's pretty cool. Have you seen her video for 'Nightmare'?"

"The vampires in her video were caricatures. Fake fangs, blood dripping all over the place and Sienna lying half naked in an open coffin like a virgin sacrifice." I laughed, but not in amusement. "Is that how you see us, Nate?" I heard Valdez snort beside me.

"Of course not." Nathan put his hand on my shoulder. "But it shows—"

"It shows Sienna's trying to jump on the paranormal trendy train. I bet she'd freak if you told her anything about Ray and what happened to him. Promise me you won't say a word to her until we discuss this, Nate. I mean it. Promise." Sienna Star. I'm admittedly a tabloid junkie and was even before I became a headliner. Young, edgy, Sienna had the kind of perfect body men lusted for.

My roommate and I had every CD Ray had ever recorded.

Every DVD of his videos too. But we'd boycotted his duet with Sienna. Because, even though Nathan was right that the song had gone platinum practically overnight, we'd hated the way the young slut had been all over "our" Israel Caine. Before we'd met Ray we'd been ridiculously obsessed fangirls. What can I say? The man can *sing* and look great doing it of course.

"Fine. I won't tell Sienna Ray's secret and I'll do something to stall her. Now you concentrate on fixing Ray. Is there anything you can do, Glory?" Nathan stared down at me. Waiting for my vampire miracle cure.

I knew of only one way to get bad blood out of a vampire's system. I stood and stared at Ray. He was really pale and still not moving. I gestured and Nate followed me to the hall again. When the three of us were outside, I shut the door and leaned against it. A quick sniff assured me Nate was the only mortal upstairs.

"This may not work. But it's the only thing I can think of. I'm going to have to feed Ray."

"Feed? But you said he can't eat. Which is a bummer. I know he really misses Italian food and Will's chili smells delicious. Ray'd really like that." Nathan scratched his chin then did a double take when he noticed my fangs were down. "Oh, I guess you mean give him your blood. Fine. Do it. What're you waiting for?"

"I already fed Ray once. Last night." Valdez growled, but hushed when I nudged him with my foot. "It was an emergency. Like this is." I told Nate about Ray cutting his foot. "Ray healed, but he still woke up sick. And without his voice. I think, though, that the more new blood he gets, the more it will dilute the alcohol in his system."

"Like I said. Get after it."

"*You get after it, mortal. Go in there and throw yourself on your buddy's fangs.*" Valdez showed some teeth.

"That's not what Ray needs, Valdez. Aged vampire blood. That's what has healing power." I couldn't help it. I took a deep breath and almost sighed with pleasure. "So I'll feed Ray right after I take care of myself first. I have to power up before

I let another vampire drink from me again." I put my hand on Nathan's muscular arm. The man obviously worked out. Hmm. "Nate, I hate to ask this of you, but, umm, you're AB negative, aren't you?"

"Here we go," Valdez muttered. *"AB neg trumps Cheetos every time."*

"What?" Nathan jumped back, his eyes wide. "You want to bite me? Drink my blood?"

I smiled. I knew for a fact Nate wasn't a vampire virgin. He'd had a little romantic interlude with a female vamp who'd taken him down a pint or two. I usually relied on synthetics myself, but to help Ray, I figured I needed some really high-octane stuff, and my fave is AB neg. I'd known from the first inhale that Nate was just my type.

"Surely you'd be willing to donate. For your best friend? I can put you under the whammy if you're afraid it'll hurt." The whammy makes a mortal have temporary or, if you want, permanent amnesia. Works on immortals too if you're lucky enough to catch one of them off guard.

Nate glanced at Valdez then gave me a really thorough once-over. I still wore Ray's T-shirt and shorts. No underwear, of course. My thong had been snipped along with my jeans. "Don't suppose this could be made part of something a little, um, more interesting."

"Watch it, Burke. Glory's not available."

"Oh, yeah? Available or not, Nathan, I'm afraid all I'm interested in right now is a little fang action. Valdez, why don't you take a chill pill, sit your butt downstairs, and do your bodyguard thing while I enjoy drinking at Nate's personal fountain?"

"Just don't enjoy it too much." Valdez bumped me with his butt on his way down the stairs.

"Remind me to tell Brittany how you've been sniffing around that dachshund in apartment 3C," I said to his backside.

"She's a min pin, a miniature pinscher. And you stay out of my love life."

"Same to ya, V." I turned to Nate. "Come on, Nathan. Whether you think this is interesting or not remains to be seen." I pulled Nathan toward one of the empty bedrooms. I wasn't about to do this in the room with Ray, even if he was practically unconscious. That seemed too much like a threesome.

"Wow. Thanks. And you don't need to whammy me, Glory. Ray's my best friend. I'll do whatever it takes to help him recover." Nate threw himself on a queen-size bed that had obviously seen some overnight action.

"You're a good friend. And this won't hurt. Not much, anyway."

Nate's eyes widened and he braced himself like he was about to be drilled at the dentist's office.

"Oh, relax, Nathan. I'll be gentle. I just need to be full strength when I feed Ray. So we can dilute the poison he put in his system." I sat beside him and picked up his wrist.

"Wait! You mean alcohol is poison to him now?" Nathan frowned as he watched my fangs descend even farther. "That would be good news. You know I was afraid Ray was about one drink shy of turning into an alcoholic before this vampire gig came up."

I inhaled Nate's delicious scent. Hoo boy. I gave up drinking from mortals decades ago. Back when synthetics were invented. It was a conscious decision because, after centuries of having to hunt and use unsuspecting mortal donors to survive, I was kind of over it. Now, though, years of denying myself that fresh taste hit me hard. Didn't hurt that his blood type was like Godiva to me. Way too expensive in the synthetics to be more than an occasional treat.

"Ray won't be hitting the bottle anytime soon. He'd be a fool to put himself through this again. He said he didn't even get a buzz from what he drank last night." I lifted Nate's wrist to my lips.

"Wait!"

"What now?" I was dying here. To be so close to nirvana . . .

Nathan smiled, suddenly all naughty bad boy. "Ray and I grew up together, you know?"

"Yes, I've heard all about your gilt-edged 'hood.' " Poor little rich kids went to all the best schools the Chicago suburbs had to offer. Then Nate had gone on to Harvard while Ray had made music his life. Did we have to go into this *now*? I was ready to just whammy Nathan and get on with it.

"He tells me pretty much everything."

"So?" Had Ray lied and said we'd slept together? Maybe I'd let him suffer with his hangover a while longer. I dropped Nate's wrist on the bed.

"I know you're just his mentor, Glory. And he really appreciates it. But he'd like your relationship to be something more. We both think you're hot."

"Oh?" Now this was interesting. I barely stopped myself from going all girly, throwing back my shoulders and tossing my hair.

"Would you, well, would you drink from my neck? Pretend we were lovers? Just so I can stick it to Ray?" Nate sat up and put his hands on my shoulders. "It'll be fun. We can pull his chain. I've seen him try some of his 'never fail' moves on you and seen you deflect them. Valdez says that's because it's you and Blade all the way."

"Jeremy Blade and I have a complicated relationship. Which is sometimes on, sometimes off." That dog was going to earn a muzzle if he didn't quit telling everyone I was in a committed relationship. Maybe I was, maybe I wasn't. Getting stuck dateless on New Year's Eve made me feel pretty uncommitted if you want to know the truth.

"Good to know." Nate popped the rubber band that had held my hair back in a ponytail and ran his hand through my curls. Then he slid one hand to the back of my neck the other to the edge of my sleeve to stroke up my arm. Seems like Ray wasn't the only one with some "never fail" moves. "The idea that you and I have been together will drive Ray wild."

I shivered. Nate's hands were warm, human warm, and I hadn't had that kind of touch in, hmm, decades. He had good instincts, lightly touching the vein pulsing in my neck, then tracing a path to my collar bone where Ray's too-large T-shirt gapped.

"Pulling Ray's chain. Sounds good." I took a breath and tried to think beyond the smell of warm blood and the feel of warm hands on my body. Nathan rolled me on top of him. Like he was getting me into position, then smiled up at me.

"Go for it, Glory. Do whatever you want. I'm game."

He was game, all right. I could feel the bulge of him nestled between my legs. Interesting. Nathan *was* a hot guy, but the only thing turning me on was being close to his warm human blood. But he did deserve a reward for this sacrifice.

"Listen, Nate. Ray and I, well, any vampire can read your mind whether you want us to or not. He'd know in a heartbeat if we lied about hooking up."

"That's crap." Nate ran his hands down my back and cupped my bottom to press me against him. "So I guess we have no choice but to make this the real deal if we want to play with Ray's head." He gently bit my wrist where it lay next to his head.

"Hate to disappoint you, but we do have a choice. I can give you a hot memory of what *could* have happened in this bed. It's what we do when we've fed from a mortal and we don't want him to remember the deed. We plant a false memory and send him on his way. So I can do that here. Then, if Ray checks out your story, he'll see you think we've done the deed, Super Stud."

Nate grinned. "Super Stud? Have you been talking to my exes?"

We both laughed. "No, I googled you, though. There are thousands of blogs about you and your prowess."

Nate slid his hands up to my waist. "Could be. You won't know until you try me for yourself. You sure you want this to be just pretend?" He had a very sexy smile and his mind was full of interesting ideas of what he could do to me.

I decided this had gone on long enough. I looked into his eyes and put him under the whammy. Nathan would think it was real. I'd know otherwise. I proceeded to give him a—ahem, pardon the expression—blow-by-blow description of us burning up the sheets. I mean, his memories were absolute scorchers. The man never had such great sex in his life. Forever after, he'd measure all encounters with "the time I slept with the fabulous Glory St. Clair."

Maybe I got a little carried away. And maybe this would complicate things, but who could resist? So, damn me, if I didn't lean into good old Nathan, who, have I mentioned, is really a looker in a tall, dark and well built way? Think Denzel a few decades ago. Yum. While I built my fantasy scenario, I kissed him and ran my hands down his body then settled in at his neck. Who was acting? I was really turned on by the AB neg.

"Damn, Glory, this is—" Nate gasped when I finally used my fangs. His eyes rolled back in his head and I figured the whole vampire experience was a little too much for him. No problem. I drew on him and felt the wonderful fresh taste burst into my mouth. I swear it was enough to bring tears to my eyes. Why had I denied myself this pleasure?

And not only was the flavor delicious, but the surge of power made my whole body jolt with renewed energy. I literally had to shove my mouth away from Nathan before I drained him. I lay for a moment against his warm chest, relieved that his heart still beat strongly. Oh, God, but that had been dangerously wonderful. I finally raised my head and saw blood trickling down Nate's neck. I'd been so far gone, I'd even forgotten to lick the fang marks closed. I took care of that, then kissed his lips and pulled his hand off my boob.

I patted his cheek and left him to sleep it off. I could tell he was okay, just a little, um, drained. I sauntered down the hall feeling pretty damned good. Valdez must have heard me coming because he met me at the top of the stairs.

He trotted up to me, then almost sat on my foot. *"Cheeks pink. And the look on your face . . . Wow, Glory. Musta been good."*

"I'll say. I forgot how great mortal blood can be. Nate passed out when I bit him." I grinned. "But he won't remember it that way."

Valdez glanced at Ray's bedroom door. *"Whatcha gonna do about Caine? Can't believe that a-hole showed those yahoos downstairs your tits last night."*

"I wanted to kill him." I couldn't meet V's gleaming eyes. He'd been one of those "yahoos."

"Let me tell Blade what happened, and you won't have to."

"No. Ray and I had a freak meeting out on the lake last night. I'll tell you about it later. But I need Ray around to help with this situation." I sighed, already coming down from my temporary high. "I'd better go see if I can help him now."

"Yeah, yeah." Valdez shook his head. *"I'll be at the bottom of the stairs. But I'll be waiting. I can't protect you if I don't know what the hell's going on, you know."*

"Yep, I know, pal. I need your help. I always do." I slipped into the bedroom, closed and locked the door, then leaned against it, trying to recapture that high I'd had when I'd taken Nate's blood. I did still feel pumped and ready for anything. Good. Because Ray was awake and tapping on the bedside table. He looked frantic. Yeah, he would since he couldn't make a sound with his million dollar voice.

Maybe you think I should be a little more sympathetic. Hey, I'd had a few adventures with alcohol myself back in the day. The fifties were big on martinis. I'd had some killer hangovers. Nights and nights of pain and suffering. But I did eventually come back, 100 percent recovery. Of course Ray couldn't wait. The voice thing. I sympathized. Really I did.

"Okay, Ray, relax. I think I know what you need, and I've got it right here." I sauntered over to the bed, prepared to make the most of my mission of mercy. Nate had said Ray wanted something more from me. Why not? Glory St. Clair is hot, hot, hot. I did a little hair toss. Wasted effort. Poor Ray was scribbling madly on the pad I'd found for him earlier. He held it up.

"I *know* you need your voice back. I'm not one hundred percent sure this'll work, but I think if you feed from me again, it'll help." So much for my sex-kitten act.

Ray fell back on the bed, tossed the pad and pen aside and opened his arms. I knew that look. He figured he'd get a little more than blood with my donation. Ah, so maybe my sex kitten had been noticed after all. Meow!

"Relax, Ray. This is all about the voice right now. Save your other moves for another time. I'll bet you're still hurting, aren't you?" Had to play hard to get, didn't I?

He shook his head, then winced and mouthed the words. "Maybe a little."

"No guarantees, but never underestimate the healing powers of aged vampire blood." I sat beside him and brushed my hair back to offer my neck. Suddenly I was flat on my back, staring up at a Ray I hardly recognized. This man snarled, bared his fangs, then pinned my arms over my head before he plunged his teeth into my neck.

"Ow! Son of a—Ray! Ease up!" I jerked my arms free and grabbed his hair so I could flip us until he was under me. I couldn't have done it if he hadn't still been weak from alcohol poisoning. "Now drink like a civilized vampire, not an animal, and try not to rip out my throat." I put my arms around him and held him close as I felt the pull of him drinking from me. Wow, I'd expected a little finesse, maybe a few nibbles before he sank his teeth into me. Instead I'd gotten a ferocious attack that still had me shaking.

"Calm down, Ray. I know what your voice means to you. But, damn it, you hurt me again like that and I'll throw you across the room. Just so we're clear." I braced myself, ready to pull Ray off of me if he went too far, tried to take too much. *I* had to be able to function when all was said and done. Sure he was desperate. And probably saying every prayer he knew that this would work for him. I was praying for him too. But I wasn't willing to die for him.

Gradually his movements became less frantic, and I closed

my eyes and relaxed into the rhythm. Now, though, I became aware of his hard body against mine and the way we were lying tangled together like lovers. I'd been in a similar position with Nathan just minutes before, but somehow, with Ray, I was way more distracted by every place we touched—bare legs, chest against chest, his hips pressing into mine and the way his hand cradled the back of my neck. Ray carefully licked the punctures closed, his tongue making me shudder.

"Want to go for best two out of three, vamp girl? I think I could flip you now that I've got juice."

I slapped his arm. "This wasn't a game, Ray. How do you feel?" He'd spoken in my mind. "Try to talk. Out loud. See what happens."

He touched my throat. "Sorry. Too . . . rough. You . . . okay?" His voice was raspy. But he could speak. We grinned at each other.

"I'm a freakin' miracle worker, but you attack me like that again and I'll hand you your ass on a platter, vamp *boy*." I yawned and stretched.

"Did I . . . take too much?" Ray sat up.

"I'd have stopped you before I let you do that. I'm okay. I fed from your buddy Nate before I came in here. So I'd be in top form."

"You and Nate? How'd . . . go?" Ray's voice was getting stronger, but still just a whisper.

"I'll never tell." I sat up and leaned against the headboard. "How're we going to go vamp hunting with Sienna Star underfoot?"

"Problem. Hotel. Tell Nate. Later." Ray sighed. "Voice . . . not right."

"Sorry." I really was. This was a hard way for Ray to learn that he just couldn't drink alcohol. "How does your body feel?"

"Better." Ray rubbed his forehead. "But still hurts."

"I'll feed you again later. Hopefully that will help. I'm trying to dilute that poison in your system. Stay up here.

We don't want to start a panic with the band. But I need to go down and talk to Will. You realize we're going to have to go out to the EV stronghold if we want to deliver Simon to Aggie."

"How?"

How indeed. Maybe going after Simon Destiny was foolish. But I saw this as a golden opportunity to rid the paranormal community of one of the worst excuses for a vampire to ever show a fang. So I was determined to try. Muscle wouldn't do it. The King of the Energy Vampires was way too powerful and the demon he worked for too scary for us to just bull our way in and drag the leader out with us. No, it was going to take some pretty clever maneuvering. We had to lure Simon away from the safety of his lair.

"Simon's bored. He told me that much when I saw him last." And hadn't that been a treat? For some reason Simon had actually expressed an interest in hooking up with me. Not that I take that as a compliment. The guy's just about as gross as Aggie. Has this unusual talent, though. He can make himself look like your heart's desire. If he decides to, of course. He hadn't bothered when I'd seen him last. "Maybe we can use his boredom to our advantage."

"Also has drugs. Go out there. Try some. Together." Naughty smile. Ray knew the Energy Vampires were famous for their Vampire Viagra. It enhances sexual pleasure for male *and* female vampires. Trust me, no male vamp *I've* ever met had ED issues. The VV is strictly to ramp up the pleasure. Think wild monkey sex for hours on end. I never said it was a *bad* thing. Except for loss of control and, of course, the fact that it costs the earth.

"I guess we *could* go out there and *pretend* to want to try some. Together." I threw Ray one of my own naughty smiles then crawled out of bed.

The doorknob rattled and there was banging on the door.

"Gloriana, baby! Are you in there with Ray? Let me in."

Five

Nathan. Calling me baby. I checked out Ray's reaction. He'd closed his eyes again. That headache. I hurried to the door.

"Nathan, be quiet. Ray's still hurting. What do you want?"

Nathan slid his arm around my waist and planted a big wet one on my lips. "You, baby. I dreamed—"

"Let's take this outside. Let Ray rest." I started to pull Nathan out the door.

"Wait!" Ray's voice was barely a whisper, but Nathan was already halfway across the room.

"Man! You can talk. Not a hundred percent, but I heard you! Glory, sweetheart, you did it." He grabbed me and tried to kiss me again, but I dodged away.

"It's the vampire blood. Thanks to your donation, Ray's a little better, but I'm afraid it'll take more than once to do the trick." I grabbed Nathan's hand and was about to get him out the door again when I saw Ray's eyes narrow on his friend.

"Nathan?"

"Downstairs. Now. You need a computer, Ray. Come on, Nate. Ray needs to google someone. I'm sure you've got a

laptop you can bring him, don't you?" Temporary postpone-
ment, but I was desperate. Maybe I should erase that erotic
fantasy I'd given Nate. Ray's friend pulled me close and
nuzzled my neck. No maybe about it.

"You and Glory, Nate?" Ray's slow smile didn't reach his
eyes. "Hot and heavy?"

"I'll say." Nate pulled my hand to his lips and ran his
tongue across my knuckles. "I'm glad to give her my blood,
for you, buddy, but I had no idea . . . Seems that kind of
fang action is a real turn-on for vampires." He grinned. "I'm
a gentleman so I'll say no more. Come on, baby. Sure I've
got a laptop downstairs Ray can use. You need more blood?
Got to admit I'm feeling a little woozy. Let me eat something and I'll be good to go again. In *every* way."

"Uh, well, we'll see. I need to confab with the paranormals we've got on the payroll. Why don't you head on down
and eat?" What had I been thinking? Creating virtual sex
with Nathan? I'd had a vampire pull that trick on me once.
And when I'd found out it had all been a sham, a fantasy, I'd
felt betrayed and like a complete fool. This had started because Nate and I had wanted to pull Ray's chain. But Ray's
narrow-eyed look could mean anything from "Go to hell" to
a knee-jerk competitive "You win the booby prize." Me being the booby—or boobies, in my case.

"Come with me, Glory."

"No, I hate to see mortals eat. It makes me sad that I
can't." I blinked like I was fighting back tears. Yuck. Nathan
bought it. He just hugged me.

"Later then." He looked at Ray. "We need to talk, bud. Sienna's due and you've got to be able to sing. Let Glory do
whatever it takes to bring you up to speed. I'll stick Sienna in
a hotel and put her off for a day or two, tell her we're waiting
for some equipment to come in. Maybe Dex can show her the
sights in Austin." Nathan patted me on the butt, then strode
out of the room.

"Nice." Ray rolled over and stared at the wall.

Since I wasn't about to tell Ray the truth, I began to

babble about the pressing need we had to figure out the Aggie situation.

"I'd better get downstairs. Maybe Brittany or Will knows something about Sirens. You stay in bed. Google Aggie and this Achelous; see what you can find out."

"Sure." Ray rasped. "When feed me again? Use Nathan?"

I took a moment to think about it. I knew Ray kept a supply of synthetic blood because, as part of my mentoring, I'd insisted he survive on it. But I had a gut feeling the real deal was necessary for this healing to work.

"No. Nathan needs time to recover from his last donation. You've got a houseful of mortals here. I'll sniff around and see if there are any who aren't drunk or stoned. Polluted blood wouldn't do you much good, just add another set of problems to your situation. I may have to go outside and check out our latest crop of stalkers and paparazzi." Hunting like the old days. I admit I got kind of jazzed about it. Decades of denial and suddenly I was in predator mode again? Man, this was crazy.

Ray rolled over and looked at me. "Be careful."

"Oh, I'll take Valdez with me. Trust me, Ray, I was hunting long before electricity was invented."

"Yeah, right." Ray picked up a pen and paper. He stared at it for a long moment, then tossed it aside. He reached out his hand and I walked close to the bed.

"What?"

"Nathan. He's my best friend. Don't hurt him. And you'd damn well better not turn him vampire." Ray obviously felt strongly about this, his voice ringing inside my head.

"I don't plan to hurt him. And I don't turn people vampire." Okay, reality check. There'd been that once . . . "Well, not unless it's a life-or-death situation. I know Nate is important to you. And you're important to him. He's donating blood for you. He knows you're a freakin' vampire and he didn't run screaming into the night. Now that's a true friend." I took a breath. "Try to rest. When Nate gets up here, don't talk, just write notes or type on the computer.

I'll come back before dawn and feed you again. Hopefully, by the time Sienna is ready to practice, you'll be able to belt out your tunes per usual."

"Hope so." He frowned and pulled the covers up to his chin.

"See you later." I headed downstairs. Valdez was sitting on the bottom step.

"Glory, would you call off your dog? My guitar is in one of the spare bedrooms and I thought this mutt was going to bite my head off when I tried to go past him. You and Ray aren't the only ones who use the upstairs." A member of Ray's band, a really hot guy who'd been with Ray for years, gave me a sly smile.

"Sorry, Dex, and the mutt's name is Valdez."

"Right. You want to help me look for my guitar, sweet-heart? Maybe play a . . . tune together?"

Valdez growled and I grabbed his collar. "Now, Dex, I don't think Ray'd like that, do you?" I winked. "Sorry about my dog. I'll take him with me." I pulled Valdez along. "Oh, and don't bother Ray right now. He's taking a little nap. Says I wore him out."

"Aw, Glory, now you're torturing me." Dex put a hand over his heart and looked me over. "If I write a song for you, will you give me some of that?"

Ray had written a song for me, "The Glory Years," that was going on his new album. Dex didn't have a clue that, with luck, Ray would have Glory *centuries*. I leaned across Valdez to pat the man's handsome cheek lined from way too much hard living. I inhaled a nice B positive, but with a little too much marijuana for him to be a donor.

"Write that song and we'll see. But I've got to warn you, Dex, I'm a one man woman. One at a time, anyway." I laughed and dragged a growling Valdez toward the kitchen.

"Glory, I'm going to head up with this laptop for Ray." Nathan stepped out of the den carrying a black leather case. "Meet me upstairs in about an hour, baby? Had a rare-roastbeef sandwich and a glass of milk. I'm reloaded and ready to go again."

I looked around to make sure we were alone, something Nathan should have done, then smiled. "Relax, Nathan. You need a full twenty-four hours to recover after giving a donation. And this is our little secret. Remember? I'm Ray's girl as far as the guys here are concerned." I stepped out of reach when Nathan moved closer.

He frowned. "Yeah, yeah, I know what they think. But I know what happened up there. You were into me, Glory. Really into me. I can give you something besides blood. Remember? We were hot together. No need to wait twenty-four hours to recover from that, baby." He gave me a hot look, dropped the laptop and grabbed my arm. It took Valdez about half a beat to grab *Nathan's* arm.

"Damn! Okay, I'm letting her go, Valdez. See?" Nathan stepped back and rubbed his bicep. He wore a nice thick wool sweater. Expensive Italian in a beautiful cream color. Which would have to be rewoven now that it had some significant punctures. At least I didn't see any bloodstains. Yet.

"Valdez, that was an overreaction. You know Nathan would never hurt me." I gave him a fierce look. "Bad dog." I said this in case one of the band members or their ladies happened to be within earshot. Valdez just glared at Nate, daring him to lay another finger on me. Which was actually okay with me for now. Nate really needed to let this go. But I had no one to blame but myself.

"Nate, I'm sorry. This isn't happening. Big mistake. Please—"

"Come on, Glory, quit teasing. I know this isn't the place to talk about this, but you can meet me upstairs. No one needs to know but you, me and the dog here. Not even Ray." Nathan had put his hands behind his back and he moved closer, his voice quiet and his eyes on my mouth. He licked his lips. "You, we . . . I've never felt like that before. You inspired me." He glanced down at Valdez and dared to inch closer. "You called me your 'Big Gun.' Never a misfire. Just bang, bang, um, bang. I lost count of how many times I pulled *your* trigger."

Valdez snorted and I bit my lip to keep from smiling. I did do mental eye rolls. Obviously I'd gotten a little carried away when doing the whole fantasy thing. I'd been stuck on Ray's hokey starting the New Year with a bang idea and the rest had snowballed from there.

I could see Nathan about to start in again, his face flushed. I read his mind and quickly put my fingers over Nate's lips. I have a pretty wild fantasy life. Which has served me well when I'm up close and personal with my state-of-the-art vibrator. In fact, if I'd made it home, I'd planned a New Year's date with my always to be counted on lover. I didn't doubt Nate could have made me very happy between the sheets if his thoughts were any indication. But he was a man, Ray's friend, and not a piece of equipment I could toss in a drawer when I got tired of it. This situation had "Handle with Care" stamped all over it.

"I'm sorry, Nate, but I can't talk about this now. I've got some serious things to discuss with the bodyguards. And don't you have the Sienna situation to deal with?"

He glanced at his watch. "Yeah. She should be picked up at the airport in about an hour, then taken to the hotel. I guess I should think about meeting her there."

"Yes, you should. Keep her away from Ray until we get his voice fixed."

"I hope to hell it *gets* fixed." Nate looked at Valdez, then snagged my hand. I had to give him points for guts. My dog just stared at him. "Call me when you need my blood or whatever." He pulled my hand to his lips. "I mean it, Glory."

"Right. You're a good friend, Nate. I know Ray appreciates it."

Nathan dropped my hand. "Ray. Sure. This is all about Ray." His face fell and he grabbed the laptop. "Of course this was all about Ray. Appreciate the sacrifice, Glory. How could I forget? Rock star trumps paper pusher every time."

Damn it. Now I'd hurt Nathan's feelings.

"Nathan, wait!" I caught him at the bottom of the stairs. "Look at me." I pulled him around until I had him in my sights. I checked to make sure we didn't have an audience. "We were great together. Forget Ray." I kissed him long and hard. "Now I've got to talk to those bodyguards. I know you understand. Security first." And with that I almost ran toward the kitchen, Valdez on my heels.

"He'd better keep that popgun in his holster."

"Do *not* make me laugh."

Valdez sniffed as I opened the kitchen door. *"Hmm. I could eat."*

In the kitchen, Will was in front of the stove seasoning a steaming pot. It smelled delicious and I wished for the ten millionth time that *I* could eat. Brittany, who's a shape-shifter, sure could. She sat at the round glass table with a full plate in front of her. She stuffed a loaded nacho into her mouth, then put the plate on the floor. It took Valdez about a nanosecond to clean it off.

"Cruel and unusual. You guys really shouldn't eat in front of me." I sat down on one of the chairs at the table. There was a roar from the den. All the mortals were glued to the tube. I'm not a football fan, but I could hear bets being made about whether the favored team could score before halftime. Will had a pained look on his face and I knew he was itching to get in on the action. Not me, I never got into the sports betting scene.

"Listen, guys, we need to talk." I nodded and the kitchen door closed. It didn't have a lock of course, but I could keep it closed with my mind against any feeble mortal trying to push it open.

"Finally. Something happened to Ray and Glory out on the lake last night. What was it, Glory? Do you need for us to go out there?" Valdez looked up at Brittany and she wiped off his muzzle with her brown cloth napkin.

"Trouble? Man, if those paparazzi have hired a boat, I'm gonna—"

"Relax, Brittany, that's not it."

"More fans?" Will tasted his concoction. Since he said he'd trained at the Cordon Bleu in Paris I'm sure it was delicious. It definitely smelled that way. "Not bad if I do say so myself." He put down his ladle. "What happened out there, Glory? Fill us in. The crew in the den said you came in wet and Ray had cut his foot. Was bleeding like a stuck pig. Which surprised me, him being vampire and all. Then"— Will grinned—"there was a topless moment that I'm sorry as hell I missed." He winked when Valdez growled. "Relax, fur face. You gonna tell me you didn't look?" Now Brittany growled and Will laughed. "Details, we want details."

"What you'll get is the bottom line. What do any of you know about Sirens?"

"Will had the smoke alarm going last night. I told him not to try deep-frying those chicken wings." Brittany sighed. "But they were delicious."

"Oil got too hot. Then two senior citizens tried to jimmy open the gate on the driveway. That set off the siren something fierce." Will grinned. "Didn't know little old ladies could run like that. One of them even threw her crowbar at me. Glory, one of them was AB negative. Delicious. Thought of you when I had my midnight snack, darlin'."

"You are so bad, Will Kilpatrick. I hope you left the woman enough for the drive home." I grinned. Will is too charming for his own good.

"Her sister was driving. I left *her* standin' around while I did the dirty." Will laughed. "But what about sirens? This house is wired from top to bottom. Keeps us hoppin' with the paparazzi and all tryin' to break in every night. Everyone wants a piece of Israel Caine."

"Or a picture of him doing something crazy like showing the world his girlfriend's tits." Valdez glared at me. *"I'd like to see what Blade would have done if that picture had shown up in the tabloids, Glory."*

"Admired them, of course. Now let's move on to a new subject, Valdez. I'm not talking about the kind of siren when an alarm goes off. I mean like in legends, myths, whatever. The kind of females that lure boats onto rocks." I sat back and waited.

"Those Sirens? Where's this coming from?" Will pulled up a chair and straddled it. "I know they're bad business. Dad used to have a fleet of ships, back in Queen Victoria's day. Lost more than one on the rocks in the Mediterranean to what must have been a Siren. Mermaids. Whatever you want to call them. One of my brothers ran afoul of one close to home. In the North Sea. She bewitched him. Can't imagine it myself. I'm partial to women with legs, not fish tails."

"What happened?" Brittany leaned close, elbows on the table.

For a moment, Will didn't answer. I think he got distracted by the way Brit's red sweater outlined her awesome breasts. Valdez edged closer to her and showed his teeth. I really felt sorry for him. Will's a handsome man with red hair, green eyes and a buff bod. Valdez might be more than a match in human form, but right now he looked 100 percent Labradoodle. Brittany's hand landed on his head and she fondled his ears.

"Will? What happened to your brother?" I needed all the information I could get. "And, for your information, Sirens are shape-shifters. They can have legs if they want them."

"Whatever they look like, they're greedy wenches. Dad finally had to pay her off. Seems this Siren was satisfied with a shipload of gold." Will grinned and shook his head like maybe he realized Brittany wasn't returning his interest. "Why? You're not telling me there's a Siren on Lake Travis."

"Yes, I am. She's out there and she's looking for male vampires. So, whatever you do, don't go out on the lake." I like Will. He definitely had his faults, compulsive gambling being one of them. But since I'm a recovering gambler myself, I couldn't hold that against him. I sure didn't want him to be one of Aggie's vamp sacrifices.

"*This is nuts. You mean when you and Ray went out in his boat you met a* Siren*?*" Valdez abandoned Brittany to sit next to me. *"And she's looking for male vamps? Why'd she let Ray go then?"* Valdez's expression said it would have been okay with him if Ray had been taken away to wherever.

"Seems she's a fan. Ray sang for her and she decided to let Ray and me go if we'd bring her three other male vampires. But we've got to do it by the full moon. That's just three weeks away."

"I don't know a thing about Sirens. You, Rafe?" Brittany looked down at Valdez, whose first name, by the way, is Rafael.

"Nope, never had what is obviously not a pleasure. Damn it, Glory, you never shoulda gone out in that boat without me."

"She caught us by surprise. You couldn't have done anything, Valdez."

"You wanna bet?"

Actually I bet my dog would have ended up fish bait, but I didn't say it.

"Sounds like she's dumb as dirt." Brittany reached for a can of soda and took a swallow. "She let you go? What's to make you ever bring her anyone?"

"She's got us on a leash. She can call us to her. Ray tested it. Tried to get the hell away from her in the boat. No go. He was *compelled* to turn right around."

"So she's more powerful than a vampire?" Will frowned. "Not that I'm surprised. My brother was whipped, but then I figured she'd been giving him great—"

"Spare us the details, Will. Let me tell you. This creature is ugly as sin, but can freeze you with a look. I mean, you can't freakin' *move*. Totally creepy. I hated it. You are completely helpless." I shuddered, remembering. "But now, if Ray and I want to come out of this with our own hides intact, we've got to bring her three vampires. And Aggie specifically wants males. She's got a deal with a goddess named Circe. The goddess hates men, hates the night, so she wants *male* vamps. Period." I knew I couldn't relax, though. If Ray and I didn't come up with the goods, I had a feeling I'd still end up tossed into Circe's circle of hell just for the fun of it.

"Aggie? Her name's Aggie? That doesn't sound like a

Siren to me. Are you sure that's what she is?" Will got up to check on his bubbling pot. He dipped the ladle in, tasted, then added a pinch of salt.

"Her real name is long and unpronounceable. You should see her. Definitely doesn't look like a mermaid. Circe did a number on her. I don't care what she is, I only know we've got to do what she says or Ray and I are going to be her vamp sacrifices and the clock's ticking."

"I hear ya, Glory. You know plenty of vampires in Austin. Got any favorites you'd like to see go bye-bye? Would seem kind of cruel to just pick random vamps, don't you think?" Brittany crushed her soda can effortlessly, her arm muscle flexing.

"Oh, we're not going to be random. I really, really want to take her Simon Destiny for one."

"Now you're talkin', Blondie." Valdez jumped up and wagged his tail. *"But you'd better not be thinkin' of going out to the EV compound after Simon on your own. There are three of us here, four with Ray. We'd be dead meat before we even reached the perimeter. We need a freakin' army. Man, I want a piece of that EV bastard."*

Simon Destiny almost killed Valdez once. My dog wouldn't and shouldn't ever forgive or forget. "We'll get him, pup. I promise. He'll be on his way to Circe before he knows what hit him."

I heard a commotion at the door. "I think the natives are ready for your chili, Will. And more beer. Must be half-time." And our game was just beginning.

Six

When I opened the door, the crowd seemed more intent on making a beer run and talking about the game than wondering why a door without a lock had jammed. One of the women opened the massive fridge and leaned down to pull out six-packs of beer.

"Love your tats." I could see a pretty vine growing up her arm and flowering across her upper back. Tattoos and vamps don't mix. The healing sleep wipes them right away. Which is why Ray's situation was such a freak-out. He wasn't *healing*.

"Look at this one." She stood and pulled down her low-rise jeans.

"Is that—"

"Dave's face on my ass. Seemed appropriate." She laughed and carefully balanced three six-packs before shutting the refrigerator door with her hip. "Had it done in San Francisco. I can hook you up if you're interested. The artist is a genius."

"Yeah, I can see. Let me think about it."

A redhead got busy filling bowls with chili, then smiled at me.

"Glory, you brought that great classic Gucci bag, didn't you?"

"Yes, I own a vintage-clothing shop. You'd be amazed what I get in." I was about to go into my usual selling spiel, then noticed she had on this season's designer boots that cost more than my shop made in a good month. So I shut up.

"Your phone keeps ringing. I had to move your bag or Randy was going to dropkick it off the deck. It's in the entry near the front door." She frowned. "The man has no respect for quality leather goods."

"Thanks for the rescue. I'll see who's been calling." Obviously Randy was not *her* significant other. I got up and headed for the front door, pushing past three other women and two of the band members, including Dex. He managed to cop a feel before Valdez showed some teeth and encouraged him to forget it. I sent a mental message for Valdez to quit growling and come with me. This might be a good time to check outside for blood donors. I found my purse on the marble-topped table near the front door.

Valdez looked over his shoulder to make sure none of the band or their women were nearby. Fortunately they were all back in front of the wide-screen with the surround sound turned up full blast.

"Bet it's Blade calling from Europe. Hope he got there all right." Valdez stood with his back to me, to make sure no one came up to within listening range. As far as the band was concerned, I was Ray's girlfriend. We'd planned to stage a breakup as soon as Ray felt comfortable going vampire on his own. Neither one of us had any idea when that would be. This latest incident was certainly a setback.

I checked my messages. Two from my former roommate, Florence da Vinci.

First message: "Glory, I've been robbed." Sounds of sobbing. "I must talk to my best friend. Call me." I hit speed dial. No answer. Damn. I hurriedly listened to her second message.

"Ricardo has calmed me down. He says to tell you I am fine, which I'm not. But at least my body is fine. Anyway, he is making me feel a little better by taking me on a short honeymoon to a place in the hills near here. So he can be sweet when he isn't a bullying—" I heard sounds of a scuffle and some Italian curses.

"Glory, Florence is being her usual dramatic self. She needs to talk to you, but we'll be gone a couple of nights. She'll call you when we get back. Trust me, this is not an emergency." Richard, Flo's husband, obviously knew how to handle my former roomie. Amazing. I heard her giggle in the background. Then the call ended. Hmm. Well at least she was okay.

Now to check on the calls from Jerry. There were three messages from him. He'd made it across the Atlantic, thank God. And had spent the day in Paris. With Mara? He left out that tiny detail. Not that he would want to be with her. I knew better, in my head, at least. But there was this stupid knee-jerk jealousy thing I had where the woman was concerned. She was so obvious in her pursuit of my guy. I hated her.

Hearing his voice made me realize how much I missed him. Sure he could be overprotective, but right now, with the Aggie threat and Ray still flat on his back and depending on me, I felt the weight of all that responsibility, big-time. Even with an ocean between us, he was still taking care of me.

"Watch your back, Gloriana. I've heard that Westwood's jet left Europe yesterday heading for Texas. I don't know if he was on it, but keep Valdez with you." Brent Westwood. A vamp hunter with me at the top of his "get" list. Swell, that's all I needed right now.

I replayed Jerry's messages twice, just to hear his voice, then realized he might still be awake over there. No luck. I bet I sounded as frustrated as he had.

"Jerry, I'm okay, but I miss you already. I'm sorry I was crabby about your leaving. I hope you find Lily and bring her back so I can get to know her. I'll figure out this time-difference thing and try to call you again later. Love you." I ended the call then dropped the phone back in my purse. I picked up the leash I carried for show and turned to Valdez.

"Now we need to go out and find a nice clean source for me to drink from."

"*Are you kidding me?*" Valdez looked shocked as he faced me. "*Since when do you drink from mortals? First Nathan, now you're going hunting for* strangers?"

"Ray needs to be fed again. His voice is still wonky." I knew I sounded defensive, but it was only the truth. Unfortunately, it was also the truth that I'd made a big deal out of never drinking from mortals. Had looked down on those vampires who hunted humans instead of drinking synthetics like I did. It's kind of the vampire version of going green.

I threw up a block so Valdez couldn't read my mind. Forget green. Right now I couldn't think of anything but red. The taste of Nathan's real, warm, human blood lingered on my tongue and in my system, as delicious and addictive in its way as Ray's Jack Daniel's probably was to him. I wanted more, more of the real deal. And had a feeling that even if Ray had suddenly burst into full-throated song upstairs, I might have manufactured an excuse to hunt anyway.

This was bad. I've known for decades that I have an addictive personality. Sessions with Gamblers Anonymous had taught me that. But right now I couldn't just slip back into the kitchen and twist the top off a bottle of one of Ray's specially marked bottles of "Health Drink." Will had to keep them locked in a special minifridge in the walk-in pantry next to the bar because anything off-limits in this house was like a magnet to Ray's band members. They were convinced Ray had some kind of special drug in his private label brew. I'd be jumped if I walked out with a bottle. And I didn't want it anyway.

I turned the dead bolt on the front door. "Come on. Do your bodyguard thing. I need to find someone who's not polluted like these people inside." We reached the end of the driveway and I pushed the button to open the iron gate. Lights flashed and a reporter came at me.

"Glory! Why are you leaving? Did you and Ray have a fight? Give me the scoop." The man took another picture. "What's with the dog? Are you walking him? How about a picture of the two of you together? What's his name? Can you spell it for me? Is he named after a former lover?"

I looked into the man's eyes and put him under the whammy, then took a whiff. Ordinary blood type but something off there, smoker with bad lungs. Didn't want his blood. Not good enough for Ray. I gave him a mental suggestion that he needed to leave and write an article for *Dog Fancy* magazine. It would be about celebrities' girlfriends and their dogs. He could use this picture of me and my cute Labradoodle. I even spelled Valdez's name for him. Then I snapped the photographer out of it and watched him take off.

I was hoping I'd run into that AB-negative granny, but there wasn't a single woman waiting outside the house tonight. Hmm. Was Ray losing his touch? Maybe the Sienna Star thing *had* been a smart move.

And speaking of . . . I almost bumped into two men waiting for what they hoped was a chance to see the sexy Miss Star. Blogs claimed she was arriving at Ray's tonight. I put them under the whammy, sniffed them both and decided the cutest one would do for Ray's blood donor. I dragged them into the bushes out of sight of the street while Valdez kept watch. My dog paced impatiently until I took what I needed. Then I gave the guys the name of the hotel I knew Nathan used for visitors to Austin and sent them on their way.

"Feel better now?" Valdez trotted ahead of me as we headed back to the house. *"The way you were goin' at it, I'm surprised you left the guy able to walk to his car."*

"I—"

"There she is, Wilson. Hit her with both barrels, and watch out for that dog."

A blast of water almost knocked me off my feet.

"Listen, if you're trying to get a picture for one of those

gossip rags, you just blew it big-time." I wiped wet hair out of my eyes and felt Valdez press against my legs, his body vibrating as he growled.

"I thought vampires couldn't stand holy water. She didn't even fall down. Blast her again, Wilson." A tall man stepped out of the shadows, his water gun, a high-powered one, aimed at my face. Before I could cover my eyes, he hit me a hard one right between the eyes.

"Throw the net, Sam."

"Now I'm pissed. Except for a shower or bath, I hate water and I've been nothing but wet since I got here. Back off." I felt the glide of my fangs as they extended. These guys had picked the wrong lady to mess with. I was about to leap when the guy named Sam tried to toss a silver-mesh net over my wet head.

I caught it in midair. "I swear to God I'm going to write a book—*How* Not *to Catch a Vampire*." I held the heavy net in front of me. "But this is cool." I admired the way the silver links glittered in the moonlight.

Valdez snarled and the men jumped back a foot, both of them giving him short blasts with what seemed to be state-of-the-art water cannons, complete with holsters. I decided I'd have to confiscate both of them. Flo and I could have some fun with those. Just let Jerry or Richard complain if we took too long getting dressed to go out.

"Hey, Valdez, this is a nice piece, sterling links. It'll look cute with my black leather mini." I tied it around my hips.

"Uh, Glory, I think they got one thing right."

"Hmm?" I looked up from trying to knot my new accessory and saw Wilson and Sam coming at me armed with ugly-looking stakes. "Well, what are you waiting for, Valdez? Let's kick some butt."

"My pleasure." Valdez turned and leaped, a blur of fur as he landed on one of the men.

This wasn't going to be easy. Both guys had on body armor with—can you believe it?—Kevlar turtlenecks. The way Sam was waving that stake around, I wished I had on my own

Kevlar, though my wet T-shirt was proving a nifty distraction. I knocked Sam back with a sharp kick to the stomach. He hit a black SUV, then went down hard, but jumped back up again. We circled each other, me dodging that stake until I managed to pop him a good one with my right foot.

This time when he hit the ground, I threw my arm across his well-padded neck. "Who are you? What do you want?"

"The last person you'll ever see, vampire. And I want you dead."

The wooden stake pricked my side and I gasped at the pain. Damn, that hurt. I pressed down, a little padding no match for my vamp strength, especially when I'm aggravated. The man's eyes rolled back in his head, the stake slipped from his fingers and he passed out. I picked up the stake and tossed it about a hundred feet away.

I could hear Valdez snapping and barking and looked over to see the man he'd attacked sprawled on the concrete. He was bleeding and unconscious but still breathing. Valdez looked ready to finish him.

"Stop. Don't kill him. I want to know who these guys are. How they knew I was vampire."

"No mystery there. Check out the SUV over there, Blondie. When you knocked Sam into it, a black film fell down." Valdez backed up, but never took his eyes off the man in front of him.

They'd come in a WD company vehicle. They'd been sent by my old nemesis, vampire hunter Brent Westwood. He'd made his billions in computers and the SUV had the logo of Westwood Digital, one of his companies. Westwood figured vampires were less than human and stalking and killing them was a public service. I was surprised they'd made the feeble attempt to disguise the logo. No need to be secretive about it. A vampire sure couldn't go to local authorities and complain or press charges, now could she?

"I'll bet he thought I'd be weak from that stuff he's been selling me and I'd be an easy get." Because he hates vampires and me in particular, Westwood had taken over the company where I'd ordered my synthetic blood and sent me a substitute that had left me pretty much powerless. Fortunately, I'd figured out what was wrong and switched brands, but I'd let Westwood think I was still drinking his weak swill.

"So he sent his thugs to pick you up. I bet he didn't want either one of them to off you but wanted to do the honors himself."

"Sure, he always was a hands-on vamp hunter." I saw the man I'd laid out start to stir and jumped on top of him before Valdez could do it. "Listen, a-hole. Tell your boss that Glory St. Clair is not going to die tonight or ever. That if he sends any more of his people after me, they'll be shipped back to him in tiny gift boxes, piece by piece." I snarled and showed my fangs. The guy under me stiffened in horror. I hadn't survived this long without picking up a few intimidation skills. Fortunately, I hadn't had to trot them out in a while.

"Your buddy over there needs to go to the emergency room. Tell them he got tangled up in barbed wire while putting up fence on his ranch."

"But they'll see the dog bites."

"Then he ran into a pack of rabid coyotes on the back forty. He'll have to take some shots, but don't you dare blame pit bulls. We like dogs around here." I glanced at Valdez. "And don't come back. If Westwood is smart, he'll stay the hell away from Austin. You got all that?"

The man nodded frantically.

"And get this. You can wrap your throat." I picked up his wrist. "But I can still drain you here." I glanced down. "Or maybe I'd just rip off your dick and take your blood down there. Believe me, it wouldn't be a pleasure for you." The man was wild-eyed and bucked under me. "But you're not my type." I bit into his wrist, drew enough blood to scare the hell out him, then spit it on the ground.

"You do exactly as I just said with your injured friend or I *will* come after you. I've got your taste now. I can find you wherever you go. And my friend here has your buddy's blood on his tongue. You disappoint us and you won't live another twenty-four hours. Now give me those squirt guns, holsters too." I stood and wiped my hands on my shorts. I waited until I had both guns and holsters in front of me, then watched the man scramble to drag his cohort into the SUV. He practically popped a wheelie tearing out of there.

"Good job, Blondie. You okay? He got you with that stake and you're bleeding. How do you feel?"

I lifted up Ray's T-shirt, which now had a jagged tear in it. "It's already healing. Don't worry about it. Did you see me go after that guy? Can I kick butt or what? Hah!" The scrape did hurt. Vamps have almost an allergy to wood when they're poked like that. But when it's not a stake through the heart, no big deal. And I was pumped. I grabbed my new toys and carried them toward the house.

"Yeah, you were awesome. Now wait here while I make sure the pair of paparazzi who're trying to make it down the hill with the video of both of us kicking butt don't send it to MTV or post it on YouTube." Valdez pushed me toward the door until I was standing under the front porch light.

"You're kidding me."

"Don't I wish. Go get Brittany. She needs to help me with this one and you need to get inside and take care of Ray." Valdez bounded off down the hill.

I ran inside, whispered in Brittany's ear, then hurried upstairs to check on Ray, only stopping to throw the water guns in a hall closet before I opened the bedroom door. He was propped up in bed with a laptop.

"You'll never believe—" We both said it at the same time, though actually Ray whispered it.

"Okay, you first." I stopped beside the bed.

Ray grabbed my T-shirt. "Hole. Blood. And you're wet. What the hell?"

"A little attack. Water cannons. Funny and, uh, okay, a little scary, but I handled it." I can't say I wasn't pleased by the worry lines on Ray's handsome face.

He shook his head, then set the laptop aside. He pulled me down next to him. "Tell me."

So I gave him a summary, highlighting my bravery, awesome intimidation skills, not to mention kung fu or whatever you call those fighting moves.

"Why—"

"Talk in my head, Ray. Save the voice for the important stuff, like singing."

"Why does this Westwood hate you so much?" Ray lifted the hem of my shirt to look at my healing wound. *"Son of a bitch. That's got to hurt."*

"Yeah, wood really stings. I had a run-in with Westwood before. He hates vampires, hunts them with a bow and special olive-wood arrows, for sport. Collects their fangs for trophies and wears them on a necklace. Two of those fangs belonged to Jerry's best friend. Pretty sick, huh?"

"He sounds like Simon Destiny. A man who's too rich and too bored. Wish we could send him to Circe too."

"Exactly! Too bad Aggie only wants vampires. Brent Westwood would be a great catch for her." I entertained myself for a moment with the thought of a world without Simon and Westwood in it. "Anyway, we had a showdown on Halloween last year and I managed to get the best of Westwood. So he's been gunning for me ever since. Bad enough the male vamps are eluding him, but when a dumb, blond vamp puts one over on him, his ego just can't take it."

"A smart man would never, ever take you for a dumb blonde, Glory St. Clair. Don't know how this guy made billions. Maybe there was a blonde helping him." Ray grinned and slid his hand over my wound.

Ooo. Felt comforting. And sexy. Very distracting. I threw up a block. Obviously Ray had stopped pouting about what might or might not have happened between Nate and me. Sexy moves. Was he feeling competitive? Trying to see if he could win me from his buddy? I wasn't about to be the prize in a macho seduction contest.

"What did you find out on the laptop?"

"See for yourself." Ray picked up the laptop and set it on my legs. *"Check this out."*

There was a Web page devoted to the mythological (hah!

If they only knew.) Aggie or rather her real and definitely unpronounceable name. "It claims these Sirens are usually in the Mediterranean or thereabouts. I'd love to know why Circe dragged her to *our* lake. Sure wish her boss the Storm God had a Web page and an e-mail account. We could clue him in on his Siren's activities. Bet he'd be none too happy to learn she's hooked up with Circe."

"That's what I was thinking. Seems we could blackmail Aggie, threaten to expose her, if we could figure out how to contact her big boss." Ray suddenly started to cough and gasped for air. Bad news. Since even a glass of water could make him sicker, all I could do was watch and wait for him to lay back and close his eyes as his breathing became even again.

"You need to feed again. I'm up for it, but I need to shower first." I looked down at my dirty shorts and the bloodstained T-shirt. "I'll read this stuff later. Why don't you lie back and take a nap?" I picked up the laptop and moved it to a dresser on the other side of the room.

"Maybe you shouldn't feed me. You were injured. You need your strength for yourself." Ray lay back and put his hands behind his head. He'd shucked the sweatshirt Nathan had insisted he wear earlier and was back to just boxers again. Exhibitionist. Of course he did have something worth showing off.

"Glory?"

"Uh, I'm fine, Ray. I fed from a healthy young guy outside. One waiting to scope out your friend Sienna when she arrives. I barely bled from this little cut."

"You went hunting outside? Are you crazy?" He sat up straight, his hand clutching my thigh under my shorts.

"I had Valdez with me." I kind of liked the way Ray seemed sincerely worried about me. And his hand on my thigh wasn't so bad either. I should move back, tell him to cool it. Of course I did none of the above.

"And you came back injured anyway. Maybe next time we should just order pizza and you can do the delivery boy."

"Yeah. Might work." And Valdez would be happy to scarf down the pizza afterward. "I'm fine. I hope I warned his henchmen off, but we need to be careful if Westwood is thinking of coming back to Austin. He has a way of detecting vampires. You're not immune from an attack either."

"*Vampire hunters? I can't think about that now.*" Ray yawned and stretched, finally letting his hand slide down my leg and away from me. Those boxers gapped and I almost swallowed my tongue. "*I still have a hell of a headache. Stupid. Alcohol never did this to me before. I could drink Jack all day and all night if I wanted and never feel a thing.*"

"This isn't before. This is after. I hope you've learned your lesson, Ray. I'm not planning to come running over here every time you have a craving for the old days and a bender." There. I guess I'd shown Ray I wasn't one of his groupies, turning to mush and willing to do whatever just because he flashed a little skin. Okay, maybe I was out of sorts because he'd just let go of me so easily. Or could he be teasing me? I gave him a narrow-eyed look.

"*No, I wouldn't expect that. I've learned my lesson.*" He touched his throat. "*Believe me. If I come out of this able to sing . . .*" He swallowed and I forgot all about ulterior motives. "*I'm scared, Glory. Singing. It's all I have. What if—*"

"Stop it, Ray." I sat next to him and put my hands over his, throwing a few healing thoughts his way. "This has got to be temporary. I told you. I've had hangovers before. Bad ones. A few days, a week at most and I was back to normal." I smiled. "Or at least as normal as a vampire ever gets. Read my mind. You'll see I'm telling you the truth."

Ray gripped my hands and looked into my eyes. "*Yeah, I can see you're being straight with me. Thanks.*" He pulled me down and kissed me on the lips, a sweet, friendly peck. "*Go take your shower. The sooner I feed, the sooner I get cured. Right?*"

"Right." I jumped up and headed for his closet. "Ray, you know I need to go home soon. I can't keep wearing your clothes. And there's the shop. Tomorrow night I really need to check in."

No answer. I looked out and saw Ray had his eyes closed.

I guess admitting his fears had worn him out. Or relieved him so much he was finally relaxed enough to sleep. My heart squeezed and I had to force myself to go back into the closet and the problem of what to wear.

I found a red silk shirt that was definitely my color. Indulgent, but what can I say? I'd earned it. I held the shirt up and realized it would only come down halfway to my knees. It would be totally sluttish of me to wear this and nothing else. I pulled open a drawer and found a pair of his silk boxers. All right. Modesty preserved. Sort of.

Before I hit the shower, I couldn't resist checking out Ray lying in bed. Not sleeping. Now he was watching me, eyes gleaming, that wicked smile on his face like he was still reading my mind. Which he shouldn't be without my express permission. How many women had thought to toy with him before? And how many had ended up just exactly where he wanted them? I wanted . . . What? A clear conscience for when Jerry came home again? Or the experience of a lifetime with a legendary rock star? What a hell of a choice.

"Glory?"

"Hmm?"

"You do great things for a wet T-shirt. Just thought you'd like to know that I noticed."

I scurried into the bathroom, my face on fire. Stupid, I know. I should have thrown my shoulders back and said "Thanks, Ray." But I'm still a fangirl and he's still a world-class rocker. I've listened to his CDs for hours. Watched his concert DVDs over and over again. And if vampires could dream, well, I'm sure he'd be a star in some pretty hot ones.

I made the shower quick. Didn't need to wash my hair, so I wrapped it in a towel to keep it dry then picked a nice lavender shower gel I found among the offerings in a basket in the bathroom. After I got out, I inspected my healing wound. It was barely a pink spot. I put on the shirt and saw that my nipples were excited to start the party. What party? All I was going to do was feed Ray. I pulled on the boxers.

See? I was decently covered. My nipples refused to face reality and calm down.

I opened the bathroom door and found that Ray had been busy. He'd lit candles. Almost a dozen of them around the room. Oh, boy. Now what had been a simple case of me giving him a dose of healthy healing blood was turning into a seduction scene right out of one of my fantasies. Yep, a vampire might not have dreams, but she sure has fantasies.

Jerry had certainly never thought about lighting candles except for light, back in the days before electricity had been invented. Nope, not thinking about Jerry now. Who was I kidding? I couldn't be with any man and not compare him to Jeremiah Campbell. Not since 1604 anyway. And all of them (and I'm not revealing numbers, you do the math) had come up short when compared to my Scotsman. Ray would probably be the same. I blocked my thoughts and smiled. Nothing was going to happen here tonight. But I wasn't about to share that thought with Ray. I wanted to see what kind of moves he made. If any.

"My shirt never looked that good on me." Ray was still talking in my head.

"Maybe you didn't think so, but millions of women would disagree with you." I walked to the bed, putting a little sway in my hips.

"When you come out looking like that and"—sniff—*"smelling like that, you give me hope that something interesting is going to happen here. Besides feeding, I mean."* Ray smiled and held out his hand. *"Lavender. I like."*

"I like too. That's why I chose it. It's supposed to relax me. No ulterior motives."

"Are you tense? I promise not to attack you this time." Ray pulled me down beside him. *"Or at least I hope I won't. I didn't intend to do it last time. I went a little crazy. That's why I lit the candles. I'm trying to make things nice this time. Last time . . . wasn't."*

"I understood, Ray. You weren't yourself. And there's nothing wrong with crazy, as long as it doesn't get out of hand." I settled next to him, facing him. I reached out and brushed the hair back from his forehead. "Quit worrying. You were in a weakened state. You've had time to recover now. I feel sure you'll be fine. Start slowly. Like you just did, smell me. Start here." I touched my neck.

Oh, pooh, my hands were shaking. So much for calm, sophisticated Glory. I'd had a thing for Israel Caine for years. Sure I was just going to feed him, but this was pretty cool. He was showing every sign of really wanting to be with me.

He nuzzled my neck and I felt the gentle scrape of his fangs across my jugular. But he didn't take me there. *"You smell fantastic. Like warm, rich blood. I can hear your heart pounding. Does it always beat this fast?"*

"No." I lay back on the pillow. "Every vamp gets off to a little blood exchange. Even when it's just between friends."

"Friends. Right. You're a good friend to me, Glory." Ray moved down my body, still just inhaling.

"I try."

First he picked up my wrist. Then he touched his lips to the crook of my elbow. Oops. A few buttons had come open on my shirt and he nuzzled the space between my breasts.

"Soft, sweet, and your pulse is calling to me." He eased down to my knees and then picked up one foot. *"You even have a pulse in your ankle. But I won't bite you here. Too bony and there are much more interesting places left to investigate."*

"I think you've gone far enough, Ray."

He kissed a path up my leg behind my knee.

I bit back a moan. "Ray, I said—"

"Don't say anything. Just let me explore. Will's been telling me about all the places a vampire can take blood." He carefully, oh, so slowly, moved his lips toward my inner thigh. *"There's a spot near here. Isn't there, Glory?"*

"Stop!" I practically flew off the bed. Ray was left looking puzzled, like where the hell did she go? Tough. I stood a foot away and put my hands on my hips. "Okay, Ray, listen to me."

"Come here, Glory, things were just getting interesting." He patted the bed beside him and gave me his sexy smile again.

"No, they weren't." I tapped my foot. "That spot you were headed for is an intimacy I reserve for one guy. I think you know who he is."

That wiped the smile off his face. *"I wasn't asking you to make love, just give me some of your blood."*

"Well, sorry, bud, but in the vampire world, giving my blood from that spot is all about lovemaking. I don't do that lightly." I looked down and realized I was definitely sending the wrong message. Clingy red silk unbuttoned down to there? No wonder Ray had headed for the Promised Land. I stomped into the closet, pulled out a black T-shirt and exchanged it for the silk. I took a steadying breath, then marched out to stand by the bed again. Ray was lying on his side, watching me.

"I get it. We're friends, not lovers. I crossed a line. Sorry." He held out his hand. *"I'm grateful to you for helping me. Maybe I'll be able to talk out loud after this session and not in my freakin' head. Even sing. I owe you. And it wasn't fair of me to use this situation as a chance to get into your pants."*

"No, it wasn't." I liked the honest contrition I felt coming from him. Ray was being real. I could feel it. And he did want me, or "in my pants" anyway. Which was a compliment I wasn't about to be insulted by. The guy was hot and famous and every woman's fantasy man, for crying out loud.

"Now can I feed? I'm feeling like crap." He managed to grab my hand and pull me down to the bed. He took my wrist and gently drew it to his lips. *"Okay?"*

"Sure. Go for it. But not there." I lay back on the pillow. "Use my neck, it's a better spot, quicker."

Ray grinned. *"And I like lying close to you too. Thanks."* He gathered me in his arms, angled his head and began to drink.

I lay there, his body wrapped around me and impossible to ignore as I felt the pull of his mouth all the way down to my toes. Glory the noble, Glory the irresistible. Glory the stupid? Had I just missed my one chance to find out what it would be like to sleep with the famous Israel Caine? I could feel the proof against my thigh that he'd really been ready to rock and roll. Hmm.

Jerry? You'd better not be falling into Mara's clutches because look what I just gave up for you.

Seven

I woke up to what had to be the most beautiful sound I'd ever heard. Ray singing in the shower. Yep. Singing. Not a CD, but the man himself. I was so jazzed, I threw open the bathroom door and then the glass shower door and jumped him.

"Oh, my God! It's back! Your voice is back!" I ignored the steamy water pounding on top of my head and soaking my T-shirt and shorts. Hey, I was used to being wet. I hugged his slippery body, then laughed like a mad woman.

"Thanks to you." Ray laughed too, then turned off the water and wrapped his arms around me. "You saved me, Glory. I'll never forget it." His eyes seemed to darken to a stormy blue as he looked down at me. "I've never been so damned terrified in my life. Not even when I woke up a vampire. You pulled me through it, lady."

"I, uh . . ." I felt a flush heat my cheeks. Sometimes my enthusiasm overloads my common sense. Ray was naked and we were both wet. I began to back out of the tiled shower.

"Wait a minute, vamp girl." His arms tightened around me.

"For what?" I glanced down, oh, yeah, then pushed wet

hair out of my eyes. No way was I going to miss one bit of that view. Ray has a piercing there with a sparkling diamond ring. I forced my chin up to meet his gaze.

"For this." He slid his hands under my thighs and pulled my legs around his waist until I was snug against him. "The celebration."

One part of me was definitely celebrating. No underwear and baggy shorts? It wouldn't take much of a push for us to be . . .

"We're just friends, remember? And you're pale. While one part of your body is obviously up for the celebration, I don't think it's a good idea even if I *was* willing." I shoved and managed to climb off of him without falling on my butt. "You want to lose your voice again?"

"Is that possible?" Ray actually looked worried and didn't try to pull me back. I'd found the magic words.

"Doubt it. But we're in uncharted territory. I don't think you want to take that chance." I handed Ray a towel.

"Somehow I have a feeling you'd be worth it." He grinned and pretended to reach for me again, but I could tell this time he was playing.

I scooted out of reach. "I admit I'm a fan. But I refuse to be one of those notches on your bedpost."

"Notches? Was I supposed to keep score? Damn. Nobody told me." Ray ran the towel over his hair, then down his chest. He took his time with his arms, feet, everywhere. Watching me, watching him.

I turned my back and grabbed a towel for myself, finally wrapping it around my hair. Calm. I'd taken yoga. I needed to meditate. Find my center. As if. With Ray less than a foot behind me combing his long hair after tossing his wet towel at my feet? I blindly handed him a dry towel then scurried out of the bathroom. I'm not immune to a well-built guy, no matter how committed I am to another one. If anything, my years with Jerry had made me appreciate men, *really* appreciate how a guy who knows his way around a woman's body can make her feel. Oh, jeez. I had to get a grip. On myself. Not on Ray.

"Get dressed. We need to talk about Aggie."

"Screw Aggie." Ray sounded out of sorts.

I didn't bother to hide my smile. "I'm sure she'd love for you to. If we don't find those three vamps for her, you may end up her love slave."

Ray finally wrapped the towel around his waist. "Whoa. Now that's a picture guaranteed to take the starch right out of a fella."

I shook my head. "Aggie could probably freeze you stiff, if you know what I mean." I patted his shoulder when Ray shuddered. "Surely it won't come to that. Let's think positive. Now that you can sing again, you can deal with Sienna and I'm going to my shop. I'll see what I can do to get us those vampires we need to satisfy Aggie."

"You know how to get hold of the EVs? Seems the sooner we can get that ball rolling, the sooner we can get Aggie off our backs. Can't imagine she'd just sit out on the lake twiddling her thumbs waiting. I expect to be summoned out to the lake any minute now for a progress report." Ray frowned. "And you're right about Sienna. She's a tyrant when it comes to rehearsals. I won't have time to mess with Aggie too."

"I bet Brittany has one of the EVs on speed dial from when she worked for Lucky. I'm sure her former employer was into their drugs."

"Oh, yeah. One of us should follow up on that." Ray sat on the side of the bed.

"I will. Right after I pull together one more outfit." There was a knock on the door. "I'll get it."

"Hey, Glory." Nathan pulled me to him and kissed me, then noticed Ray wearing nothing but a towel. His face fell. "Oh, obviously I interrupted something."

"Not at all. We were celebrating. Ray's voice is back." I'd had enough of this drama. I stared into Nate's eyes, ready to put him under the whammy.

"Stop it, Glory." Ray stepped between us. "Listen, bud. Glory's been playing her mind games with you."

"Hey, you did get your voice back!" Nathan grinned, then looked at me. "What's this about a game?"

"You gave your blood so I could help Ray. In return, we decided to make Ray jealous. So I planted a hot memory of you and me together. It never happened." I shrugged and noticed both Ray and Nathan watching my T-shirt. I couldn't help smiling a little. Sure I looked sluttish, but the guys weren't noticing my hips and thighs now, were they?

"Man, I hate that mind control you guys do." Nate frowned. "Glory, you mean we didn't do the *Top Gun* thing?"

"Sorry, but no. We're friends. You and me. Ray and me. You and Ray. No sex for any of us."

Nate looked at Ray. "Damn."

I smiled at Nate and shook my finger in his face. "Come on, Nathan. Did you really think I was that big a slut? That I'd just hop into bed with you? Both of you know I'm with Blade."

Nathan grabbed my hand and kissed it. "A guy can dream. Did we make you jealous, Ray?"

"Hell, yes. Glory won't give me any, and then you strut in here like you got it all? I woulda ripped out your throat if I hadn't felt like shit."

Nate backed up and put a hand on his neck. "Damn. Don't even joke about it. I love you like a brother, Ray, but this vampire thing still scares the hell out of me sometimes."

Ray ran a hand over his face. "I know, guy. Me too." He looked up and smiled. "I owe you. Big-time. For the blood you gave." Ray slapped his friend on the shoulder. "Took guts."

Nathan staggered and rubbed his shoulder. "Obviously you're back to full strength. Just in time. Barry's here. He's got some phone interviews lined up and I was going crazy trying to stall him." Nathan glanced at me. "Barry's our PR guy. This is part of the Grammy hype." Nate grinned. "Sing something, Ray, so I'll know this is for real."

" 'Oh, I get by with a little help from my friends.' " Ray belted out the line from an old Beatles song.

"Hot damn!" Nate yelled. He and Ray high-fived. "Glory, you're a miracle worker."

"I've been trying to get her to celebrate with me." Ray winked at me.

"That'll have to wait. Sienna's downstairs. She ordered me to come up and drag you out of bed if I had to. She's ready to rehearse and isn't going to be put off. Dex spent the day taking her around town. They caused a few riots when they went public, paparazzi had a field day. In private, Dex tried some of his tricks. Now he's limping because Sienna dug a stiletto into his instep."

"I've got to meet this woman." I grinned, grabbed my purse from the nightstand, then disappeared into the large walk-in closet. "I'm getting dressed now. You guys better take care of business because Valdez and I are out of here in about ten minutes." I shut the door and found yet another T-shirt and khaki shorts. I took a few minutes to throw on some makeup and pull my wet hair back into a ponytail. Then I stuck my feet into a pair of rubber flip-flops, picked up my suede boots and threw open the door.

Ray was on a cell phone. Nathan stood by the door whispering with a tall, thin man with a shaved head and a gold earring. He was dressed in casual elegance in expensive trousers and a white silk shirt open at the neck. He looked me over, grinned, then gave Nate an elbow.

"Oh, Glory, meet Barry Donaldson, Ray's PR guy." Nate glanced at Ray and lowered his voice. "You two need to get together."

Barry took my elbow and hurried me into the closet and shut us inside. "Great to meet you, Glory. The press loves you. I can't wait to set up some interviews." He whipped a card out of his pocket. "Here are all my numbers. I know you're a busy woman, but we've got to get you on local TV. Fantastic publicity for your shop too."

"Thanks, Barry." I stared down at his card. I should have

known. He was from a prestigious Los Angeles agency. Here in close quarters I could tell he was B positive with an overlay of Dolce & Gabbana's "Masculine."

While he chattered on about possible Austin publicity opportunities, I read his mind. He was wondering if he could talk me into joining one of the national weight-loss clinics. Do a commercial and combine publicity with getting some of the extra pounds off of me.

I was about to write him off as a shallow jerk when I saw that he did think I was cute and respected Ray for picking someone who wasn't a celebutante for a change. He'd also checked out my fan club, one that protested the way the tabloids picked on my size—four thousand members and counting, thank you very much. He liked the publicity there too. I waited, but he didn't bring up the subject of my weight. Not that I could diet. Believe me—been there, done that. At least I've tried to cut down on the fluid intake. Vamps just can't lose. Healing sleep, you know.

"Local TV doesn't exactly love me, Barry. One reporter in particular keeps trying to make something of the Vintage Vamp's thing. Like I'm a vampire. Can you believe it?"

We both had a good laugh at that. "I say we run with it. The mysterious Glory St. Clair. Only comes out at night. I've seen the pictures. The agency has a file on you, of course. Started it as soon as Ray was seen with you the first time. That vampire mural on your shop wall is dynamite. Great draw for the store. I'd say you're a marketing genius." He grinned and turned when the closet door opened.

Ray stuck his head inside. "Do I have to throw a jealous rage here?" He threw his arm around me. "Glory, let me know if Barry tries to overschedule your life. I'll make him back off. You should see the list of phone interviews he handed me a few minutes ago."

"Right. And Chicago's next. I'll get them on the line." Barry held out his hand and took the cell phone from Ray. "Great to meet you, Glory. I'll be stopping by your shop.

Got to see that mural for myself. Oh, and I already met your dog." He shuddered. "Heavy duty, isn't he?"

"You'd better believe it." I watched him look at a list on his BlackBerry, then begin to punch numbers into the phone before he sat on Ray's bed and started to talk.

"You okay with this?" Ray kept his arm around me.

"Sure. Publicity for the shop. But let's cool the idea of playing up the vampire angle. Not my style. I'm into blending."

Ray frowned. "You'd better teach me that whammy thing soon then. Barry can be made to forget all about it. If he gets out of hand, that's your answer."

"Right. Now I've got to go."

Ray walked me to the door. Since Barry was now standing next to him with the phone, he obviously felt compelled to lay a kiss on me, a lingering, full-throttle kiss that curled my toes in those much-too-big flip-flops.

"Come on, Glory, I'll introduce you to Sienna." Nathan opened the door and we almost tripped over Valdez. "Your sentinel is on duty as usual." He closed the door behind him.

"Woof." Valdez looked around to be sure we were alone. *"Wait'll you see Sienna Star, Glory. Ooo, baby."*

Nathan grinned since everyone in close range can hear Valdez talking inside their heads just like I can. "She's got looks *and* attitude. Just ask Dex. Watch yourself, Valdez. Not sure what she'd do if a dog talked to her. I hear she packs a gun in her designer bag."

"I'm immortal. All a gunshot would do is slow me down a little."

"But you'll keep your mouth shut anyway. You've been wounded enough lately."

"Listen to her, Nathan. Glory's worried about me."

"Sure, I'm worried. The way you play hero, it's a miracle you've lasted this long." I stopped at the top of the stairs. "Let's go. I need to get to the shop. But I want to talk to Brittany first." I looked back at Valdez. "Remember Brittany? The woman you are supposedly crazy about?"

"Hey, I can be crazy about Picasso, but that doesn't mean I can't admire a Van Gogh."

"Wow, listen to the art references." Nathan stared down at Valdez. "The canine has hidden depths."

"The canine has been living with me and my art-loving roomie, Florence, for too long. Flo's slept with every major artist since Leonardo da Vinci and has the stories to prove it." I patted Valdez on the head.

We trooped down the stairs and I heard the piano being played in the living room. Not the hard rock I'd have expected. This was a beautiful classical piece. But not one I recognized. Not that I'm all that conversant in such things, but I've been exposed to culture, even if I'm not particularly highbrow. Jerry loves stuff like the opera, the ballet and the symphony. Go figure. Another guy with depths. I'm about as shallow as a discount store cheek cream.

"Come on, you've got to meet her." Nathan grabbed my hand and pulled me toward the living room. The song reached a crescendo and it actually gave me goose bumps. I looked out through the open drapes and saw—oh, my God!—Aggie leaning on the rocks, listening and swaying to the music. I hurried over to the wall of windows and pressed the button for the automatic shades to close just as the woman sitting at the keyboard lifted her fingers from the keys. The sound lingered in the room for a few breathless seconds.

"Bravo!" Nathan clapped and stepped forward. "Is that one of yours?"

"Yes, but it needs work." The tiny woman stood and looked at me. Her spiky hair was a collage of blond, pink and purple that trailed halfway down her back. She had piercings on both eyebrows with a sapphire on the left side of her nose that matched her eyes. Her skin was pale and flawless, her eye makeup stripes that matched her hair. Full fuchsia lips pouted for a second before she grinned and stepped forward, right hand outstretched.

"You've got to be Glory. I've read so much about you."

"Please don't believe that trash." I found myself smiling in return even though she made me feel like an absolute Amazon. I took a second to admire her pink leather miniskirt and blue sweater before reality set in. I *had* to get outside and make sure Aggie got away from Ray's deck before anyone else saw her.

"Sorry I closed the shades like that. I thought I saw one of those paparazzi trying to scale the rocks with a camera. I'd better alert the bodyguards. They usually hang out in the kitchen." I was shaking inside. Sure, I could whammy Sienna, but what would Aggie do next, slither up to the door and ring the bell?

"I can do that, Glory. They should be out on patrol." Nathan started toward the kitchen.

"No!" I leaped to put my hand on his arm. "I have to walk Valdez anyway."

"Thanks for running them off." Sienna made a face and shuddered. "Did you see the picture of me on the topless beach in Cannes? I looked like a boy. Didn't help that it revived rumors that Ian is gay. Which I'm here to tell you that, as far as *I'm* concerned, he's definitely not."

"No, I guess I missed that one. But in person you have a great figure." I smiled. Always nice to meet a fellow victim of tabloid abuse. And I was glad to hear her boyfriend, a hot British movie star, wasn't gay. I'd had some nice fantasies about him.

"Well, fifteen million other people didn't miss it." Sienna plopped down on the sofa and kicked off her four-inch Louboutin heels. "I don't believe anything I read in those rags. For instance, you're so much smaller than your pictures. Those creeps obviously use Photoshop. Bastards!" She held out her hand for Valdez to sniff. He shamelessly licked her palm, then moved in for a full head rub. "What a sweet dog! I'm on the road so much. No time for a pet. What's his name?"

I loved this woman. I was "smaller" than my pictures? Obviously my Sienna Star boycott was over. I looked around. The house seemed curiously empty after the crowd of the last few days and apparently a cleaning crew had been in downstairs while Ray and I had slept.

"Valdez. It's a Spanish name. The tabloids figure he's named for a former lover." I forced a smile. "Whatever."

Valdez laid his head on her knee, and she ran her hand over his back. He suddenly jerked.

"Oh, no!" Sienna held up her hand, her opal ring now sporting a hunk of his black fur. "I'm so sorry." She looked at me. "Did he say 'Ow!'?"

"Of course not. 'Bow wow!' What else?" I grabbed his collar and inspected the new quarter-size bald spot on the middle of his back. "Don't worry it'll grow back."

"Oh, gosh, I guess I'm not a dog person after all. Or maybe it's because, according to the tabloids this week, I'm an androgynous alien who is the long-lost granddaughter of Marilyn Monroe. Which is kind of cool actually. The Marilyn Monroe connection anyway." Sienna stood and laughed. Valdez got up his nerve and approached her again for a head rub.

I turned to Nathan. "Where's the band?"

"I told them to go home. Sienna and Ray need to practice alone. The guys understood. We've got studio time lined up and they can meet there if they want to work on their own tunes." Nathan moved to put an arm around Sienna but she headed back to the piano.

"Did you say Ray was on his way down, Nathan?"

"He's on the phone. Interviews. Give him ten more minutes."

"Go hurry him along." Sienna was suddenly all business. "We've got a lot of work to do and not much time. This performance has to be perfect."

I glanced at Nathan. He shrugged and headed back upstairs. "Guess I'd better leave you to it then. Glory, you're alerting security?"

"Thanks." Sienna was already making notes on some sheet music.

"On my way." I tried to read Sienna's mind. No go. Some mortals are like that. All you get is white noise. But I recognized a hard-driving professional when I saw one. She and I looked about the same age, early twenties, but I had a few hundred years of experience under my belt. I'd have liked to have told her to relax, enjoy this early fame, but she'd never listen to a nobody like me. In fact, I was pretty sure she'd already forgotten that I was in the room. She was humming the famous duet she and Ray were going to sing. It had sold millions. A love song that couples probably danced to at their weddings. Very sexy. And the video they'd made showed them with some great chemistry.

I felt something that was an awful lot like jealousy poke me in my size-twelve midriff. Sienna was a zero, size two max. Flat chested or not, she put off a sensual vibe that men responded to. I heard a sound from outside that brought me back to reality. Aggie or a fog horn? Didn't matter. I didn't have time for imagined jealousies. I had a real problem to deal with.

"Nice to meet you, Sienna."

"Oh, you too." Sienna looked up and smiled. "It's good to see Ray with a real woman, not one of those plastic Barbies who usually pursue him. Don't let those tabloids get you down, Glory. I'm really sorry about hurting your dog."

"Thanks. And don't worry about Valdez; he'll be fine. I'm sure I'll see you again before you leave town." Real woman? If Sienna only knew. I hurried to the kitchen, where Valdez stopped to show Brittany his wound.

"What happened to you, Rafe?"

"*Sienna Star.*" Valdez craned his neck. "*Hurt like hell. How does it look? Am I completely bald?*"

Brittany made sympathetic noises, but I didn't have time for this.

"Look, I've got an emergency outside. V, you coming with or should I go it alone?" That got his attention. Valdez rocketed out the door as soon as I opened it. He jumped into the elevator.

"So what's the emergency?"

"You'll see when we get downstairs." Sure enough, Aggie was lounging on Ray's boat like she owned it.

"Are you freakin' kidding me? What the hell is that?" Valdez's jaw dropped open, then he seemed to remember that he was supposed to defend me. He growled and was about to spring when he dropped like a stone, frozen in place on the wooden decking.

"I'm your friend Glory's Siren, fur ball. I'm not a 'that,' I'm a 'who.' A shape-shifter like you, only usually much prettier, thank you very much." Aggie ran a claw down her scaly body.

"Why are you here? God, Aggie, anyone could have seen you outside that window. How can Ray and I function if you cause mass hysteria among the mortals he has to live with?"

"I guess I don't give a flying flip how you 'function,' sweetie, as long as you get the job done. You made any progress? You got somebody for me yet?" She lifted her green snout and sniffed. "I smell a vampire in the house, and it's not you or Ray. Bring him out. It would be a start."

Will. Oh, God, please let him stay inside. "What's your range on pulling in vampires? Can't you get him yourself?" My stomach heaved and I glanced up at the deck off the kitchen, terrified that Will would suddenly appear and swan dive down to the water next to the boat dock.

Aggie frowned. "I wish. Why do you think I had to sing to get you two? But once I have your scent, up close and personal, you're mine, sweetie. Forever. So get cracking. Start with that fang banger in the house there."

"No. I want to bring you *bad* vampires. Vampires who deserve to die, not my friends. Can you blame me?" I took a shuddery breath. "You have friends, Aggie?"

"Sure I do." Aggie pondered a long claw and frowned. "At least when I'm not looking like the wrath of a goddess. None of my friends would come near me now even if they knew where to find me here in the back of the beyond." She glanced at Valdez, who actually stirred. "Never mind. Your dog is pretty powerful. I never had a shifter able to break my freeze before. You get him to stay in line or I'll take you to Circe anyway. Got it?"

"Yes, I've got it. Now. get this. I need the full three weeks. If you want to listen to music, sneak up here to the dock, but stay out of sight. Ray and Sienna are going to be practicing here. I'll tell him to open the windows and you should be able to hear some pretty awesome tunes." Why not throw Aggie a bone? Keep her in a good mood? Because Aggie in a bad mood . . . Well, I sure didn't want to think about *that*. "But if Ray sees you out here, he'll move them to a studio downtown and you won't hear a thing. Wouldn't that be a shame?"

"Hah! He'd move downtown if he could move at all. But I hear you, sister." Aggie frowned when Valdez wobbled to his feet and shook. "That woman sure can play the piano. Bet she can sing too. But she needs a new hair stylist. And Ray . . . I can't wait to hear him sing again." She stood and glared at Valdez. "Listen to me, dog. Don't try to come at me again. I can take your vampire down easy as pie. Watch this." She waved a scaly hand and I froze.

"Glory?" Valdez circled me.

Yeah, I could tell he was doing it, but couldn't freakin' move a muscle. God, I hate the freeze thing.

Valdez growled and launched himself at Aggie. I swear if I could have yelled, I would have been hysterical. Was the mutt trying to get me or himself *killed*? There was a blur of fur and scales. Some cursing like you wouldn't believe. Finally Valdez staggered back to the deck and spit out a chunk of green scales. Aggie collapsed on Ray's white bench seat and dropped a hunk of black fur into the water.

"That was fun."

"Speak for yourself, woman. Gack. You taste like the bottom of a cesspool."

"You drink at a lot of cesspools, fur ball?" Aggie snickered. "Now, listen up. You can't beat me, so don't try again." She actually grinned.

I couldn't believe it. While I stood here in frozen agony, my bodyguard and the badass Siren were trash-talking each other. I'd have loved to throw in a comment or six myself. But noooo. I couldn't even freakin' breathe.

"You gonna let up on Glory anytime soon? She hates being stuck like that. If she can't talk, she'll die."

"Naw, she's immortal. Or she *thinks* she is. Now once Circe gets hold of her, I'm pretty sure that'll be the end of her. Don't know. If Circe thinks Glory can be useful, she might send her out on missions. Like she does me." Aggie frowned. "Death might be better come to think of it."

"Stop the pity party and let my boss go." Valdez sat and licked at a new bald spot on his left hip. *"Damn. Good thing I heal fast, or I'd be butt ugly."*

Aggie laughed. "Funny. Okay, I'll unfreeze her just because you asked so nicely."

I fell to the deck. "Well, I'm glad you two are having such a good time. I hate being frozen. Aggie, if—" I stopped when I saw the look in Aggie's eyes. One more word and I was a statue again.

"Let's get clear, shall we? I'm in a pretty good mood right now. Your dog is a fighter. I like that. But I want another kind of action. Soon. Yeah, you have three weeks, but I hate waiting. So I want regular reports. Something to keep me amused. Or I'll call you out just to play with you. Got it?"

Valdez and I both looked at Aggie and nodded.

I pushed down a serious case of nerves and blurted out what I was thinking. "I've got a question for you, Aggie."

"Fire away, but no guarantee I'll answer it." Aggie dipped a claw in the water.

"Why'd Circe bring you to *this* lake? In Austin, Texas? Seems a strange choice of location for a Siren."

"No kidding." Aggie looked up when there was a thunder clap. "But goddess knows best. And she'd heard there was a special male vamp here. One she really wants. One she hates with a passion." Triple thunder boomers. "I was supposed to ask for him specifically, but in the excitement of seeing and hearing Israel, I forgot." Aggie frowned when lightning sizzled so close, my hair haloed around my head like a bad fright wig.

"Who is this special male vampire? Maybe I know him." Wouldn't it be perfect if Circe wanted Simon Destiny anyway? I'm sure he had enemies all over the world. The man sucked out energy for a living. And, as a drug dealer, he was bound to have done people dirty more than a time or two.

Aggie sighed and Valdez and I both backed up from the blast of putrid fumes. "You got to give the goddess credit. She's big on women's rights and hates guys who are playboys. You know, the love-'em-and-leave-'em types?"

"Aggie, would you just give us a name already?" Valdez obviously figured he and swamp thing were buds now.

Surprisingly, Aggie didn't knock him off the dock. "Casanova. Circe heard that the vampire Casanova lives around here somewhere. Is it true?"

I glanced at Valdez.

"Oh, my God! It is! You hear that, Circe? They can bring us Casanova!" Aggie did her version of a break dance around the boat. Not a pretty sight, what with the sloshing and the fumes and all. The sliver of a moon shone brightly and night birds sang. Circe was obviously thrilled.

Me, not at all. Flo's brother Damian claimed to be the original Casanova and he sure had the chops to hold the title. He had dark Italian good looks and moves on women that made even starchy matrons dissolve into puddles of moaning ecstasy at his sultry "Come and get it, baby" stare. He'd played a few dirty tricks on me, but no way was I sending my best friend's brother to hell.

"Now children, play nice." Aggie always read every thought in my head practically before I had it. She shook her finger in Valdez's face too. So he couldn't block her either. "And I already have enough holes in my body, shifter, thank you very much. Sorry if you like this guy, but what Circe wants, Circe gets. Right, Goddess?" Moonlight glinted on

Aggie's upturned face. "She wants him. Plus two very, and I do mean very hot male vamps along with him. No substitutes."

I felt tears fill my eyes. How could I do this to my best friend?

"Sorry, chickadee, but that's the deal. Be glad you know where Casanova is. Now all you have to do is figure out how to get him into my range. Piece of cake."

Valdez and I heard a rumbling sound and it wasn't thunder. What the—

"That reminds me. I'm starving out here for some decent eats. I want a snack next time. Cake would be nice." Aggie's uneven eyes zeroed in on Valdez. "Twinkies you say. Yeah. Those would work. A case or two. I'm sick to death of this fish diet."

"Isn't there anyone else Circe would accept?" I couldn't see how I could do this. Sacrifice Flo's brother? I might as well stake Flo too.

"Forget it, Glory. You and Ray get with the program or resign yourselves to taking the hit." Aggie smiled up at the twinkling stars and the clear sky. Obviously her goddess was pleased she was spouting the party line. "You can make new friends. Suck it up, figure out a way to get that womanizing SOB out here, and all your troubles will be over. Except for those split ends that lightning strike just gave you. I'm afraid your bad hair days are just beginning."

I opened my mouth, then shut it again. I was all out of snappy comebacks.

"Ah, I'm leaving you speechless. My work here is done. I'll be seein' you and when you least expect it. Bring those Twinkies next time. Don't think you can deny Circe, kids. Believe me, I tried and look at me now." Then she jumped over the side of the boat into the water with a noisy splash.

"Bad news, Glory. Flo's gonna kill us."

"No kidding. How can I do this to her?" I put my hand on his shoulder. "You all right, puppy?"

"Guess so. Feel like I just took a shot in the butt with a taser."

"You impressed Aggie. Me too. When she froze Ray and me, we couldn't move an inch. Not even an eyelash."

"Yeah, that freeze thing creeped me out. Never got stopped in my tracks like that before. I failed you." Valdez took a step, staggered, then finally seemed to get himself together and walked to the elevator. *"Aggie whipped my ass. She was toying with me, Blondie."* He hung his head. *"I couldn't take her."*

"She's freakishly powerful, Valdez." I rubbed his ears. "You were incredibly brave to try to take her down, one-on-one." I took a shaky breath. God, Aggie really could have *killed* Valdez. I knelt down and gave him a quick hug, then wiped my eyes. "Damn it, now do you see why we've got to do exactly what she says?"

"Yeah." Valdez's warm brown eyes studied me for a moment, then he gave me a gentle head butt. *"Come on, Glory. Don't wimp out on me now. We'll figure this out. We've got to. Can she really draw you to her like a magnet?"*

"Afraid so. Ray tried really hard to get away from her. No go. She pulled him right back to her side. And she says she can do it from anywhere, even from as far away as my shop. I hope to hell we don't get a demo of that." I stood and looked out at the dark lake. No wind tonight so the water was calm. No sign of that Creature from the Black Lagoon either. But she was probably listening to our every word.

"Yes, Aggie, darling. You win this round. We're playing your game. So you'll be hearing from us. Soon. Happy now?" I swear I could hear her husky cackle from across the water.

"Come on, V. Let's go up and talk to Brittany. I want to contact the EVs and I'm sure she has a number where we can reach them. As far as I'm concerned, some EVs would be fine for a vamp sacrifice. I'd rather work on that angle than imagine what I could possibly say to Flo. What do you think?"

"I think we need to send that freak-a-zoid and her goddess back where they came from. If a few EVs go with 'em, even better."

Valdez jumped on the elevator. *"Hit it, Glory. We're going up, and that Siren's going down."*

We both winced when thunder shook the deck and lightning crackled mere feet from Ray's boat nearby. Okay, we were definitely taking the stairs.

Eight

"Glory, *mia amica*, I tell you I was robbed." Flo, trailed by Richard loaded down with shopping bags, rushed into the shop close to midnight three nights later.

Three long nights when I'd been going crazy playing phone tag with Jerry and leaving messages for the Energy Vampires. Ray and I had talked on the phone to complain about lack of progress when he could get away from Sienna, which wasn't too often.

"Glory? Did you hear me?"

"Of course. What happened? Are you all right? They didn't steal your shoes, did they?" I quickly blocked my thoughts, which had been gloomy to say the least, and threw down the receipts I'd been trying to check. If Flo thought she had problems now, wait till she heard my news. No way was I spilling this without Ray by my side. He was coming by later. We'd do the deed then.

"No. This is a *disastro*. Worse." Flo grabbed my arm and dragged me toward the back room. "Can your clerk take over? We must talk."

"Sure. Bri?" My stomach clenched. Worse than shoe larceny? I glanced at Brianna who was wide-eyed. The shifter who helped me most nights abandoned the dress rack she'd been inventorying and moved closer, eager to hear the latest gossip. Flo was always good for a story.

"Sure, Glory. Not much going on right now. There's a customer in the dressing room." She gestured at Valdez, who looked ready to take on whoever had "robbed" my ex-roomie. "Maybe you should leave your dog out here, for protection. If there's a problem . . ." Of course Bri hoped I would fill her in later, I usually did.

"You're safe. Flo's——" Richard started to smile, but quickly got serious when Flo gave him a look that could have stripped paint off a wall. "Upset about something. Figure of speech. No actual robbery——" Another look from Flo and he shut his mouth with a snap.

"My life is *terribile*. Ricardo, I love you, but you are a man, no?"

"Of course, my darling. You need Glory to understand your pain." Richard followed us to the storeroom and set the bags down with a thump. "Here are the magazines you wanted."

I glanced at the one that slipped off the top of one of the overstuffed bags. *Bride Monthly*? "Flo, how were you robbed?"

"Isn't it obvious?" She picked up the magazine and waved it like a flag. "I finally, finally after centuries——" She paused when Richard shut the storeroom door. I did have a customer. Of course she was afraid now to venture outside. Robbers, you know.

"As I was saying, after centuries of refusing to commit to one man, I finally decide that this is the man I will love *per sempre*, forever." She smiled and rushed to press herself to Richard, giving him an openmouthed kiss that curled *my* toes, and I wasn't even involved directly. Suddenly she pushed him away and wiped her mouth.

"Pah! What am I doing? What does *he* do? He takes me to *una caverna*! A cave!"

"It was the catacombs, dearest. Under the Vatican. There was candlelight. You said it was romantic."

"*Insano!* There were rats. And damp. The man who married us was not handsome."

"Paolo has been a close advisor to His Holiness. And to half a dozen popes before him!"

Flo ignored this, her bosom heaving as she pulled another magazine out of the bag. "Look at this. So beautiful. A garden. Bridesmaids. What did I have? Three old men in long dresses." She threw *Heavenly Brides* across the room.

"Cardinals, my precious. You should feel honored. I had to erase their memories afterward."

"As if witnessing our marriage is something shameful? Not to be remembered?" Another fat magazine sailed across the room, this one at Richard's head. His vamp reflexes came in handy and he caught it before it clipped his ear.

"Richard, why don't you find a twenty-four-hour car wash or something. Flo and I need to have some girl talk."

"Good idea, Glory. That drive into the hills left the car filthy." Richard grabbed Flo around her tiny waist. "Remember the last few days, my love?" He leaned down and whispered something in rapid Italian into her ear and she turned scarlet. Wow. Must have been some trip.

Finally she pushed at him, but she was smiling. "Go, wash your car."

"You want a fancy wedding, go for it. I'd marry you a thousand times in a thousand places. Just tell me when and where." He kissed her, then jerked open the door and headed out.

Flo and I looked at each other and blinked back silly tears.

"That was romantic." I rescued the magazine Richard had dropped by the door and shut it again.

"Yes, but he has escaped and left everything up to me, no?" Flo smiled. "I love him. So I marry him again." She pulled out another magazine, this one with colored stick-on flags marking pages. "I want at least six bridesmaids. You will be maid of honor, of course." She flipped open a page. "How you like this dress for you? I complain, but I did like the red the old men were wearing. You look good in red. What do you think?"

I gazed at the size-zero model and tried to imagine my curves in the strapless number with the tulip skirt. Flo was tearing pages out of the magazine and muttering about three-tiered cakes and centerpieces. I didn't dare mention that as far as I knew Flo didn't have six girlfriends to act as bridesmaids. Oh, boy, and I thought a Siren was trouble.

"I think I would love to be your maid of honor. Maybe we can go shopping. I should try on some dresses."

"Yes. And we'll need the right shoes to go with it. I am thinking a March wedding. Ricardo checked the weather on the Internet. Austin in March is *perfetto* for the outdoor wedding." She looked dreamy for a moment, then grabbed another magazine.

"Look at this. My dress! I fly to New York soon to see if I can get it in a hurry. I don't want to wait for a special order." She held up a picture that was a designer original. Obviously there were no budget limitations here. I knew Flo flying meant shifting. I guess the dress would come to Austin in a more conventional manner.

"It's beautiful, Flo." I tried to imagine myself planning a wedding. To Jerry. He'd go along with whatever I wanted, just like Richard was doing. But I'd always refused to consider that kind of commitment. Now . . . Well now I probably wasn't going to *have* a future.

"My brother will expect to give me away of course. I don't know. Is he prettier than me?" Flo wheeled on me when I gasped. "You're blocking your thoughts. He is! *Diablo!* I will walk myself down the aisle. Damian can stand by the guest book for all I care."

"No! Of course you are much more beautiful." I jumped off the table and hugged Flo. Now was definitely not the time to get into the Casanova thing. I hadn't even told Ray yet. In a complete fit of nerves, I'd just hit the road that night, after Valdez and I'd had our face-to-face with Aggie.

I'd been desperate for a change of clothes and the normalcy of getting back to my own place and my shop.

Flo held me off and examined me with her dark eyes. "Your hair's a mess, like you need a good conditioner, and you look like you want to cry. What's up with you, girl-friend? What did you and Jeremiah do New Year's Eve? Did you have a fight?"

"I don't know what Jerry did, other than fly across the Atlantic. I spent the night with Ray." I fingered my fried hair that I'd tried to hide with a vintage scarf. It was getting a hot-oil treatment as soon as I had time. Unfortunately, a vamp's healing sleep doesn't extend to hair and nails. So vampires had to deal with those issues like mortals do, with one great exception—we never go gray. Cool, huh? At least Aggie had left me alone for the last few days, but she'd been right about those split ends.

"*Mio Dio!* I want details." Flo grabbed my arm.

I gave Flo a quick, down-and-dirty version of New Year's Eve and beyond. I left out the Aggie encounter for now. I'd get to that when I could sit down with Flo *and* Richard *and* Ray.

"You fed Israel Caine? Don't tell me it didn't get a little hot. Come on now. I know how you are." Flo sighed. "I know how *I'd* be. Poor Ray, unable to sing. My heart breaks. And then you are the only one who can save him. It's better than one of our favorite soap operas."

We DVR two of them shamelessly. Hey, it's like reading a great book that never ends. And some of the guys on there are hunk-a-licious.

"Well, yes, it was awesome. Ray *needed* me. I had to drink from mortals beforehand. So my blood would be full strength."

"Of course. Go on." Flo sat in the chair and crossed her legs. She wasn't a bit shocked. She drank from mortals all the time and had little patience with my usual reliance on synthetics. I must say her natural diet agreed with her. She looked great as always. My former roomie is a size six and a shoe addict, and had just discovered the joys of designer jeans, which hugged her tiny butt perfectly. I'd hate her if she weren't my best friend.

"I drank from Nathan, who happens to be AB negative."

"Your favorite! And he's Ray's best friend. This just keeps getting better."

"We kind of . . . well, Nate and I made Ray think we'd done more than just the blood thing."

"Ooo. So was Ray jealous?"

"Not for long. We're just friends, Flo. Really."

I jumped when my cell phone rang. Jerry.

"Gloriana. Finally I get you instead of that damned voice mail. How are you?"

"Fine, Jerry. Any luck over there? With the daughter hunt?"

"Yes. I've tracked her and her boyfriend to the mountains of Transylvania." Jerry growled. "He calls himself Dracula. If it wouldn't drive a wedge between my daughter and me before our relationship had even started, I'd have already killed the bloody bastard."

"He sounds like an idiot. But keep in mind that Lily's been a vampire for better than five hundred years. I doubt she's looking for a protective father at this point." I felt Flo breathing down my neck. Of course she wanted to listen in. Why not? This was good stuff. "So how did Lily take the news? That she has a new daddy?"

"You're right. And Lily's not inclined to believe her mother any more than I am. We both know Mara's not above lying to get what she wants."

Jerry left unsaid that what Lily's mum wanted this time was Jerry, *my* Jerry, as hubby number two. Her number one had been Jerry's best friend Mac. When he'd been killed by Westwood, Jerry had tried to help Mac's widow any way he could. Recently she'd dropped the bombshell that the child she'd always been perfectly happy to claim as Mac's was actually Jerry's offspring. Great timing. Can you blame me for hating the manipulative bitch? Jerry knows how I feel so I didn't waste international cell phone minutes dredging up all that.

"Is Mara over there with you?"

"No. I left her in Paris."

"I'm surprised she didn't want to press Lily personally to take the DNA test, since she's so sure her daughter is yours."

"She's left that up to me. Lily does have the look of the Campbells, like my mother claims."

His mother actually *likes* Mara. And was eager for a Jerry-sired grandchild. Mother Campbell also ranked me right below whores and polyester. Anything or any*one* who could lure Jerry away from my side had Mag Campbell's vote.

"Gee, Jerry, seems like Lily would want that test. To know one way or the other."

Flo snatched the phone out of my hand. "You can always trick her, Jeremiah. Steal a sample of Lily's spit on a glass or pull some of her hair out. Got to be by the roots, though. That's important for some reason. That's what they did on *The Bold and the Restless. Mio Dio,* what a catfight. Then . . ." Flo fended off my grab for the phone. "Anyway, if it turns out she's your daughter, then *you* can decide whether you want to claim her or not. With her taste in boyfriends, sounds like not."

"Thanks for the advice, Florence. Now can I speak to Gloriana again? Say hello to Richard for me. Tell him he should come over here and assess this situation. There's a lot of work to be done with these out of control vampires."

"Oh, no, Jeremiah. Richard is no longer an enforcer of anything. Much too dangerous. He is mine now. And I forbid you to mention this 'situation' to him. You must come home soon. Ricardo and I are to have *un grande* wedding. He will want you to be his best man I think. But I shouldn't have said anything. Ricardo can ask you himself." Flo waved me off again with a smile I didn't trust.

"Now I want you to ask Glory about her New Year's Eve.

You really shouldn't have flown away like that. A girl's got to keep busy, you know." Flo dropped the phone in my hand, took one look at my face, then hurried out of the storeroom as fast as her stilettos could carry her.

"What does she mean? What did you do New Year's Eve, Gloriana? I assumed—"

"Just a minute, Jerry. You're breaking up." I looked toward the storeroom door Flo had closed so carefully, already planning a sneak attack on my former roomie's favorite Ferragamos. Flo thought jealousy kept a man on his toes. Granted, she should know. She had a good three hundred years more experience under her tiny belt than I did. Might as well go with it.

"Can you hear me now, Gloriana? I stepped outside. What's this about New Year's Eve?"

"Yes, that's better. No big deal. Ray had a problem. Didn't believe the warnings I'd given him about alcohol and got into booze anyway. He was really sick. I had to help him recover. Let him feed from me. New vampires." I made a noise, like what do you expect?

"He fed from you." Jerry said this like Ray and I'd shagged ourselves silly. British term. One we'd picked up watching the BBC.

"It was the only thing I could think of to help him. He'd lost his singing voice. It was really pathetic, Jerry. I felt sorry for him." Now *I* was the one sounding pathetic, making excuses. "Anyway, he's okay now. Valdez went with me, I'm home again and everything's back to normal." Yeah, right, if normal included a Siren in vampire-hunting mode and me suddenly craving mortal blood so much I'd actually thought about dragging one of my customers into the back room for a little late-night pick-me-up.

Oh, yeah, and then there'd been that wrestling match with Westwood's water buffaloes. I glanced at my trophy water cannons, propped up where I could see them. For a moment I was tempted to brag about my takedown, but I knew Jerry wouldn't see it as a good thing; he'd just issue more orders and double my guard. Hey, he'd done it before.

"Watch out for Caine, Gloriana. I know you're mentoring him, but he wants you for more than that. I wouldn't be surprised if he staged the drinking thing just to get you to come be with him." Jerry sounded serious. Jealous? Hmm. Maybe Flo was on to something. "I'll be home as soon as possible. Are you sure you're all right? You're keeping Valdez with you at all times?"

"Didn't I just say so? And you be careful. I can't imagine a guy who calls himself Dracula is discreet."

"He's a young fool."

Hmm. "Young" to Jerry is any vampire less than two hundred years old. Jerry's ancient, but looks all of thirty-two. And have I mentioned how hot he is? I wished he was here right now. With his clever hands all over me. Then I wouldn't be so vulnerable when Ray made moves on me.

"Dracula's not your problem, Jerry. Do what Flo says, grab a hank of Lily's hair and get your butt back here."

"Why, Glory, you must really miss me."

"I do. Come home and I'll show you just how much." I heard Jerry growl, a hungry sound that always makes me hot.

"I like the way you think, lass. But not yet. I can't leave Lily in this situation. Even if she's Mac's daughter and not mine, it's too dangerous. She's involved with this group led by her boyfriend. They're careless, preying on mortals, sometimes getting greedy with disastrous results. Now they've got the countryside here stirred up. The paparazzi are after them. You know how that can go. If the reporters for the tabloids can't find anything concrete, they make it up."

"Bad news." And why I was happy I'd found Austin, where vamps kept a low profile and no one did anything stupid like leave a victim lying around with a throat torn open. Or at least not often. I shuddered.

"There are even stands in some of the markets selling

stakes, crosses and vials of something called a vampire repellant. Whatever's in it reeks. It sure repelled me." Jerry laughed, but he didn't sound amused. "Superstitious nonsense."

"Sounds pretty serious. Be careful, Jerry. Drag Lily back here if you have to. And leave the weirdo boyfriend there." There was a knock on the back door that led to the alley. "I've got to go. Call me again soon. You're obviously better at figuring out the time difference than I am. Okay?"

"Sure. And, Gloriana, it's good that you're mentoring Caine," Jerry said grudgingly. "That's what these young vampires needed. A firm hand in the beginning. Just don't let him take advantage of you."

"I want him to get the right start. I'm glad you understand, Jerry." But would Jerry understand how Ray and I kept seeing each other naked or nearly so? A fist pounded on the back door again. "And, Jerry, I remember how you helped me get used to the vampire life. This is kind of payback."

Jerry groaned. "Gloriana, we spent your early days as vampire in bed. The only thing I taught you was the most erotic place to drink from. You wouldn't let Caine—"

"No! That's your spot, no one else's." I swallowed, just thinking about it, and I knew Jerry was thinking about it too. I cleared my throat. "Someone's at the door, Jerry. I really have to go."

"All right. And I do understand your involvement with Caine but I don't have to like it. Take care, Gloriana. I'll be home as soon as I can. Good-bye." Jerry hung up.

Hmm. No "I love you." Well, not surprising. Such declarations weren't the norm with us. And the jealousy thing felt pretty good. Maybe Flo's shoes were safe from a blast with my water cannon. I laid the phone on the table and went to the back door.

"Who's there?"

"Greg Kaplan. Simon sent me. We heard you want to meet with him."

"Finally." Actually I dreaded a face-to-face with the King

of the Energy Vampires. The last time we'd met I'd given him attitude. Truth be told, he scared the shit out of me. But it wasn't Simon Destiny standing in my alley, it was one of his minions, one I knew too well. Hated him, but wasn't scared of him. I blocked my thoughts and threw open the door. Surely I could handle an old boyfriend who'd joined the dark side. Valdez was only a scream away.

"Hi, Greg. I don't want to meet with Simon, but my boyfriend does."

"Blade? I find that hard to believe. He hates Simon as much as you do. I don't believe for a minute you're suddenly part of the EV fan club." Greg followed me into the storeroom. He and I had a history, most of it bad. Now he worked for the Energy Vampires as a gofer. I'm not sure why Simon kept giving him second chances. Greg was all about Greg and I knew he could be bought. Not that he was in *my* budget, but now I had Ray in my corner. A man with deep pockets. I turned to Greg with a smile.

"Blade and I are taking a break. He's in Europe. I'm with Israel Caine, the rock star. Simon knows that. He invited me to bring Ray out there sometime to the EV headquarters. Ray's hot to try the Vampire Viagra."

"You don't have to go out there to sample the VV." Greg pulled a packet of white pills from his jeans pocket. "Here's a free sample from Simon. He figured your rocker would be interested. Caine wants more, we'll e-mail him a price list." Greg grimaced. "Costs the earth, but I'm sure your guy can afford it."

I pretended to study the four pills. "Waste of money. Trust me, Ray needs no help in the sex department. But Will's been filling his head with stories. Ray's all about trying something new." I shrugged and tucked the Baggie between my breasts.

Greg tore his gaze from my cleavage. "If it's new highs he's after, you two should come out to headquarters. The VV isn't the only thing we've got going." Greg grinned. "We've got special guest quarters. You'd love it under the right circumstances. Though if I were you, I'd send Caine and stay the hell away from there. You've got to know Simon still hates your guts."

"The feeling's mutual. But surely he's willing to bury the hatchet if I have a boyfriend with money to burn. And Ray's definitely rolling in it." I tossed my hair, which snapped, crackled and popped, then picked up my cell phone. "You got a number where I can reach Simon directly?"

"Not a chance. Go through me."

"Ray's used to VIP service, Greg. Not dealing with middlemen. And he'd want future deliveries brought out to the house. You're right, I'm in no hurry to revisit your outpost of hell." Greg knew I'd been out there before, to save Valdez when he'd been held for ransom. We'd both barely escaped with our lives and I'd humiliated Simon Destiny. One of my finer moments, but not something the King of the Energy Vampires would likely forgive and forget. Maybe I shouldn't go out there. At least not without some serious protection.

Valdez had come out barely alive, all his energy sucked out by the goddess Simon reported to. Seems there must be a sorority of evil goddesses down below. Simon's Honoria and Circe were probably sisters. Divine justice if Simon landed in Circe's lap. And what about Greg here? He had a charming smile, good looks and absolutely no conscience. Oh, yeah, he was definitely a good candidate. But how on earth were we going to get EVs from their compound deep in the hills of Austin to Lake Travis? I'd say they were at least fifty miles apart.

"Drugs I can deliver, but there are special facilities out there you've never seen, although I bet you've heard about them." Greg moved closer, but I backed up. "And not even Israel Caine is going to deal with Simon directly unless Simon decides it's okay. I'll take your request to him and see what he says."

It was a start. A drug delivery would get one of them to Ray's house. But once the first one disappeared, we'd be toast as far as the EVs were concerned. If we wanted Simon for Aggie, we needed a lure. Something he wanted badly enough to venture out of the safety of his compound, a compound guarded by a she-demon reportedly even worse than Circe on a bad day. Ray and I had to figure out what Simon valued above all else. A reconnaissance trip was in order. I'd just have to find the nerve to go out there again and figure a way to come back in one piece.

"I'm not saying Ray might not want to come see the place for himself, Greg, just that I don't trust Simon. You know why I feel that way. How do I know we'll come out of there alive?"

"Are you alive now?" Greg chuckled. "Vampire humor. Got to love it." He glanced at my serious face. "Or not." He tried to sling his arm around my shoulders, but I stepped out of reach. "Relax, Glory. Nothing's going to happen to your precious rock star. The guy's high profile. Simon can't afford to attract that kind of attention. And I'll bet you'll make sure everyone in the uptight and proper vampire community here knows when you and Caine go out there. Just make sure Simon knows you're really important to Caine, not just a temporary fling."

"Oh, we're tight. And you'd better believe I'll broadcast our whereabouts. As insurance." I managed a little smile. "If our first visit is successful, maybe we'll come back and bring some of those uptight and virtuous vampires with us. You'd be surprised at how loose they can get."

"Are you kidding? *You'd* be surprised at who you'll meet out there. Some of them are already on our VIP list as regulars."

Greg chattered on about the joys of working for the Energy Vampires. I pretended to listen, still blocking my thoughts. This was exactly what I'd been hoping for. An opportunity to bring in an army with us. Though there was no way I could rationalize taking Valdez out there again.

"Okay, okay, Greg. Can the small talk. I've got the sample, now go."

"Fine. Try your Vamp Viagra." Greg sighed and put his hand over his heart. "You know what the idea of you and another man enjoying this stuff together is doing to me? I remember—"

"Don't, Greg. I'm not interested in a history lesson from you." I walked to the back door and flung it open. "I'll expect to hear from Simon next time. Obviously you're only the delivery boy. Now take off." I practically shoved him out the door. Seem harsh? Yes, Greg and I had been together, but I don't remember one bit of it because, after it was over, he'd done the whammy on me. So he wouldn't have to deal with a bad breakup. Boy, did I hate the idea of chunks of my memory missing. The more I thought about it, the more I liked the idea of Greg going to Circe with Simon.

I opened the door to the shop and came face-to-face with Barry the PR guy and a group of reporters.

"Here she is now, fellas. Glory, sorry about lack of notice, but these guys are on a press junket and wanted about five minutes of your time. To ask you about your relationship with Israel Caine. How about a few pictures? Let's go outside and get one in front of that cool neon sign with the name of the shop."

Before I even had time to redo my lipstick, I was herded outside, posed in front of the sign, my glass windows and door, then ushered back inside.

"Just a few questions, people. It's late." Barry had set up a mini press conference in front of the vampire mural.

"Where'd the fascination with vampires come from, Ms. St. Clair? Like the mural behind you. Is Ray into this scene with you?" This from a reporter representing an entertainment magazine. She was dressed in the latest style, very hip, very expensive. I really admired the eggplant leather handbag she had slung over one shoulder.

"There is no *scene*. Actually a vamp was a kind of femme fatale back in the 1920s."

"Seems odd then to paint a bloodsucking vampire on the wall." The woman was determined to press the issue.

"A friend did it as a joke and we do get a lot of Goths in here."

"Why're you open twenty-four hours a day?" Another reporter, from a music Web site. "Cool, though. The whole Sixth Street scene is cool."

"I love the Sixth Street vibe and the twenty-four-hour thing is part of it. Ray enjoys it too. He's a night owl like I am. We have that in common."

"You're not his usual type, are you? Does it bother you to be compared to his former girlfriends like Heidi or Margo?"

Superthin supermodels. I gritted my teeth, my fangs itching to do a little ripping and tearing. This reporter was from a women's magazine that was obviously trending toward edgy. The covers usually featured waiflike starlets who wouldn't eat a slice of bread, but probably put assorted substances up their elegant noses on a daily basis.

"Study Ray's background and you'll see he enjoys all kinds of women. All sizes, shapes, colors." I shrugged. "Personally I'd hate to live on lettuce leaves and bottled water all the time. And"—I leaned closer, like I was about to impart a juicy tidbit—"honestly, you don't have much energy when you starve yourself, if you know what I mean. You need a lot of it to keep up with Ray." I grinned and threw back my shoulders. There were dozens of camera clicks.

"You've got a fan club, you know. A MySpace page dedicated to Save the Blueberry, complete with blogs and message boards. It's all over the Internet." The reporter busily tapped into her PDA.

"Yes. It's the coolest thing that some people have been so supportive when the tabloids . . ." I made a face. "I won't deny I was hurt at first. Ray just shrugs it off. But I've always been a private person. Anyway, I had on a blue outfit for my first outing with Ray. The tabloids couldn't quit talking about my plus-size blueberries. I can tell you are all *real* journalists so you won't be asking me my bra size. Isn't it amazing what some people fixate on?" I looked down. Black sweater. "Anyway, tonight I guess you could call them blackberries. What can a girl do? I have assets and know how to use them. Ray doesn't complain."

Obviously ready for a subject change, Valdez woofed and ambled up to stand next to me.

"What's with the dog?" The man from the music Web site.

"Protection. Being open late can get a little dicey. It's nice to have him around, and he has good instincts when it comes to people." As if to prove that, Valdez sniffed around and began to growl in front of a large man with a khaki messenger bag.

"Not a drug-sniffing dog, is he?"

Everyone laughed.

"No, but if you brought a sandwich, he wants half." More laughter.

"There's a video on YouTube of you with fangs drinking blood. I bet you attracted a weird crowd that night. I still don't get the vampire fixation." This reporter, from a Houston daily newspaper, was back on the vampire theme.

"Oh, come on. I told you. It's all a joke. That was part of a marketing campaign. To go with the mural. Sure some weirdos came out, but they also boosted my Christmas sales. The 'blood' was tomato juice. Customers got a kick out of it. If I'd known him then, I'm sure even Ray would have shown up in a Dracula cape, just for the hell of it."

I looked down at my twentysomething body, in clothes that any woman my age would be happy to wear to work or out for a drink. Probably not the boots. They were pinching my toes and I couldn't wait to get them off.

"Check me out. Do I look like a vampire? Seriously?" I batted my eyelashes and made eye contact all around.

The reporters studied me for a second, then there was general laughter. Oh, yes, we were having a fine time. Have I mentioned that I'm great at blending? Still, all this talk of vampires was making me nervous. My clerk knew it too. Brianna dragged a cardboard box out from behind the counter.

"Here are some souvenirs from that night. Help yourself." She handed each reporter a set of plastic fangs. "Glory is a genius when it comes to advertising. See? Here's the flyer to go with the fake fangs. 'Sink your teeth into some great vintage fashions at Vintage Vamp's Emporium on Austin's historic Sixth Street.'"

"Thanks, Brianna." I gave her a grateful smile. I politely refused several shouted requests to put in a set of fangs for some picture taking.

"How do you feel about Caine's close association with Sienna Star? Are you going with him to the Grammys?" This from a female reporter whose badge tagged her from a women's magazine I admired. I also admired her Prada suit and black suede pumps. I gave her a big smile, really glad to be off vampires.

"I like Sienna. She and Ray make beautiful music together. But that's all. We're friends. She was just telling me about her vacation with Ian Pembrook." I took a breath. Jeez, Ray and I should have discussed the Grammy thing.

Barry saw my hesitation. "Great question, Gretchen. Ray told me he hopes to lure Glory to the Grammys, but she'll have to figure out her work schedule. The lady's got her own career. Look around. I don't imagine this shop runs itself, does it, Glory?"

"No, though I have some great help." I smiled at Brianna. Was Barry trying to discourage me from going with Ray to the Grammys? I was about to read his mind on the subject when the bell on the door rang and two customers pushed inside, both of them Goths. More camera clicks. Which sent the Goths right out the door again.

"Obviously we're bad for business. Let's leave the ladies so they can get back to work now." Barry deflected a few more questions while he herded the reporters out the door. "Thanks for coming. Call me tomorrow if you need any more information."

He hurried back to my side as soon as the last reporter was put into the waiting limousine idling at the curb. "Sorry about that, Glory. I literally hijacked the group. They were here to do preliminaries for the South by Southwest Music Festival that's here in March. I caught them coming out of a venue down the street and strong-armed them into making a stop in your store." Barry grinned and winked at Brianna. "You two were great."

"Thanks, but some of those questions . . ." I sank onto a stool, then looked down. Yep, I could just see my packet of VV still tucked into my bra. But it wouldn't have shown in the pictures. A good amount of cleavage would have, but that seemed to be my trademark. I wished I'd had on black leather pants instead of red—nothing like accenting my butt. Damn. Barry should have given me notice. I could have at least squeezed my thighs into some Spanx.

"Next time warn me if you bring in photographers, Barry. I want to pick out a better outfit. It's bad enough that I have to deal with paparazzi every time I go out with Ray."

"You looked fantastic, Glory. You handled the whole thing like a pro. Thanks. Oh, and Ray sends his love. He says to expect him around two, when he and Sienna are done for the night." Barry grinned. "Good thing you're used to his weird hours. I'm about to crash, myself. 'Night."

He started to head out the door, then stopped and came back to hand Bri a card. "Great to meet you, Brianna. I'll be in town a few days. If you have time to show me the sights, call me. Maybe we could do lunch or dinner. My cell number's on there. 'Night, ladies."

"He's cute." Brianna sighed as Barry left. "Mortal, of course. So it would never work."

I looked quickly around the shop, but, except for Valdez snoozing by the door, we were alone. Brianna is a werecat, sister to Lacy, my day manager.

"A relationship with a mortal can work, but it can be complicated, at least for a vampire. Not sure about the cat culture, though." I said this quietly.

"Trust me, my momcat is all about cats with cats. Not that Lacy has ever cared what Mom thought." Bri yawned. "You mind if I take a quick break? Hunt up some supper? I'll be back in thirty minutes. Promise."

I looked at my watch. "Sure. No problem. I'll want to

leave here with Ray at two." I was going to call Flo and see if she and Richard could meet with us upstairs. So we could fill them in on the Aggie situation. Then I could tell all three that Casanova was a wanted man. Oh, God, I didn't see any way to make this come out right. I was either going to hell or about to lose my best friend.

Bri took off and I faked my way through customer service while I fought the urge to feed and downed about three bottles of synthetic blood trying to take the edge off my thirst.

"Oh, my God, you were right. She *is* here." Two women rushed into the shop, Brianna right behind them.

"Glory, you have two members of your fan club here to meet you." Bri grinned and held up a basket. "And they brought you something. You'll never guess what."

Nine

"I'm Tina and this is my mother Ellen Anderson. Mom's President of the Blueberry Fan Club!" Tina snatched the basket from Bri, straightened the blue satin bow, then handed it to Ellen. Tina was a younger version of her mother, both of them pretty with the kind of voluptuous figures that had been popular in certain centuries. In this century and the previous one there was an unreasonable prejudice against generous curves. I should know, I've been fighting against it the whole time.

"Wow!" I smiled. "How nice to meet you."

The women wore coats because the temperature outside hovered in the forties. Tina's was a conservative black, her mother's a red wool. Props to Mom for the color, which looked good with her dark hair. But Tina's black was more slimming. I had a ton of it in my own closet.

Ellen stepped forward and lifted a blue dish towel from the contents of the basket. "I hope we're not bothering you, but I couldn't resist. I made these myself. From scratch. Muffins. Blueberry, of course."

"Mom's a great cook." Tina flipped her long, dark hair over her shoulder.

"This is so nice." I laughed. "I guess I'll never live down the first picture the tabloids printed of me with Ray."

"In a blue sweater. Sure. We have it on your MySpace page. I'm in charge of it. The caption said, 'Check out those Blueberries.'" Tina rolled her eyes. "I told Mom you probably hated that."

"Do you? Hate it, Glory? We could call ourselves something else. I thought 'Glory Hallelujah' would be a cute name for the group." Ellen thrust the basket into my hands.

"No, sounds too biblical." Especially for a vampire. I sure didn't say *that*. "I'm okay with the Blueberries. I always say if you've got it, flaunt it." I lifted the dishcloth and inhaled. "These muffins smell absolutely delicious." No lie. My eyes watered and I could practically taste them. Surely just one bite wouldn't kill me.

"Eat one! Mom's dying to know what you think." Tina moved closer and dragged her mother with her.

"Let me see, Glory." Brianna stepped around them, stumbled and slammed into me.

"Woof!" Valdez took a leap at the same time.

The basket and all the muffins flew into the air. I managed to juggle two of them, but Valdez proved faster, his jaw snapping as he gobbled them in midair.

"Noooo!" Ellen and Tina fell to their knees and began desperately trying to snatch muffins from Valdez's jaws of death. My dog was way ahead of them, devouring them as fast as his tongue could sweep them into his mouth.

"Oh, my God! I can't believe I was so clumsy! I'm really sorry!" Bri accidentally stepped on a muffin and kicked another one into Valdez's open mouth.

"Forget it, Mom. They all hit the floor and now the dog's slobbered on them." Tina helped her mother, who was muttering about the three second rule, to her feet.

"I'm sure they were delicious. Look! My dog loved them." As if on cue, Valdez gave a satisfied belch. "Well, pardon him. Anyway, you were so nice to think of me." I put my arms around them and walked them to the door. Brianna pulled out a broom and began sweeping up crumbs.

"Not sure they're good for dogs. Keep an eye on him. I wouldn't want him to get sick." Ellen frowned. "For *your* sake."

"Oh, lighten up, Mom. You can make more. But we can't leave yet, Glory." Tina pulled a notebook out of her Coach tote. "We have questions! For your MySpace fan page. Right now it's pretty dull."

Ellen unbuttoned her coat and dropped it on a chair. Whoa! Scoop-neck sweater and push-up bra. Ellen had taken my "if you've got it, flaunt it" philosophy to heart.

"Tina's right, Glory. We've tried to google you. No luck. So if you have a few minutes . . ." She looked around the deserted shop. "I hope you've checked the site out. You have over a thousand friends and tons of hits every day. I'll blog about meeting you, of course. And about your dog." Valdez got another dirty look.

"Let's keep me a woman of mystery. And don't be too hard on Valdez. He does provide protection around here." I grabbed the notebook. No way was I answering any of those on their list. Where was I born? They'd love to hear how I popped out in my ma's bed in London before electricity and epidurals were invented. What was my sign? Keep out. The questions went on and on.

"But the Blueberries just want to help. The tabloids are saying the most awful things about you, you know." Ellen snatched the notebook back and pulled out a pen. "Surely you don't mind telling us about your family."

"No family, except my good friends who are like family to me." I threw an arm around Bri, who looked startled, but hung in there, smiling like she was my new best bud. "And Ray's taught me to never read the tabloids. Says they're all lies."

"Of course. Trash. I use them to line my cat's litter box. Cats are such *easy* pets." Ellen smiled at Valdez when he growled. "What about old boyfriends? Surely Israel Caine's not your first serious guy."

"No, I was going with a local businessman, but we were taking a break when I met Ray." I felt Valdez staring a hole in me, but kept going. "He's a private person, so I'm not going to share his name. It would make Ray jealous, of course. Can't have that, can we?"

Ellen and Tina both shook their heads.

"I'm a private person too. Or used to be before I hooked up with Ray. Now I've got to think about identity theft. I'd no more post my birth date than I'd post my weight."

"I hear that." Tina glanced at her mother. "We'll describe your shop. Add some pics. Let me snap a few now. That will spice up the site."

"Sure. Thanks for understanding." I waited while she dug out a digital camera. Identity theft. Good excuse. Because assuming a new identity was such a pain. I was still making payments on the Gloriana St. Clair papers I'd had to buy when I'd left Las Vegas to relocate to Austin. I'd been Gloria Simmons, dancer, in Vegas. That gig had lasted years longer than it should have because, except for a gambling debacle, I'd had a ball there. When I knew it was time to move on, I'd needed to buy new ID. The vampire network had set me up, but it didn't come cheap. Fortunately, I could arrange a payment plan.

I posed for Tina while her mother browsed the shop. Ellen came back with a short black cocktail dress cut low in front and back.

"I'm trying this on."

"Mom, do you think—"

"Yes, I do. I'll be right back." Ellen flounced off to the dressing room.

Tina rolled her eyes, then made me stand in front of the vampire mural I was beginning to hate. "Mom thinks she's magically turned into a size twelve. But you inspired her to get out."

"How?"

"When she saw a clip of you on one of those entertainment shows, she said, 'Hey, look at that girl. She's got boobs and a butt yet Israel Caine is all over her. If she can get him, maybe I can get a regular guy to look at me.'" Tina looked sheepish. "Sorry, did I offend you?"

"No way. I do have boobs and a butt. Always have had." I looked down. "And they're not going anywhere."

"See? That's cool. You're not starving yourself trying to become one of those toothpick chicks." Tina paused with her camera ready for the next shot. "Are you?"

"No. Ray likes me the way I am."

Tina sighed. "I just knew it! He's amazing, isn't he? Israel Caine likes a full-figured woman. Good to know since"—she unbuttoned her own coat—"it would take surgery to whittle down this body."

I looked. Yep. Valdez would say she had a nice pair. I glanced at him. Sure enough, he was checking them out, his eyes gleaming.

"You have a great figure, Tina. You should show it off. Your jeans are too baggy, and that high-waisted top isn't doing you any favors." I steered her to the sweater table. "This red V-neck would look great with your dark hair. The extra large will fit. Use your cleavage, girl."

Tina grinned. "You're right. Who cares if some people think it looks sluttish?"

Hmm. Had that been a slam? But Tina was holding on to the sweater and her smile *looked* genuine.

"You see cleavage everywhere now. Especially on TV." I picked up a turtleneck, then threw it down again.

"And guys dig it. I get that. So does Mom. After she saw you with Israel she got up off the couch. Decided to take dance lessons. Even enrolled in night classes in—can you believe it?—archaeology. So she could meet men."

"Good for her." Why hadn't I ever thought of that? I could dig archaeology. And my fake papers included a high school diploma, even a little college.

"Are you telling all my secrets, Christina?" Ellen swirled

out of the dressing room. "Check me out. Dancing burns lots of calories. You girls should try it."

Oh, yes, she *had* managed to get into that size-twelve cocktail dress. And her own berries were swelling out of the top of the dress.

"Wow, Mom! You look . . ."

"Amazing. That dress was made for dancing." I grinned and clapped.

"That's what I thought." She did a twirl, hummed a tune and did a fancy two-step around the coat rack. "I'm taking it."

"Great. My clerk will write it up and, Bri, give her a ten percent discount."

"Thanks, Glory." Ellen dashed over to give me a hug. "Don't worry, we'll make you another batch of those muffins and put them in a sealed container this time."

"I guess I'd better step up my own game. Can't let my mom show me up. She's meeting men and I'm the one renting DVDs." Tina fingered the red sweater and sighed. "Tell me about Israel Caine, Glory. Is he as hot in person as he is in his videos?"

"Hotter." I sat on a stool and pulled off a boot to rub my toes. "You can quote me on MySpace. Glory says Ray's even hotter in person and he sings her to sleep every night." Okay, maybe that last was a mistake, but it felt really cool for the world to think I was with a guy so many women lusted after. I'm only human. Formerly, anyway.

"Wow, I can't imagine it." Tina frowned and scribbled this in the notebook her mother had left lying on the counter. "Anything else for your blueberry groupies?"

"I hate to say this, but I wish they wouldn't bake for me. Sure, I'm proud of my curves, but they're generous enough. Maybe one of you could put something on MySpace discouraging gifts of food." Valdez woofed an objection from by the door.

"People are just trying to be nice, Glory." Bri just had to

speak up. "Makes me wonder what else people might make with blueberries."

"Your clerk's right. There's a lot of buzz on the site. People are having fun exchanging blueberry recipes. Told you it was dull." Tina smiled wryly. "The riveting reading for tonight was supposed to be Mom's post about how you liked the muffins."

"Instead post a warning not to bring me things to eat in the shop when my dog is here. Look what happens when someone comes in carrying food." I gave Valdez a fierce glare. He put on an innocent look, complete with lolling tongue and tail wag.

"No kidding." Tina was writing in the notebook. "But when could they know for sure? Some of them seem pretty determined to do the blueberry thing. I say, 'Get a life.'"

I didn't comment on that. Tina obviously wasn't as enthusiastic about the MySpace thing as her mother.

"Daytime." Bri was obviously looking out for number one. "Glory only works nights. She's a real night owl, just like her honey."

I gave her a smile and a nod. "Yes, I keep musician's hours now and I always bring Valdez with me. But that's a good idea, Bri. If my fans want to make me blueberry anything, they'll have to bring it in during the day." Valdez's tail was really wagging now. Obviously he and Bri were anticipating a split. "But totally not necessary, of course."

"Seems like it's risky having a dog in here. Some people might be afraid of dogs. And look what he did tonight. Maybe you should leave him at home." Ellen walked up with the dress on a hanger.

"Can't." I grimaced. "You should see what he does if I leave him home alone. I'd lose my security deposit for sure." I pulled off the other boot and hopped off the stool. "And I'm really sorry about earlier. He's usually fine here. It was the food that set him off." I dropped the boot on the floor. "The dress looked great on you, Ellen."

"Sure did." Tina whipped out her credit card. "My treat,

Mom. For your birthday. I'm proud of my hot mama. And, here, I want this sweater." She laid the red sweater on the counter.

"Thanks, honey. And thanks, Glory, for the compliment and the discount." Ellen scooted out of the way when Valdez wandered up to stand next to me. "You need the Dog Whisperer, Glory."

I looked down when I felt a paw on my bare foot. Nice. Valdez was making sure I knew he was pissed about the ban on baked goods when he was around and the slam on his behavior.

"No, I need the Dog Shouter."

Once the transaction was completed, I smiled at both women. "Thanks so much for the muffins. Valdez thanks you too. And when you come back, I'll make sure Ray has autographed his latest CD for each of you. If I'm not here, Bri or the clerk on duty will have it behind the counter." I took the empty basket and towel Bri handed me and gave them to Ellen.

"You're so nice, no wonder Israel loves you!" Ellen flushed. "We'll definitely be back. Bye, now." She and Tina headed out the door.

"Quite a stunt you two pulled with those muffins." I looked down at Valdez, then back at Bri.

"I could tell you were going to eat that thing. No way was I going through another Cheetos incident." Valdez collapsed by the door, his stomach swollen. *"You should appreciate my sacrifice. Hey, Bri, you got any antacid in the back?"*

"Uh, sure thing. And, Glory, I thought you'd want me to intervene. I know vampires can't eat. The ladies had put you on the spot." Bri swept the last of the crumbs into a dustpan. "Sorry if I overstepped."

"No, you were right. Valdez was right." And V was not going to let me forget that a Big Grab of Cheetos had called my name not too long ago and then left me wishing for death, like Ray's nightmare hangover. "But next time, let's try a less violent approach. Maybe, Bri, you could have reminded me I wanted to be sure I could get into my Grammy dress. Or made up an allergy to blueberries." I shook my head. "I know that's what *I* should have said, but the muffins smelled so delicious." I smiled wistfully. "Pure torture."

"They were *delicious. Best ones I ever ate."* Valdez burped again. *"Bri?"*

"Yeah, bicarb coming right up. Wish you'd saved one of those for me, Valdez." Bri stopped on her way to the back room. *"Are* you going to the Grammys with Caine, Glory?"

"Good question." Valdez looked up from his stupor.

"Don't know. I haven't been invited yet." And didn't that wipe the smile off my face.

"I got another question for you."

"What's that, V?" I flipped through my evening gown selection. Pitiful since I'd had decent New Year's Eve sales. If I did get to go to the Grammys, I had nothing to wear anyway. Would one of those famous designers offer me something fabulous? Yeah, right. Which one designed for women with my figure type? Valdez still hadn't said anything, so I turned to look at him.

"Well? Spit it out. Or is that hangdog look all from muffin overload?" I crouched down beside him. "You angling for a tummy rub?" He did look pretty bad—head on his paws, tail tucked.

"Okay, I'll tell you what's bothering me." He lifted his head and glared at me. *"You'd better hope like hell that Blade doesn't have a clue about MySpace because what you just told those women would hurt him. Bad."*

I jumped up. "I didn't say it to hurt Jerry. It was part of my cover. As Ray's girlfriend."

"Yeah, right. You should have seen your face. 'Ray's so freakin' hot. He sings me to sleep every night.' You know what kind of picture that'll put in a guy's head? Especially a guy who loves you. I'm just sayin' maybe you should think before you give out quotes next time. One minute you say you're a 'private person,' the next you're blabbin' what sounded an awful lot like pillow talk."

"There has been no pillow talk. Jerry and I are solid. I

talked to him just a while ago, Mr. Nosy Paws. So relax, will you?" I rubbed my aching head. "You think I'm worried about my love life right now? With what Aggie said to us? Jeez, V, cut me a break. I've still got Flo to deal with."

"Oh, yeah. Well, good luck with that." Valdez stood and rubbed against me. *"Sorry, guess your plate's a little full right now. I think those muffins had something funky in them."* He winced on his way toward the back room. *"What's keeping you, Bri? I'm about to belch 'The Eyes of Texas' out here."*

I watched him head to the storeroom, his conversation with Bri background noise as I realized that once again, I'd let my mouth overload my tiny brain. Sure, I'd added to the Ray cover story, but if Jerry saw that quote, and I was sure the tabloids would pick it up and run with it, then he would be hurt. I thought about calling him, telling him about it before he could read it somewhere. Explain. What? That I got off to bragging that I slept with a famous rock star? Oh, sure. That made me look really special and shallow and just as worthless as his mother kept telling me I was.

I pulled my boots back on and picked up my cell phone. I'd call Jerry and leave a loving voice mail. Just to reassure him in case he did happen to hear about my stupid brag. So now I was shallow, worthless and selfish. Surely he knew this was all part of the mentoring package. Yeah, right. Okay, the question of the night was: Why *couldn't* I have two hot guys panting after me? I loved Jerry because he was my rock. And I got these tingles around Ray because he was my rock star. Is there a rule somewhere that says I can't have them both? I think not.

"What's going on, Glory?" Ray strolled in a few minutes after three in the morning.

His smiling, casual attitude hit on my last nerve. Just wait till we got upstairs and he heard the latest in Aggie's demands. I was so freaked-out I could hardly speak. But you knew I'd manage, didn't you?

"I thought you were going to be here at two. Richard and Flo are waiting for us upstairs."

"Sorry. Once Sienna gets her talons into you, it's hard to tear loose." Ray grinned at Brianna. "Lookin' good, Bri. That a new outfit?"

"Actually it is." Bri blushed and fussed with her vintage pink twin set. "I got it here. Employee discount."

"No flirting with the hired help, Ray. And you do look cute, Bri. I should have mentioned it." I grabbed Ray's arm. "Let's go. Any more fans come in, tell them I'll be here to-morrow night, early shift."

"Sure thing, boss. 'Night, Mr. Caine."

"Ray. I hope my fans aren't bothering you, Bri." He gave my clerk his patented "guaranteed to melt the panties off a statue" smile.

"Not yours. Glory's." Bri showed signs of falling under his spell with her flushed cheeks and a hair toss. Next thing you knew, she'd be sporting a "Lick my candy, Caine" T-shirt. No, I'm not kidding. I had one upstairs myself. I know, gross. But if you wanted the complete Israel Caine collection, you had to have one.

"The Blueberries, Ray. I have quite a following." I pulled him away from the counter. "Bri, we're heading out."

"Wait. I want to hear more about these fans. Speak to me, Bri." Ray leaned against the counter, pulling me off balance as he gave Bri his full attention.

Bri glanced at me. "I'll let Glory tell you about them. I'd better check on a customer in the dressing room."

"Come on, Ray. We're late." I dragged him toward the door.

"'Night, Bri. Patience, Glory. Not jealous are you, babe?" He pulled open the door and glanced outside. "No paparazzi? Must be our lucky night."

I grabbed Ray's arm. "Wait. Valdez goes out first." I held Valdez's leash but didn't bother to snap it on. "Valdez, go across the street and do your thing." The door to the apart-ments upstairs, including my place, was just a few feet away.

Valdez burped as he went past, not even sparing Ray a glance.

"The dog's in a mood. Sorry you had to wait for me. You know I think you *are* a little jealous." Ray was still grinning.

I smiled back. "Don't be ridiculous. We're both free agents. As you'll see when Jerry gets back from Europe." That wiped the smile from his face. "You want to hit on Bri? Go for it. Just remember I need her to work most nights for me."

"You know we can't publicly date other people yet." Ray moved in on me. "The tabloids would have a field day. Think of the added stress when we've got Aggie to deal with." He brushed my frizzy hair back over my shoulders, then frowned when I backed away from him.

"You have no idea. It's worse than you think. I'll tell you upstairs."

"What? Tell me now." He moved close again.

I glanced across the street and saw a woman follow Valdez into the bushes. "Is that—"

Barking, yelling and a scream drew Ray and me across the street at a run.

"What's going on here?" Ray stopped in front of me and I ran into his solid back, almost knocking us both down.

I peeked around him. Valdez was standing over a woman who lay crying in the mud. She wore his paw prints on her red V-neck sweater. And no wonder. She had a leash in one hand and pepper spray in the other.

"I—I was just trying to catch your dog for you." She sat up and waved the leash, almost hitting herself in the face with the metal fastener. "I saw him escape when you came out of your shop. Then he ran across the street."

"Why'd you try to spray me in the face with pepper spray, lady?" Valdez sneezed and rubbed his face on a small patch of dead grass. *"Good thing I've got great reflexes or you'd have blinded me."*

"Oh, God! I'm hallucinating! I must have hit my head

when I fell." The woman collapsed again and closed her eyes.

"Tina, what the hell are you doing here and why *did* you use your pepper spray?" I snatched it from her hand.

"You know this woman?" Ray put his hand on my shoulder.

"She was just in my shop. She's one of my fans." I stepped between Ray and Tina. "I don't get it, Tina. Why'd you try to spray Valdez?"

"I—I was afraid he'd bite me." She sat up again and looked at me instead of Valdez. Apparently I was less threatening than a talking dog. Though, with pepper spray in my hand and my temper rising, she was dead wrong.

"Did he growl at you? Lunge?"

"No." She stood and brushed off her baggy jeans. The moon came from behind a cloud and she shrieked. "Israel Caine! It's really you!" She wobbled and I thought for a second she was going to go down again.

"She tried to sneak up on me. I was doing nothing but my business. Then ssspppit, she zapped me with that spray and came at me with the leash. Of course I had to defend myself."

She'd come after my dog. What was her agenda? A quick trip through her mind didn't help. She was all about seeing Ray in the flesh. I was shaking with the urge to pepper spray her until seeing anything was a dim memory. I stepped back.

"Practice your whammy, Ray. Look her in the eyes and paralyze her."

"What?" Ray glanced at me. "I don't—"

"Israel. I've dreamed of meeting you. I go to all of your concerts." She edged closer and reached out a muddy hand to touch his sleeve. "You're really standing there? With the talking dog, I thought maybe I'd slipped into a coma. After falling down and all." She shrieked again and covered her face. "Don't look at me. I'm a mess! That damned dog. I'm covered in mud." She went on a rant about how she'd wanted to look perfect when she finally met Ray.

"Come on, Ray. You've seen me do it dozens of times.

Stare into her eyes. Touch her hand. That physical connection makes it easier. Use her name. It's Tina or Christina Anderson. It helps if you can call her name. Ask her what she's doing out here. Then tell her she's going to forget all about the talking dog."

Ray took her hand. "Look at me, Tina."

I thought she was going to jump out of her ballet flats.

"Yes, Israel."

"What are you doing out here, Tina?"

"Stealing that horrible dog."

I gasped and looked at Valdez. He sneezed again and showed his teeth. Damn it, his eyes were red, irritated by the pepper spray.

"What the—"

"Why did you want to steal the dog, Tina?" Ray's voice hardened.

"Because it belongs to that fat bitch you're sleeping with, Israel. I've been watching her shop. Waiting for my chance. Even went inside today." Tina's jaw suddenly trembled and two tears slid down her muddy cheeks. "Look at her. Gross."

Ray dropped her hands. "She's nuts. I'm not doing this."

"Yes, you are, Ray." I squeezed Valdez's leash, fighting my kill urge. "Keep going."

Ray focused on her again. "What are you doing here, Tina?"

"I want to give you what you need. She's nice." Tina spat it, like it was the worst of four letter words. "I'm naughty." She reached for Ray, but he held up his hands and she backed off.

"You want sex? Have sex with me, Israel. I'll do anything you want. Anywhere. As many times as you wish." She ran her hands over her breasts, the red sweater clinging to her ripe curves.

Had I really sold her that? Now it was all I could do to keep from leaping on her, ripping it off her and cramming it down her throat. Right before I drained her dry and tossed her body in those bushes, of course.

"I've been studying, reading. I know lots and lots of positions. And I have toys, outfits. I bet she's boring in bed. Please give me a shot. I even have a certificate, a clean bill of health from my doctor, in my purse." She gestured toward a tree to her right.

Ray's stare gave me chills. Tina just kept talking, on a roll.

"Israel, please. Listen to me. I guarantee you'll never go back to Fat Ass there after I get through with you."

I heard a snarl. Oh, that was me. The fat ass. Ray reached over and squeezed my hand. Valdez was pressed against my leg on the other side, his growls promising he would be happy to finish her at my signal.

Clueless Tina, a breath away from death, just kept talking. "I love you, Israel. Give me a chance to show you how much."

Add tears to the pleading. But Tina was obviously under the influence of the whammy during the whole "Love me, Ray" recitation, her voice monotone, her stare never leaving Ray's face. Good thing, because one look at *my* face, and she'd run screaming if she was as smart as she thought she was.

"Well, that's the power of the rock star at work." My lips curled, my fangs more than ready to rip. Fat Ass? Nice was about to turn really nasty. Sorry, but I'd seen Tina's curves and they weren't any smaller than mine. Talk about delusions. Underneath the eau de pepper spray she reeked of Juicy, a perfume one of Ray's former girlfriends had declared his favorite scent.

She also smelled of B negative, which under normal circumstances would have called my name. Right now it was calling all right. "Drain me," it whispered.

"Why the dog, Tina?" Ray didn't even smile. Which showed more character than I'd given him credit for. That free sex offer should have at least made him waggle his eyebrows, wink, something. Instead he was focused on the threat to Valdez.

"I figured losing her dog would show that bitch the dangers of being with a rocker. I'd send a note, of course. So she'd know why he went missing. And whose stew pot he went into. I'd also let her know that if she didn't leave you alone, she'd be next."

"Holy shit. The woman's psycho." Valdez looked up at me. *"What is this? A bad remake of* Fatal Attraction?"

"Damn, I'm sorry, Valdez. You'd be surprised how many obsessive fans I've seen. Usually they're fairly harmless." Ray walked over to the tree and picked up Tina's tote. He pulled out a wallet and handed me her driver's license. "We'll give this to Nathan tomorrow night. He'll know who to notify to make sure she doesn't hurt anyone else."

"That makes me feel better. Problem is, that psycho helps with my MySpace page and has a really nice mother." I felt my fingernails bite into my palm and took a few seconds to struggle for calm.

"Nathan will know what to do. I'll tell him to be discreet." Ray tossed the bag aside. "Though why the hell we should worry about discretion, I don't know. Women like this are unpredictable, Glory, and with the power of the Internet . . ."

"So we send her home with a nice new memory. Okay, here's what you do now. Make eye contact with her again, Ray. Suggest to her that she forget about Valdez, about this wild-ass plot to steal my dog, and that the dog *did not* talk. I don't think you can erase her whole Israel Caine obsession. Too strong. But you can send her home thinking that she waited in the park and you came out of the shop. That you talked to her and were really nice. Here, sign her purse." I grabbed a pen from my own bag and handed him her Coach. I know, I considered it a desecration to write on a designer leather bag, but an obsessed fan would probably treasure it. "Write 'To Tina, a great fan.' And sign it."

"You sure this will diffuse the situation?" Ray did what I said.

"It's worth a shot. Like I said, she's connected to my fan

club. It's complicated." So why did I feel like I was wimping out here? "She'll get home and tell her mother. They'll blog about her Israel Caine meeting on the site. Probably not remember that Valdez or I were even here."

"Good. I don't want her within a thousand feet of you." Ray threw her purse to the ground and issued his orders. We watched as Tina sleepwalked through picking up her purse and heading to her car.

"You sure you shouldn't just rip out her throat and be done with it?" Valdez rubbed his head against my leg. *"She could still decide to come after you, Glory."*

"Tempting, V. I can't stand the way she went after what she thought was an innocent animal." I scratched his ears. "I can handle a psycho bitch, anytime, anywhere. But say the word and I'll send her to hell right now." I saw Ray's eyes widen. Did he think I was kidding? I let him read my mind.

"Son of a bitch! You guys don't fool around, do you?" Ray stared at me then at Valdez. "What—"

"Naw, not worth the effort. We going upstairs now? I still feel like I have pepper up my nose. It's been hours since I ate those muffins. I think I need a snack. At least a dozen Twinkies."

"You got it." I turned to Ray. "Good job on the whammy, Ray. Think you could do it again?"

"Yeah." Ray cleared his throat. "Welcome to my world. One rocker's girlfriend had her hair set on fire." He put his arm around me. "Of course she wasn't a badass vampire as far as I know. I remember that Freddie Mercury ran with one chick who might have been a zombie."

"Yeah, I heard that." We both chuckled and I relaxed against Ray for a moment. "Welcome to my world too. Sometimes we have to use violence. You might as well get used to the idea. And I know this wasn't your fault."

"Maybe it was. The name sounds familiar. I think she's been sending e-mails, snail mail, packages. Nathan keeps track of that stuff. Or rather his assistant Dru does. We should have taken Tina seriously." Ray ran a hand through his hair as we crossed the deserted street. "Dru's in New York. I guess we should think about moving her out here if I stay much longer. There's probably more of this kind of thing I'm letting slide."

"Forget long-range for now. Think short-range. Aggie. Flo and Richard need to be clued in and they're waiting for us. And just wait till you hear the complication Aggie's cooked up for us. Flo's already called me three times and Richard's getting tired of watching your old music videos and reading bridal magazines." I saw Ray's mouth open. "Don't ask. Let's go. I want to bring them and *you* up to speed. Among other things, I made contact with an EV tonight."

"*When? Where was I?*" Valdez practically leaped up the stairs after I punched in the security code to let us inside the building.

"You met with someone alone?" Ray put his hand over mine when I was about to unlock my apartment door.

"Well, yes. I handled it." Ray and Valdez both stared at me like I was a first-class idiot. "Quit ganging up on me."

"You shouldn't be taking chances like that. And you definitely won't be walking Valdez in that park anymore without backup. Got it?"

"Man, you're sounding like Jerry. Am I going to have two overprotective males in my life now?"

"Three. Valdez, am I right?" Ray put his knuckles down and Valdez butted his head against them.

"*Damn straight.*"

"Look, I'm perfectly capable of looking out for myself. I'm the trainer, you're the trainee, Ray. Remember?"

"I know I'm not Jerry. He's a hell of a lot more powerful than I am now. Valdez too. But I do care what happens to you. Give me a hundred years or so and I bet I'll be able to kick both Jerry and Valdez's butts to hell and back, see if I don't."

"*Yeah, yeah, yeah.*" Valdez sniffed. "*I could stand around here and compare packages, but I think I smell something good cooking on the third floor. There's a shifter up there who likes me, Glory.*" He sat and rubbed his face with one paw. "*She can feed me while you two tell Flo and Richard about that freak-a-zoid Siren. See you later. Keep giving her hell, Caine. Glory, I'll be back before sunrise. Don't you dare leave this building without me."* He headed up.

"More orders." I looked at Valdez's furry backside as he disappeared around the turn in the stairs. "I'll do what I damn well please, mister! You think I don't know why you're headed upstairs? You're scared of Flo. You're not a dog, you're a chicken."

"Where Flo's concerned? Cluck. Cluck."

"What? Are you in third grade?" Ray grinned at me.

"They didn't have grades when I went to school back in the dark ages. Didn't have school for girls at all actually. My mum taught me what I needed to know. Picked up everything else later. Much later." I leaned against the door and studied Ray, trying to imagine both of us in a hundred years. Oh, we'd look the same, but what would the world be like? Where would we be? Roasting in hell if we didn't handle the next few weeks right.

And if we somehow managed to salvage this situation would we stay in touch? Doubtful. It was rare for immortals to keep the same friends for centuries. I guess that was why I was so close to Jerry. He'd made the effort to keep track of me. I'd never had the resources to do the same for him.

"I keep forgetting that you're so much older than I am. You look young, talk young." Ray ran a finger down my cheek. "I'll always keep in touch with you, Glory." He'd been mind reading again. "I know you didn't turn me vampire, but you're making sure I'm going to do this gig right. I owe you. You need me, anytime, anywhere, give me a shout. At the very least, I can sing something for you. It helped with Aggie."

"Your singing has helped a lot of people. Don't let fanzilla Tina's reaction to it bring you down." I breathed in his now familiar scent. Ray hadn't asked to be made vampire and it was playing hell with his life. Some things he had always loved, like the sun, were now permanently off-limits. But, except for that brief bout with the booze, he hadn't whined, just accepted the inevitable and moved on. I admired him. Go figure.

I put my hand on his chest. "I've neglected your vampire lessons. Like the whammy thing. We should have gone over that sooner. You've got lots of powers you've yet to discover. I'm going to get Richard to work with you on some of the macho vamp things like fighting tricks he knows." I slid my hand along Ray's shirt, a nice black Egyptian cotton tonight.

"That's good." Ray stared into my eyes. "But I don't feel much like fighting now. If I practice my whammy on you, can I make you do something for me?"

Ten

"You shouldn't have warned me. Now I'll refuse to meet your eyes. Unless . . ." I met his gaze head-on. "I'm willing to risk it. Because I trust you not to make me do something we'll both regret."

"Well, hell. Now you're counting on me being a gentleman. Which I can be. Or not. Right now, not so much." Ray lowered his head and gently bit my lower lip. "I won't whammy you into doing things with me, Glory. Won't need to, will I?" He smiled against my mouth. "I'm not the only one feeling the heat here. Am I, babe?"

"I think you're still stirred up from Tina's promises. We're just friends, remember?"

"Tina grossed me out. You, though . . ."

Ray's hands were on my waist. I relaxed against him, not averse to a little harmless one-on-one flirting. It beat thinking about what waited on the other side of the door.

"Would you two get your butts in here? We have vampire hearing, you know." Flo's voice was clear and irritated. "I want to see what you're doing out there. If we could eat, *cara*, Richard and I'd be having popcorn and a Coke with our entertainment."

I grinned and felt Ray's smile against my lips. *"Don't say a word. Just breathe heavily. Moan a little. I'm going to bump against the door a few times."* I said all this in Ray's head, of course. I'd hate to spoil Flo's fun, probably the last she'd have for a while.

"Why pretend when we can give them the real deal?" Ray leaned into me, his kiss open, wet and wild.

I guess I bumped against the door. I'm sure one or both of us moaned. By the time I came up for air, the door was open and we both fell into the living room, our faces flushed and Ray's shirt unbuttoned. Flo clapped her hands, Richard grinned, and the Israel Caine DVD on the TV came to a soaring conclusion. I, for one, needed a drink.

"Well, you were having some fun, eh?" Flo followed me into the kitchen and watched me pull two bottles of synthetic out of the refrigerator. "I am so jealous. I love Richard, but, just once, I'd like to kiss Israel Caine. To compare, you know."

"Don't risk it." I stuck my head in the freezer, finally grabbed a few ice cubes and pushed them down my sweater. "Oops, here take this before I ruin it."

"Mio Dio! Where did you get this?" Flo waved the Baggie in the air and darted back into the living room. "Ricardo, we are going home."

"No, you can't." I ran after her and snatched the bag. "You can have this after we talk."

"What is it?" Ray took the bottle I handed him, looked at the lumps in my sweater, then grinned when he saw an ice cube slide out of my bra. "You hot, Glory?"

I dug out the ice cubes and threw them at him. "Not anymore."

"It's Vampire Viagra." Flo sighed. "You *are* going to give it to me, aren't you, my friend, *mia amica?*" She put her hand on Richard's shoulder. "I know you don't like it, but, with me, *amante*, you will be transported to paradise. I promise you a night you'll never forget." She gave him a look that could have melted the polar ice cap.

"Let's go. We'll discuss whatever you wanted to talk about another night." Richard shoved to his feet, his hand out, ready to take the Baggie from me by force if necessary. I didn't have to read his mind to know that.

"Please. Give us a few minutes. Then you can play all the love games you want." I tossed the bag to Ray. "Guard this."

"No problem." He frowned at the bag. "I don't need a drug to push my love button to 'on.' "

"It's not like that for vampires, Ray. My Ricardo's love button, as you call it, is always on." She gave Richard a dazzling smile. "But this little pill . . . Mmm. It will give us such a pleasure . . ." Flo sighed. "I can't describe it. So I sacrifice two of the pills. Try it. You and Glory will be amazed."

"Keep your damned pills. I lost my voice just by drinking alcohol. No way am I putting a drug in my system. I've got an important gig coming up. I can't take a chance." Ray tossed the Baggie on the coffee table. "Flo, you and Richard can have all of it."

"No one's leaving yet." I grabbed the bag and stuck it down my bra again. "The VV and you, Flo, can wait a few more minutes. Sit down. Ray and I have a serious problem and we need your help. Richard, you might know about this. You ever have dealings with a Siren?" I twisted the top off the bottle of synthetic and took a swallow. Bleck.

"You mean like a mermaid? Sit, darling. I have a feeling that if I tried to take the pills from Glory's bra, Ray would have something to say about it." Richard pulled Flo down beside him on the couch.

"Damned right." Ray took a drink from his own bottle and made a face.

"No fighting in my living room. Flo, quit giving me the stink eye. You'll get your VV." I settled into a chair.

"Patience, my love." Richard patted Flo's knee. "Let's hear your friend out." Flo huffed and puffed and shot me looks that made it clear *she* had no problem shoving a fist down my bra. But she finally settled beside him, tapping her fingers on his thigh.

"Sirens, mermaids. Come on, Richard. What do you know?"

Richard frowned. "I've come across a few, in the Med, but you're not implying you ran into one around here, are you?"

"Unfortunately. Aglaophonos. Aggie for short. She's staked out in Lake Travis. Caught Ray and me on New Year's Eve."

"Caught you doing what? I wonder if I have Jeremiah's number on speed dial." Flo grabbed her red leather purse.

"Florence, quit trying to make trouble. This could be serious. A Siren is no laughing matter." Richard grabbed Flo's purse and dropped it back on the floor.

"Did I laugh?" Flo looked hurt. "I've heard of mermaids. Wanton witches. Luring men to their deaths. But what can they do to a vampire? Pah! Surely you didn't let this Aggie scare you, Glory."

"She scared the shit out of me. She's more powerful than a vampire. Can freeze you where you stand. Lucky for me she's an Israel Caine fan. Ray sang and she finally let us go. But we had to make a deal with her."

"What kind of deal?" Richard addressed this to Ray.

"She's in league with a goddess." Ray grimaced. "This so-called goddess cursed her. Man, you should see the results. Aggie sure as hell doesn't look like a mermaid. More like a nightmare after too many bean burritos." Ray saw Flo and Richard's blank looks and laughed. "Right. No burritos for you guys. Take my word for it then. She's butt ugly. Ask Glory."

I nodded. "Scaly, stinky, disgusting. Green! She must have really pissed off Circe."

"Circe! That bitch!" Flo jumped to her feet. "*Mio Dio!* Now we're in for it. No one hates male vampires like Circe. She took a lover from me once. Just sucked him right down to her level of hell." Flo paced around the coffee table, her cheeks pink. "Put a Siren and Circe together and you have serious trouble. We're leaving Austin immediately. All of us." She turned to Richard, hands on her hips. "Ricardo, I forbid you to go within a hundred miles of this vampire gobbling fiend. Do you hear me?" Her voice had risen and she was now officially red-faced. If she could have seen her reflection, she would have been mortified.

"What's the deal you made?" Richard got up and led Flo back to the couch. "Calm down, darling. We'll figure this out. No one is running away and no one is going to suck me down to any level of hell. I'm a former priest, remember? God knows I still do his work here."

Ray looked startled and I smiled at him.

"Richard's right. He's one of the good guys. No way is he destined for fire and brimstone. Ray and I can't run anyway, Flo. Aggie's got us on a leash of sorts. Ray, tell Richard what happened with Aggie."

So Ray gave Richard and Flo the whole story as far as he knew it. "You see, we need three vampires ASAP. Aggie's not patient, but she's given us until the full moon. Two and a half weeks away now. Glory contacted the EVs, that's how she got the Vampire Viagra. We're trying to lure Simon and two of his cronies out to the house. If we can get them close enough, Aggie can sing her Siren song and do the rest."

"I'm afraid it's not that simple now." I knew that word would get a reaction and I was right.

"Simple?" Flo jumped up. "Sirens in an Austin lake and dealing with Simon Destiny is not simple. I think this is going to ruin my wedding."

I put my hand on her shoulder. "More than you know. She wants Damian."

"What?" Flo looked at each of us. "What is this? A joke? You said we would send her bad vampires. Damie is naughty. Is true. He breaks women's hearts. But they have a good time with him, no?" Flo took a breath. "You tease me. Give me the Vampire Viagra. We go, Ricardo."

"No, Flo, I'm serious. Circe wants Casanova." I looked at Ray.

"When the hell did you find this out?" Ray obviously didn't like to be blindsided.

"Valdez and I had a face-to-face with Aggie, Ray, when you and Sienna were practicing the other night. I asked her why she was in Austin. Seems Circe heard the Latin lover was in these parts. The goddess is a big advocate for women. She figures Casanova has broken enough hearts."

"But Damie *loves* women. So what if he leaves them a little, um, broken. *Mio Dio.*" Flo collapsed on the couch. "We can't do it. I won't do it. What happens to you if you don't give this Siren my brother, Glory?" She leaned against Richard, who took her in his arms.

"Then Ray and I are going to hell at the full moon, along with any other bad vamps we can drag along with us." I pulled the Baggie out of my bra and tossed it on the coffee table. "Here's the VV. We all need time to think about this."

Richard kissed Flo's pale cheek. "Darling, we'll think of something. Your brother is not going to hell. And neither is your best friend. What kind of wedding would it be without either one of them?"

Flo sniffed but didn't say anything. I glanced at Ray. "I think we should go ahead and try to get Simon and another EV out to Ray's house. Ray and I plan to go out to the EV headquarters and see what we can learn that would lure them out to the lake."

"Madness. I don't want anyone going out to that EV chamber of horrors." Flo clutched Richard's thigh. "I had a very bad experience out there. Glory, you did too. I don't think Simon would let you leave there this time. Not unless he is sure Israel is really your protector. I don't know. It was *terribile*. A nightmare. Now that I think about it, maybe I shouldn't take the VV." She looked longingly at the packet Ray had picked up and was dangling from his left hand. "I got hooked."

"Want me to flush them down the toilet?" Ray stood and made a move toward the bathroom.

"No!" Flo jumped up and grabbed the bag. "I can't get hooked if I don't have more. I'll take one. Ricardo, you take one. I must think. But not tonight. Glory, I won't call Jeremiah. You know that. Right? Or speak to Damian yet." Her lips trembled and she looked at the pill in her hand. "See. This is already starting trouble for me. But I take anyway because I don't want to worry about all this other stuff now. Glory, Ray, meet us here tomorrow night. Tonight is for love. I need it." She popped a pill in her mouth and swallowed.

"Now, *caro* Ricardo, you have ten minutes to get me home before I start tearing off clothes. Yours, mine"—she looked across the coffee table—"Ray's."

Richard put a pill in his mouth. "Let's hit the roof and shift out of here then. We'll see you tomorrow night. Surely one of us will come up with something." He grabbed Flo's hand. "We're outta here." The door slammed behind them.

Ray stared down at the two pills left in the Baggie. "Should I flush them?"

"No. Let me have them." I blocked my thoughts. Maybe I'd use them with Jerry when he got home. Ray handed the pills over without comment. I could see the question in his eyes but deliberately ignored it as I stuck the VV behind a book, *Getting the Love You Deserve*, on my shelf. I have a lot of self-help books. I've been helping myself for a long time. I turned to Ray.

"We're obviously not going to solve the Aggie problem tonight."

"Guess not." Ray picked up his bottle of synthetic and took a swallow. "So Damian, Flo's brother, is Casanova? Like in the history books?"

"That's what he claims."

"Maybe it's just male bragging and Circe's wrong."

"That would be convenient. But I'm not counting on it." I rinsed my empty bottle out in the sink and left it for recycling. "Getting him out to your place will be a problem if Flo tells him—" My voice cracked. Ray was beside me in an instant and put his arms around me.

"I get it, babe. I keep wondering what I would do if this was Nate's brother we were talking about. I sure couldn't send him to hell. Or ask Nate to agree to it." Ray's arms tightened around me.

"So we've got to figure out a way to get Damian out of this. And without frying our own butts." I eased away from Ray and glanced at his bottle of synthetic, still half-full. "Aren't you going to finish that?"

"It tastes like crap." He frowned at it. "Since I'm basically stumped and you're basically stumped, I say we take a break. Unless you're willing to do the 'love' distraction like Flo and Richard."

"Nope, sorry." I grabbed the bottle and emptied it in the sink.

"Then let's go out and get some fresh air. You need to take me hunting."

"You shouldn't—" I set the bottle next to mine.

"Did you or did you not drink from Nathan when I was sick?"

"I did, but—"

"And I assume you've fed from other mortals from time to time."

"Well, sure. Over the years." I looked down and pretended to study a chip in my red nail polish. "They didn't have synthetics back in the day."

"I want to learn how to hunt. And I don't want you foisting this off on Will. I want you to teach me how to do it right. You're always so careful to 'blend,' as you call it. I'm sure you'll be the best teacher."

"Well, when you put it like that, how can I say no?" And my fangs were already zooming into place at the mere thought of mortal blood. I was so in trouble. How had I gone years living on synthetics? I had to do something about this. Later. After I got Ray fully trained. Yeah, later.

"Okay, since we really can't do anything about Aggie tonight anyway, we might as well go out. And we don't need Valdez. There are two of us. We should be able to handle whatever comes along. And I don't think the paparazzi will be out at four o'clock in the morning. Let me change clothes first.

These red pants are too noticeable. You wore the perfect clothes. Dark shirt, dark jeans."

"Sure, I can sneak up on anybody." Ray followed me to my room, but I shut the door in his face. "Come on, Glory. I can watch you change pants. You got on one of your thongs? Bet it matches those pants. I love you in red."

"Forget it." Even Ray's flirting couldn't distract me from my excitement for the coming hunt. I shucked the leather pants and found some old jeans in my closet. Tennis shoes next. Heels made too much noise. Jeez, I was as excited as I'd been the first few times Jerry had taken me hunting. See? He'd taught me more than those feeding pleasure points.

I grabbed my keys and threw open the door.

"Okay, Ray, I'm ready."

"About time." He took my arm and hurried me out of the apartment. "Give me a rundown on what to expect."

"Well, we won't see many mortals this time of night, but that's why Sixth Street is such a great location for me. There *will* be a few, coming from the after-hours clubs. Where you live, you'd have a hard time finding anyone besides the mortals who work for you. I'm sure you don't want to use your bodyguards as a source."

"No kidding. I can't imagine drinking from Buster or Sam." Ray followed me down the stairs. "What if there *are* paparazzi waiting?"

"If you don't want them for your source, you'll whammy them and send them on their way. You're always going to use the whammy after feeding. Erase memories so you can get away."

"Sure, you'd have to." Ray punched in the code and opened the door carefully. No reporters. Fine. Mugs and Muffins, the coffee shop next door, was also open twenty-four hours. There was only one customer inside, a man wearing noise-canceling headphones. He was sitting at a laptop and nursing a cup of coffee.

"What about him?"

"Diana and I have a policy. We leave each other's customers

alone." Diana Marchand was the vampire who owned the coffee shop. She and I weren't exactly best friends, but we respected each other as two single businesswomen trying to make it on our own.

I glanced in my shop and saw Brianna helping two women in scrubs pick out dresses to try on. Good. Nice to have customers during what was usually a slow time of night.

"Let's try to stay in the shadows, away from the streetlights."

"Makes sense." Ray looked excited too. "Maybe we should be going down the alley."

"No. Too many bad things have happened back there. When we find our prey, then we'll pull him or her into a dark area, a doorway or behind a Dumpster." I was constantly on the lookout. A police car sped by, but I didn't worry about it. Ray and I were just a couple out for a late-night walk.

"You said prey." Ray put his hand on my arm. "That's the first time you've really sounded like a vampire to me."

I turned and showed Ray my fangs. "Get used to it, youngster. I'm vampire and proud of it. Watch this." I leaped through the air and landed next to a man who'd just walked out of a doorway. I pulled him to me, stared into his eyes and then yanked him down a dark path next to the building.

"Come on, Ray, don't just stand there. I'm about to get this party started." My bloodlust was rising and I felt like striking immediately. The man stood there as I'd commanded and I turned to Ray impatiently. "Hurry!"

"Glory, what the hell's gotten into you?"

"I'm here to teach you to hunt. Are you interested or not?" I inhaled. Not bad. The guy had been drinking, but not a lot. Maybe he'd been playing in a band at the club he'd just left. Ray hadn't been taught about blood types yet. I'd start with that.

"Okay, I'm here. What's first?" Ray looked at the man. "I don't want to drink from him."

"Why not?" I checked out the man again. "He's clean, young, healthy. What's not to like?"

"He's a man. I don't want to snuggle up to a guy. I want to drink from a woman. Preferably a hot one." Ray smiled at me. "Tell me you didn't pick this one because he's a good-looking guy."

"Give me a friggin' break." I put my hands on my hips. "I picked him because he was the first available mortal to cross our path that wasn't soaked in cheap wine." I waved my hand toward the empty street, barely visible at the end of the building. "You want to go out there and troll for good-looking women, help yourself. I'll take this guy."

"Fine. Tell me your process while you're going at it." Ray leaned closer. "It's cool that we can see so well in the dark."

"Yes, it is. First I want you to take a whiff. His blood type is B positive. Memorize that smell. Once you've tried different types you'll probably decide you have a favorite."

"What's *your* favorite, Glory?" Ray was right behind me. He put his hand on my shoulder. "This guy's? It's the same as mine."

"Sorry, but I'm a sucker—ha-ha—for AB negative. Your buddy Nathan happens to be that type. So you see it was a treat to be able to drink from him during your hangover."

"So glad I could help you get off." Ray's hand slid away from me.

"I don't fool around when I'm out on a hunt. You shouldn't either, no matter how hot your prey. Just tilt the head back and get a bead on the jugular." I looked back at Ray. "See the blood pumping? I'm sure you can hear it too. It's calling to you, isn't it, Ray?" I'm sure my eyes were glowing. It's a bloodlust thing.

"What's calling to me is how excited you are." Ray moved closer again. He put his arms around my waist and pressed against my back. "Take him, Glory. Let me see you drink from him. This is unbelievably hot."

Ray didn't have to tell me twice. I heard myself growl before I sank my fangs into the sweet spot. I drank, feeling the reviving flow fill me. Ray's body against mine was an extra bonus. He urged me on, his hands touching me and stroking me until I realized I was getting carried away. I pulled back and licked the wounds closed.

I was panting like I'd run a marathon so I leaned back against Ray, letting the stranger's body settle against the brick wall behind him.

"Damn. I almost drank too much." I reached out and checked the man's pulse. "He'll be okay. But you have to pay attention to what you're doing. Not be distracted."

"Oh? Did I distract you?" Ray leaned down and kissed my neck behind my ear.

"I'm not playing here, Ray. What if I'd killed the poor guy?" I turned in Ray's arms and stared up at him. "It can and has happened. You want that on your conscience?"

"Hell, no." Ray finally seemed to be listening but he kept his arms around me.

"Then always be aware of the limits you can push with your source. This guy's tall, about one-eighty. He could spare quite a bit and still not feel much but a little light-headedness when he snaps out of it. But a hot, young thing like you want to drink from won't be able to give you much without serious consequences."

"Speaking of hot, young things . . ." Ray pulled me up against him. "You have any idea how hot *you* were just now? The way you went after what you wanted. God, Glory. There's only one woman I want to drink from. You. Right now."

I could see his fangs glinting in the dim light from the faraway streetlights. His eyes were glowing. So the blood-lust had gotten to him too. I threw back my head and offered my throat. Why not? Sweet words and the feel of his hard body against mine were more than enough to pull me closer. I wanted to connect with him, and closed my eyes, waiting for him to take me. Then I heard the man I'd used fall to the broken pavement.

My eyes popped open and I pushed Ray back. "No, wait. Let me finish what I started. I have to show you . . ." I turned to pick up the man and threw him over my shoulder to carry him toward the street. There I looked out to the

deserted sidewalk and realized my best bet was to leave the
guy sitting next to the doorway where I'd taken him. I gently set him down, then got in his face.

"You must have fallen when you came out of the club." I
patted his cheek. "Hey, are you all right?"

"Oh, I—I must have fallen." The man blinked and
looked around.

"My boyfriend and I were walking by and saw you. Think
you can get home all right?" I looked at Ray and winked.
"Want us to call you a cab?"

"No, I—I feel okay, just tired. I don't live far." The man
pushed to his feet, swayed for a moment, then looked down
the street. "I'll be all right. Think I'll stop at the all-night
coffee shop. Have a muffin. Starving. Thanks for checking on
me." He wobbled off down the sidewalk.

"That seemed easy enough." Ray stuck his hands in his
pockets.

"This time it was. No witnesses interrupting."

"Just you interrupting what promised to be a highlight.
I guess you're not going to let me drink from you right
now."

I shook my head and looked down the street. "I've been
thinking about that. Not tonight. Let's go through with the
plan. Find you someone to feed from. You need the practice
so you can be independent. I'm not going to be with you
forever."

Ray put his hand on my arm and turned me to face him.
"You could be, you know."

"Get real, Ray. Even Jerry and I take breaks. And you and
I . . ." I tapped my foot. "I'm a novelty for you now. And I
admit we click on some level."

"Oh, was that the sound I heard when I kissed you outside your door? A click?" Ray grinned. "Sounded more like
a moan to me."

I found it hard to resist Ray when he played like this. So
I didn't try, just headed off down the street where I knew
we'd find some of the clubs that stayed open really late. A

group of women emerged from one of them just as we got to a corner. Ray was recognized immediately and I realized we'd have a problem with the whole hunting thing. Especially if we hoped to cut one filly out of a herd. Sue me, but it had been a country western venue and the girls were in jeans and boots.

"Israel Caine. Sign my shirt. Please!" The squeals were enough to draw a few more people out into the street. A police car slowed, then pulled up next to the milling crowd.

"Problem here, ladies?" The cop got out of the car, slapping a nightstick on his palm.

"It's Israel Caine and his girlfriend!" Moans, cheers, more squeals.

"Do I need to call for backup?"

"No, thanks, officer." I gestured to the cop to come closer so I could whisper to him. "My boyfriend is famous. The singer, Israel Caine. These women are fans. But Ray and I are just exhausted. Could you help us get out of here?" Ray was being gracious, signing bar napkins, shirts, even a boot with a sparkly pink gel marker one girl produced from her purse. That started a whole new slew of requests.

"Sure, hop in the car. You got far to go?"

"Just down the street. Vintage Vamp's Emporium. My store."

"You got it." The cop began working his way to Ray, politely but firmly informing the crowd that Mr. Caine was ready to leave now.

Ray and I ran to the police car and threw ourselves into the backseat. In less than five minutes we were back in front of my apartment building. We waved good-bye to the policeman, then looked at each other.

"Well, that was a bust," Ray said with a grimace.

"You got busted? What did you do? I'm getting on the scanner, so don't bother to lie about it, Caine." A reporter appeared at my elbow. He snapped pictures and managed to get one of the police car as it sped away.

"We just caught a ride. There was no arrest." Ray

frowned and looked like he was about to start smashing a
camera.

"Drugs? Your eyes look red." The reporter pulled out a
cell phone. "Damn, this is huge. I'm finally gonna get that
piece in the *Enquirer*."

I got in the guy's face, but he just kept punching in
numbers. My whammy wasn't working, probably because I
couldn't seem to concentrate. "Stop it. There were no drugs.
We got ambushed by a bunch of kickers outside a club
down the street."

Ray grabbed the guy by the shoulders and forced him to
look at him. "Stop using the phone."

Suddenly the man froze.

"Way to whammy, Ray."

"Yeah, worked like a charm." Ray looked around but this
was the only photographer in sight. Even Mugs and Muffins
was empty.

"What do you say we give this guy a story? You have to feel
for him. Out trolling for a scoop at four thirty in the morning
and it's probably damned cold for a mortal." I glanced at the
wall thermometer outside Diana's shop. Thirty-four degrees.
No wonder the man was shivering despite his overcoat.

"You're feeling sorry for him? After the way the tabloids
have talked about you?" Ray shook his head. "What kind of
story you got in mind?"

"I don't know." I grinned. "You could come out of the
closet."

"Way too late for that. Didn't you hear? I fathered Brit-
ney Spears's last baby."

"Well, there's always an alien abduction."

"I'm in the wrong car. I've got a terrific race car at home
in Chicago that would look like a space vehicle in the right
light." Ray looked down and squatted to pick up something.
"Wow. Treasure. Someone dropped this."

"It's a ring from the gumball machine in Mugs and
Muffins. More than one Goth couple has gotten engaged with
one of those."

Flashes went off. "Thanks, Caine. Engaged. Man, what a scoop!" Running footsteps.

"Should I chase him?" I was ready to take off.

"Forget it. There's the story." Ray turned to the first reporter, who was still standing silently under the whammy.

"No, wait. What are you thinking? Your fans will go nuts. You engaged to *me*?" For a moment I actually imagined the reality of me rock-star worthy. Yeah, right. The alien abduction would play better.

Ray hugged me. "What's wrong with you? Maybe some of these wacko fans will actually back off if they see I'm off the market."

"Or lose it completely. We might have to put Valdez in body armor. Forget it, Ray. Bad idea. No one's going to believe you'd hook up with me permanently." I could see the blogs now. Caine loses mind. Joins fat-thigh cult.

"Glory, you'd honor me if you'd pretend to be engaged to me. I know you don't dig the marriage thing. Being immortal and all. But it would give this guy a real scoop." Ray put his hands on my shoulders. "Besides, Flo said you and Simon Destiny have a really bad history. He wants my business and wouldn't dare take out a guy with my kind of notoriety. Hell, my publicist would blow his cover wide open."

"Yeah, I could see Barry making the EVs the cover story in every fanzine in the country if something happened to you out there."

"There you go. So what if you went out to that EV place as my fiancée? That would be pretty good protection for you, don't you think?"

Ray had a point. I'd been worrying about seeing Simon again in his natural habitat. And convincing him that Ray and I were really together after I'd obviously been with Jerry ever since I'd arrived in Austin. An "engagement" would certainly do the trick.

"This is a pretty serious decision, Ray. You got other women out there who are going to get their feelings hurt when they read about this in the tabloids?"

"Naw. I've been playing the field. Especially lately. On the road way too much. And I'm not much into marriage myself. Never even been engaged. Not after that time I almost proposed in New York. You know the one I mean."

"The unlucky time with Lucky. Sure." Lucky was the woman who'd turned Ray vampire. Good thing he hadn't *married* her. Obviously Ray'd been reading my mind again. I should block my thoughts around him. Shouldn't have taught him to read them in the first place. "Are you serious? You'll do this?"

"I think it will make you safer and this guy will be forever grateful. Watch and learn.

"Hey, photo guy. I just got here with my lady. Wake up and get the latest on Israel Caine." Ray snapped his fingers and the reporter suddenly came alive.

"Caine! Give me a quote! Where have you been tonight?" The man began taking pictures.

"You're one lucky bastard 'cause Glory and I just went ring shopping. You're going to get details and pictures no one else will." Ray got down on one knee and looked up at me. "Gloriana St. Clair, will you do me the honor of becoming my wife? I love you more than I've ever loved any woman. I want to write songs about you for the rest of my life."

I thought the reporter was going to pass out. I was going to be lying on the concrete right next to him. Ray's blue eyes glinted in the glow from the streetlight, and he sounded so sincere that I almost believed this was real. I found my eyes welling and my lips trembling.

"Answer him, lady." The reporter hopped around us, trying for new angles, different shots. "Yes or no, either way it's a hell of a story."

I hadn't been an actress back in the day for nothing. I smiled down at him. "I love you too, Ray. Of course I'll marry you." After he slid the plastic ring on my finger, I dragged him up and threw my arms around him. The big kiss that followed was probably the money shot. We were both just doing it for the camera of course. Uh-huh.

"Wow! This is big. Thanks!"

"Now I carry you over the threshold." Ray swung me up into his arms then carried me into my shop. Bri looked up, did a double take, then got busy distracting a customer who was checking out vintage hats.

"I think you're supposed to wait for the honeymoon for the threshold bit." I stared up at Ray when he shut the door in the reporter's face. "And I really wish you hadn't done that. They'll probably put that butt shot on the front page."

"It's a hell of a butt." He patted it as he headed to the back room and set me on the large oak table then turned to close the door to the rest of the shop.

"I hope we don't regret that. I didn't think it through. What's Jerry going to say? I need to call him. Explain."

"Can't say I care. What I do care about is that we didn't get to finish what we started down the street." Ray pushed up to the table. He stood between my legs, his eyes hot. "I want to drink from you. Watching you feed . . . You were on fire out there, Glory, filled with bloodlust. I want some of that."

"Ray, we were acting. I . . ." I couldn't look away from him as I fell back, Ray on top of me.

"Come here, vampies. I want to know how you're doing. RIGHT NOW."

"Nooooo." Ray and I looked at each other, then at the back door.

Eleven

First Ray climbed off of me, then he helped me to sit up. Forget resisting. Believe me, Ray tried. He was a man with a mission. And I wasn't exactly throwing up stop signs either. But Aggie's grating voice chanted inside our heads, urging us to get out of there. I grabbed the case of Twinkies I'd picked up for Aggie.

"What the hell is that?"

"Our mistress craves sweets. I don't know about you, but I don't want to see her in a bad mood."

"No shit." Ray grabbed the box. "My car's in the alley. No sense taking on the paparazzi out front again."

Outside, Ray hit the remote and we climbed into his black Escalade. We didn't say much. Too frustrated. So, driving just over the speed limit, Ray took the most direct route back to his house. We had about an hour before dawn. Which was the only good thing I could think of about this demand to go see the Siren. The meeting would have to be brief.

Ray parked in the circular drive and we both were almost running as we hit the elevator down to the boat dock. Stupid, but it was a compulsion. Aggie wasn't on the boat.

"Come on out to my little retreat on the lake. I have a surprise for you. Just follow your noses. Can't miss it."

"Does she realize we'll fry if we're out after dawn?"

"She'd better think about that next time. Circe probably wouldn't give her credit for our charred bits if that happened." I helped Ray throw off the ropes tying the boat to the dock. The roar of the engine probably didn't endear him to his sleeping neighbors. "But we still have time. What the hell does she think we have to report? The very thought of an Aggie surprise makes me want to throw up."

"Yeah." Ray stowed the Twinkies in the locker under the bench seat, then steered the boat away from the shore. "I'm feeling her guiding me. I guess I just follow my instincts. Hang on, Glory. I'm opening her up." He hit the throttle and we practically hydroplaned across the water. I grabbed for the railing and prayed. What fun if I bounced off the damned boat and disappeared into Lake Travis. Fish and other assorted creepy crawlies would nibble on me until Ray finally found me, if he ever did.

Sure, in an emergency I could shape-shift. But you have no idea how much I *hate* that. Being fish bait would almost be better.

"I'm making a sharp right. Don't let go."

"No worries there." I'd never loosen my death grip. Finally I saw a pile of rocks ahead and what looked like an island. Ray slowed down and coasted into an inlet surrounded by boulders. Aggie sat on a huge rock. She waved a claw.

"Just leave the boat there and swim ashore. I have something to show you. You bring my snacks?" Aggie was grinning. Bad sign. Aggie pleased scared the hell out of me. "Don't worry about the boat, it's not going anywhere. One of my powers."

"Good to know. Yeah, we've got Twinkies. That what you want?" Ray turned off the motor.

Aggie's cackle of glee was our answer.

"Put on a life vest, Glory. They're next to Aggie's treats under the bench seat. I'll pull you to shore and you'll have to hold the Twinkies up out of the water. I know you're not crazy about swimming."

"This will be fun. I'm not too good at swimming either." I grabbed the vest from the locker in the back of the boat. Not only do I hate swimming, I hated the whole idea of getting wet again. At least I'd changed out of my leather pants, but if I had to cut off another pair of jeans . . . I glanced at Aggie, juggling rocks like she didn't have a care in the world. Right now jeans were the least of my worries.

We climbed down the ladder at the back of the boat, Ray catching me when I jumped into the icy water. He towed me to the sandy area below Aggie's perch, then we stared up at her.

"Okay, we're here, your Siren-ness. What's the big surprise?" I shivered. Wind, cold water, wet hair dripping down the back of my neck. Still January. Still winter. Damn. Even a vampire isn't *totally* impervious to physical misery.

"Hand me those cakes. Yum." She ripped open the carton. "While I chow down go look. I made a nice little hidey-hole for when you bring me your vampires. In fact now you only have to bring me Casanova and one more." Aggie grinned. Oh, those teeth.

"Why?" Ray and I ran over the rocks in the direction she pointed. This could not be good news. Sure enough, Will Kilpatrick stood in a cave with iron bars across the entrance.

"Glory! Ray! Thank God! Get me the hell out of here. That freak ambushed me when I went out for a smoke." Will's red hair was wild, his beard two days old. He'd obviously had no chance against Aggie. That freeze thing.

"Didn't I tell you not to go outside?" I looked at Ray. "But I also told Aggie not to touch our friends. Damn it."

"Now, vampies, I see William here as a little insurance policy. A bird in hand so to speak." Aggie waddled up behind us, a Twinkie in each hand and a smear of cream on her snout. Of course I'd smelled her coming. "Foolish boy. He tried to sweet talk me into letting him go. He can't sing worth a damn, Israel. Not like you, dear one."

"Aggie, you made a deal with us. We've still got more than two weeks. Let the man go. You don't need insurance. Look how quickly we got here when you called." Ray waited until she'd polished off another cake then took her claw in his hand. I had to admire his guts. I wouldn't voluntarily touch that sea urchin on a dare.

"You had no choice. But I needed to report some progress to Circe. She was very happy to know I already had one birdie. With two more on a string." Aggie stroked Ray's face with the back of her other claw. "I wish it wasn't so near dawn. I could use a love song right now."

"And I could use some fair play." I stomped my foot, my tennis shoe squishing. "Release Will this instant."

"Issuing orders, Glory? How'd you like to join him in lockup?" Aggie's snout quivered and smoke puffed from her ears. "I could let Israel handle the procurement for me."

"No, Aggie, this is Glory's turf. I don't know squat about Austin vampires. And this Casanova deal's really screwed things up. I'm new at this game. Glory's the one that's got the best shot at getting him for you." Ray hummed a bit from one of his hits. "You've been listening to Sienna and me practice, haven't you?"

"Of course. Oh, goddess, but that's a beautiful song." Aggie swayed when Ray hummed some more. "One of my favorites."

"We've got to get this deal with you wrapped up before the Grammys or my career's in the toilet. You know that, don't you?"

"So wrap it up." Aggie gave me a dirty look. "What's the hold up, Glory?"

"I'm working on it. But if I have to worry about my friends . . ."

"A little worry is incentive, chickie. Hop to it. Ray, get your adorable butt out of here before the sun hits you. Don't give William another thought. Except for a few rug burns on his backside because I miss my Charlie and I need *someone* to help me get my, um, exercise, he'll be fine."

"Oh, my God!" Will's cries tore at my heart.

"Don't hurt him, Aggie." I tried to tune out Will's whimpers. "He's a fabulous cook. You want something better than Twinkies to eat, don't you?"

"Are you kidding me?" Aggie wrinkled her snout. "I don't believe you."

"It's true!" Will was about to crawl through the bars. "I've studied with master chefs from all over the world." He glanced at me. "I'm a better at cooking than anything I do horizontally. Ask my old girlfriends."

Ray and I looked at each other. Who knew? And if Will got out of this, I'm sure he'd deny he ever said it. Hey, I knew a desperate man when I saw one.

Aggie licked cream off her claw. "Well now, seems I caught myself a real prize. There's a vacant house on the other side of the lake. I could . . ." She looked at Ray. "Didn't I tell you to leave? If you vanish in a puff of smoke, I'll never forgive you. Run along. Go! Both of you!"

I stared at Will and sent him a mental message. *"Why don't you shape-shift and crawl or slither out of there?"*

"Give it up, Glory. William has no powers when he's under my control." Aggie gave me a stern look. "He can't shift. He can't even hear your little messages. Now move out before my darling Israel becomes a crispy critter." She flapped her flippers.

"We're going, Aggie!" Ray grabbed my hand and jerked me away from the cave entrance.

"I hate to leave him like that," I said after we'd climbed back into the boat.

"No choice, babe. Will's a desperate man. I think he'll talk his way out of exercising Aggie, but it's up to us to bring in a substitute for him." Ray started the boat, then pulled a blanket from his storage locker and threw it over my shoulders.

"I know." I shuddered and clutched the blanket. "Damned Siren. It's a good thing vamps don't dream, because what we just saw tonight would be giving me nightmares for sure."

"Me too." Ray looked at me and grimaced. "Kind of funny, though. Exercising Aggie? Sex with a sea monster like that would burn more than a few calories."

I punched his arm. "Funny until it's you on the bottom of that pile."

When we pulled up at the dock, Brittany was waiting for us and grabbed the rope Ray tossed to her. They both tied the boat to the dock, then Ray helped me climb onto dry land.

"Wet again?" Brittany wasn't smiling. "Have you seen Will? Last night he was supposed to be off. But tonight he was a no-show. I'm starting to get worried."

Ray glanced at me. "Sorry, Brittany. Should have told you. He's helping out in town. Glory and I had a problem in the park earlier tonight. I called him to stay near the apartment in case that fan came back. The woman was a real psycho."

"Oh, wow. Leaves us shorthanded out here, though." Brittany shook her head. "You'd both better get out of those wet clothes. That Siren still giving you hell?"

"Of course. We're heading upstairs to change right now." I glanced at the sky. "Guess I'm staying here tonight, Ray. No way we can make it back to my place."

"Fine with me. We've still got some unfinished business, anyway." Ray slung an arm around me. "Brittany, why don't you do a last swing around the grounds? And don't worry about staff. You've got plenty of mortal guards. You should be okay."

"I was afraid Will . . ." Brittany looked out over the water. "That Siren's not interested in shifters?"

"Will's fine. And you'll be fine too. The Siren's only after vampires this trip." Ray really was an excellent liar. A handy talent unless you needed to trust him. I shoved that thought aside.

"That's a relief. See you tomorrow night then." Brittany headed off into the night.

Ray and I stepped into the elevator and headed up. Once we were in the kitchen, I glanced at the refrigerator. "You want a last bottle of synthetic? You never did feed."

"No way." Ray grabbed my hand and pulled me toward the stairs. "You were about to let me drink from you when Aggie called. Come on, lady, we're going to finish what we started."

"You'd better take what you can get, Romeo. It's almost dawn, Ray. I'm sure you can feel it. I know I can. I'm really dragging." We headed up to his bedroom. "We don't have to share a bed."

"Sure we do. You think the housekeeper who cleans the rest of the house while we sleep doesn't report to those paparazzi outside? I'm betting she supplements her income with whatever she can find out."

"Fire her then."

"Now, Glory, you know it doesn't matter where we sleep. It's the next few minutes you're trying to avoid." Ray threw open his bedroom door. "I'm feeling weak. You got yours tonight, now it's my turn."

"I'm changing out of these wet clothes. I suggest you do the same." I charged into the closet I was coming to know way too well. I stripped off and hung up my jeans, sweater and underwear. Hopefully they'd dry without shrinking by the time I woke up tonight. I slipped into a black T-shirt and then realized the boxers were in a drawer in the bedroom. Oh, well. If Ray thought he was going to get more than a quick drink at the Glory fountain, he was doomed to disappointment. I opened the closet door.

Ray was lying in the middle of the king-size bed. He had on a pair of red silk boxers. Poser. And, damn, did he look good.

"Come here, Glory." He grinned and patted the bed beside him.

"Fine." I flopped down next to him and held out my wrist. "Take what you need. Just get it over with."

"Are you kidding me?" Ray sat up. "What is this? The vampire version of 'Not tonight dear, I've got a headache'?"

"Now that you mention it . . ." I hid my smile. "I'm not refusing you, Ray. This is more like offering you a five minute—" Ray put his hand over my mouth.

"Don't say it." Ray pulled my wrist to his lips then swept his tongue across my vein. "At least you didn't send me to the bathroom with porn. That's what one girlfriend did."

"Oh, that's what happened in the kitchen. I guess you missed it. I forgot to mention I'd flash my fangs while you drank your synthetic if it made you feel better about it."

Ray nipped the inside of my elbow. "Do I feel a chill? Or is that the usual vampire body temp?" He kissed his way down to my wrist again. "I'll take your pity offer and enjoy it. Because your taste does more for me than my Jack ever did. If I try to take too much, yank on my hair." Ray settled on top of me, a lover about to make me his, only it was my wrist he was putting to his mouth.

I felt the slide of his fangs as he took me and the pressure of his hips against mine. Oh, God, but this shouldn't be such a rush, yet it was a sweet, sweet feeling as I gave and he accepted. Ray was so much more than the plastic rock star I'd worshipped from afar every time I heard him sing. The man behind the hype was funny and really good at making *me* feel good.

I tugged on his hair. "That's enough, big guy. I'd say we've got just enough time to get under the covers before the sun comes up."

Ray shuddered and licked the wounds closed, then laid his head on my breast. "That was damned good, Glory girl. I think I *would* marry you. We could do this every night." He looked up, then propped himself up on his elbows. "Well, not this. A hell of a lot more than this." He rolled us over and slid his hands under my T-shirt. "Umm. You're going commando. Now that's my kind of woman."

" 'Night, Ray." I could feel the sun coming up in every cell of my body. Somewhere I found the strength to crawl off of him.

" 'Night, Glo—"

• • •

I woke up to pounding. Ray staggered to the bedroom door and it didn't take vampire hearing to get the message that Sienna was ready to rehearse.

Ray headed to the bathroom, where I could hear him brushing his teeth. When he came out, he was wearing a towel, his hair wet, and I realized I must have dozed off.

"I've got to get downstairs." He sat on the edge of the bed and pushed my hair out of my eyes. "Come down when you're ready and we'll make an excuse to get out of here."

"More rehearsals?" I dragged the sheet up to my chin.

"Sienna's freaking out about the Grammys. I get it. She's young. This is her first time." Ray took my hand and pulled it to his lips.

"Oh, no wonder she's so obsessive about rehearsing."

"She was that way before we cut the track for the album too. But this is even worse. I'm trying to be patient, but if she doesn't back off soon . . ." Ray nibbled my fingers.

I smiled and sat up. "Now, Ray, cut the girl some slack. Go rehearse, but you know we've got to be out of here in a few hours. Sienna's just going to have to deal with it. You've gotten pretty good with the whammy. If you have to, use it."

"I hate to. Especially with someone I know." Ray stood and dropped his towel. "Frankly, though, this Grammy thing is pretty far down on my priority list right now. With Will in Aggie's hands . . ."

"I know. I can't forget how he looked behind those bars." I was proud that I managed to choke out that sentence with Ray walking around naked in front of me. He turned to dig out a pair of boxers from the drawer and I sighed. Oh, wow. The way the muscles flexed in his perfect butt made me want to slide my hands down his back then around his front and . . .

He glanced over his shoulder and winked. "See something you want, Glory?"

"Get over yourself, Ray." I pretended to study a chip in my nail polish.

"Better block your thoughts next time then." He laughed and stepped into his shorts.

I chose to ignore that. "Anyway, what I *really* want is to come out of the Aggie thing alive."

Ray grinned. "That too. But doesn't mean we have to quit living now. Just so you know, I'm perfectly willing to keep Sienna waiting if you want to take advantage of me."

He ducked into the closet when I threw a pillow at him. With him out of sight I could think and breathe again. I had to admit, though, that his playing did lighten my mood, which tended toward gloom and doom.

Ray came out wearing jeans, a navy sweater in his hand. He shoved his feet into black Cavalli loafers, then pulled the sweater on over his head.

"The clock is ticking even faster now. I sure as hell don't want to wait until the full moon to get Will out of there." Ray tucked his wallet into his back pocket, picked up a comb, then walked back to the bed. "Would you do this for me? I still haven't gotten used to the no reflection thing."

"Sure. Sit." I waited while he settled on the edge of the bed again, then dragged the comb through his wet black hair. It was silky and straight and hitting past his shoulders now. He usually tied it at his neck or tucked it behind his ears. I combed it straight back, the way I liked it best. So I could see every bit of his handsome face and those blue, blue eyes. He'd shaved and I indulged myself, brushing a droplet of water off his strong jaw.

"Now you're ready. I'll be down in about an hour. Is that enough rehearsal time?"

"It'll have to be. Come here." Ray put his arms around me. "I've been thinking. Aggie says she can pull us to her no matter what, but I could charter a jet. We could make a break for the West Coast. Surely—" We both grabbed our heads at the same time.

"Forget it, Israel. Suck it up and take care of my business. Now behave. Will's fixing me crepes. I do not want to be disturbed again."

Ray and I sagged against each other.

"So much for that idea." I sighed when the pain disappeared. "Go practice. I'll be down in a while. Then we can at least see what Flo and Richard have come up with."

TWO hours later, we were still trying to escape from the house.

"Sienna, it sounds great. Doesn't it, Nathan?" I looked at Ray's friend who was just as anxious as I was to get this rehearsal over with. Nate was supposed to be taking Sienna out for a late dinner.

"The arrangement is brilliant. I swear the final notes still give me goose bumps and I've heard it—What, Glory?— seven, eight times tonight?"

"Ten, but who's counting?" I walked up to Ray, who was sitting at the piano, and put my hands on his shoulders. *"Get us the hell out of here. Please?"* Our silent communication was really handy in situations like this.

"Ray, I think the harmony on the second line of the chorus is wrong. Play it again." Sienna frowned at the sheet music in her hand. "No, move over. Let me play it."

Ray stood and slammed the lid shut on the grand piano. "No! I'm tapped out. It's perfect, Sienna. Has been perfect since Monday. Will you leave it the hell alone?"

"Excuse me?" Sienna didn't seem put off by what was the first temper tantrum I'd seen Ray throw. "I'll say when it's perfect. You just don't take this seriously, Ray." She tossed the sheet music into the air and turned on her heel. "Nathan, get me out of here. The big rock star is satisfied. Why am I bothering? I'll have my manager call the Grammy committee. I feel laryngitis coming on."

"Now, Sienna. Don't be foolish." Nathan shot Ray a look that said, "Apologize." Ray shook his head.

"You guys obviously need a little break. Why not just knock off for tonight and pick it up again early tomorrow night?" I ran to catch Ray as he headed for the front door. "Wait, baby, let's discuss this."

"Nights. What's that about?" Sienna was right behind

Ray and almost shoved me out of her way. "You can't be bothered to wake up before the sun sets? I'm sick of your screwy
schedule, Israel Caine. I may be younger and newer to the
game, but I've got a string of hits, mister. My last single sat
on the top of the charts a hell of lot longer than yours did."

Oh, crap. Ray's back was rigid, and I could read his
thoughts, a string of expletives that raised my eyebrows.
Sienna was lucky he was determined to keep his vampire self
under control, because he was really thinking about trying
the rip-someone's-throat-out method of venting fury. He
turned slowly and the three of us—Sienna, Nathan and I—
jumped back when we saw his face.

"Thank you so much for reminding me that I'm a washed-
up has-been. Are you sure you want to share a stage with a
loser like me? Oh, yeah, it was *your* agent who approached
mine with the idea of this duet in the first place, wasn't it?"
Ray's fists slowly unclenched.

"Ray, I, that was uncalled for. I know—"

"Shut up, Sienna. I'm not through." I saw Ray's mouth
working. I knew what he was doing. Trying to control his
fangs. Yep, Sienna smelled delicious. Fresh, young and a
nice A negative.

We all waited, afraid to speak.

"I *haven't* been taking this seriously. I have some other
things on my mind." He reached out and I took his hand.
"Glory understands. She's helping me through this . . . I
guess you'd call it withdrawal. Whatever. It's got me on my
last nerve."

I gave Sienna a "back off" look. "You're doing great, Ray.
Don't be so hard on yourself."

"No, I owe Sienna an apology. Give me a week, and I
promise I'll have my shit together and we can start again.
There's still time." He looked at Sienna. "What do you think,
Sienna?"

"I think I'm an idiot. I know you've just quit drinking.
What a bad trip. Of course you're strung out. And you're doing it without rehab." Sienna shook her head. "A whole week.

I, uh—that's tough, Ray. What if I just leave Austin until Monday? Ian's on location in Wyoming, shooting a picture. I'll surprise him with a visit, and maybe when I come back, you'll be ready to work again. Okay?"

"Call me then. If I can't pull it together, maybe we can get the Grammy people to schedule you for a solo instead of the duet." Ray grimaced when Nathan made a noise of protest. "Hey, she's just starting out, Nate. I've made my name. Besides, I'm pretty sure it won't come to that." He lifted my hand to his lips. "Right, Glory?"

"Right." Oh, God, I hoped I was telling the truth. I wrapped my arm around Ray's waist. This was costing him so much. The Grammy thing was huge for him. I'd heard Nathan talking to Barry about it. Ray's career needed the boost. But Aggie was about to ruin all that. Of course a career meant nothing if we were residing in the bowels of hell with Circe.

"Come on, let's get out of here. Sorry, Sienna. Glory and I like to go for a ride in the hills. Seems to clear my head. Maybe we'll go to her place. Doesn't matter. You and Nate have a nice dinner. Sorry for the meltdown." Ray pulled me out the front door before we had to listen to any more from either Sienna or Nate.

I let Ray help me into the Escalade. My jeans and sweater hadn't quite dried and I was anxious to get home to change. Would Flo and Richard be waiting for us? Or would they have snapped to the fact that Aggie didn't have *them* on a leash and they could gather up brother Casanova and head for parts unknown, leaving Ray and me to our fates?

"Wow. I never saw you go ballistic like that before, Ray."

"It happens." Ray patted my bottom. "You know, you might consider leaving some clothes here. Especially now that we're 'engaged.' I'm not objecting, but those jeans are definitely tighter than they were last night and they're still damp. Can't be comfortable."

"No kidding. But don't change the subject. Why'd you go off on Sienna like that?"

Ray got in and started the car. "I'd reached my limit. Sienna goes over the same thing a zillion times. Changes something, then changes it back. When all I can think about is you, me and Will in that cage. Will and I taking turns being Aggie's boy toy before she hands us over to Circe." Ray drove through the iron gates and cameras flashed.

They wouldn't get much, not with the dark tinted windows on the SUV, but I could hear shouted questions about a wedding date. Hmm, news travels fast. I should call Jerry before he read it somewhere. But I bet he had better things to do in Transylvania than hunt up an American tabloid.

I'd had no idea how really freaked-out Ray was by this whole Aggie business. I guess I'd dodged so many bullets myself through the centuries that I'd actually turned into an optimist. This time, though, I needed a searchlight to find the bright side of this situation.

"You okay today, Ray? You didn't get to feed much last night." I glanced at him as he drove fast through the hills toward my apartment.

"You think I don't know that? I had to fight the urge to take a bite out of Sienna, though for some reason Nate smelled really good to me." Ray grinned. "That would be totally weird, though."

"He's a rare blood type. Only natural you'd crave a taste of it. I told you, his type is my personal favorite." I'd lusted after it myself. But as an older vampire, I actually could go a few days between feedings when I'd had the real deal like I'd had on Sixth Street. I needed to drink the synthetic way more frequently. So maybe that wasn't a particularly "green" way to go after all. Think of all those bottles I had to recycle. Okay, now I was rationalizing.

"Glory, did you hear me? I said I'm feeling really, um, thirsty. Either you've got to feed me for real this time instead of a puny little wrist snack, or we've got to hunt a mortal for me to drink from."

"Right. And it's got to be a hot girl."

"Well, sure. Why not?" Ray pulled into the alley behind

my shop. He turned off the engine and we climbed out of the car.

"You are such a guy." I stood next to Ray, automatically looking around to make sure we were alone. "What if no hot girls are available?"

"Okay, if I were starving, no choice, I'd take what I could get. But I say we should do this right for my first time with a stranger. Like a man would do for a virgin, you know?" He reached out and put his hand behind my neck, pulling me to him.

"Make it good for me, baby." His whisper sent chills up my spine and heat right down to, well, you know.

"Fine. Let's go." I looked up when I heard barking from the roof above us. "Oops. Seems I forgot someone last night."

"What the—" Ray jumped back as Valdez took a flying leap off the top of the four-story building and landed next to us.

"Damn that was fun."

"I hope so because you just scared Ray half to death." I checked Valdez out. I knew he was okay. He had some really awesome powers that he rarely had to use. I figured the jump had been easy for him.

"Can I do stuff like that?" Ray looked up at the roof. The building is old, with one floor of shops and three stories of apartments above them. It had been quite a distance.

"Sure. I'm not crazy about it, but I can jump. I've even levitated a few times. Not that high, but I guess we could try it. Coming down's easy. You just leap and you'll land softly if you don't rush it. Won't hurt a bit." I grinned. I figured we could both use some fun. "What do you say, Valdez, can you go up as well as down?"

"Oh, aren't you in a great mood. Here I was so worried I chewed my toenails off and you're laughing and planning to freakin' levitate?" Valdez chuffed. *"Oh, what the hey? I've been bored to death and obviously you're okay. Go for it, Glory. See how far you can get."*

"After Ray feeds. Right now he'd be lucky if he got a foot off the ground. Valdez, you're on guard duty. You know what to do." I looked down the alley and saw a pair of Goths come out of the back door of the tattoo parlor next to my shop. The girl was pretty if you could get past the hardware decorating her eyebrows and nose.

"Ray? Check her out. Can you handle the piercings and tattoos?"

"No problem. Let's go." Ray pulled me along. "You take the guy. I assume you want to feed again." He walked up to the couple. "Either of you got a light?"

They turned, the boy digging for a lighter. I had him frozen in an instant. I heard Ray talking to the girl, taking longer, but getting the job done.

"Glory, what's this blood type? I like the smell of it."

I leaned over and sniffed. "Ordinary O positive. But that's good. Universal donor. Happens to be my blood type."

"Ah. That explains my craving for it." Ray grinned.

"Move her out of the light to a dark place. Over there between the car and the Dumpster. Valdez will bark if anyone comes down the alley."

"Man, this is exciting. My fangs are down without even trying. How cool is that?" Ray led the girl by the hand. "She's a little thing. I won't hurt her, will I?"

"Just don't take too much. Count to thirty slowly while you're feeding. You know, one thousand one, one thousand two, like that. Then stop, no matter how great it tastes." Might as well fill up while I had the chance. I was about to put my arms around my guy when I caught a whiff of something in the air.

Twelve

"**Okay**, I'm ready."

"Wait, Ray. Smell her again. Anything familiar there?" I knew he was acquainted with it. It had been on his deck New Year's Eve and you couldn't convince me he hadn't enjoyed his own share in the past.

"Shit. She's been smoking weed. What'll that do to me?"

"Might make you a little high. Depending on how much she's had. Can you deal with that?"

"Will it hurt my voice? Like the Jack did?" Ray's eyes were glowing and I could tell he really didn't want to stop and think about things at this point.

"I've run across it a few times and it never gave me a hangover like the booze did. You have to decide."

"With Aggie threatening to take us out anyway? I say I might as well go for it."

Couldn't blame him. He'd really missed the buzz from alcohol. I decided to take care of myself. In a few seconds, I realized I should have paid more attention to my own donor. Whoa. My guy had enjoyed a *lot* of weed tonight.

"Uh, Ray. Don't forget . . . wipe her memory. She saw your pretty face." I noticed something interesting a few feet away so I threw my guy at Ray. "Here, take care of mine too." I headed down the alley.

"Glory, what the hell's the matter with you?" Ray grabbed my arm.

"Huh?" I reached into the Dumpster. "Wow! Why would anyone throw this away?" I picked up a half-eaten Snickers and was about to pop it into my mouth when Valdez leaped up and snatched it. He gobbled it down in one bite.

"Hey, you almost bit off my hand. Bad dog." I wagged my finger in his face and stumbled.

"You're stoned."

"Am not. You see my guy's tat?" I giggled. "Ray, you should get one." I grabbed him around the waist and held on. "With my name on it. Tabloids'd love it. They'd have to catch it quick, though. Vamp sleep would wipe it out." I pulled open his shirt, popping a button. "Put it right there." I patted his chest. Mmm. Nice chest. I smiled up at him. "Probably hurt. Would you suffer for me?" Funny. I laughed until I hiccupped.

"Don't think Caine would go for it. Even temporarily. Unless you got him high like that loser who, by the way, is still over there where you guys left him and the chick." Valdez wasn't laughing. *"Someone else could come out of that tattoo parlor any minute."*

"Yeah, yeah, but about that tat . . . He's right, but what did it say?" Ray held me up when my knees went limp. "Wow, you really are smashed. Your guy must have smoked a buttload of pot."

"Umm-hmm. It was dee-licious." I pushed Ray away and headed for the Dumpster again. Was that a Cheetos bag? "Naked guy in chains. Said 'Stacy's Sex Slave.' Cute, huh?"

"I'd be happy to be your sex slave, babe, but no need to put it in writing. Now I'd better get those mortals out of here. Valdez, you keep an eye on our girl." Ray pulled on me again but I shrugged him off. "Glory, stay away from that Dumpster."

I heard Ray, but forget him. He was a new vampire. Probably eaten Cheetos a million times. Not like me, who'd only had them once and then suffered agony afterward. I finally got the bag just as Valdez's teeth clamped down on my pant leg. Empty. The bag, not the pants.

"Let go, Valdez, I'm coming out."

"You'd better be." Ray lifted me out and into his arms.

I grinned up at him. "Hey, cutie." I gave him a loud kiss. "Nothing but trash. Buy me Cheetos, fella, and I'll give you anything you want." I nibbled on his lips.

"Forget it, Blondie." Valdez bumped my butt with his head. *"Put her down, Caine."*

"Mind your own beeswax, dog. I like it here." I bit Ray's ear. "Ray and I need some alone time."

"Now she says it." Ray set me gently on my feet. "Let me deal with these mortals first. Then if you want to stay down here and make out, we can send the pooch up to the roof first."

"Sounds like a plan." I swayed for a moment and grabbed a handful of fur. "Oh, sorry, pup."

"You're not sending me anywhere." Valdez led me to a wall.

I leaned against it until I slid to the ground and closed my eyes.

Some time later Ray squatted down beside me. "You okay, Glory?"

"Sure. Help me up. I haven't forgotten, Ray. Time to lev—uh, lev—float."

Ray helped me stand and I looked up at the roof. The earth swirled around me for a second, then steadied. "Let's go."

"Fine. Maybe the cold air up there will clear your head." Ray smiled and held me when I wobbled.

Valdez sat beside me. *"Glory, I don't think you can do it, not with the buzz you've got going."*

"Buzz? Me?" I reached down for an apple core but Valdez beat me to it. "Ouch. That time you bit my finger."

"Would you quit trying to eat?" He chewed, then swallowed. *"Gack. Snap out of it, Glory. I'll bite you again if I have to."*

I stuck my finger in my mouth. He'd barely grazed me. "Okay, forget eating." I sighed. "Ray, I'll tell you how to float." I leaned back against the building. "Look at me, Ray. At my *eyes*."

"Can't help it, Glory. Your sweater shrunk last night. I like you like this. Relaxed. Not so guarded."

"Watch it, Caine." Valdez showed his teeth. *"A gentleman doesn't take advantage—"*

"Give me a break. Oh, right. I forgot you and the rest of Glory's friends come from prehistoric times or something like that." Ray threw his arms around me. "The best thing about Glory coming from back then is that she's the real deal. So many women these days are made with manufactured parts. Plastic." Ray squeezed me until I pushed him back.

"Yeah, I'm real, handsome. And I'm here. Quit talking to my dog and talk to *me*." I smiled at him. "So you like what you see and, um, feel?"

"Damn it, Glory." Valdez growled. *"Back off, bozo. She doesn't know what she's saying."*

"Relax, fur face. I know she's buzzed. Look at her eyes. Unfocused. And her silly smile." Ray kissed the corners of my mouth. "Sweet. I tell you, Valdez, worst invention of this century? Botox, my man. Women are ruining themselves with that stuff. Hell, you can't tell what they're feeling. Blank faces. Like nobody's home."

I snuggled against him. "I'm *always* home, Ray. Want a demo?" I slid my hand inside his shirt. I really liked his chest. Too bad he wouldn't get that tattoo.

"Glory, if you think I'm going to stand here and watch you—" Valdez snorted when I smiled and nodded.

"You'd better. Or I'll make sure Blade fires your furry butt."

"That's it. Glory, you're wasted." Ray quit smiling. "We'd better get you upstairs. Valdez, can you tell me what to do or should we take the stairs?"

"In a minute." I gave Ray a full-throttle kiss that made Valdez growl. I pulled back and grinned. "Aw, calm down, Valdez. Ray appreciates me. That was a thank you."

"You bet I do." Ray kept his hands firmly planted on my

butt. "You seen the lips on some of the actresses I dated? In-
flated like they've been hooked up to a bicycle pump too
long. Hell, I was scared to really kiss those lips. What if
they pop?"

"So kiss me again, Ray. I really like the way you kiss."
Valdez's growl was getting louder, but I ignored it.

"Nope. I figure your bodyguard's patience is stretched
pretty thin." Ray put some space between us. "Sorry, Valdez.
Seems you've really got it rough stuck there in a dog body.
Wouldn't blame you if you hated Blade. It's not right. A de-
cent boss would let you shift to whatever the hell you wanted.
Blade must not trust you around Glory as a real man."

"Hush, Ray." Maybe I was finally coming down to earth,
but I could see how this was hurting Valdez's pride.

"You don't know what the hell you're talking about." Valdez
stalked toward Ray and I jumped between the two.

"Valdez, cool it. Ray, get off Valdez's case. He's my friend.
Now I'm aggr— aggra— pissed." I sent Ray a mental message.

His eyes widened. "Glory! A lady shouldn't think words
like that."

An arrow whizzed past me and hit Ray in the arm.
"Damn!" Ray grabbed it, then threw himself against me. "Get
down!"

My vampire reflexes, even impaired, were good enough to
help us dodge more arrows as they hit the wall all around us.

"Not down. Go up." Valdez peered into the darkness when
there was a brief lull in the barrage. Maybe the enemy was
reloading or something. *"Go straight up, Glory."*

"Hang on to me, Ray." I was suddenly stone-cold sober.
Staring Death in the face will do that to you.

"Save yourself, Glory." Ray grunted when I wrapped my
arms around him and stared up at the roof just as more arrows flew past our heads and hit the wall behind us. Way
too close.

"I'm saving both of us. Come on, Valdez. No heroics now.
Forget going after them. You're coming too." I issued orders

as Ray locked his arms around my neck, the smell and feel of his blood dripping near my mouth a distraction I couldn't afford. I took a breath, held on tight to Ray and soared.

To my relief, Valdez came flying past us like he wore spring-loaded tennis shoes. Thank God it took only moments for Ray and me to reach the roof and land on the flat surface.

"Let go of me, Glory. You all right?" Ray pulled back and looked me over.

"Me? I'm not the one with an arrow through my arm. Sit down, Ray. No, lie down."

Ray looked at the blood dripping from his wound and sat suddenly. "Holy crap that hurts."

Valdez glanced at us to make sure I was okay, then trotted over to check out the alley below.

"Well? What do you see, Valdez?"

"Westwood's back and he brought along those two bozos who came after you at Caine's house. Guess their paycheck's bigger than their brains. He armed them with bows and arrows too but, lucky for us, they can't shoot worth a damn. Surprised Westwood missed, though. Guess the injury Blade gave him Halloween is still bothering him."

"Yeah, Westwood definitely wasn't shooting up to par or I'd be dead right now. Lie down, Ray." I hated to leave him, looking so pale, but there was something I had to do. "I'll be right back."

"Where do you think you're going?" Ray jumped back up again, clutching his arm and leaving a blood trail.

I ran to the ledge, ready to jump off and end this Westwood feud once and for all.

"No way in hell, Glory." Valdez grabbed the waistband at the back of my jeans with his teeth. *"You're outnumbered. Take care of Caine."*

"Screw that, Glory. You stay up here because down there is suicide." Ray grabbed my shoulder with his good hand. "Get back. He might try to take another shot."

"Damn it, Valdez, Ray. Westwood keeps hurting my friends." I swiped the tears off my cheeks. Don't you hate it when you cry because you're mad? "I want to rip out his throat. Valdez, you and I together could take that man apart. The two guys with him are clowns, we could handle them in our sleep. Sorry, Ray, but you're in no shape to be more than a liability."

"*I swear to God, you jump and you're going bare-assed, 'cause I'm not letting go of your jeans.*" Valdez growled and I heard cloth tear.

"And, liability or not, you jump and I jump with you." Ray was right beside me, his face white as paper.

"You two don't get it. Westwood shouldn't get away with this. I'm tired of being afraid to walk in my own freakin' alley behind my own fr-freakin' apartment." I swiped at another tear and backed up a foot. I knew better than to try to get physical with Valdez. He wouldn't hurt me, but he could and would keep me from doing something he thought was too dangerous. And Ray was just idiot enough to jump with an arrow in his arm and get himself staked in the process.

"*He won't get away with anything. We'll take care of him an-other night. In the meantime, while we've been having this debate, Westwood's not stupid. He's gone. He peeled out in his SUV as soon as he saw you look over the ledge with fire in your eyes.*" Valdez let go and stood beside Ray. "*Caine looks shocky to me. Since you like him so much you play kissy face with him, take care of him.*"

"Ray!" I put my arm around him and got him down. "Oh, God, I'm sorry."

"What did *you* do?" Ray stared at the arrow sticking out of his arm. "Who the hell uses a bow and arrows?"

"Brent Westwood. That's an olive-wood arrow. If it had hit you in the heart, you'd be dead. Just like being staked. Jerry knifed him in his arm on Halloween but he got away." I gave Valdez a dirty look. "Just like tonight. He's got a real hate on for me and vampires in general, of course."

"Of course." Ray lay back on the concrete. "You come off your high yet? That was some pretty impressive floating just now."

"Guess watching you get shot was a real buzz kill." I teared up again. "Forget me. Let me take care of you."

Ray grimaced when I touched his wound. "Guess we were lucky Westwood didn't come after us before."

"He's been in Europe, trying to get his arm fixed. Jerry warned me he might be headed back to Texas. Guess he was right." I saw that the wound had quit bleeding. "Uh-oh. I've got to get that arrow out. Because you just fed, you're already healing. Unless you want to wear that thing as a permanent badge of courage, I'm going to have to rip it loose."

"Gee. Get graphic, why don't you?" Ray shuddered. "Fine. Do it fast." Ray looked at me, then at Valdez. "But send him downstairs. I think the dog's going to enjoy watching this way too much."

"He helped save your life, Ray. You guys should call a truce."

"When dogs fly." Ray managed a slight smile. "Oh, wait. They just did."

"Sure, I'd get off watching you torture him, but I think I'll head downstairs and let Richard and Flo know that Westwood is back in town. Got to say something first."

"What?" I looked up from examining Ray's wound and realized Valdez was just a foot away.

"This is my fault. The attack. Caine's injury. I'm just damned glad it was him hit and not you, Glory." Valdez laid his head on my shoulder.

"Now how can you blame yourself? You didn't put those guys in that alley."

"No, but I shoulda sensed them there. They got the drop on us. Instead of doing my job, I was shooting the breeze with you two. Acting like we were buds instead of me bein' your bodyguard. And, yes, you should tell Blade to fire my furry butt. It's what I have comin'."

"He's right, Glory." Ray struggled to sit up. "Why didn't you sense those three mortals before they hit us, Valdez?"

"No excuse." He backed up and stared down at the concrete.

"Yes, there is. Ray and I had just fed and reeked of mortal

blood. And the Dumpster reeked of everything else. Not to mention that, with weed in my system, I was pulling all your focus to me, acting out." I rubbed the top of Valdez's head. "I don't want to fire your furry anything. But I guess we all need to be more on guard from now on. This was a wake-up call. Right?"

"Yeah. But I'm planning to make full disclosure to Blade about this when he gets back." Valdez turned and headed for the door. He stopped at the doorway and looked back. "Caine, try not to squeal like a girl when she jerks out that arrow." Valdez trotted down the stairs, ignoring Ray's shaky gesture.

"He's a stand-up guy, even if he is an interfering pain in the ass." Ray lay back down and closed his eyes. "All right, Glory, just do it."

"I'm sorry, Ray." I took a steadying breath then broke the arrow in half, tossing the feathered end aside before pushing the pointed end on through the fleshy part of his arm.

"Holy crap, that stung!" Ray hit the concrete three times with his fist and said a few choice words.

"Now hang on while I heal the wound. So you can play the piano again when you get home." I shoved his shredded sweater sleeve up so I could see the angry red tear in his skin. I said a few choice words myself about Westwood.

"Oh, yeah, I'll really be in the mood to play. Something loud and—" Ray sucked in a breath when I pressed my hands on his wound, but his face relaxed as I concentrated on healing thoughts.

"How does that feel?" I studied his arm, relieved to see the ugly red scar was already fading. "You lost a lot of blood, so you may be a little weak."

Ray sat up and moved his arm around. "I can't believe this. I feel pretty good. Considering I was wearing a stick through it a few minutes ago, my arm's great." He took a breath of the cold night air and looked up. "The stars are beautiful up here. But, damn it, that sliver of moon is getting bigger. I sure as hell don't want to die just when I've found out I can live forever."

"Neither do I."

He looked into my eyes and reached out. "Come here, woman."

"What is it, Ray?"

"This." Ray pulled me into his arms and kissed me like we wouldn't have a tomorrow. I knew the feeling. Those flying arrows had been a pretty concrete reminder of how vulnerable vampires are to some things. So I gave in to all those urges that had been building for days and just rode the wave. When you're facing Death, well, you really don't want to leave a lot of "if only"s behind. Finally Ray pulled back and smiled.

"Whew, that was some kiss." I put my head on his chest and listened to his pounding heart. I knew my own was pumping double time. "If we get through this, we'll have to do some more of that."

"Oh, yes." Ray rubbed my back. "Wasn't long ago that my biggest worry was whether my album was going to go platinum or not. Now . . ."

"I'm not giving up, Ray, and neither should you. We'll beat this Aggie thing. I haven't survived all these years just to let a slimy seaweed-wearing *thing* take me down. And Westwood? His days are numbered. He's pissed off way too many vampires with his bow and arrow." I pulled back and grabbed Ray's hand. "Let's go. Flo and Richard are waiting."

"I don't know how you've survived all these years, Glory. And mostly on your own." Ray walked with me toward the stairs.

"Hey, 'I get by with a little help from my friends.'" I sang as we headed down the stairs.

"Glory, promise me something," Ray said as we stopped outside my door.

"What?" I had my hand on the doorknob.

"Let me do the singing from now on?" Ray grinned and we both heard Flo and Richard's shout of "Please!"

Valdez greeted us at the door. *"With Westwood back in town, Glory, you'd better not sneak off without me again."*

"Ray and I left here last night because Aggie called us

out to the lake." I looked at Flo and Richard in their usual spots on the couch. "She's got Will Kilpatrick, guys. If we don't come across with Casanova and those EVs, she's going to take Ray, Will and me to Circe."

"*Mio Dio!* Will is such a handsome one. Though he is not always so good, eh, Ricardo?" Flo shrugged. "I suppose . . ."

"No, I won't let him be sacrificed." I couldn't believe my former roomie could be so . . . detached about this. But then Flo is always practical. She'd think one down, only two to go for us to take to the lake. I'd expected her to be tearing her hair out about Damian. Instead, she was actually flipping through yet another bridal magazine. Had she had some sort of breakdown? Maybe temporary amnesia?

"*Will? That's bad news. But there's no way in hell that green thing's taking you anywhere. You've got to let Blade in on this.*" Valdez paced a circle around me.

"Why? So he can get on Aggie's to-do list? We're handling this without him. Flo, did you talk to Damian?"

Flo smiled. "No worries. My brother will be by later. Relax, Glory. He will help us with our little *problema*."

Little problem? Ray and I gawked at her, then at each other. Richard looked enigmatic as usual. Valdez was pouting by the door and didn't seem inclined to comment. Maybe he was waiting for his chance to burst into a chorus of "I told you so"s when this whole mess blew apart.

I could tell Valdez was going to argue with me when my phone rang. I glanced at the caller ID. Blocked caller.

"Hello."

"Gloriana, I understand your boyfriend is interested in our VIP services."

I'd know that voice anywhere. The phone number was blocked because apparently Simon Destiny called *you*, not the other way around.

"Yes, Simon, I've heard about your sunlight rooms and told Ray about them. He's really anxious to try them. He wants to come out there this weekend."

Flo gasped. Richard and Ray looked grim, but nodded.

Valdez was snarling and dancing around like he'd rip the phone out of my hands with his teeth if he could. He knew better but I'm sure I'd get an earful as soon as I got off the phone.

"We usually book those rooms well in advance."

"Are you saying it can't be arranged? Why don't I put Israel Caine on the phone and you can tell him that? Oh, and we need a suite with two bedrooms. We're bringing another couple."

"My, aren't you the pushy little thing. Please, put Mr. Caine on the phone."

I handed Ray the phone but punched the button for speakerphone first.

"This is Israel Caine. You're on speakerphone, Mr. Destiny. Are you going to be able to accommodate me and my party?"

"Good evening, Mr. Caine. Gloriana tells me you want to come this weekend. Our services are very much in demand."

"No problem. My friend Richard here has been telling me there's a resort in Sedona run by a vampire group that can offer me some unusual experiences. Maybe I'll charter a jet and take Glory and our party out there for the weekend."

"Not necessary, Mr. Caine. I've just been informed we've had a cancellation. I'll expect your party some time after sunset on Friday night. A limousine will pick you up in front of Ms. St. Clair's shop then."

"We'll want that sunlight room Friday *and* Saturday nights." Ray smiled at me. "I won't lie to you, Destiny. I miss the sun like a son of a bitch. That's the only reason I'm considering coming out to a place my fiancée frankly doesn't have fond memories of. You *will* make sure Gloriana and our friends are treated to first-class service, won't you?" Ray and Richard exchanged glances like there was some serious mental messaging going on.

"Naturally. Gloriana's previous experience was unfortunate. Did you say she is your fiancée?"

"I did." Ray grinned when Flo gasped and muttered something about Jeremiah. "I'm sure you'll see the news of our engagement in the tabloids if you read that trash. But Glory has honored me by agreeing to become my wife. I expect her to be treated with every courtesy by you and your staff."

"Of course. Please assure Ms. St. Clair that our past disagreement is totally forgotten on *my* part. You have my word that she and your friends will be treated as favored guests, just as you will be."

"I'd expect no less." Ray smiled at me.

"As for the sunlight. You'll love it. Guaranteed or your money back. The Energy Vampires have spent a considerable amount of time and expertise creating the sunlight experience. I'm sure you'll find it well worth the price. And, don't worry, we accept all major credit cards."

We stared at the phone when it became clear that Simon had ended the call.

Ray laughed. "Credit cards? Damn. Now I've heard everything."

"Unfortunately, no, you haven't." Richard looked grim.

"Glory, how can you break Jeremiah's heart this way?" Flo threw down her magazine. "You know he is the man for you."

Valdez was right beside her. *"She's right. Are you out of your freakin' mind?"*

"Relax, Flo, Valdez. Not that it's any of your business, V, but I'm not marrying anyone." I glanced at Ray. "I didn't want to go out to the EV headquarters without some serious protection. Ray and I figured an engagement would keep Simon from trying his tricks with me."

"Tricks?" Valdez practically leaped over the couch. *"Honey, attaching a vacuum tube to your belly button and sucking out your life force is way more than a 'trick.' Been there, done that. Saw the white light before you got there and saved me."*

"Holy shit." Ray sat down. "Maybe we should forget this."

"I know it was horrific for you, V. That's why you're staying here. Just Flo and Richard are going with us."

"I don't want to go out there, Ricardo." Flo looked down at her lap, her shoulders slumped.

"Nonsense. You will do as I say. Gloriana and Ray need us. And you heard Destiny. He gave his word we would be well treated."

"But they were so mean to me before. I don't trust Simon's word." Flo sniffed and looked up, her eyes swimming with tears. "Please, none of us should go. I remember that horrible machine. And their demon. A she-devil—"

"Enough! You'll speak when I give you permission, is that clear?" Richard's voice was firm and I gasped.

"Yes." Flo's shoulders shook and we could barely hear her whisper. "I'm sorry."

"What the—" Ray looked at me. "Don't force her to go, Richard. I didn't want to drag anyone else into this. Glory thought you'd want to help."

"Flo, honey, you're not going out there." I knelt by Flo's side and gave Richard a hard look. "What's the deal, Richard? Last night did the VV push your love button the wrong way? No one treats my roomie like that. Flo went through hell out there. She doesn't have to go back."

"Hah!" Flo jumped to her feet and pulled me up to hug me. "Glory, it's okay." She turned to Richard. "We fooled them, eh *amante*? I knew we could do it." She grinned. "I'm fine, Israel. Richard and I were playing with you. Simon would never accept that I would come out to his hellhole willingly after what he put me through before. So I become the submissive little woman."

"Florence is quite an actress, isn't she?" Richard hugged her and kissed her lips. "Anyone who knows her, *really* knows her, can't imagine my beloved really letting me get away with treating her like I just did."

"I'll say. I really bought your act, Flo. I was trying to read your mind, but all I got were unhappy thoughts. How'd you do that?" The truth. Flo hadn't blocked my mental probes, which she usually does.

"It's a trick Ricardo taught me. One you and Ray must learn before you go out to the EV place." Flo pulled Richard down beside her on the couch. "Sit, I show you."

"I was about to punch your lights out for being an abusive bastard, Mainwaring." Ray sat in a chair across from the couch.

"You could have tried. And not succeeded." Richard grinned.

Valdez stopped pacing around the room. *"Glad you are all so cool with this. But forget it. An EV visit is not going to happen. Are you crazy? You can't go out there like it's a freakin' vacation. I won't allow Glory within a mile of that cesspool of insanity. And Simon's word on anything is not worth shit."*

"Sorry, pal, I know you just want to protect me, but you're not my keeper. I go where I please. You're staying here, I'm going." That declaration of independence got Valdez's attention. He planted himself between Ray and me.

"Caine, you act like you care about Glory. Put your foot down. Don't let her go. Blade would never allow it if he were here."

"Blade orders her around?" Ray looked from Valdez to me. "No wonder she never married him."

"T-hat tears it. I've watched you grope her, kiss her and, God damn it, talk about drinking from her. Now you're putting down Blade?" Valdez snarled and lunged at Ray. I threw myself between them and took a hard hit on the forearm. I landed on the coffee table and reduced it to a pile of sticks.

"Glory!"

I lay in the ruins of my table waiting for the dizziness to pass while three vampires and a shape-shifter in canine form screamed at each other, placing blame and blows anywhere they could reach. I closed my eyes when I heard glass shatter and actually hoped it was one of my Israel Caine collectibles. I think it had been Ray's fist that had hit me in the arm. Accidentally, of course. He'd be horrified when he realized it. So would Valdez. Damn them both and their excess testosterone.

The action seemed to be dying down when I pulled a table leg and a crumpled copy of *Cosmo* out from under me. Well hell. I hadn't read the twenty tips for the ultimate orgasm yet and the page was ripped. Finally I lifted my sweater and watched blood ooze from a cut on my side.

"Hello? Would someone get me a towel? I don't want to bleed on the carpet. I might lose my security deposit."

"No, *mia amica*, my brother owns this worthless building. He wouldn't dare keep your deposit." Flo cradled my head in her lap. "These men. They are *stupido*. Fighting. It solves nothing. We are going out to the EV place and we are getting that bastard Simon Destiny for your Siren." Flo sniffed. "Look at you. You are hurt. And, *insano*, but your blood smells *squisito*. We are vampires. No?"

"Yes. And I'm sorry I upset you." All that Italian. Flo must really be worried about me. "I'll be fine. I just fed before I came up. I'm drinking from mortals now. Totally fallen off the synthetic wagon." I caught a drop of blood and sniffed. "Yeah, not bad. Where are the guys?"

"Israel tried to go to you, but my man says no, he must not touch. He and Valdez have done enough hurt to you. Ricardo took them to the roof to kick their butts into some sense." Flo sighed. "I don't say that right but you know what I mean. Let me help you up and into the bathroom. You can clean up. Change clothes. Why you wear such things? Damp, tight and ripped in the back."

"The damned Siren keeps making me jump into the lake. Blame Valdez for the rip." I let Flo help me undress and get into the shower. I was too battered to even care that she saw my thighs. My tiny former roomie doesn't have thighs, damn her. Anyway, a hot shower did me a lot of good. By the time I got out, the men were back in the living room, the remains of the coffee table had disappeared and things were, on the surface at least, back to normal.

"Sorry, Glory." Valdez trotted up to me, his head down. *"Report me to Blade. He'll probably fire my ass. Deserve it."*

"Forget it, V. Just don't attack Ray again. We're going to do what we have to now. Don't get in our way." I liked the way that sounded. Assertive. I turned to Ray. "Well? You apologizing too?"

"Of course. I'm really sorry you got in the middle of that. How are you feeling?" He gave me a careful hug.

"I'll be okay. But you and Valdez owe me a coffee table and a new copy of *Cosmo*."

"Done. I'll give you a credit card, and you can order whatever you want." He shot Valdez a stern look. "The dog and I don't agree on a lot of things. I guess it was bound to come to a head sometime."

"Just not in my living room next time, okay?" I walked over to a chair and sat down with a sigh. "Good thing the healing sleep will take care of this. Right now I'm a mass of aches and pains."

"Do you need to feed again, Glory?" Flo looked at Richard. "We can bring you someone."

"What? Vampires have delivery and takeout?" Ray sat in the other chair.

"Use your imagination, Caine." Richard had obviously had enough from a new vampire. "Florence, finish explaining to them how to protect thoughts. When you two get out to the EV compound, you're going to have to be especially careful. One slipup, and Destiny will know about your plan to lure him to Caine's house for the Siren."

"Yes, you're right. The few times I've been around him, Simon blasted right through any blocks when I tried to keep my thoughts from him." I shuddered, remembering. "Just like Aggie does. Hell, she can read my thoughts and Ray's from the lake. Right now if she's tuned in." A pain hit me and I winced. "Guess she's *always* tuned in."

"Maybe this won't work with your Siren, but will work with Simon." Flo leaned forward. "A while ago, when I was pretending to be dutiful, all you could see in my mind were my silly, sad thoughts. That's because I was forcing them to fill my head." She turned to Ray. "Israel, it would probably be easy for you to load your head with your music. Anytime you're around an Energy Vampire, not just Simon, you should concentrate on singing inside your head. So when they try to read your mind, they'll think 'Oh, he's a stupid singer with nothing in his empty head but his songs.'"

"Am I supposed to have something else in there?" Ray

grinned, obviously really liking the idea and glad to be off the topic of his fight with Valdez.

"I could think about my wardrobe. My shoes, my clothes, reorganizing my closet or my inventory. Simon would expect it of me. Because of the shop if nothing else." I rubbed my healing side. It still stung, but was already better.

"You've got it, *cara*. If you're careful that way, Simon won't sneak into your thoughts and figure out your plan. He'll think you just want the sunlight. And, Israel"—Flo flushed—"I know you'll love it. I remember your music videos when you sang on your island in the Caribbean or on your boat. You loved the sun."

"You guys are serious about this sunlight thing? We're really going to get to see the sun out there?" Ray looked excited by the idea.

"That's the rumor. Flo, did you see the rooms? Valdez?" I couldn't deny sunlight would do it for me too.

"When I was out there, I didn't see anything but a cage and a giant machine trying to suck the life out of me." Valdez collapsed by the door. *"But why ask me? I'm a bodyguard. I don't count. I just follow orders."*

Oh, great. He was sulking. I felt bad laying down the law like I did, but he simply couldn't go out there with us. And I wasn't staying away on his say-so. The only bright side to our stalemate was that Valdez had admitted he couldn't communicate with Blade while he was in Europe. It was too far away for their mental link to work.

"I saw one of the rooms." Flo grabbed Richard's hand. "It was like Tuscany where we summered when I was a child. Very golden and warm, ready for a picnic in a meadow. *Fantastico.* Too bad we couldn't have our wedding out there, Ricardo. Is very romantic." Flo sighed. "Anyway, there are several rooms for the sunlight. Simon bragged about them. One will be perfect for you, Israel. It's like a beach in the Caribbean."

Ray leaned forward, his eyes bright. "Tell me more. I'd kill to lay out on a beach again and just soak up the sun."

We all jumped when there was a knock on the door.

"Must be my brother. Let him in, Glory." Flo and Richard exchanged glances, but their thoughts were definitely blocked.

I still couldn't get over how calm she was about his whole Casanova sacrifice thing. I glanced through the peephole and saw Damian's handsome face. He wasn't smiling for a change. Okay, so at least he was taking this seriously. I threw the dead bolts and let him in.

"Hi, Damian."

"*Cara*, you look . . . What happened to your beautiful hair?"

I touched the frizzy mess I'd made the mistake of trying to blow dry. "This is what happens when you back talk a goddess."

"Poor Glory." He gathered me into his arms and kissed my cheek. "And you've been worried about me." One of his hands strayed down to my left hip. "Charming."

Suddenly I had Ray on one side and Valdez on the other.

"Let her go, Casanova." Ray practically jerked me out of Damian's arms.

"Careful, macho man. I've been wounded, thanks to you." I smiled at Damian. "Why the heck aren't you and"—I glanced at Flo—"your sister worried about you?"

"Because I am caught. Eh, *mia sorella*?"

"*Sì, mio fratello.*" Flo leaned against Richard. "I didn't want you to walk me down the aisle anyway. You are too pretty. Now . . ." She sniffled and Richard pressed a white handkerchief into her hand.

"No! Surely we can figure something out!" I felt a hot poker stab my brain. "Stop it, Aggie!" I grabbed my head. "Ow! Oh God! She's killing me!"

"What is it?" Damian reached for me, but backed off when Valdez growled and showed all his teeth.

"Aggie can hear our thoughts. Even from out by the lake. She's reminding Glory and"—Ray winced—"me that we'd better cooperate. Circe wants you. Are you saying you're willing to go to hell for us?"

"No. This goddess wants Casanova." Damian locked eyes

with Flo. "I have a shameful secret. I bring ruin on my family. Of course Florence doesn't want me at her wedding."

"Did I say that?" Flo jumped up and threw her arms around her brother. "So you tell a few lies, break a few hearts. It's what we do, eh? To survive." She hugged him and wiped her eyes. "You *must* be at my wedding. Because I have decided it will be on your terrace. With the lights of the city behind us. Romantic, no?"

"Perfect. Maybe Richard will let me be a groomsman. Or, what do you say I pay for everything? My wedding gift to you."

Flo broke into rapid Italian, suddenly all smiles as she grabbed a magazine from her ever-present shopping bag.

"Wait!" I threw myself between Damian and Flo when she started to show him "the dress." "What secret? What lies? Why is Damian so sure he'll be here for your wedding, Flo?"

"Simple, Glory. Damian isn't the real Casanova. It is, how you say, a game." Flo found the flag she wanted and told Richard to turn his back. Bad luck for the groom to see the wedding dress before the wedding.

Bad luck? Aggie gave me another shot to the left temple.

Flo laughed and hugged her brother when he agreed to fly to New York with her and take his Platinum Card with him. Ray and I reached for each other. We were doomed.

Thirteen

"Florence, darling, Glory needs for you to explain. Look at her face. Look at Ray's." Richard risked his beloved's ire by snatching her magazine.

Flo said one more word in Italian that made both Damian and Richard raise their eyebrows, then she turned and really checked me out.

"Glory! I'm sorry. The wedding. It's all I think about. You are thinking about hell of course."

"Of course." I sank down on the couch, Ray right beside me. "I can practically feel the flames. We needed Casanova."

"And you shall have him." Damian leaned against the door. From his dark hair cut expertly to look like he'd just run his fingers through it, to his leather loafers, Italian of course, on his narrow feet, he was the picture of elegant male. If he wasn't Casanova, he was a heck of an imitation.

"How?" I glanced at Ray. "We can't foist a fake on Circe. Aggie probably has to report stuff like that to the goddess."

"You got that right, vampy. No Casanova, no deal. Nice to hear you finally get it."

I shook my head. "She's talking to me right now. What can we do?"

"The real Casanova is here in Austin." Damian stepped away from the door. "Alberto and I have been rivals for centuries. It amuses me to take his name from time to time. Because it makes him crazy. When he heard I was doing it again here, he flew in to confront me. Women would pay to see that fight, eh, Florence." He laughed when Flo punched him in the arm.

"You are both too handsome for your own good, *fratello*. But Alberto is a pig." She kissed her brother on the cheek. "You never would treat a woman as he does. I should know; Berto and I were lovers once."

We all jumped when Richard snarled.

"Calm yourself, *amante*. It was long ago. My name was Analisa then. So you see it cannot concern you." Flo pushed Richard into a chair then plopped herself onto his lap. She stroked his cheek and whispered in his ear.

The rest of us exchanged glances, trying to understand Flo's logic, though my experience told me it was a waste of time.

"Bertie makes women fall in love with him, seduces them, then drops them most painfully. He likes to see women publicly humiliated." Flo leaned her head on Richard's shoulder. "I tell you this so you understand why I'm glad we send the *bastardo* to hell."

"What? Maybe you shouldn't tell us anything else, Flo." I know I had some bad breakups in my past I'd never trot out for public consumption.

"No, is time." Flo took a watery breath, her handkerchief wadded in her fist. "He made me think I was his only lover. Then he came to a party at my villa with another woman! He hoped I would cry, beg, you see, for him to send her away."

"He didn't know you very well, did he, my love?" Richard held her close. "Does he wear your initials carved on his ass?"

Flo giggled. "He would if he didn't heal in his sleep."

"He's still in town?" Ray was obviously all about the, pardon the expression, bottom line. Truth be told, so was I right now. "You think we can get him out to the lake?"

"*Sì*, if you dangle the right bait. I tell him you have beautiful women there. Gloriana." Damian bowed toward me. "Perhaps Florence can loan you a wig, *cara*."

"*Tell him Sienna Star's out there too. She's hot and a famous rock star.*" Valdez planted himself next to my knee. "*And Glory's hair is fine, Sabatini.*"

"Two beautiful women. Yes, that should do it."

I touched Valdez's shoulder. "Thanks for the kind words, but tumbleweeds have more style than my hair right now." I turned to Flo. "This Casanova guy's really handsome?"

"Oh, yes." Flo leaned forward. "And, Glory, he has an enormous, um, you know."

"Really!" I know my eyes were wide.

"I thought women didn't care about stuff like that." Ray gave me an elbow.

"We don't." Flo and I grinned when that came out like a duet.

Flo patted Richard's cheek. "As I said to my dear Leonardo more than once: It's not the size of the paint brush; it's the skill of the artist, no?"

"She's never had to say that to me." Richard grinned at the other guys.

"Can we get back on track here? Casanova. Great. We still need two more hot vampires. I'm hoping for Simon, but who else can we send to hell with a clear conscience?"

"I have others in mind." Damian managed to sit on the couch on my other side. It was a tight fit and made Ray and Valdez both give him warning looks that he ignored. "You know, Gloriana, I would be devastated if you were treated so unfairly by this Siren." He ran a finger down my cheek.

"*This guy has one smooth line. Wish I could see him. Sounds like Circe material.*" Aggie's voice rasped inside my head.

"Careful, Damian, now you've got Aggie interested in you. Don't think you want to be on our short list." I grabbed his hand, which was headed for my left ear. "But I appreciate the sentiment. Who are you thinking about? Anyone I know?"

He pulled my hand to his lips for a brief kiss before I

eased it away from him. "Fortunately not. Florence, what do you think about Maurice?"

"That murdering butcher? *He's* in Austin?" She grabbed Richard's hand when Damian nodded. "Yes, he must go."

"He and his sidekick arrived last week. Maury's been here trying to get into the Energy Vampires. Simon Destiny won't meet with him. What does that tell you?" Damian put his arm around my shoulders. "Florence, would you say they are handsome?"

"Yes, as the Devil must be." Flo shuddered. "They both are perfect for hell, Glory."

"I guess so, but I still want Simon to go too. He can fake handsome, especially if he sees Sienna at Ray's." Aggie didn't poke me, so I guess she wasn't a stickler on that point.

"If Simon doesn't work out, Glory, this sidekick sounds like a good backup. Simon could be the bait to get him out to the house. For that meeting this killer wants." Ray obviously wasn't as gung ho about the "Send Simon South" plan as I was.

"I don't like how this whole party thing is shaping up. It's a security nightmare. You're inviting a sexual predator, a serial killer and his sidekick, whatever the hell that means, and the freakin' King of the Energy Vampires." Valdez was up and pacing my tiny living room. *"I'm not sure Brittany and I can guarantee your safety."*

"No worries." Damian's arm tightened around me when Valdez got really close and showed teeth. "I mean, I have help for you. I've formed a council. To take care of vampires who disturb the peace here in Austin." He leaned around me and looked at Ray, who was already throwing visual daggers his way. "Like that crazy woman who turned you vampire, Caine. Never should have happened. My council would have run Lucky out of town before she'd ever have had a chance to pull a stunt like that."

"Sounds good, Damian. Who are these guys?" I decided to get off the couch. Too much testosterone. I'd already been the victim of that once tonight.

"Vampires with lots of power and"—he smiled at his sister—"handsome, of course. Florence helped me select them."

"Of course. Richard, you might like them to be grooms-men at our wedding. And they will be wonderful help if fights break out."

"The council can handle anything." Damian got up and walked to the door. "I'll be working on Casanova and Maury." He turned and smiled. "The dog is right. This will be quite a party. If Circe doesn't take out these bastards, then my coun-cil will. Austin will be a safer place after that."

"If we live to see it." Had I said that? Oops. Guess my optimism had really run out this time.

"You have any idea how much I dread this?" I threw an ex-tra scarf into my suitcase, though a session with a deep con-ditioner had given my hair some of its shine back.

"You're the one who said we have to go." Ray had been watching me pack.

"You're right. Besides, Simon would be stupid to suck the energy out of a famous rock star's fiancée." I smiled down at the rock on the third finger of my left hand. "Unless you decide to dump me this weekend."

"Not a chance." Ray grabbed my hand. "I should have let you pick this out. Flo says the diamond's too little."

"Flo thinks the Hope Diamond's too little. It's beautiful, but I hope this is a CZ." I looked down at the five carat twin-kler. An engagement ring. I'd never had one before. Oh, Jerry had offered. Even bought me a few. I wore the ring he'd given me that I'd actually accepted, a beautiful sapphire, on my right hand.

What the hell was I going to do when Jerry came back to town? Which would be soon. I'd been a complete wimp and let his calls go to voice mail all week. No way could I explain all of this over the phone. The phony engagement. The Siren. The trip to the EV compound. Which he would absolutely forbid if he knew about it. He'd probably be home by Monday. After this weekend.

"Earth to Glory. Would you quit worrying about Blade?" Ray stood behind me and massaged my shoulders. "I'd never buy any woman a fake diamond. It's the real deal. Just like you are. You want to call off this EV thing? I can feel your nerves wound tight."

"We've got to go through with it. You're right. As long as Simon's convinced you and I are together, then I'll be okay." I leaned into Ray's hands on my neck and finally relaxed a little.

"All right then. Finish packing. Where's your bathing suit? Toss it in there. I don't see a sexy nightie, either, but I like you better without anything at all anyway."

I ignored the flirting and slipped out of his arms. "Ray, you still don't really get how old I am, do you?"

"What do you mean?"

"Jerry turned me vampire in 1604. Now I know you didn't go to college." I had a copy of his unauthorized biography on my bookshelf. "Neither did I. But I bet you have a sense of history. Think. Did women go to the beach back then?"

"No, guess not. But this is the twenty-first century."

"Right. I never see daylight and I hate the water. So why would I own a bathing suit?" Not to mention the fact that my thighs are not something I'd deliberately put on parade.

"I'm sorry, baby." Ray put his arms around me and rested his chin on top of my head. "I never thought. You've really missed out on a lot of things, haven't you?"

"I don't choose to look at it that way. And I'd advise you to adjust your attitude right now if you really do get to live forever." I eased out of his arms and decided to add a few things to my suitcase. Extra jeans—no, make that shorts. Flo had mentioned a beach scene in the sunlight room. With my luck, I'd end up wet again.

I slipped in a black silk nightgown that I'd bought before Christmas. For a night with Jerry. I took a moment to wallow in guilt. Nope, not necessary. Ray and I weren't going to, uh, you know. This was all about saving our butts, and "acting" engaged was part of it. Sleeping in my Snoopy jammies wouldn't cut it. Surely Jerry would understand that.

Ray had watched with interest as I stuffed my suitcase. "That's better. So tell me what attitude I should have."

"That if we take care of business and get to live past the full moon, you're going to get to see things mere mortals today can only dream of. Colonies on Mars maybe. Who knows what else?"

"Cool. I'd like to see freeways in the sky. You know, aerial snowmobiles. Up and away." Ray laughed and mimicked steering skyward.

"Anything's possible. Think, Ray. I've seen electricity invented. Airplanes fly. Space exploration. Microwaves and cell phones." I grinned at him and slammed my suitcase shut. "Not to mention the wonderful, amazing television and iPod."

"Right. Sixteen hundred till now. Wow, you've seen it all, haven't you, old girl?" A horn honked and Ray lost his smile. "That's our limo."

Richard and Flo appeared in the doorway. "Ready? We're going on down."

"We're right behind you." I zipped my suitcase closed. "Flo, are you all right?" She'd gone from nervous chatter earlier to pale and silent in the last few minutes.

"I'm freaking out, Glory. So I say nothing."

"We'll have to watch what we say out loud all weekend. I'm sure they have surveillance equipment everywhere, even in those sunlight rooms." Richard put his arm around Flo. "I wouldn't advise reading Florence's mind right now. She *is* freaking out and curses like a Venetian sailor chained to his oar."

"Do you blame me, *amante*?" Flo bit her lip. "Simon the snake *will* be spying on us. At least he has to be close to read our minds, not like that Siren of yours, Glory. But there will be video cameras. Glory, you and Ray must act the lovers every minute."

Ray put his hands on my shoulders. "Who's acting?"

Ray's playful attitude was hitting on my last nerve. I started to say something snarky but there was no use spreading the angst.

"Let's just be sure to leave there with a commitment from Simon to come out to your house, Ray. Soon. So we all need to keep our eyes and ears open to figure out what would lure him there."

"I could offer him Sienna. She'd make a hell of a vampire."

I was in Ray's face before he could blink. "Never. I mean *never* joke about making someone vampire." I pointed to my bed. "You remember waking up right there and finding out . . . ?" I took a breath and closed my eyes.

"Glory, I was kidding. Hell, you know I'd never do that, don't you?" Ray pulled me close. He must have sent a message to Richard because Rich and Flo muttered something about seeing us downstairs and left.

"Sorry. I lost my sense of humor when I woke up tonight and realized I was really going out to that EV hellhole."

Ray stroked my back. "We should cancel this then think of something else. I don't like seeing you scared like this."

"Yep. I'm scared. But I think Aggie's even more powerful than Simon. So I can put up with a little discomfort for the chance to see that vermin in hell."

"I think it's stronger than discomfort for you, but if you're determined to go through with it, let's get it over with."

Ray picked up my suitcase, then grabbed his own.

"*Stop right there, Blondie.*" Valdez stood blocking the door out to the hallway.

"Valdez, we had this conversation. I'm going. Move out of the way." I knew I couldn't physically budge him. Even Ray and I together would have a tough go of it.

"You heard her, fur face. Move your butt." Ray obviously had a death wish, even making a move toward the dog.

"*Listen, you empty-headed a-hole. You don't have the first idea what does go on out there. Simon hates Glory. She made a fool out of him in front of his followers. You think he's just forgotten that?"*

"Valdez, it's okay. He wants Ray's business. I'll be under Ray's protection. This sparkler on my left hand guarantees Simon knows that. You can't stop me, pup." I squatted down and looked him in the eyes. "I know you mean well, but I'm going, end of story."

"Blade—"

I held up my hand. "I know Jerry wouldn't like it. But this doesn't involve him. Just Ray and me." I stood and sighed. "If Jerry tries to blame you later, I can say you did everything you could to keep me here."

"Right." Valdez leaped and knocked me flat, sitting on my chest while staring at Ray, his teeth bared, his growl the stuff of nightmares.

"Damn it, V!" I shoved at his paw and got a mouthful of fur for my trouble.

"Are you hurt, Glory? You son of a bitch, you've gone too far." Ray lunged and Valdez shifted just enough to grab Ray's duffel bag and toss it across the room.

"Stop it, Ray! I'm okay. He's no lightweight, but"—huff, puff—"let me talk to him."

"I'm not moving, Glory. I can sit here all night. You tell your new boyfriend that the healing vamp sleep won't grow him a new right hand. If he tries to reach for you again, I'll tear his off and swallow it."

"Ray, don't." I could see Ray's frustration. "He means it. Listen. Take the suitcases downstairs. Valdez and I need to talk privately. I'll be down in a minute."

"I can't leave you like this. The son of a bitch must weigh a ton."

"I'm fine. He'll get off once you're out of here." I shoved at Valdez's furry butt. "Right?"

"No promises, but your boyfriend isn't helping. Put down that chair, Caine. Glory's already had her coffee table busted this week, thanks to you."

"I'd feel a hell of a lot better if I broke this chair over *your* empty head. Wasn't just me knocking Glory on her ass, and I didn't see you stepping up with a credit card to replace her table. Get off her now or I'm not leaving."

Wow. Points to Ray for standing up to Valdez. Air gusted into my lungs when the dog actually stood and stepped off of me.

"There. Now get out so I can talk some sense into this woman."

"Right. Like you and sense have made each other's acquaintance. See you downstairs, Glory." Ray picked up the bags and stepped into the hall, leaving the door ajar.

I sat up and took a minute to relearn breathing.

"Okay, Valdez, I get that you're the great protector, but I'm in charge. Jerry has always made that very clear to you. Am I right?"

"Simon Destiny hates you. Am I right?"

"The King of the EVs is all about money and power. Ray represents both. Simon won't risk losing such a valuable client. I'll be okay out there. Richard and Flo will have our backs." I put my hand on Valdez's head. "Now brace yourself. Ray called Brittany and told her you have the weekend off. She's on her way over. Forget your contract for once and shift out of this dog body. Take a shower. You've got till late Sunday night to enjoy your freedom. It's long overdue, my friend."

"I can't—"

"This isn't a request, it's an order. You've been tense. On edge. I know you're conflicted. Working for Blade, but watching me become close to Ray. It's been tough and you can't do your best work when you're wound up like this." I rubbed his ears. "Richard left some clothes in Flo's old bedroom. I don't know if they'll fit. Hey, if you're lucky, you won't need them. There are rib eyes in the freezer, wine in the pantry that Will left here. Knock yourself out. You've earned it."

"Damn it, Glory."

" 'Night, V." I ran out the door, my heart pounding. Ray was waiting at the top of the stairs. "You heard?"

"Yep. Think he'll do it?"

"He's not supposed to disobey a direct order."

"He sure was worked up about this EV visit."

"He had his reasons. Don't be fooled by the pretty setting, Ray. You heard what Valdez said before about how he was treated out there. Obviously bad things happen behind the scenes. This time you're a paying guest, a celebrity. So you'll be okay. And I'll be under your protection. That means a lot in the vampire world. So throw that phrase around a lot. Say, 'my fiancée, Glory, who is under my protection,' every chance you get. We just need to find out what it would take to get Simon to come out to your house. And it needs to be next week. We can't wait."

"Gotcha." Ray punched in the code and we stepped outside.

Flo and Richard were already inside the limo, Flo with her head down, Richard smiling like he was king of the world. Greg Kaplan lounged against the long black SUV stretch smoking a cheroot. He straightened when he saw Ray and me and grabbed our bags.

"Ray, this is Greg Kaplan, our limo driver." I smiled sweetly. "No uniform, Greg?"

"Just filling in for the regular guy." Greg nodded. "Pleasure to meet you, Mr. Caine. Mr. Destiny will greet you personally when we get out to the compound."

"Of course." Ray was into his "I'm a rock star and don't you forget it" persona. "Glory, baby. Did you pack the sunscreen?"

"Oh, Ray, silly. You won't need it. Vampires don't sunburn." I frowned at Greg. "But, wait. Do they, Greg? In this sunlight room I've heard about?"

"No, Glory. But you'll see. It's a great experience. Worth every penny. But then I'm sure Mr. Caine doesn't care about the cost." Greg gave me a look, like how did I land this big fish?

"Just send the bill to my business manager. I'm surprised there's not paparazzi everywhere with this thing parked here. Destiny's not exactly subtle, is he?" Ray had his sneer down pat.

"Only the best for our guests." Greg grinned. "And he took care of the photographers earlier. I brought reinforcements. They cleared out all the reporters. Let's just say some of them will wonder how they ended up with snaps of the polka tournament at Schulenburg."

I hid my grin. "I hope you didn't hurt them. They're only doing their jobs, Greg. And Ray doesn't mind a little publicity."

"But we can't let them tail us out to the compound. So they had to go. They'll be okay, but of course if they had good quality juice, they were donors for the guys. That's a given." Greg held open the door.

I ignored him and let Ray help me into the backseat.

"Where is this place?" Ray patted my bottom as I climbed into the car.

"In the hills south of here. We keep our location a secret. You'll notice you can't see out those specially tinted windows. Nothing personal, Mr. Caine. Just the way we do business. We're very security conscious. Drive will take about forty-five minutes. There's a variety of some new premium synthetics in the minibar if you're interested."

"No, thanks, we've gone back to hunting." I laughed at the look on Greg's face. "Oh, yes. Now I don't have to recycle all those bottles. So much more earth friendly. I hope you have plenty of mortal donors on hand out at the compound."

"Of course. Any type you wish." Greg slammed the car door and walked around to the driver's side.

"I think you surprised him, baby. You two have a history? Should I be jealous?" Ray nuzzled my neck.

"Of him?" I laughed. "I scraped him off my shoe long ago, lover. You're all I'll ever need." I saw Greg watching us in the rearview mirror. "Put up the privacy window, driver."

I swallowed a lump of dread and leaned against Ray while he and Richard discussed basketball of all things.

Surreal, but male vampires are men first, and don't you forget it.

"Nice place you've got here, Destiny. Reminds me a little of Istanbul." Ray held my hand as we strolled the grounds of the EV compound. Richard and Flo were right behind us. "What's in the gold domed building? Are we going inside?"

"That's a holy place for us, Mr. Caine. I'm afraid it's not open to visitors." Simon turned and looked at Flo. "Did you say something, Florence?"

"She did not." Richard frowned. "We are all anxious to see our rooms, unpack and visit the sunlight rooms. Am I right, Ray?"

"You bet." Ray turned to me. "I want to do this for my fiancée, Glory, who is under my protection. You do understand that, don't you, Destiny?"

"Certainly. Gloriana and I are starting over." Simon smiled and I had to hide my shudder.

"Glory hasn't seen the sun in hundreds of years so she's forgotten how wonderful it feels. I can't imagine going that long without the warmth, the, well, you know." Ray hugged me. "She's not as into this as I am. I guess we all have our secret cravings. She's more into the food thing."

"Now Ray, I'm sure Simon doesn't care about that." I filled my head with thoughts of Cheetos and chocolate truffles in case Simon decided to probe my mind.

"No, I find this fascinating. So, Gloriana, you would like to be able to eat like born vampires do." Simon was trying to catch my eyes, to whammy me.

I looked at Ray instead. "That used to be a big deal for me. Now I'm into whatever Ray wants."

"That's my girl." Ray kissed my lips. "What would do it for you, Destiny? Any big cravings on your hidden agenda?"

"What more could I want?" Simon swept his arm around the cluster of buildings that seemed to be straight out of the Arabian nights, complete with minarets and stucco. The centerpiece was the huge gold dome atop a massive building that I knew housed their demon Honoria and the energy-sucking device that kept her happy and everyone else around her miserable.

"It's a nice place, but a little isolated. I like action myself. This vampire gig is cramping my style. The sunlight room is a great start, but I'd like to be able to go out in the daytime. Don't suppose you've got a magic bullet for that in your bag of tricks, do you?" Ray was suddenly serious and I wondered what he was up to.

"You've probably seen those vampire shows on television." Simon laughed, which was a pretty creepy sound, I can tell you. "Actually, we're working on it. You're not the first customer to express an interest. There would be a big demand for a drug that would allow for an adjusted body clock."

Richard put Flo behind him and moved closer. "Are we going to stand around here all night?"

"Not at all." Simon gestured and a woman hurried from the shadows. "Mindy will show you to your suite. Then provide you with whatever you need. The sunlight rooms are at your disposal. Contact me directly if you can't find what you desire, and I'll see what I can do. The number is on the telephone beside each bed. Have a good evening." Simon nodded and walked away.

"Please, follow me." Mindy led us to a cottage that contained two bedrooms connected by a large living room. A fire blazed in the fireplace, the vibe a cozy southwestern feel. Our suitcases had been unpacked and I figured that meant someone had snooped through our things.

"Ms. St. Clair, there is a selection of bathing suits available in the dressing room if you wish to wear one to your sunlight room. Of course that is up to you. Terry robes are also in the dressing room. When you're ready to go, I'll escort you there." Mindy threw open the door to a decadent bathroom with an adjoining dressing room and closet.

A variety of bathing suits in every size and configuration were on shelves. I guess I wasn't the first vampire to arrive who didn't own a suit.

"There you go, babe, you can have your pick. Want to model some for me?"

"I'd rather fall on a stake." I smiled and slammed the door in Ray's face. Oops. Forgot. We were supposed to be engaged. I opened it again. "Sorry, love, but I'm a little self-conscious about my figure flaws. Let me do this by myself. When I think I have one I like, I'll show you. Okay?" In my head, I told Ray to cut me a break and give me some privacy. He just grinned but finally gave me a thorough kiss in case there were video cameras in the dressing area. Ick.

"Fine. I can't wait to see you. I'll put on my suit. Hurry. I want to have as much time as we can in the sun. I'll be out in the living room talking to Richard."

So I began the utterly humiliating task of trying on swim-suits. Yes, I'd read the articles and the funny cartoons about women in dressing rooms refusing to come out or having identity crises before swimsuit season. Hah! Now I felt their pain, especially since I kept trying to figure out if I was on video with Simon laughing somewhere. So I hid behind doors and used the terry robe as a sort of curtain.

I started with the one-pieces. No, not working. Because my top and bottom weren't quite the same size. I finally ended up with a red bra top that barely contained me. Ray would like the cleavage. Surprisingly, I liked a bikini bot-tom with a cute red ruffle on the diagonal to match the top and to distract a little from the width. My waist is not all that bad. I have what used to be called an hourglass figure. Of course my hour ran more like ninety minutes. I was try-ing to talk myself out of the dressing room before dawn when Ray tapped on the door.

"Glory? Babe? We're burning daylight."

"Coming." I sighed and grabbed one of the terry robes, frowning at the embroidered EV logo, then slipped it on and

tied it. I scraped my hair back into a ponytail and wished for
sunglasses. I'd never owned a pair. Sunlight. Yep, I was excited. I stepped into the living room and found Ray talking
to Simon.

"Where are Richard and Flo?"

"Already gone to their sunlight room. It's the one that's
like Tuscany. Florence was very excited to revisit a place like
her childhood memories." Simon smiled indulgently and
my skin crawled. "Richard certainly knows how to handle
her."

"Destiny's brought you a present, Glory." Ray was grinning with what looked like real excitement. Which was
scaring the crap out of me. Didn't he remember anything
I'd told him? I hurriedly filled my head with all the bathing
suits I'd just tried on.

"Why? I mean, what?" I realized Simon was holding a
tray with chocolate truffles on it. "Not candy. You know better than that, Simon." I pouted and clung to Ray. "Please
don't be mean."

"These are very special, my dear. Try one. They won't
make you sick. They're specially formulated. Made with the
best of synthetic materials, yet taste like the finest chocolate." Simon was still smiling as he held out the tray.

"They're not drugged, are they?" They did *look* delicious.
Like those I'd seen in expensive shops in the mall. My
mouth watered.

"Glory! Surely Destiny realizes it would be a very grave
mistake for him to do anything to harm my fiancée while we
are here and you are under my protection." Ray gave Simon
a hard look. "I know you and Glory have had your differences
in the past, but I was warned about you and your organization. So I took precautions."

"Oh?" Simon moved the tray out of my reach. "What
kind of precautions?"

"You know the tabloids follow me and my career with interest. So if anything happens to my fiancée or me or my
guests this weekend, I've arranged for information about

you and your organization to go public on a massive scale."
Ray pulled me to his side and wrapped his arms around me.
"Would be a shame to do that, since you seem to have so
much to offer out here."

"I assure you, Mr. Caine, I have done nothing but brought
Gloriana a little treat. There will be no need to publicize
anything. Except your enjoyment of the facilities to other
vampires, of course. I would love to have your personal endorsement for our Web site."

"Those kinds of deals are handled by my business manager. If things go well out here, maybe I can arrange a meeting with him." Ray finally smiled.

"Excellent." Simon popped a chocolate into his mouth.
"Now, Gloriana, please consider trying one. See? Delicious.
Here, Mr. Caine, taste one yourself. These chocolates are very
dear, of course. And only available on-site. Our way of insur-
ing that our made vampires return to us on a regular basis."
He smiled and watched Ray tentatively pick up a truffle,
smell it, then take a bite.

"Damn, Glory, it tastes like the real thing. Bet you've
never had one of these, babe." He held the half-eaten chocolate to my lips. "Try it. I guarantee you'll be hooked."

Well, you knew I'd go for it. Chocolate? Oh. My. God. I
closed my eyes and savored. The flavors burst in my mouth
and my eyes watered. I swallowed and waited for some kind
of pain or nausea. Instead the pleasure just kept on coming.
I reached for another truffle, intending to nibble, but instead popped the whole thing into my mouth.

"Sorry, my dear, but that's all for this visit." Simon took
the empty tray with him to the door after I'd polished off
the last truffle. "Mindy will show you to the sunlight room.
Enjoy."

"Ray." I held on to him as we walked to the door. "I ate a
chocolate truffle." Truth? Four chocolate truffles.

"Yes, baby." Ray reached up and wiped a smear from the
corner of my mouth, then licked his finger. "Come here." He
kissed me slow and deep, finally pulling back and looking

into my eyes. "I believe watching you eat those truffles for the first time was one of the sexiest things I've ever seen."

I laughed and leaned against him. "You do know how to make me feel good, Israel Caine." We followed Mindy to a building set back from the others. We walked down a path through the woods, the dark soothing and not a bit creepy. Which in a way was disturbing as hell. We were in the freaking Energy Vampire stronghold, surrounded by the worst evildoers on the planet and only yards away from a demon who could suck the life out of you, and I was *happy*? What was wrong with this picture?

Fourteen

Sunshine and blue, blue sky. I knew it was special effects—an Imax screen maybe—that provided fluffy clouds, the sun and the waves breaking toward us and the infinity edge pool. I lifted my face to it anyway, felt its warmth and luxuriated in the fantasy. Ray stretched and lay beside me on a mat. At least the sand was real. White sand that Ray said was similar to the beaches on the island he owned in the Caribbean. The sun reflected off the small pool in front of us. Even the sounds and smells were right, down to the squeal of gulls, the rustle of palm fronds and a sea breeze with a touch of salt in the air.

"Damn, this is fantastic. I'd love to know how they make the sunshine seem so real. I've got to get back to the island." Ray rolled over and grinned at me. "Even at night, it's magical. You'll love it there."

I started to say something in my head about Aggie and our ticking clock, but couldn't bring down Ray's mood. He was high on the whole experience, like a kid with his first treat.

"I'm sure it's wonderful."

"*You're* wonderful. And you look great. How does it feel to be wearing your first bikini?"

"Strange. Like I'm wearing underwear in public. But then this is a private beach, so I'm okay with it." I scooped up a handful of sand and let it trickle through my fingers. "Thanks for this. I'd forgotten what the sun feels like. And, honestly, I never felt this much on my body before."

Ray looked very at home in his brief black swim trunks and he certainly had the body for them. He had the broad shoulders and strong arms and legs of a swimmer and not an ounce of fat on him. He'd been tanned when he'd been turned vampire and would always stay that way. No tan lines. So his island had been clothing optional. The very thought made my heart race and I licked my lips and looked away, pretend- ing to be fascinated by the abundance of potted palms cir- cling the pool.

"You and Blade never . . ." Ray ran a finger down my tummy to the edge of my bikini bottom. He certainly knew how to bring my attention back to him, us. That dangerous finger anyway.

"Jerry was vampire when I met him. We never did day- light together, except the virtual-reality kind. He can play some terrific mind games, though." I had to get away from Ray and his touching. I sat up. "Water looks good. I think I'll test the temperature."

"I get it. Me and my big mouth. I never should have mentioned the ex." Ray grabbed me and brought me down beside him again.

"He's not—" My mouth was suddenly covered with Ray's.

"Cameras, Glory. Simon thinks you and Jerry are done. Play along." He prolonged the kiss until I finally had to push him away, though I tried to make it look playful.

"I think you should cool off, big guy. We've got all night." I forced a grin and got up again. *"And I'm not letting you take advantage of the camera thing."*

Talk of Jerry made me uncomfortable. I should have called him. Given him a heads up. But then again, what was the point? So he could rail at me and then stress over being so far away when I was in danger? No, avoidance had been the right thing to do.

"You're right. Let's get in the pool." Ray walked over to sit on the edge, then jumped in. "The temperature's perfect. Look, it doesn't even hit my shoulders. Come on in. You couldn't drown if you tried."

"Want to bet?" I did sit down, though, and stick my feet in the water. The sun was almost too warm, but felt great on my back. "I swear this could be the real deal. The EVs are creepily clever." I figure Simon would be suspicious if I didn't knock the EVs a little. Our bad history and all.

"Must be magic of some kind. I'm impressed. I really don't care how they do it. I just plan to enjoy it. Come here." Ray pulled me in and wrapped my legs around his waist. "How does that feel?"

I grinned. "The water? Or that bulge I'm sitting on?"

Ray laughed and walked me around the pool, laying me back until I was floating.

"Don't let me sink, Ray. I'm not the swimmer that you are."

"I know. How about making this more interesting? Ever been skinny-dipping?" Ray reached for the tie at my neck.

"Sure. Well, in shallow water anyway. I'm not a prude as you well know." I sat up and grabbed his hand, then leaned close to whisper in his ear. "Stop. I'll not strip off for Simon the snake and his video cameras."

Ray nuzzled my neck, his breath hot against my skin. "You have nothing to be ashamed of. I bet Simon watches this clip over and over again to get his rocks off."

"You have just officially grossed me out." I sent that message in my mind. Before I could stop him, Ray slipped off my top and flung it toward the mats.

"There, doesn't that feel better? Freer?" He pulled me to him, his chest hard against mine. *"Play along. I won't do anything to embarrass you in front of Simon."*

I couldn't deny that this felt really, really good. Warm sun on my back, warm man on my front.

"Relax, Glory. Our voyeur can't see a thing that happens underwater." Ray's skimpy briefs didn't disguise the fact that he was ready to make this video X-rated.

"I want you." He nipped my earlobe, sending shivers all through me. Then he kissed a heated path down my neck, his hands roaming around my back to cup my bottom. Hot, cold. I clutched his shoulders to keep from laying back so he could pull my aching nipples into his mouth. It would be too easy to forget we had an audience.

"You're beautiful. Perfect." Ray looked into my eyes and saw what he wanted to see, me reacting in predictable Glory fashion. Melting. Resistance practically nonexistent when it came to a man with clever hands and a good line.

But Ray wasn't just any man, now was he? We'd been doing this mating dance for weeks now. Letting the tension build until I, for one, was practically thrumming with it. And the lust was mixed up with all kinds of other things. Like how he "got" me as an independent woman. Oh, God, but I was tempted to quit analyzing and start doing.

Ray smiled, all sensual, confident male. Most women would have already let their hormones do the talking. Mine were shouting "yes." I told them to shut up and let me *think*.

"Let me make love to you, Glory. You can feel how much I want you, and you know you want me too. What do you say?"

"I'd like to hear the answer to that."

I jerked back and looked toward the deep male voice that I would know anywhere, anytime.

"Jerry!"

"Well, Gloriana, answer the man. Do you want him or no?"

I shook my head and pushed away from Ray. He didn't try to stop me and I was a coward, afraid to look at him, to see what my rejection was doing to him. I tried to hurry, but felt like I was running through molasses. After an hour or so I finally grabbed the side of the pool and pulled myself out. Jerry stood there, my skimpy top dangling from his hand.

"This is a surprise. I'm glad you're back." I snatched the top and tried to shove my breasts into it, finally giving up and grabbing the terry robe I'd left by the door.

"Are you? Really? Looks to me like I'm interrupting. I was dumb enough to think you might be in danger and needed my help. Obviously I was wrong." Jerry didn't take his eyes off Ray. "If you'd answered your phone this week, Gloriana, or checked your voice mail, you'd have known I was coming home tonight. But maybe you did know and didn't give a damn."

"Jerry, listen to me. I, uh—"

"Don't bother. Valdez explained everything to me. What you've been up to while I've been gone." Jerry's jaw worked, and I saw him swallow.

"Jerry—"

He held up his hand, and I couldn't say another word even if I could have thought of one.

His voice was rough when he finally spoke. "Valdez. Yes, imagine my surprise when I arrived at your apartment to find your bodyguard had shifted into human form to enjoy a weekend off. Caught him shagging your lover's bodyguard on your couch. And where are the two bodies he and Brittany are supposed to be guarding? Only in the most dangerous place they could possibly be."

"Jerry, Jeremiah, I can explain. Later. When we're alone." I reached for him, but he moved away. *"Not here, Jerry, there are hidden cameras. Things we can't let Simon overhear."*

"I have no interest in being alone with you." Jerry turned his back on me as if I'd never spoken in his mind. "Well, Caine, are you man enough to come out of the damned pool or not?"

"I am. But I'd like to see Glory safely out of here first. I don't like the look in your eyes, Blade." Ray rested his elbows on the edge of the pool like he was in no hurry to start the coming fight. Or worried about the outcome.

I wanted to bash Ray over the head with one of the potted palms until he came to his senses and ran for his life.

Oh, God, was there any way to make this right? Jerry was hurt, furious and looking to kill someone. Lucky for me, Jerry still had enough of his old Scottish warrior's code that he'd never harm a woman or child no matter how they infuriated him. Unlucky for Ray, men were not only fair game, they were the target of choice.

Jerry could be so cold when he was enraged. I felt that chill now, like that iceberg I'd seen once when a ship I'd been on had passed too close to it. Yep, I'd so rather be sitting in a rowboat in the freezing North Atlantic than where I was right now.

"You think I'd hurt her? Physically?" Jerry still wouldn't look at me. "You don't know me. Gloriana does. Would I hit you, woman?"

Oh, how I wish he'd called me lass. "No, of course not. Jerry, please listen to me. Ray and I, uh, we're not, uh, serious. I mean, we haven't even set a date yet." I looked around. Damn. Of course there were hidden cameras. I sent another mental message. *"Jerry, we're pretending to be engaged. Ray and I were acting out for the surveillance cameras. I'm sure Simon's watching us."*

Finally Jerry swept his eyes over me, from my wet head to my bare toes, then back up to linger on my hands clutching my top and holding my robe together.

"I know what I saw, Gloriana. You're as good as naked and wearing his fucking ring! I'd say that's serious unless you're just playing the whore for him."

I gasped and tears filled my eyes. Never, never in all the years we'd been together had Jerry disrespected me. I'd been proud that he'd always treated me like a lady. Ray snarled and vaulted out of the pool. He hit Jerry in the middle of his back and the two men went down, their fangs out, their fists flying.

I knew better than to try to get between them. I threw open the door and screamed for help. Men came running from buildings on the grounds. I couldn't look when I heard flesh hitting flesh and smelled blood. I recognized first Ray's blood type, then Jerry's. I leaned against the building, tears streaming down my face as three burly guards ran inside and tried to pull the men apart. I heard one of them talking on a cell phone and soon two more men appeared. Finally, the five of them managed to separate Jerry and Ray.

I turned and saw Ray first. His ear was torn. He had cuts on his chest and his arms were bleeding profusely. Both his eyes were almost swollen shut and he was being held back by two men. He was still swearing and trying to get to Jerry.

Jerry didn't say anything or struggle against the three men who held him. He just stood silently, his lip swollen, his shirt ripped open and his head bleeding where it must have hit something hard. Obviously he'd decided that I wasn't worth fighting over after all.

Simon hurried down the path, a serious look on his face. "What's going on here? Gloriana?"

"As you can see, Blade has returned from Europe. I guess he doesn't read tabloids because he didn't know that Ray and I are engaged. He didn't take the news well." I took a shuddering breath and made myself walk past Jerry to Ray's side. Oh, God, but those were the hardest ten steps I'd ever taken. I forced myself to fill my head with one of Ray's songs in case Simon was trying to read my mind.

"Blade, you attacked a paying guest. I'll have my men escort you off the premises. If you come here uninvited again, you'll be subject to grave penalties." Simon gestured toward the gold dome, visible above the trees. "I believe you've heard of our demon and her powers."

"I'm not scared of you or your demon." Jerry lifted his chin. "But I'll be happy to leave. There's nothing for me here."

"Jerry, I—"

"Gloriana, don't waste your breath. I have nothing to say to you. Clearly my mother has had the right of it all these years and you have never been the woman for me." Jerry looked at the men who still held him. "Release me and I'll shift out of here. You won't be bothered by me again."

Simon studied Jerry and was obviously convinced he meant what he said. I didn't dare try to read Jerry's mind, sure what he was thinking would break my heart. Finally, Simon nodded. We all watched Jerry walk stiffly down the path to a clearing, then, with a cry of pure rage, shift into a blackbird and fly into the night.

"Mr. Caine, please let me bring you a donor with your favorite blood type. To speed your healing. What would you like?" Simon gestured and the guards melted into the woods.

"Nothing. I like to drink from Glory. She prefers AB negative. That's right, isn't it, babe?"

"Yes, but I don't feel like feeding now. Not from a mortal. Just bring us some synthetic of that type."

"Nonsense. I can have a carafe of the real thing brought to you and some glasses. You won't have to see the mortal at all." Simon snapped his fingers and a woman I hadn't noticed hurried away.

"Thanks. And we'll stay here until almost dawn, then go back to our room to sleep. I'm not going to let Blade ruin Ray's night in the sun." I rubbed Ray's chest where he'd obviously taken a really hard hit, the bruise darkening. "I'll heal everything for you, honey, as soon as I feed."

"Thanks, babe." Ray kept his arms around me.

"I'll leave you then. There's a phone next to the door. Press one if you need anything else. I'm sorry about this. I'll make sure there's a guard posted outside to keep you from being disturbed further." Simon turned on his heel and left.

Ray waited until the woman had delivered a tray before he looked into my eyes. *"Are you okay? Blade was really harsh with you. Or was that an act?"*

"No act." I drank and nibbled on the chocolates Simon had included on the tray. I was so upset I was nauseated, but I was convinced the truffles would settle my stomach. And I did feel marginally better after the second one.

"I've never seen him so furious. And—and he's lost his respect for me. After all these years." Tears filled my eyes and ran down my cheeks. I leaned against Ray and pretended to be hugging

him. Putting on a show. How could I do this for another twenty-four hours? With a broken heart?

"When we get back, Ray, I have to go see him to try to explain."

"You'd better give him time to cool off. You really hurt his pride. And what was that about his mother? Sounded like a slam to me." Ray pulled me back into his arms and we lay in the sunshine, his wounds healing from the blood he'd decided to drink from the goblets Simon had had delivered.

"It was. He knows I hate his mother. She's always called me a low-class climber." I sniffled and decided to hell with the pity party. Now I was mad. *"Forget Jerry's pride. What about* mine? *He called me a whore. I may never forgive him for that."*

Ray kissed my cheek. *"If Blade were here, I'd beat the hell out of him all over again."*

"No more fights, please." I smiled against his shoulder, pretty sure Ray had gotten the worst of it. *"Have I told you how great you've been about this? I know I didn't treat you well, just hopping off of you like that when Jerry got here."*

Ray rubbed my back. *"I get it. Blade had you first. But I'm still here, Glory. I'm still here."*

Time to talk out loud. "All right, Ray. Lay back and let me put my hands on you. I think I can heal that ear faster."

"Who cares about my ear? Did I tell you that son of a bitch kneed me in the groin?" Ray grinned.

"You are such a bad, bad man." I looked up to where I was pretty sure there was a camera. "How can I not love you?" I touched his ear and finally let him drink from me. As videos went, I'm sure this would be one for Simon's keeper shelf. Seminudity, violence and a little vampire fang action. Add some killing and this one would have it all.

It was almost dawn when we got back to our suite. Richard and Flo were in the living room, curled up in front of the fire, the picture of a contented couple. They both jumped up when they saw Ray's face. Sure, it had almost healed, but he'd obviously been knocked around.

"What the hell happened to you?" Richard looked around, like for a weapon. *"Simon?"*

"Blade." Ray managed a shrug. "He got back in town and Valdez told him where we were. Caught Glory and me . . ." He had his arm around me and snugged me closer. "Well, you can see that he didn't like what he saw. Couldn't handle the fact that we're getting married."

"They fought over you?" Flo rushed to my side. "Glory, how, um, awful for you." She sent me a mental message. *"Who won?"*

I blinked back tears. *"As far as I'm concerned everybody lost. Jerry hates me, Ray almost got killed, and we haven't found out anything useful."* Out loud I said, "It was horrible. Five men had to pull them apart. Jerry left voluntarily or Simon would have fed him to the demon."

"It was an unforgivable breach of security. Blade came into your sunlight room?" Richard looked like he was getting a glimmer of an idea.

"Yes. You'd think the Energy Vampires could protect their guests better than that. I came here expecting some alone time with my baby and paid big bucks for it. Hell, what next? Paparazzi popping out of the closet?" Ray was on board.

Yep, Simon owed us. I liked where this was going. "When I saw Jerry attack Ray, I was totally traumatized." I tugged on Ray's hand. "Now, though, I can feel the dawn. Time for bed. Hopefully, you'll be all better by sunset, lover boy. One more night in the sunlight room. It had better be uninterrupted." I pulled his face down and gave him a lingering kiss. "Poor baby, Ray had to fight for his life. There's no excuse for that kind of thing to happen. Now let's go to bed. 'Night, Flo, Richard."

I heard their murmured good nights as Ray closed our bedroom door.

"That was some kiss. Come here and do that again." Ray pulled me against him.

"Shower first. You've been rolling around in the sand." I smiled up at him.

"I just want one more kiss." He didn't let go and this suddenly didn't feel like playing for the cameras.

"I know where your kisses lead, mister. Hit the shower. You're not getting sand in that bed." I made it clear I wasn't in the mood and Ray stepped back. I felt the dawn coming. Dread knotted my stomach. Daylight was a vampire's most vulnerable time. And I didn't have Valdez here to watch over me. Sure, the Energy Vampires would all be dead to the world too, but they had plenty of creeps on their payroll who weren't vampires.

"Glory, quit freaking yourself out. Simon would be stupid to do anything to us while we slept. And he's anything but stupid." Ray had been reading my mind. *"You heard me warn him off too. Right?"*

I nodded. Even Simon couldn't control the tabloids once they got rolling with a juicy story. Secret vampire hideaway with weird cult would be right up their alley. Add in a rock star, and you had weeks of front-page material.

"Relax, baby. You're still upset about that fight, aren't you?"

I nodded again, suddenly a freaked-out bobblehead.

"Don't worry. Blade won't be back," he said for the cameras. "I'll take that hot shower. When I come out I want to see you in that sexy nightie you brought." He winked and headed to the bathroom.

A sexy nightie. Ray was nuts if he thought I was going to pretend to make love in that king-size bed for the cameras. I walked into the closet, hid behind the door where I was pretty sure there couldn't be a camera and put on one of Ray's T-shirts and my own panties. I tossed the bikini in a hamper and hoped I could figure out some way to avoid the bathing suit option for the next night. Sunlight had lost its appeal.

The next evening I woke up, relieved that I'd survived the day *and* managed to find another bathing suit in the seemingly endless supply. We were walking to the sunlight room again when Simon stepped into our path. He had a woman behind him this time. When she moved to Simon's side, Ray and I stopped in our tracks.

"Tina?" I couldn't believe it.

"What the hell are you doing here?" Ray moved into a protective position, placing himself slightly in front of me.

"Your fan followed the limo to our headquarters. Believe me, the men responsible for ensuring this doesn't happen have been dealt with." Simon stroked Tina's shoulder-length hair and she snuggled closer to him.

I fought my gag reflex. "Uh, so what are you going to do with her?" Frankly I was surprised she was still alive.

"And why the hell is she acting like that? Like she's crazy about you." Ray apparently didn't care about being tactful.

"She thinks I'm you, of course. The great Israel Caine." Simon smiled, leaned down and gave Tina a kiss. When he started to pull back, she grabbed his suit coat lapels and jerked him down for another big kiss, tongues and all. Simon finally forced her to release him. "Insatiable female. I'm finding it interesting keeping up with her."

Okay, the chocolate truffles definitely weren't staying down after that one. I pressed a hand to my mouth and breathed through my nose. Ray just looked at me like, huh?

"I have a unique ability, Caine. I can make myself appear as someone's true desire. Apparently, little Miss Tina's true desire at this time is you." Simon laughed.

"She's been stalking me. That's why she followed the limo. She tried to kidnap Valdez, was going after Glory next. I thought I had taken care of that. Used some mind control."

"Her obsession was obviously too strong for that trick. She still hates Gloriana. Because you plan to marry her. I'll take care of her permanently once I'm no longer amused by her. For now, she makes an interesting pet." Simon patted her bottom and she giggled and whispered in his ear. "Later, my dear."

I shuddered. "Simon, she has a nice mother. She can't just disappear. What about—"

"Apparently Tina is quite adept with a computer. I'm putting her to work out here. She's already e-mailed her mother that she's taken a temporary job with a very large salary. Which is true." Simon gestured toward a building behind him. "She'll keep up our Web site. Things like that. I'm much better at mind control than the ordinary vampire. I won't have to terminate Tina when I'm done with her unless she does something to displease me."

"Good to know." Ray slung his arm around me. "But this is the second serious breach of security in your operation. Blade, now a stalker who could have harmed Glory. I think you owe me a favor, Destiny."

"Really? What kind of favor?" Simon leaned down, said something to Tina and she hurried away.

"I'm having a little get-together at my home next Wednesday. I'd like to show some of the local people that I'm not such a new vampire, that I have some connections. You know what I mean?" Ray stepped away from me, like it was time for a man-to-man talk.

"Well, you *are* very new at this." Simon's smile was indulgent.

"Right. But I'm used to being a star. With the kind of respect that brings. The vamps around here don't get it. They aren't showing me the proper deference." Ray squared his shoulders. Even in a terry robe and flip-flops, he was still the kind of man a woman couldn't take her eyes off of. "Hell, I've won Grammys, been on TV, own an island and have more millions than I could spend in a hundred lifetimes." Ray grinned. "Now I'll be living long enough to try, you know what I mean?"

"Oh, yes." Simon visibly relaxed, obviously sensing a kindred spirit. "It's why I love being King of the Energy Vampires. I'm feared, yes, but also respected. Some of the clients who come here are nothing. Living hand to mouth. No talent, nothing special about them. I can see you deserve to take your rightful place as a leader in the vampire community."

"See? I knew you'd get it." Ray glanced at me. "Glory,

she doesn't understand. I know you and she had some issues. Old news. Now that she's under my protection, she's safe from any reprisals from you, am I right?"

"Of course." Simon smiled at me. "Would you like my oath on it, Gloriana?" ·

I nodded, sure if I spoke I'd spew chocolate all over his expensive Italian loafers.

"Very well. I swear on Honoria and the EV bible that I will not harm Gloriana as long as she is under Israel Caine's protection."

"Excellent. Feel better, baby?" Ray put his arm around me.

I nodded again. Oh, the nausea. Would we ever get this over with? In my head I was busy counting winter skirts in my closet. I'd already done the purses and the shoes.

"Now, about that favor. What did you have in mind, Ray, if I may call you that?"

"Sure, Simon. I just want you to drop by the house. At this little party I'm throwing. Just come by and hang out for a few minutes. Show that I'm the kind of guy who has powerful friends in the vampire world. Wednesday about ten o'clock. Think that'll work? Afterward, maybe we can talk about that endorsement you wanted."

"I wouldn't come alone, of course. And some of your new vampire friends may be afraid of us. Even hate us." Simon looked at me, like he knew that behind the stack of sweaters I was sorting, I hated him with a passion that bordered on the kind of obsession Tina had.

"Even better." Ray got a firm set to his chin that surprised me. "Hey, I'm not in this to make friends. I *have* friends. May even make my best friend vampire before all is said and done. Thing is, respect is what I'm after. I have a feeling you understand that."

"Yes. And perhaps one day we can sit down and discuss what it would take to make you an Energy Vampire. I think you would enjoy the perks. Like constant access to the sunlight rooms." Simon's cell phone vibrated, and he shook his head. "Sorry, I'm expecting a call and need to take this. Please enjoy your last night in the room. I guarantee you'll not be disturbed. I'll post two guards at the door. And I'll see you Wednesday night. Ten o'clock."

"Great." Ray reached out to shake Simon's hand, but I grabbed it and tugged Ray toward our room.

"Come on, baby, I'm ready to see the sun. You've kept me standing here so long, I've had time to totally reorganize my winter wardrobe."

"Oops, better go. Later, dude." Ray waved and we watched Simon walk off talking on his phone. *"What was that about?"*

"Never shake his hand. He can do some kind of mind meld on you and know everything despite you singing the top forty in your head. Trust me. You don't want to touch him."

We spent the rest of the night playing in the water, soaking up the sun and keeping our swimsuits on. I'm sure Simon was disappointed in the video, but I was just anxious to get this visit over with so I could go see Jerry. Mission accomplished as far as Aggie was concerned. Wednesday night all we had to do was lure Simon and company out to the deck and Aggie would take care of the rest. So since it seemed I might live past the full moon after all, I'd better see if it would be with a certain Jeremy Blade in my life or out of it.

Fifteen

Sunday night I drove to Jerry's house, a morose Valdez in the passenger seat. We might have to walk home or call a cab. The Mercedes convertible actually belonged to Jerry. My old Suburban was dead, though, in the alley behind my shop. The repairs to fix it would cost more than it was worth. Time to either buy a new car or . . . Well, I really couldn't think about practical stuff like that now. I was too busy trying to figure out how to fix things with Jerry.

"So what exactly did you tell Jerry when he found you?"

"*For the hundredth time, I said you and Caine were out at the EV headquarters trying to figure out a way to get Simon to the lake. So the Siren could send him to hell instead of you guys.*"

"See? And we did it. So that part worked out. And here I am. Safe and sound." I gripped the steering wheel. "And you still have a job."

"*First he fired me. Because I broke my contract.*" Valdez snorted. "*Brittany was the one who explained that you ordered me to shift. I wasn't about to go begging for my job back.*"

"Brit did the right thing."

"*Yeah, yeah, but I ended up giving him an extra year tacked onto the end of my contract. Letting you go out there to the EV hellhole*" *was a big mistake. If nothing else, I should have had Brit make a call to Blade. Letting him know what you were up to."*

"I don't know why Jerry is keeping you on anyway. He's through with me." I was not going to cry again. No point. I'd made a big mistake too. Jerry had caught me with my top down. He had a right to be mad. But we weren't exclusive and he'd said unforgivable things. *I* had a right to be mad. This circular argument had been running nonstop in my head every waking hour since the big showdown. I should take my pride, turn the car around and go home. Let Jerry come repossess it if he wanted it back.

"You still got a chance there, Blondie. Go. Grovel. If Blade didn't still love you, he wouldn't have gone off like that." Valdez, mind reading as usual, looked over at me when we stopped at a red light. *"I mean, you weren't actually doing it with Caine when he walked in, were you?"*

"No! We didn't, haven't, done 'it.' I'm attracted. I admit it. He's Israel freakin' Caine. You know how I feel about Ray's music. There's something about actually being around the singer of the sexy songs . . ." I accelerated when the light changed. "Hell, I'm getting off to the attention as a rocker's girlfriend too. I've got figure flaws and yet this incredibly hot man is making serious moves on me. Isn't even ashamed to pretend to be engaged to me. Oops." I slipped off my engagement ring and dropped it into my purse.

"Yeah, that would be cool. Walk into Blade's house wearing another guy's ring." Valdez used his paw to lower the window then stuck his head out, the cold air blowing his fur around his face. *"I bet Blade really went ballistic when he saw that."*

"Oh, yeah." I blocked my thoughts. I'd refused to tell Valdez the gory details of just how "ballistic" Jerry had gone. Not even Flo knew it all. Jerry's disdain for me had hurt too much. I pulled up in front of his house and saw the lights were on. Garage door was down so I didn't know if his car was there or not, but I sensed he was inside. I always knew when Jerry was near, and didn't that bring fresh tears to my eyes.

Was I insane to think he'd even let me in? My stomach

knotted and I almost hit the accelerator and kept going. But I wasn't ready to give up on us and I had something I needed to say to Jerry. *If* he'd listen to me. So I turned off the engine, took a breath and looked over at Valdez.

"You going to be okay if I just park you out on the front porch, V?"

"Sure. I'm not jonesing to witness your humiliation." Valdez laid his head on my thigh. *"Sorry, Blondie. Sorry as hell. You have a right to your feelings. Whichever guy you want, go for it. Just think about your history with Blade. He's been taking care of you for a long time. The man deserves respect. Ya know?"*

"I love him, V. I do. But Ray's my friend. I admit he's been pushing to make it into something more but . . . Well, Ray didn't deserve to be attacked like that. Jerry didn't give either of us a chance to explain what was going on out there." I tucked my impossible hair behind my ears. "Oh, hell, it looked worse than it was."

Valdez raised his head.

"Never mind. I do owe Jerry an apology. For dodging his calls and being gutless about this whole Siren thing. I should have come clean about it from the get-go."

"And worry him when he was an ocean away? No, you did what you had to. Quit second-guessing. Just get in there and say what's in your heart." Valdez chuffed. *"Jeez, listen to me. Dear Abby in fur."*

I leaned down and put my cheek against his head. "Thanks, old pal. I need a friend right now. I can't afford you, but if Blade *had* fired you, you'd always have a home with me if you needed it."

Valdez looked up, his eyes gleaming. *"You haven't seen me in human form, but I'll remember that. Flo's room is empty. I'm claiming it."*

"Fine." I opened the car door and climbed out, then waited while Valdez hopped out and trotted to the front door.

He stopped on the porch, his growl alerting me that all was not right in his world.

"What's up?"

"Blade's not alone. There are at least four other vampires in the house. And three of them are not good guys."

I rang the bell and pounded on the door. If Jerry didn't answer in less than two minutes, Valdez and I were going right through the leaded glass insert. No, wait, I had a key. I was digging in my purse when Jerry flung open the door.

"Well, I guess I'd better ask you in before Valdez decides to tear someone apart." He looked at my dog. "Stand down. These vampires are under my protection."

"You sure, boss? I'm not liking the vibe I'm getting here."

"Are you questioning me?"

"Guess not." Valdez tucked his tail. *"Glory asked me to wait on the porch. Where do you want me?"*

"Porch is fine. Come in, Gloriana." Jerry wasn't smiling, but at least he hadn't left *me* on the porch.

"Who else is here, Jerry? Did you bring Lily home with you?" I followed him into the living room. A nice fire blazed in the fireplace. A woman and three men sat on the sectional couch in front of a big-screen television watching a particularly gory slasher movie. They were laughing and pointing out how lame the details were. Nice.

Jerry picked up the remote and hit a button, pausing the action as a werewolf bit into a woman's breast. The men high-fived each other.

"Cool, Blade. Let's see if we can do that all the way through." One of the men tried to grab the remote.

"After I leave the room. I have a guest. Lily, let me introduce you to Gloriana St. Clair. Glory, this is Lily Mac-Tavish."

"Oh, the infamous Glory. The one my mother hates. Great to meet you, Glory. Anyone Mother hates is a friend of mine." Lily got up and stood next to Jerry. She had Jerry's dark hair, her mother's pale skin and a fabulous figure set off by a tiny T-shirt and low riding jeans. Her feet were bare.

"Great to meet *you*, Lily." I nodded and smiled, liking her immediately.

"And these gentlemen," Jerry said the word like he

didn't even begin to mean it, "are Dracula, Benjamin and Lucifer."

"Call me Drac. I'm Lily's guy. Benny and Luke are my running buddies. We're here to protect my lady." He jumped up and gave Jerry a warning look. "Seems this guy's trying to make a claim on her."

"As my daughter, Drac. I hardly think that will harm her." Jerry glanced at me, then tossed the remote between Benny and Luke, who had remained on the couch.

All three men were beautiful in their own way. Drac had dark good looks, very edgy with a restless energy that kept him moving around the room, touching a book here, a silver box there, all the while watching Lily with a hunger that was easy to interpret.

Benny looked like a fallen angel, blond, with startling turquoise eyes and long golden lashes. He smiled and I almost gave him a reflex smile back until I saw his tongue flick his fangs, a sensual invitation in the vampire world.

I turned my attention to Luke, Lucifer. Oh, yes. Another angel, this one Dracula-dark. He had a calm about him, like he could wait forever for his prey, then would happily enjoy ripping it into pieces. I shivered as he watched me with dark eyes then smiled and nodded.

"A pleasure to meet you, Gloriana. Perhaps you'd like to sit here and watch the movie with us." He patted the couch next to him.

"No, she would not." Jerry gave all three men a warning look then put a proprietary arm around me. I took it as a good sign and was bold enough to take advantage, slipping my arm around his waist.

"Gloriana and I are going upstairs. If you leave to go hunting, remember what I said. Be discreet. If you kill a mortal or leave a witness remembering your feeding, I'll make sure you regret it." Jerry said this so firmly that even I got a shaky feeling in my stomach. The men merely nodded.

"Gee, Dad, lighten up. They gave their word." Lily grinned at me. "Blade's really protective, isn't he? He's worried we'll get caught and staked or something. I think it's cute. We're doing the DNA thing this week and I almost hope he *is* my father, though I loved MacTavish of course. He was the best of dads." She blinked and looked down. Drac rushed to her side to hug her and murmur in her ear.

"You *should* be careful. Jerry, Westwood made an attempt on me the other night. Did Valdez have a chance to tell you?"

Oh, boy, Jerry did not want to hear that yet another secret had been kept from him. "No, he did not. Lily, men, there's a hunter in Austin who uses olive-wood arrows and shoots with a bow. Watch out for him. He has a ranch west of town. When he hunts he wears special goggles that allow him to identify vampires. Take care if you see anyone suspicious wearing dark glasses or goggles."

The remote hit the coffee table and skidded to the carpet.

"All right!" Benny and Luke jumped up.

"We've got ourselves a challenge, boys." Drac rubbed his hands together and his grin was full fanged. "Let's find this hunter. What's his name again?"

"Westwood. Brent Westwood. If you can take him out, I'll personally pay a sizable reward." Jerry smiled grimly. "I expect you to bring me proof, of course."

"Ah, I love it. I say we chop off his head. That would be excellent proof. Right, Blade?" Drac actually had the nerve to slap Jerry on the back. A look from Jerry sent him back toward the couch.

"Hey, Benny, did you bring your ax?" Drac picked up a black cape and threw it over his shoulders.

"Of course. Never travel without it. You know, I was afraid this trip would be boring. Let's get the hell out of here." Benny and Luke threw on similar capes, Benny pulling a lethal-looking ax out of his. He grinned at me. "What do you think, Gloriana?"

"Uh, awesome." I refused to cringe when he sliced the air near me.

Lily looked at Jerry and me and rolled her eyes. "Don't

worry. I'll go with them and make sure they clean up any messes they make." She sat down and slipped on black suede boots, then picked up her own black cape and followed them toward the rear of the house. We heard the back door slam.

Jerry stepped away from me as soon as the men left the room. He picked up the remote and turned off the television.

"Why does she run with that crowd?"

"She says they amuse her. But it goes deeper than that. She made Drac over a hundred years ago and feels responsible for him. And his gang keeps her on her toes and away from her mother. You heard her attitude about Mara."

"Yes." I looked toward the staircase. Would we still go up to his bedroom? I wasn't sure if I was for or against that idea.

"Why did you come, Gloriana?" Jerry sat in a chair, not even waiting for me to sit somewhere. Still not treating me with respect. And not heading upstairs.

"To apologize. I'm very sorry that you saw what you did out there. I made a mistake. Ray and I set up a phony engagement. To protect me from Simon. Anyway, we knew we were on video in that sunlight room. Things obviously got out of hand." My knees felt weak and I sat in a chair across from Jerry, where I could see his face.

"I know what I saw. And things don't get 'out of hand' unless you're feeling something." He glanced at my hand. "Where's his ring?"

"I just wear it for show, Jerry. It's part of the act. And what you saw . . ." Here was the hard part. I looked him straight in the eyes and opened my mind to him. "Okay, I admit it. I'm attracted to Ray. It's a lust thing. That's all. But I'm not in love with him." I bit my lip and felt sappy tears well in my eyes. I blinked them back, determined not to use that old female trick to soften him.

"I've loved you for a very long time, Jeremiah Campbell. Even you have to admit we've gotten comfortable together."

I took a steadying breath. "Ray was something new and, for a while there, maybe I forgot how special you make me feel. And how I feel about you." I got up and walked over to Jerry.

I couldn't read his expression but he *was* watching me. There wasn't exactly warmth in his gaze, but none of the chill that had frozen me in the sunlight room either. Here it was. If he rejected me now, I guess it was all over.

"Jeremiah, I know you have a lot of pride. So do I. You hurt me deeply when you called me a whore. I feel that you've wronged me too. I have *not* made love with Israel Caine. I've been true to you. To what we have. If you don't believe me, then I'll leave and that's that." I stood very still and breathed through that urge to cry again.

Jerry stood. I didn't try to read his mind. That would be cheating. If he wanted to read mine, fine. He'd see that I'd told him the truth. To accept me or reject me, he was going to have to say the words. I didn't breathe again. Just waited.

"I do have a lot of pride, Gloriana. It's how I was raised as heir to the laird of Clan Campbell. Maybe it's made me arrogant, but I thought that I was enough for you." He shook his head.

I wasn't about to comment. Arrogant? Some would call Jerry confident. Whatever, it was one of the reasons I knew I could lean on him, why he made me feel safe when no one else could. I felt myself sway toward him but resisted the urge. He wouldn't look at me, but stared at a spot over my head. Not a good sign. I let my hand fall to my side.

"I know we've taken breaks before. Usually by mutual consent. This time, I thought we were still together when I left here. That's why when I saw you like that with Caine, it hit me like a knife between the ribs." Jerry put his hands on my shoulders and finally looked into my eyes.

I held very still, afraid that this was sounding like a kiss-off. Oh, God, no. I wanted to close my eyes, but couldn't, in case this was the last time he'd let me this near to him.

"I consider you mine, Gloriana. He had his hands on you.

Your breasts were touching his body. God damn it, woman, those beautiful breasts should be seen by no man but me, touched by no man but me." He crushed me to him and took my mouth with his.

I stopped thinking and tasted him, tasted blood where his fangs scraped against my tongue. And I didn't mind. If I was his, then he was mine. No love words yet, but I could wait for those. Or could I? He slung me up into his arms and carried me toward the stairs. I grabbed the post at the bottom and stopped him in his tracks.

"Wait. I have to know, Jerry. Do you believe me? Or is this just a territorial thing? If we're not okay, you can put me down right now." Yeah, maybe my timing sucked, but once we hit the sheets, I didn't want to have to rehash things. I wanted this settled.

"Aye, lass, I believe you. I think I'd know in my gut if you'd lain with another man." His smile was rueful. "Maybe that's crazy."

"Which is it, Jerry? Do you believe me or your gut?" I stared up at him.

"Gloriana, I want us to be together. You came here. To me. Not to Caine. That's all the proof I need that I'm the only man you want. Now can I carry you up the damned stairs or not?"

"One thing." I nipped his neck, not entirely satisfied with his answer but willing to let it go for now.

"What?" He growled and stroked my backside.

"Let Valdez in off the porch, will you? It's cold out there, and I don't want Drac and his buddies to get the idea that he's fair game."

"That shifter deserves to freeze his balls off for letting you go out to the EV headquarters unguarded, but as you wish." Jerry carried me over to the front door and reached around me to open it. "Inside. Don't say a word. The lass here thinks you should have a place by the fire. I'd as soon you had icicles on your arse." He kicked the door closed and carried me up the stairs.

I waved at Valdez over Jerry's shoulder and the dog winked at me before he ambled over to settle in front of the fireplace. Jerry stepped inside his master suite and slammed the door shut behind him. A fire was going in the fireplace near the king-size bed and provided the only light in the large space. The bedclothes were rumpled, like he'd flung out of bed at sunset and hadn't bothered to straighten the covers. As if he would.

I expected him to lay me on the bed. Or toss me on the bed as he'd done a few times before. He did neither. Instead he carried me to the rug in front of the fireplace. It was a fur throw, dark, soft and probably cost the earth. Didn't matter. I lay back and watched the firelight play on the contours of his face, waiting for what Jerry would do next. He sat beside me and stared into the fire.

"You said we were comfortable together."

"Yes. It's a good feeling." I sat up, well aware that the black miniskirt I'd put on in hopes of stirring some lust in Jerry had ridden up to panty-revealing heights. And those panties were of the skimpy-thong variety. I tugged off my black leather coat and tossed it aside. If Jerry bothered to look, he'd see a red satin blouse that I'd unbuttoned to the edge of the corset I wore underneath. The shiny fabric glinted in the firelight. Not that Jerry was noticing.

I crawled over, pressed myself against his strong back and put my arms around him. "That seems to bother you."

"Hell, yes, it does. Comfortable to me means boring, predictable." Jerry took my hands and pulled both my thumbs to his lips. "Caine must not be any of those things."

"We will not discuss that man in this room." I used a vamp move to leap over Jerry and land in his lap. "I never said you bored me. Right now I can't wait to see what amazing things you'll do to me." I unbuttoned my blouse. "Especially when you see this." I pulled off the satin and flung it across the room.

"You do have a most interesting wardrobe." Jerry fingered the lacing between my breasts, his eyes dark.

"Occupational hazard. Vintage clothing is my specialty. This little number was worn by a courtesan in New Orleans in the eighteen nineties." I arched my back when he cupped my breast.

"I'm not here for a history lesson. But why don't we visit that den of iniquity?" Jerry leaned forward and ran his tongue along the edge of the corset.

"Umm. I like the way you think. But can you afford me, monsieur?" I pushed him back, stood and walked away from him, twitching my bottom as I circled the foot of the bed.

"Depends. What services do you offer?" Jerry grinned and was suddenly behind me, his hands making quick work of my skirt. It dropped to the floor and I kicked it away. I kept on my high heels, liking the way they added a sexy sway to my walk.

"Everything, of course." I looked back over my shoulder. "Well, almost everything." I winked. "I'm not really into pain, but if you want me to hurt *you* . . ."

Jerry ran his hands up my thighs to my waist, then turned me to face him. "I'd like to see some of your tricks."

"I am very particular about my clientele." I pushed on his chest and backed up. "You wear too many clothes for me to judge whether you are even worthy to see my price list." I clapped my hands twice. "Undress. I must judge your, um, attributes."

"You're confused, mademoiselle, or is that madame?"

"Mademoiselle, of course. I shall never marry, despite rumors to the contrary." Oops, too close to a recent issue. "Now what is this confusion?"

"If I'm paying, I should see *your* goods, shouldn't I?" His eyes raked over me, head to toe and back up again.

"You're seeing most of them." I untied the bow on the corset and loosened the ribbon. My breasts took advantage, popping free until I was definitely showing nipple. I did another turn around the room, staying out of Jerry's reach. "Now take off your shirt. Do you have a manly enough chest? I wonder. I hate a thin, weak chest on a male."

Jerry grinned and ripped off his dark blue shirt, buttons flying. I'm sure his housekeeper would have fun when she got to vacuum some night. He pounded on his hard chest like he'd just left his cave.

"This manly enough for you?"

"Well, it *looks* firm enough. Let me feel." I moved closer and ran my hands over him, teasing his nipples with my fingertips. When he reached for me, I danced out of the way. "No, no, no. Not yet. I haven't seen the most important part. Your equipment. The pleasure center. It must be of a size to touch me"—I slid my fingers inside my thong—"deep inside."

"Gloriana," Jerry groaned. "This game is going to kill me."

"No, it's not. It's going to be a bit uncomfortable for a while, but that's the point, isn't it? We don't *want* to be *comfortable*." I smiled and reached for his belt buckle. "Now take off you pants, monsieur."

"You do it. I hope I don't shock you, mademoiselle. I am ready to please you. Bursting to please you." He stood still while I unbuckled his belt and unzipped his pants. I slid them down his legs and he stepped out of them. His boxers strained with his erection.

"You have a very proud gentleman here." I peeked inside the elastic waistband. "And he is eager to come . . . out." I pulled down his underwear and tossed it aside. I stepped back to study him, tapping my chin and frowning as if trying to decide if he would do or not.

"Well? Is he up to your standards?" Jerry didn't touch me but his face was flushed and I could tell he was on the verge of tossing the game out the window and me on the bed.

"Don't rush me. I'm thinking." I ran into the bathroom and found a washcloth, wetting it with warm water. I strutted out to the bedroom and found Jerry still standing in the same spot as if he was afraid to move or he might lose it, if you know what I mean. I dropped to my knees in front of him and ran the warm cloth over and around the length of him. I reached between his legs, using the cloth to stroke his heavy sacs.

"What the hell are you doing?" He put his hand on my head.

"I've decided he'll do, but we have procedures here, monsieur. We always make sure our customer is clean before we do this." I smiled, then took Jerry into my mouth. His gasp of pleasure was all I needed to hear. As ready as I'd made him, Jerry is a vampire after all and was more than up to the task of allowing me to take my time to please him.

I felt his hands in my hair as I used my lips and just the slight touch of my fangs. "You have quite remarkable staying powers, monsieur."

"You're torturing me, Gloriana. Lie back and let me love you."

I ignored him, sliding my hand between his legs to touch the base of his sex. His gasp was my reward. Did I want him to suffer? Well, he *had* made that remark about his mother . . . I finally leaned back and smiled up at him.

"What would you like to do now?"

"First I want to see more of you. I like this corset, mademoiselle. So I will not use one of my knives on it. Kindly remove it." He sat on his heels and watched me slowly pull the ribbons apart. When they were loose enough, he pulled the corset off over my head.

I still had on my matching red thong, but he made no move to take it off yet. Instead he lay me back again and made love to my breasts, his lips moving over every inch of them. He pulled first one nipple into his mouth and then the other. He drew on them until I thought the pressure would drive me mad. Just when I thought he would surely tire of this, he started all over again. He slowly circled one nipple with his fangs, then the other and I felt shivers run down my body all the way to my toes. Next he used his tongue to trace the same sensual path. Finally, he used his lips, pulling them inside his warm mouth and suckling until I gripped his hair.

I didn't try to read his mind, but I wondered if all this attention above the waist wasn't to erase Ray's touch. By the time Jerry had thoroughly explored every inch and suckled my nipples, I was wild and begging for him to move on.

He lifted his head, his eyes bright. "Move on? How about here?" He placed his palm against my mound. "There is something very sweet behind this very tiny panty." He plucked the lacy front then ran his finger underneath to tease my folds. I moaned and parted my legs.

"You are very eager. One would think you had not had many clients recently."

"I told you. I am very—oh God, yes!—particular." He pushed another finger inside me, stroking me until I trembled.

Jerry eased his hand from me and kissed my stomach. He sat back and studied me, his eyes dark and his hair wild. God, but he looked good to me, all that was masculine and strong. His firm lips, his taste, I wanted all of him. He smiled and I saw his fangs gleam in the firelight. I reached for him, but he shook his head.

"Our game is not done. I can afford more of your time and you are so very pretty. Roll over. I want to see the back of these panties again."

The hell with our game. I bit back an objection and rolled over. He toyed with the thin string that rested between my buttocks and I had to admit it stirred me and made me want him even more.

"Interesting. Why do you bother? Or perhaps this is more costume, for your clients, and not underwear at all. It can't be comfortable."

"It's fine. But you are certainly free to remove it. I hardly notice it anymore." I sighed, then shuddered, when I felt his tongue trace that little string, then his fangs follow. "Please. Take it off if it is in your way."

"Yes." He pulled it off, then lifted my hips, kissing a path down between my thighs. I cried out, so sensitive, so desperate for him to take me.

"I . . . Jerry, it's been so long. I need you. Please, please take me now."

"Jerry? Who is this man? I'm a customer, nothing more. I'm paying for your services, mademoiselle, and *I* will say when I take you."

Okay, this game had definitely stopped being fun. I rolled over and sat up, my arms across my breasts. "Monsieur, your time is up. Pay the madame when you go downstairs. I have another client waiting. One who is kinder."

"Gloriana, I—" Jerry reached out. "I'm sorry. I guess I wanted to hurt you. I can be a bastard, can't I?" He tried to pull me into his arms and I allowed it.

"Yes." I rested my head on his shoulder, thinking. So he'd forgiven, but not forgotten. Who could blame him? If I'd walked in on him and Mara doing what Ray and I'd been doing? Hell, I'd have tried to scratch her eyes out, and then I'd have figured out a way to make Jerry pay, even while probably taking him back so Mara couldn't have him.

"Shit, I blew it, didn't I?" Jerry settled me in his lap, both of us still naked. It wasn't exactly the ideal way to have an important discussion about our future together, or lack thereof.

"No, I guess *I* did. You're still seeing Ray and me together, aren't you?"

"Hell, yes. You were in sunlight. I'd never seen you in real sunlight before. You looked beautiful and happy. And as good as naked. With another man. I really wanted to kill both of you."

"I understand. I do. I can't ever erase that memory for you. All I *can* do is ask that you give me a chance to prove that you can trust me. That we can make more of our own memories together. And, Jerry, you're going to have to keep dealing with Ray. Seeing Ray and me together, while we pretend to be engaged for a while longer. You can't kill him. And I hope you didn't really want to kill me."

Jerry's arms tightened around me. "It makes me crazy that the man attracts you. Of course I see your interest when you look at him, and it's not all because you're such a fine actress.

Damn it, Gloriana, I think I should be enough for you. Let me prove to you that I can be." He rolled me under him and kissed me like we were going to die in the next moment.

I opened my mouth and my heart to him. We touched everywhere, setting small fires and blazing infernos. The heat from the fireplace was nothing compared to ours as we claimed each other. Jerry's mouth was a torch that set fire to all parts of me.

I tasted him and knew just what he liked and where he liked it. There was much to be said for the familiar, the warmth of a comfortable fire on a winter's night or the light in the window of home after a long journey when one has been lost. I was home now, found. Why had I ever given in to wanderlust and forgotten how much this meant? I loved this safety, this perfect harmony as we moved and held each other. Jerry shouted just when I cried out, together reaching the same insanely perfect place where no one existed but the two of us. Safe. Warm. Together.

If only we could shut out the rest of the world. But even one uninterrupted night was probably too much to hope for.

Sixteen

"I like Lily. She looks like you, you know." I lay next to Jerry in the bed, finally relaxed enough to carry on a normal conversation. Which meant we'd made love three more times and seemed to have worked out our mutual frustrations with each other. Not that we'd discussed them. Jerry was typical male, not into talking about feelings. But I'd take the nonverbal cues. Like the way he held me and looked at me without the shadows in his eyes.

"I wish she didn't have Dracula and his gang with her. I think she has real potential to be a fine person. But she rebelled against her mother years ago and has kept up the pattern." Jerry rubbed my arm. "If the test shows she's mine, I'm taking a stand with Mara. She's going to have to let me work with Lily to try to change her ways."

"Good luck with that." I sat up and stared down at him. "Lily's an adult, Jerry. A woman who's been on her own for centuries. She obviously doesn't give a flying fig what her mother thinks. You can no more control Lily than you can control me."

"Back to that, are we?" Jerry sat up next to me and looked me in the eyes. "Fine. I'm a controlling bastard.

What's new, eh? If you hate it so much, walk away. Take up with your new lover permanently."

"Stop right there." I put my hand on his mouth. "He's not my lover. You said you believed me."

"Aye." He nipped my palm. "But I'm still jealous as hell. You'll just have to put up with it."

"Fine." I put my hand behind his neck and pulled his face close to mine. "And as for your controlling nature, I think you can change, Angus Jeremiah Campbell the Third. Just as you've changed your name and the way you speak over the centuries." I kissed the corners of his firm mouth, then used my teeth on his earlobe. "You just don't *want* to change. You *like* controlling me. You *love* controlling me."

"That I do." Jerry rolled me under him and surged into me, proving once again that he had the stamina of a stallion. "But I guess if you were easy to lead, you'd have bored me long ago."

"Hah!" I grinned up at him, gasping as he picked up my hips and pressed into me harder. "Now who's been in control? You think that hasn't been my plan all along?"

"Witch." Jerry pounded into me, then leaned down to drink from me, taking what I so gladly offered.

I held on to him and breathed in his familiar scent, the sweet mingling of our bodies and our life force. I'd often wished I could give him a child. And now he had one. Because I'd seen something in the set of Lily's chin, the cast of her head, that left little doubt in my mind that she was Jerry's get. I sighed as he made love to me and offered me his own blood. I decided I would love Lily as if she were my own. And she would bring us closer together. That is what I wished for as we held each other and found release.

Much later, near dawn, I sat up suddenly. "Do you think Valdez will be all right downstairs?"

"Lily will make sure Drac and his crew won't bother him." Jerry reached for me and yawned. "Besides, the shifter is a guest in my home. They harm him at their own risk."

"Valdez would tear them apart anyway." I settled down again, my eyes closing.

"That he would."

Monday night I was in a good mood as I straightened inventory and waited for Jerry to come by. Valdez had survived Drac and company's return, though he'd reported that they were unhappy since they'd had no luck running down Westwood. Benny had threatened to use his ax on Valdez to make Lily a fur coat. All three male vamps backed off when Lily sided with my dog.

"Glory, I give up. Next time Ellen comes in, tell her no more eats in the shop. Say we're gettin' a roach problem." Valdez groaned and sat by my feet. *"Don't suppose I could talk you into a tummy rub."*

"Fat chance." I looked down at his swollen stomach. "And I do mean fat. You and Bri scarf everything down so fast, a roach doesn't stand a chance. What was it today? Blueberry scones?"

"That's not all." Bri pulled a disposable plastic tub out from under the counter. "Take a gander at this. Blueberry spaghetti. What twisted sister thought up this one?"

"I'm not tasting it." Valdez stood up and stretched.

I grinned. "Wow, you have standards?"

"And limits. I'm worried about Ellen. Her last batch of cookies could have doubled as Frisbees. She says daughter Tina hasn't called her once since she took on her new job you know where."

I shuddered, imagining what Tina and Simon were up to out at EV headquarters. "That's bad. I shouldn't care, but I hope that somehow Tina comes out of there in one piece and over her Ray addiction."

"Hey, she tried to kidnap me. Pepper spray me. I say what goes around, comes around. If she didn't have a swell mom, I wouldn't give a rat's ass what became of her." Valdez took an antacid chew from Bri and they both crunched and breathed a sigh

of relief. *"For Ellen's sake, we send a nice wreath to psycho chick's funeral."*

"Valdez!" I had more to say, but a customer came in. Bri dumped the blueberry spaghetti, sealed so we didn't have to worry about those fictional roaches, and we went about our business. Valdez was in his usual spot by the door when Ray, Sienna and Nathan came in a little after midnight. By then there were no other customers, which gave my rock stars a break, but meant my business was in a bit of a slump.

"Wow. Rehearsal must have gone well for you to quit this early." I met them halfway, playing the dutiful fiancée as I lifted my face for Ray's kiss. When I turned my cheek at the last minute, I didn't miss Ray's frown.

"It was great. Ray finally put his heart and soul into the song. Just what I'd been waiting for." Sienna looked around the store. "This is such a cute shop. I see something already I have to try on."

"Are you into vintage clothes?" I followed her to the dress rack.

"Are you kidding? I dig them. Watch old movies all the time. For the costumes. Oh, look, you've got a black lace cocktail dress. Love this." Sienna began pulling out dresses and handing them to me while she chattered about her favorite stars and the clothes they'd worn.

"Glory, why don't you let me help Ms. Star?" Bri approached cautiously. "I'd love to show her our stuff."

"Call me Sienna." The singer grinned, grabbed the clothes and transferred them to Bri's open arms. "Glory, you go hang out with your guy and Nate. I'll be fine. What's your name?"

I left Bri stammering out a reply and walked over to the men. "Nate, do you mind if I steal Ray for a minute? I need to talk to him. In the back room."

"Sure, Glory. But brace yourself. Barry's on his way over. He didn't like the fact that you two leaked an engagement to the tabloids without telling him first. He wants something he can hand to his close contacts that no one else has. Be thinking of a factoid you can give him."

"Like what?" I looked at Ray, who shrugged.

"I don't know, make up a story. Like maybe Sienna's going to be a bridesmaid." Nate looked longingly at the singer. "That would be cool. I figure I'll be Ray's best man. I don't suppose you'd consider making Sienna maid of honor. We could walk down the aisle together."

I'd heard enough. I grabbed Nate by his jacket collar and pulled his face down near mine so I could whisper. "Earth to Nathan. This is a *fake* engagement. There will be no bridesmaids. Got it?"

"Oh, yeah. Sorry, Glory." Nate's eyes bulged. I realized I was cutting off his air supply and let him go.

"So I won't be going into wedding details." I patted his chest. "*I'm* sorry. This has been a little stressful."

"Sure. Bridal nerves." Nate grinned and held up his hands. "Kidding. So instead say something about how you're going to meet Ray's mother next week."

"What?" Ray was suddenly interested in the conversation.

"Sorry, bud, forgot to tell you." Nate looked sheepish. "She's coming. Tried to call you this weekend, but you had your cell off. And you know you can't be reached during the day. Anyway, this engagement story's got her thinking grandbabies. So she's booked a flight to meet your lady." Nate squeaked when Ray seized the jacket this time. "You guys sure get physical. You ever heard the phrase 'Don't shoot the messenger'?"

"Heard it, don't believe it. Come on, Nate, you couldn't head her off?" Ray glanced at me. "Not that I'm ashamed of you, babe, far from it. But no way am I dealing with my mother right now."

"I get it. Ray, let the man go. One crisis at a time. Next week is a lifetime away. Am I right?" I was happy to see Ray release Nathan so he could stagger to a stool and sit.

"Man, you guys have any idea how strong you are? Glad Sienna's hip-deep in dresses or she'd wonder what the hell's up over here." Nathan grabbed a bottle of water Sienna had left on the counter and took a gulp.

"I guess I'm glad she's our only customer, though this isn't helping my bottom line. Come on, Ray, I need to talk to you. Nate, you okay?" I waited until he nodded. "Good. We'll be back in a few. Knock on the storeroom door when Barry gets here if we're not out before then."

Nate nodded again, still drinking water.

Ray followed me to the back room and closed the door behind us. "Well? You and Blade make up?"

I could see he was hoping the answer was no. Flattering and discouraging. I didn't want to play this game and hurt him. Or myself. Every time I kissed him in public, it was harder to pretend it didn't matter that Ray was trying to make something real out of it and I was trying to pretend that I didn't feel anything, yet act like I did. Hello? Did that make any sense at all? Probably not. That's how confused I was.

I sat on the wooden table. Hmm. The last time I'd sat like this Ray had been about to drink from me and Aggie had interrupted. I could see the memory in Ray's eyes and I made sure I kept my ankles crossed like a lady should.

"Yes, we made up. It will take a while for Jerry to get what he saw between you and me out of his mind, but Jerry and I are working on our relationship." I gestured at the chair next to the table. In true contrary Ray fashion, he sat on the table beside me instead.

"If that makes you happy, fine." Ray picked up my hand. "But you're still wearing my ring."

"For the cameras, Ray. There were three paparazzi outside when I came to work tonight." I didn't snatch my hand away, though. That would be childish. Hand-holding was no big deal. Innocuous really. And let loose, his hand could touch dangerous places.

"Hear this, Gloriana St. Clair." Ray pulled my hand to his

mouth and nipped my knuckles, his tongue playing with my ring before he tucked my hand against his chest. "Any relationship you have to 'work' on doesn't stand a snowball's chance. But go ahead, knock yourself out. I'll be here for you. For a while anyway. But I'm not a patient man. So what if I've got forever? I'm not into celibacy, if you get my drift." He released my hand and hopped off the table.

I just stared at Ray. He smiled, obviously pleased that he'd left me speechless.

"You know, I'm feeling pretty good about what we accomplished last weekend. We've got Simon and Damian working on Casanova and the Butcher for Wednesday. Now all we have to do is invite them down to the dock and Aggie should be able to take care of the rest."

"Uh, yeah." I was still reeling from Ray throwing down his "I won't wait" gauntlet. Not to mention the whiplash from that abrupt subject change. "Uh, I figure you can take them down in the elevator to see your boat. Flo said she'd call Damian and let him know Wednesday's the day."

There was a knock on the door into the store. "We're set then." Ray grabbed my waist and swung me down off the table, holding me against him for a moment. "Blade didn't come down too hard on you, did he, Glory? He was really rough out there. I didn't like the way he treated you."

There was real caring in Ray's bright blue eyes, enough that for a moment I felt the stupid urge to cry on his strong shoulder. Cry? About what? Jerry loved me. Ray seemed to still want me. Hey, Glory was riding high. I took a breath.

"Jerry was pissed. And rightly so. I kept a lot of things from him while he was gone. For the wrong reasons. Because I knew he wouldn't approve of what we were doing."

"You always need his approval?" Ray was still so very close, our thighs touching, his hands on my waist.

"Don't twist my words, Ray. He worries about my safety. You and I went into a dangerous situation. Jerry would have tried to come up with a safer alternative than going out to the EV stronghold." Why was I defending my relationship with Jerry? It was none of Ray's business. "This subject is closed."

"Good. I'd rather not talk about the other man in your life. I'd rather there not *be* another man in your life." Ray brushed my hair back over my shoulders. "My mom would love you, you know."

"Doubt it. There will be no grandbabies." I smiled sadly. "My fault."

"Will tells me my swimmers can't do the deed anymore either." Ray couldn't muster up even the semblance of a smile.

"He's right." I touched his cheek. "I'm sorry. And your poor parents. You're an only child so there will be no grand-children in their future."

"Yeah and how do I explain . . . ?" Ray hugged me and rested his chin on my hair. "Guess I'll tell them I had a diving accident down on the island. It happens. Maybe I just found out. 'Cause you and I were talking about starting a family and wondered why I'd never fathered any children." Ray leaned back and smiled sadly. "Tabloids would love to get hold of this."

"No kidding. They already think my big butt and our sudden engagement is all about me springing the 'baby trap' on you. No wonder your mother is thinking she's going to be a grandma. Didn't you warn her against reading the tabloids?"

Ray frowned. "Sure, but she devours those things anyway. You should see her scrapbook."

I reached up and smoothed away Ray's frown lines. "So call her, let her down gently. No need to tell her the really bad news now."

"No, I won't. I'll say she can visit after the Grammys. Maybe we'll have something to celebrate." He grabbed my hand and kissed my palm.

"A Grammy, sure. You can celebrate with your family." I eased my hand away. "But after the full moon she'll be reading about our breakup. I'm really sorry, Ray, but I did go back to Blade and that's how it is." I reached for the doorknob.

"For now." Ray put his hand against the door. "I don't think he's what you really want anymore, Glory. He's a habit you've had for centuries. And I can see that you're different around him. So I'm going to ask you to do something for me."

"What?" Different? Was I? Valdez had told me to grovel to get Blade back, but I hadn't done it. I'd acted like the same independent woman I was right now, hadn't I?

"Just step back a little and watch how you are when you're around Blade and then how you are around me. When are you freer? Happier?" Ray wasn't touching me, but was so close I felt surrounded by his scent and the warmth of his body. His arm was mere inches from my lips.

My breath caught in my throat as his eyes drifted down my body. I'd worn a black cashmere V-neck that dipped low enough to show the edge of my lacy bra. My hips were jammed into black cords with my high heels. I wished I had on a turtleneck as Ray looked down the valley between my breasts. But it was too late. Ray had seen what was under these clothes. Touched me. Tasted me. And I'd encouraged him. Even had moments when I'd wanted him. I remembered to breathe again.

"Ray . . ."

"No, don't say anything now. Maybe I'm wrong. Maybe I'm just seeing what I want to see. 'Cause if I don't get inside you soon, Glory, I'm going to blow apart." He inhaled, like he was memorizing my scent.

I closed my eyes to it because it was a vampire thing I recognized and knew only too well. Part of the mating game we played with each other. I didn't need to inhale him. I already knew his scent as well as I knew Jerry's and wasn't that a hell of a thing?

"Ray, please. This is only going to hurt you." I *had* to

look at him. He was watching me, studying me and trying to read my mind. I was smart enough to block the chaos that passed for my thoughts right now.

"Hear. Me. Out." He touched my cheek, then traced the vein in my throat with his thumb. "Sometimes relationships outlive their usefulness. Me? I think it may be time for you to cut the Scotsman loose. For both your sakes." Ray stepped back from the door. "Think about it."

I stood there a moment trying to figure out how I was going to act halfway calm after *that*. Finally I jerked open the door. I expected to see Barry waiting impatiently. Instead, a nervous Nathan, surrounded by two of the three visiting nightmare vampires, had lifted his fist to knock again. I could see Lily and Drac on the other side of the store talking to Bri and Sienna.

"Benny, Luke, I see you've met a friend of mine, Nathan Burke, and this is Israel Caine. Perhaps you've heard of him. Nathan and Israel are under my protection, men. Which means they are under *Blade's* protection." I crossed my fingers. Hopefully Jerry would back me up on that.

"Israel Caine! Sure. Dig your music." Luke and Benny knocked knuckles with Ray, who actually managed to smile and not cringe. Props to Ray on that. Surely he'd picked up on the serial-killer gleam in their eyes. Nathan linked arms with me and whispered in my ear.

"They showed me fangs, Glory. More vampires. I don't think you want this to become a hangout, do you? Bad PR." He shuddered. "They kept talking about my blood type. You said it was rare. Guess I'm like the daily special. Do me a favor? Tell them again that I'm off-limits?"

"Sure." I saw that the water bottle was empty. "And, Nate, there's a bathroom in the back room. Stay out of sight as long as you can. I'll suggest they move on." I gestured behind me. I smiled as Nate made a wide detour around the vampires. I turned up the classic rock station on the radio. That should help keep Sienna from overhearing while I tried to get rid of my visitors.

"Glory, you have a great shop." Lily walked up with a frowning Dracula in tow. He kept looking over his shoulder at Sienna, who was heading into a dressing room. "Drac, you will *not* bother Sienna. This is Glory's business. You can't use her customers as a filling station."

"Thanks, Lily. And none of you will bother any mortals who are in my shop, especially not my friends." I introduced them to Ray and Nathan. Nathan quickly excused himself and headed to the back room. I blocked an attempt by Luke and Benny to follow him.

"Dude, didn't know you were one of us." Drac looked Ray over.

"Yeah, it's not something I advertise, understand?" Ray didn't smile.

"Totally." Drac glanced at his buddies. "We survive by the same code, man. We won't out you; you do us the same favor."

"Absolutely." Ray put his arm around me and I saw Lily's eyebrows go up.

Hmm. She knew I was with Jerry, now Ray was acting possessive. Well, vamps are complicated. I just smiled until I caught a whiff of something familiar.

I sniffed and moved closer to Drac. "Masculine."

"Yes, isn't he?" Lily hugged him. "That's why I turned him over a hundred years ago. I just love a man with a great body and that whole macho vibe, don't you?"

"No, I mean, yes, of course Drac is masculine, but he smells like a men's cologne called 'Masculine.' Ray's publicist wears it." I narrowed my gaze on Dracula. "Did you feed recently near this shop?"

"Why do you ask, dear lady?"

"That's not an answer, Dracula. Where is he?" I got up in his face and Valdez was suddenly right beside me. Bri hurried to the door, threw the dead bolt and turned the sign to Closed.

"Glory, what the hell are you talking about?" Ray put his hand on my arm, obviously concerned that I was getting aggressive with a vampire a foot taller than I was.

"The mortal who wore the cologne?" Dracula looked unconcerned. "In the alley, I suppose. I didn't take much. I don't *think* I was overeager." Drac looked at Lily. "Blade asked us not to kill mortals on his turf."

"When was this? When you went outside for a smoke?" Lily grabbed Drac's arm.

"Sorry, darling, but he was so perfectly fine. B positive. Turned out to be quite thin, though. Not the blood, the man. I barely started when the idiot fainted." He shook his head when Lily snarled. "Quit overreacting. There was a heartbeat when I tossed him in the Dumpster."

"You threw Barry in the Dumpster?" Ray ran toward the back. "I swear to God, if he's dead, asshole, *you're* dead."

"Like to see you try." Luke and Benny jumped in front of Ray and showed their fangs.

"Stop it!" I pushed between them, almost tripping over Valdez.

"Get the hell out of the way, Blondie." He snarled, putting himself at Ray's side. *"Bring it on, fellas."*

I looked behind Luke and Benny. "Lily? Some help here?"

"Let's all go out and see what the damage is before we start ripping out throats." Lily had her father's calm. Or at least that's the way I saw it. "Drac, you're crawling into that Dumpster."

"But, darling, I have on my new Gucci loafers." Drac pouted as he followed Lily out the back door. We were quite a parade into the alley. I heard a flush as we went through the back room.

"Nathan, stay where you are and keep the door locked. Don't come out until I tell you to."

Luke laughed. "That flimsy door isn't going to protect anyone."

Valdez growled. *"Keep talking and you'll see who protects who around here."*

"Calm down." Lily had stopped outside next to the Dumpster. We all groaned. Mugs and Muffins had obviously dumped some soured milk products recently. The enhanced vamp sense of smell really wasn't helping matters. "Drac, get in there."

"He's probably dead. This is good waste disposal. Don't you think?" Drac looked around for approval.

Luke and Benny were all for it. "Clever, Drac."

"Efficient."

"He'd better not be dead. And you're not getting out of it. Take off your shoes. Those look like expensive jeans. Drop them if you want to and climb in. Pull the guy out. We want to check his vitals for ourselves." Lily had her hands on her hips, obviously the alpha in this pack.

"I'm going commando, love. I might shock Glory." Drac grinned in my direction.

"What'll shock her is how little your package is. Now get in there."

Valdez and Ray slapped paw to hand while I did my best to keep a straight face. Drac gave them a dirty look. Luke and Benny weren't laughing, which made me think Lily pretty much spoke the truth. Drac muttered an obscenity, rolled up his jeans and leaped up and into the stinky mess.

"Here he is, on top of a pile of, shit, well, not shit, but what must be egg shells and old baked goods of some kind. I'm throwing him out."

"No!" Ray and I screamed it at the same time.

"You'll kill him that way, *darling*." Lily looked at me and rolled her eyes, like that's what you get when you choose beauty over brains. "Carry him out and bring him into Glory's back room."

We all watched Drac leap out of the Dumpster, a limp Barry in his arms. Drac walked over to the back door, then laid the mortal on the oak table. Luke carried Drac's shoes inside and we all crowded into the room to assess the situation.

"I can see him breathing." Ray hovered over Barry. "Nate, get out of the bathroom and bring some wet paper towels."

"The rest of you can go back into the shop." I glanced at Drac's filthy feet. "After you clean up, Drac."

Lily shook her head. "I'm sorry, Mr. Caine. I guess this is a friend of yours?"

"My publicist. And a friend." Ray took the wad of paper towels from a wide-eyed and speechless Nate and began washing Barry's pale face. "Glory, what do you think?"

"You're right, he's still breathing. I'll look at him more closely in a minute. Lily, I appreciate what you did with Drac." I saw him come out of the bathroom, roll down his jeans and slip into his shoes. He had a sullen look on his handsome face and he really wasn't happy with his lover. When he'd stepped into the store and closed the door, I continued. "Drac's quite a handful, isn't he?"

"Yes, but I made him during a lust-filled weekend when I was basically out of my mind, so he's my responsibility. I should have known better." Lily sighed. "I may have to stake him some day if he goes too far. But I'm quite fond of him. It's a tough choice."

"Well, I hope Blade *is* your father. Because you're a daughter he'd be proud to acknowledge." I hugged her.

"Thanks, Glory. I'd better get out there. Sienna's just his type. We have an open relationship, but I still have to keep an eye on things. You know what I mean?"

Oh, God, did she sound like her father. "Yes, I do." I turned to look at Barry. Besides the puncture wounds at his neck that Drac hadn't bothered to heal, he was obviously weak from blood loss. He probably could benefit from a transfusion, but that wouldn't be happening. You don't just show up at an emergency room and ask for one. And our blood would turn him vampire. Definitely not happening. He was going to have to sleep it off.

"He'll be okay, Ray. I'll heal those puncture wounds and he should be fine by tomorrow. Lily, do you think Drac bothered to erase Barry's memory of the feeding?" So far, I didn't have reason to believe Drac had done anything right.

"I wouldn't take a chance that he did or didn't." She leaned down and licked the puncture wounds closed. "Here, let me show you a trick I learned in Europe." She put her hands near his heart and pressed. Like a vampire version of CPR or a shot with high voltage. Barry suddenly sat up, alert and wide-eyed. Lily immediately locked eyes with him and told him that he had had an accident and had fallen in a Dumpster. His clothes were a mess and he was lucky that his friends Ray and Glory had found him and brought him into her shop. Then she snapped her fingers.

"Oh, my God! Ray? I swear I only had one martini with dinner. That Dumpster came out of nowhere." Barry tried to get off the table but fell back.

"They must have made it a triple, my friend." Ray helped Barry sit up. "Hate to tell you this, but you reek."

Barry sniffed. "No lie. Glory, sorry about this. I need to talk to you soon about the engagement. Get a quote or two. Not tonight. Still feel woozy." Barry rubbed his head. "Better call me a cab."

"Will do. You lie back and rest. I'll come get you when it gets here." Ray helped Barry settle back down again and the rest of us left the storeroom. Valdez trotted back to the front door, which Bri had unlocked again.

Sienna was at the counter with three dresses and a sweater. "There you are. Glory, I just love this place." She leaned closer. "So many hot guys. Girlfriend, this is a treasure trove." She glanced at Drac, who was giving her hungry looks. "I slipped that one my private number."

"Uh, Sienna, please. He's not . . . That is, his girlfriend's really jealous. I wouldn't go there. They say they're free to date others, but I don't believe it." I began to ring up her sales. "I'm giving you the family discount, not that you need it, of course. And Bri gets the commission."

"Thanks, boss." Bri happily wrapped up the sweater and left the dresses on the hangers.

Sienna whipped out a credit card. "What about the other two guys? I can dig the Goth look and they are so incredibly hot. Oh, what am I saying? I'm leaving Austin in a few days. Long-distance relationships don't work. Ian and I broke up this weekend." Her eyes filled. "That's why the retail therapy."

"I'm sorry." I put my hand on hers. "But you're right. Wait till you get home to L.A. Then you can find someone."

"Los Angeles?" Luke strolled up to the counter. "My hometown. I'm heading there next. This was just a quick stop." He leaned close to Sienna and began talking about hot spots and bars in L.A., even Rodeo Drive, convincing me, at least, that he'd actually been there. I tried to read his mind, but no go.

This was bad news. And Sienna was leaning into him, smiling and tossing her hair. Great, nothing like starting a vampire coven of rock stars with Ray as the first in the circle. I wouldn't put it past Luke to use some mind control on Sienna to get her interested. But, unfortunately, he was hot enough not to need it.

Nathan hovered nearby, obviously trying to decide whether taking on a vampire would be a suicide mission or not. I could read his mind easily. He was determined to be the one to leave here with Sienna. That determination, along with his rare blood type, made him a marked man. I grabbed Ray's arm and whispered instructions in his ear.

Blade walked in just as Sienna was signing her charge slip. He looked around, quickly assessing the situation like he always did. What he saw obviously didn't make him happy. He ignored my huddle with Ray for the moment and crooked his finger at Lily. Surprisingly, she walked up to him.

"What the hell is this gang doing here?"

"I had to bring them somewhere. I wanted to see Glory's shop." Lily kept her chin up and didn't sound a bit defensive.

"I don't like it."

"Lily is welcome here." I felt Ray's arm slip around my waist but decided flinging it off would be undignified. "She was very helpful earlier."

"With what?"

Hmm. Not a question I wanted to answer. Of course at that moment a cab honked out front.

"I'll be right back, babe." Ray grinned and kissed my

cheek, then headed to the back room. He came out with a pale, weak and reeking Barry, who staggered through the store and out to the waiting taxi. Since Barry also smelled strongly of vampire, Jerry didn't have to look far to figure out what Lily had needed to help with.

"What's wrong with Barry?" Sienna rushed to the publicist's side.

"Food poisoning. And an accident with a Dumpster. Grab the door, would you, Sienna?" Ray was handling Barry gingerly, like he really didn't want to come away with milk slime on him.

"A Dumpster?" Sienna stepped back when she got a whiff of him. "God, what else was in there?"

"Don't know. I'm lucky to be alive," Barry mumbled. "Ate bad clams, maybe, or something in that martini at dinner. God, I feel weak. Don't touch me, Sienna. Maybe it's the flu. Might be contagious."

Bad timing. The cabbie heard that and sped away.

Ray looked at me. "Okay, looks like I'm giving you a ride to your hotel, Barry. Glory, baby, see you later. Nathan, you take Sienna to her hotel for me. I'm counting on you, bud." Flashbulbs popped. Paparazzi. "Fellas, give us a break. My publicist got food poisoning. You want a headline? Israel Caine on mission of mercy. Takes ailing friend to doctor. What? Not sensational enough?" Ray shot the finger. Okay, that got him some flashes.

I shook my head. Sienna followed him out, Nathan behind her, his arms full of clothes. The paparazzi went crazy, screaming questions. She stopped and posed.

"Here's your story, guys. This little store is the place to come to meet hot guys. I personally saw five of them in thirty minutes and not one of them had on a wedding ring. I don't know what Glory St. Clair is doing, but she's a man magnet." Sienna turned and blew me a kiss, then headed down the sidewalk. Nathan was by her side, and he turned to give me a grin and a thumbs-up. The photographers trailed them, asking Nathan to spell his name for them.

"Oh, great. Now we'll become the next singles' hook-up scene in Austin." I slammed the shop door before the cameras turned on me.

Bri giggled. "And what's wrong with that?"

Drac growled and looked at Lily. "Yeah, I'm all for it. Time for me to hook up with someone new."

This time it was Lily who shot the finger before she stormed out of the shop. Jerry looked at me, then went after her. Which left me alone with Valdez, Bri and three of the nastiest vampires I'd ever met. Good times.

Seventeen

Jerry was back in less than thirty minutes. It just seemed like an hour. Because I had some regular mortal customers I had to protect from my bloodsucking ones. I finally left the customers to Bri and got the three stooges into the back room to tell them more about Westwood. Valdez stayed with me, ready to defend me if the vamps made a wrong move.

"Guys, I'd really like to see you go after this hunter. Valdez took an arrow in the hip right back here in my alley. Israel Caine was shot in the arm."

"Sounds like the guy's not that swift with his bow and arrow." Benny smirked. "We get the drop on him and he's ours." He pulled his ax out of his cape and ran his thumb over the blade. The resulting droplet of blood had all three guys murmuring excitedly.

"Relax, hotshot. If he was an easy get, we'd have taken him down already." Valdez stayed between me and Benny's ax. *"He's a freakin' billionaire and has lots of high-tech toys he plays with. No tellin' what he'll come up with next."*

"This one of them?" Benny picked up my water cannon and played like Rambo, he and Drac doing mock battle until a bored Luke called a halt.

"Can we get down to business, gents? I, for one, could use a drink. Drac fed, but, Benny, you and I might get lucky if we head out now."

"Listen to Valdez. Remember Westwood took out Mac-Tavish, Lily's father." I was glad Lily hadn't returned. She didn't need to hear this. "The creep takes the fangs as souvenirs, then leaves the bodies in the sun to go up in smoke."

"Mr. Sensitivity, eh?" Luke pulled a derringer out of his cape. "We'll get him. For Lily."

"Thanks, guys. She'll appreciate it." Drac kept opening the door into the shop. Watching for Lily? Or for another hot girl to hit on? I really didn't like him.

"Westwood's been in Europe and he just got back. I've got a map here of his ranch. Maybe you can figure out a way to get the drop on him there." I pulled out one of the copies Jerry had left in the shop the last time there had been a Westwood hunting party. This finally got Drac's full attention. The three men huddled around the map while I eased out of the back room and came face-to-face with Jerry.

"I told Lily not to bring them here again." He looked past me to where the three gestured and talked strategy. Luckily the loud music kept my customers from overhearing. And the black capes they wore were not unusual for this part of town at this time of night. There were two other Goth types in the store right now.

"She's got her hands full. I don't think she can control any of them, though she tries." I reached behind me, gestured for Valdez to come on out, then shut the door. "Ray and I are having a 'party' at his house on Wednesday night. For, um, our Siren. Those three could be our backup plan. In case Simon and company don't show. Think Lily's heart will be broken if we have to use them?"

"I don't know about her, but mine sure won't be. I'll talk to her." Jerry put his arm around me. "I hate that you've had to deal with this creature by yourself. I want to help any way I can."

"No." I smiled to take the sting out of it. "Circe wants

men." I glanced at a customer who was only a few feet away browsing the purses. "You're just her type. I don't want you anywhere close to where she can get her claws on you."

"I'm a man who can handle himself, Gloriana. Or have you forgotten?" He moved in on me, pinning me against the door.

"Ooo. Honey, I heard that." The customer blushed and looked Jerry up and down. "Why don't you take him somewhere private where you can work out your differences?"

"Great idea." Jerry grinned and bowed in the woman's direction. "Glory, we have our marching orders."

"I can't leave. Bri needs my help." Just then Lacy walked in, early for her morning shift. "Well, maybe I could slip out. After you make sure the back room is clear, if you know what I mean."

"You bet." Jerry grinned and winked at the customer who seemed rooted to a spot in front of the purses. "Madame, tell the clerk that your purchase is to be charged to Jeremy Blade. My treat."

"Oh, are you kidding?" She looked around, like what could she buy that would break his bank?

"Jerry, that's a little extravagant, don't you think?"

"Not at all. You can send me a bill, can't you, Glory?" Jerry watched the woman stop in front of the fur coats. "This is a vintage-clothing store, not Tiffany's. How bad can it get?"

"Hey, it can get pretty good from my point of view." I grinned, sent Valdez to his post by the shop door, then followed Jerry into the back room. Benny was arguing with Luke about the best way to approach the Westwood ranch.

"All right. Listen to me." Jerry's voice had the ring of authority and the three men actually stopped and looked at him. "The guards on that ranch all have the vampire detection glasses. They'll make you before you cross the fence line unless you shape-shift into something small and crawl inside. Try that." Jerry turned to me. "Glory, you got a picture of Westwood?"

"On my laptop. Give me a minute." I ran back to the

counter and grabbed my computer, then brought it to the
back. I quickly accessed the file that took me to the picture
of the ordinary-looking man who had made my life hell for
longer than I wanted to remember. "There he is."

Drac snorted. "*This* is the guy who's been stalking you?"
He elbowed Benny, then said something in a foreign lan-
guage that made Luke and Benny laugh.

I glanced at Jerry, who was so not laughing. He stepped
up to Drac, his hands fisted.

"Listen, you piece of shit. Go on out there and try your
luck. Bring back Westwood's head and then you can mock
the Austin vampires all you want. Until then, keep your
filthy mouth shut."

I looked from Jerry to the suddenly silent and sullen
Drac and his buddies. I really wished I was better at lan-
guages. But it was obviously time to get them moving on
out of here before we had a smackdown that would disrupt
the business on the other side of the wall.

"Uh, okay. Now about the ranch. You guys have a car?" I
put my hand on Jerry's fist, just as a precaution.

"Why?" Benny seemed genuinely puzzled.

"Forget I asked. You shape-shift and fly everywhere?" I
couldn't imagine it since I personally don't like doing it at all.
The very idea of shifting whenever I wanted to go somewhere
turned my stomach. "Okay, just head out, then when you get
close to the ranch you can have your discussion about strategy
out there." I could see Jerry was spoiling for a fight and taking out his daughter's boyfriend would be worse than a bad
start to their relationship.

"Trying to get rid of us?" Luke was definitely the smartest
one of the bunch. He tucked his derringer into the inside
pocket of his cape. "We're gone. No worries. Come on, guys.
We've worn out our welcome here."

"We've only got a few hours of dark left anyway. May have
to make this a reconnaissance night. Go back tomorrow for
the full attack." Benny put away his ax.

I wondered why it didn't cut a hole in his cape and he grinned.

"Your mind is so transparent. Anyone ever tell you that, pretty lady?" He showed me a heavy leather head cover for the ax under his cape.

"Stay the hell out of Glory's mind." Jerry growled for good measure. "Now move out." He threw open the back door. "Lily is at my house. Drac, if you don't make it home by dawn, do her the courtesy of calling."

"Aye, aye, sir." Drac gave a mock salute, shifted into a bat and flew after his two friends.

The sky lit up with flashes of lightning and there was a tremendous clap of thunder. No rain yet, but I wondered if they'd blow off hunting Westwood tonight and head back to Jerry's after all. Maybe I should lure Jerry upstairs to my apartment. Valdez could stay down here in the shop and we'd actually have some privacy.

"Creeps." I shuddered as Jerry shut the door and threw the dead bolt.

"Forget them. They're gone. You *are* a pretty lady. I don't say it enough." Jerry pushed me against the door and kissed me like he meant it. He leaned back and ran a finger across my lips. "Caine was acting possessive again tonight."

" 'Acting' being the operative word. He gets off to making you jealous. Don't play into his hands. Play into mine." I pulled him against me. "Kiss me again. I liked it."

I was lying on the oak table, Jerry's hand inside my pants, when I heard the voice in my head. *"Come here, vampy. I've got my sweet Ray, but I need you here too, Glory. Come to Aggie. NOW."*

"Oh, hell!"

"What?" Jerry was busy opening the front fastening of my black bra with one hand.

"Aggie. Inside my head. She wants me out at the lake. Right now."

"Ignore her. This is more important." He popped the

clasp and my breasts sprang free. "There. Isn't that better? I don't know why you bind yourself this way. You have perfect breasts." He pulled my sweater down and sat back to admire the effect. "Now look at that. Round, as nature made you. And the way the wool clings to your nipples . . . Much better." He touched them and I shuddered. "Breasts like this should be free to move." He leaned down to gently tease a nipple with his teeth.

"I'm sensing reluctance to obey, vampy. Move your butt or you'll regret it. How about this?"

I felt a piercing pain in my head that made me scream and clutch my temples. "Oh, my God!"

"Glory?" Jerry sprang off of me. "What the hell?"

"It's Aggie. I can't ignore her. She's trying to kill me."

"Not kill you. Just make you wish you were dead. Yes, of course I can hear you and him. Quit playing and start moving. Out here. Now. Or do you need another demo?"

"No, I'm coming." I sat up, snapped my bra closed, zipped up my pants and shoved my feet into my shoes. "Sorry, Jerry, but I've got to go. You know she'll keep giving me headaches unless I get out there. It must be something important. Or maybe we need to give her an update. I don't know, just that I've got to get to Ray's and the lake."

"I'm going with you." Jerry followed me out to the shop where I grabbed my purse from under the counter.

"No way. Hi, Lacy. Sorry I flaked out on you earlier, Bri, but I've got to go." I sprinted for the front door as a new pain hit my right temple. Not the full-throttle can't-stand-it pain, but sharp enough to get me moving even faster.

"I'm going and that's final." Jerry looked back when Lacy practically tackled him.

"Did you really authorize a Marge Sandowski to charge one thousand and five dollars to your account, Mr. Blade? She's still in the dressing room. It may go higher." Lacy bit her lip, like she was worried Jerry had brought his mistress in here or something.

"Whatever she wants. I've got to go with Glory."

"It's okay, Lacy. Jerry can afford it. And, no, lover, you're not coming with me. Valdez, let's head out." I opened the door and realized the sky was falling. Not literally, but there was a downpour the likes of which I'd seen only a few times since coming to Austin. Seems this town either had a drought or minor flooding. This was obviously flood time.

I grabbed a vintage seventies umbrella, pink and orange polka dot, that I'd intended to sell, and decided this was an emergency. I popped it open.

Jerry took my arm. "You're not leaving here without me. I'll drive you. That little Mercedes won't be able to handle some of the low-water crossings in this weather. I'm sure there are some between here and Caine's place since it's on the lake."

"Yes, there are." Austin has these dips in the roads they call "low-water crossings." Any rain at all and the low water gets high. Why road crews don't just fix them and smooth out the dips, nobody will say. Instead, they spend the money to post signs, even put up measuring sticks so you can see how deep the water is and if you think your vehicle can make it through or not. The way this rain was coming down, my little car wouldn't make it.

Yeah, Austin's weird. That's why I love it and fit right in. Another pain. Aggie. And if she got hold of Jerry . . . I studied the set of his jaw. He was determined. No way was I going to keep him from heading to Ray's, even if he had to follow me. Might as well let him drive his big SUV with the four-wheel drive.

"We'll talk about this in the car." Another pain hit, the left side of my head this time. "Come on." I ran toward Jerry's car, which, fortunately, was parked nearby. The wind caught my cute umbrella and I almost did a Mary Poppins. I wailed as it sailed away into the night.

Jerry hit the remote and the door was unlocked by the time we got there. Valdez hopped into the back before I slid inside and Jerry ran to the other side. We were on the road so fast, I barely had time to stammer out directions while I pushed wet hair out of my eyes and behind my ears.

"Sorry, guys." Valdez shook and water sprayed every-where. *"Damned reflex when I'm in dog body."* He looked out the window. *"Man, this is some storm."*

"Be careful, Jerry. Not just driving. When we get there. I'm serious. Aggie is desperate for male vampires to give to Circe. You'd be a fine sacrifice. No way am I letting that happen." I reached over and put my hand on his thigh.

"I don't intend to let it happen either." He covered my hand with his, then frowned down at my engagement ring.

I slipped it off and stuck it in my purse. "Fine. Stay in the house and you should be okay." The car jolted as we sloshed through some mud and rain. The thunder was loud and lightning seemed to strike all around us. I gasped when a tree was hit next to the road and burst into flames. I grabbed Jerry's hand again.

"That was close." Valdez stuck his head between the seats. *"Aggie still hurting you, Glory?"*

"Every once in a while. Like a cattle prod to the brain." I sighed. "Jerry, when we get there, I don't suppose you'd consider just dropping me off then turning around and driving home." I squeezed his hand.

"No." He dropped my hand and gripped the steering wheel. I looked at the windshield and saw why. The rain was coming down so hard that it was almost impossible to see the road. What we *could* see were sheets of rain blowing so hard they were almost horizontal. The heavy car rocked as wind hit it. I screamed when another pain ripped through my head.

"Damn it, Aggie, we're trying to get there. Do you see this weather?"

"See it? Who the hell do you think caused it? Get your chubby ass out here and help me with this, or we're all going to need Noah's ark."

I moaned and leaned against the dashboard. No, I didn't have on my seat belt. Sue me, but I'm a fairly indestructible vampire, remember? Well, unless Circe got hold of me.

"What's the matter, Glory?" Jerry put the car in park.

"Don't stop. We've got to keep going."

"Can't. The road's impassable."

"Then I guess there's only one thing to do." I felt like crying. Now, that would be swell. Here I'd been so proud of myself. Glory the strong independent woman, blah, blah, blah. And I was about to fall down in a weeping fit because I was going to have to do the thing I hate most in the world. Can you guess?

Yep, girls and boys. I was going to have to shape-shift. Not only that, I was going to have to get the hell out of here into the storm of the century. Okay, I deserved a meltdown. Unfortunately, I didn't have time for one. Aggie gave me a hard right to the temple to make sure I remembered that.

Valdez bumped my shoulder. *"Just wait till I get hold of that slimy slug. Where's the fire, I'd like to know?"* He nudged me again. *"You gonna make it?"*

"What choice do I have? We've got to get across the water. What do you think? Ducks? Fish?" I worked up a smile. "I'm not much for swimming. Maybe one of you could give me a ride."

Jerry grabbed my arm. "You expect to go out in this?"

"No choice. When Aggie calls, Glory listens and obeys." I peered through the windshield. The wipers were going triple time, along with the defroster, but the scene was still hazy. I could see a torrent rushing past a few feet from the front bumper. "Pull over. You can't block the road, they'll tow you once the storm stops." There was a brilliant flash of lightning and I recognized a house.

"Pull into that driveway. The house is vacant. It's for sale and isn't that far down the hill from Ray's. Good news. Once we get across this river, we'll be home free." I ignored the sinking feeling in the pit of my stomach as Jerry swung the steering wheel and parked the car. When he turned off the motor and stared at me, I realized it was time to put up or shut up. The rain lashed the heavy car and it rocked, just to make me feel better. Uh-huh.

"No way are you going out in that."

"Tell your man to shut up and help you, vampy. I need you here ASAP!" Aggie shot a lightning bolt into my brain as an incentive.

I squeezed Jerry's arm until he winced. "This *is* going to happen, Jerry. Now what's the best plan? Or do I just jump out of the car, shift into a bird and try my wings?" I put my hand on the door handle.

He hit the door locks. "You'd be mad to fly in this weather."

"Not helping and childish, Jerry, trying to lock me in. I can break the glass. I do have vampire strength. A fact you usually choose to overlook." I glanced around the comfy leather interior of his very expensive top-of-the-line SUV. "Be a shame to get this wet, and I'd cut up my arm pretty badly, but I'd heal. I'm sure Ray would let me drink from him to speed the process."

Valdez pulled his head back from between the seats and lay flat. Wise dog.

"You threaten me?" Jerry hit the steering wheel with his fist. "Damn it, Gloriana. I'll not—"

"Not what, Jerry? Let me go out in this weather? Or let me drink from Ray?" I smiled and scooted close to cover his fist with my hand. "Give it up and help me out. Advise me. If I shouldn't fly, what do you suggest?" Sure I was trying to turn him up sweet—I'm not exactly a novice in the Jerry manipulation game. He knew it too, and I could see the frustration in his eyes.

"She's still hurting you?" He touched my forehead.

"Why did you have to ask that?" I grabbed my head as the mother of all pains tried to split it in two. "Holy crap, Aggie, I'm getting there as fast as I can!"

"All right, Gloriana. I see this can't be avoided. Why don't I shift into a mastiff? You can become a small animal, a mouse or bird, something I can hold in my mouth. That way I can carry you across. You won't even get wet." Jerry rubbed my eyebrow with his thumb. "Wetter."

"Are you crazy?" I jerked back. "And what if your animal

nature took over? And you accidentally gobbled me up and swallowed me? Not to mention the slobber factor." I shuddered and turned to look at Valdez, who was trying to smother his laughter in the seat cushion.

"Unlike the shifter back there, who can't even control his shaking instincts"—Jerry nodded toward the back—"my animal nature *never* takes over. The slobber is what it is. You'd be safe anyway."

"Not a plan. But I like the mastiff idea." I leaned back to rub the glass and look at the water rushing down the crossing. "Are you sure you can swim strongly enough not to be swept downstream?"

"Don't worry, Glory. He can do it. I'm sure I can do it. We may look like ordinary hounds, but we're not, remember? Our superpowers are still with us." Valdez had ventured closer again. *"I could give you a ride. You wouldn't even have to shift."*

"No, I'm too heavy for either one of you if I stay in human form, especially in that current." I sighed. "There's no help for it. I'm going to have to shift and I know just what I'll be. Something that can cling to you, Jerry, and not let go."

"Let's do it then before that Aggie person hits you with another pain. Brace yourself, I'm opening the door." Jerry hit the locks and opened the door. "Valdez, you go across first. I want to see how the current's running before I take Glory across. Glory, I'm shifting now. As soon as you get out of the car, you'd better start to do the same."

Oh, God, did I hate this. I opened the passenger door on my side and eased over so Valdez could leap out.

"Be careful, pup."

He didn't even look back, just jumped into the water, which promptly pulled him under, then swept him downstream and out of sight.

"Valdez!"

"He'll be all right."

I looked over and Jerry had changed into one of the biggest dogs I'd ever seen. He was powerful with broad shoulders and a square jaw, and the rain pounded on him while he waited for me to get out of the car. I slammed the passenger door shut, already wet from the rain that had poured in, then crawled over to the driver's side. Jerry must have put the keys in his pocket before he'd shifted. Fine. My turn. I jumped out into the rain, closed the door and heard the locks engage. The wind and rain buffeted me as I screwed up my courage and pictured in my mind the animal I intended to become.

"Are you sure this is going to work? Valdez—"

"Look. There he is on the other side."

Sure enough, when I peered through the driving rain, I could see that my dog had made it to the other side. He was a wet and muddy sight, panting from exertion, but he had clearly survived.

"Okay, then. Here goes." I closed my eyes and felt the change shudder through my body. When I opened them again, I was looking up at Jerry. "I'm going to hold on to your back."

"Hop on. Whatever you do, don't let go." Jerry didn't talk inside my head like Valdez did, just used his lips. Very strange coming out of a huge dog.

I leaped up on his back and clung to him like the monkey I was. Yep, I'd decided to be one of those cute little squirrel monkeys. They're the ones with the big brains and agile bodies. Right now I needed all the brains and agility I could get. I dug my fingers into his fur. Not satisfactory. Ears. Yep, those floppy ears made good handles and my feet and toes had good gripping powers too as Jerry leaped into the icy water.

The water moved fast, pushing us away from Valdez, who ran along the other side shouting encouragement. A tree branch came out of nowhere and tried to knock me off. I let it hit me in the back and smelled blood. Damn, that hurt. I wrapped my tail around Jerry's furry back and shivered as I felt the ripple of his strong muscles fighting to keep us from going under.

Water splashed into my face, and I coughed and decided to bury my face in his fur and quit breathing for the duration. I did that just in time, because water rushed over my head and another stick prodded me, trying to break my hold. I gripped Jerry's ears until I smelled *his* blood. My bad, but I wasn't about to let go. I'd kiss it and make it better if we got out of this before dawn. Crap. I would have to think about that possibility.

Finally, finally, I realized the rain was beating on my furry back again and that Jerry was straining up a slope. He staggered to a spot under a carport and lay panting on the concrete. Valdez sat next to him.

"Get off of him, Glory, so he can shift back." Valdez nudged me with his nose. *"And, for God's sake, let go of his ears, you've about ripped them off."*

I looked up and realized my dog was right. I loosened my grip and saw blood on my fingers. Jerry's blood. Tears came to my eyes and dripped onto his fur. I finally allowed myself to breathe and crawled off to land on the concrete beside him.

He looked at me, one moment a dog with bloody ears and wet fur, the next a man who had wet and muddy clothes and bloody ears. He still needed healing.

"You make a cute monkey, Gloriana, but I think you need to shift now, sweetheart." He leaned back against a steel beam and smiled. "Use those vamp powers you were bragging about a few minutes ago."

"A few minutes? Seemed like an hour. Sorry I hurt you, Jerry. I guess I got a little tense out there." Tense and terrified. I checked out my tiny hands, my ugly, tiny clawlike hands. I felt the familiar anxiety building. Could I shift back? Would I ever be the old Glory again? Or stuck in monkey body? I looked around me, shivering.

"Quit stalling, Blondie. Shift back. Aggie's waiting." Valdez bumped against me, knocking me on my furry butt. *"Monkeys don't do it for me. I'd like to see you as a cute little poodle, though. Think Ray or Blade would go for you then? Naw, you'd be all mine."*

"In your dreams." Valdez's teasing had relaxed me a little. I closed my eyes and "saw" myself back in human form. The icky wet feeling of shrinking corduroy jeans clued me in that I'd actually managed it nicely. I sagged down beside Jerry and touched his ear, then kissed him on the lips. "That's a huge relief. I may be getting better at this." A stabbing pain in my head cut the celebration short.

"You just need practice." Jerry touched my forehead. "She's hurting you again, I can see it in your face. Don't worry about my ears now. We can deal with them later. How far is Caine's house?"

I could barely make out the address on the curb. "It's just a few blocks away. We're already wet, let's go." I darted out into the rain, Jerry and Valdez right behind me. Fortunately, Ray's house was uphill after this—hard on the legs, but it meant there was no chance of any more floodwaters to cross. We arrived in less than five minutes. I punched in the code at the security gate even though Valdez was all for leaping over it.

"Enough stunts. You and Jerry used a lot of effort swimming. Save your strength. Now I've got to face Aggie. Jerry, no arguing. You're waiting in the house. If she gets a whiff of you, you'll end up in Aggie's jail, slated for deportation to Circe hell."

Jerry started to argue but I just held up my hand. "I mean it." My voice quivered and a tear slipped down my cheek. "I really can't handle the stress of worrying about you right now. Okay?"

"God, I hate this. Valdez? You'll be with her?" Jerry followed me into the house.

"Every step."

Nathan greeted us inside. "What are you guys doing here? How'd you get in? And where's your ride? Sienna left something here, then when we tried to leave, the road was flooded so we're trapped. She's asleep in one of the guest rooms."

"Don't worry about how we got here. Nate, has Ray clued

you in about Aggie?" I'd had no problem with Nathan knowing about his best friend's vampire world. And he knew Jerry, Valdez and lots of other paranormals. But I was afraid that even a brilliant Harvard-educated man like Nate was eventually going to overdose on all this weird stuff.

"Who?" Nate looked confused.

"Aggie's a problem Ray and I have to solve. I'm sure Ray will tell you all about it tomorrow night. Why don't you go to bed? Jerry's going to need some dry clothes. Can you fix him up with some first?"

"Sure. Come on." Nate gestured toward the stairs.

"Be careful, Gloriana." Jerry gave me a kiss that would've moved mountains if you had a mountain that needed moving. Me? I was too busy fighting off an Aggie pain to notice. Not much anyway.

"Stay inside," I said as I shoved back and ran toward the back door, Valdez on my heels. We both left muddy prints on the floor, but I couldn't work up much concern about that. In the elevator down to the boat dock we could feel the storm still raging. The miracle was that the power hadn't gone out. Why, oh, why had I even thought about that? I prayed I didn't get stuck in the elevator with Valdez while my brain blew apart. We both breathed a sigh of relief when the door opened at the lower level.

The lake was rough, whipped to a froth by the strong winds. Ray's boat bounced up and down at its mooring. Fortunately, Aggie and Ray were settled at a table under the wooden decking that stuck out from the house above. They were still getting hit by spray, but were out of the rain for the most part. Valdez ran to the shelter, then stood there dripping. Finally, my head quit hurting. Ray was as wet as I was so I figured he'd been summoned like I had. He jumped up and helped me to a seat on a bench as far from Aggie as I could get.

"Took you long enough." Aggie stared at Valdez. "I didn't invite the fur face."

"Too bad. I go where Glory goes."

"I don't have time to enjoy a pissing contest with you." Aggie turned her back on him.

"Have you seen this weather? That's why we were late. I had to shape-shift and swim across a river to get here." I put my head down on the table in front of me. "And all with a migraine you gave me."

Ray put his hand on my back. "Shit! You're bleeding! Damn it to hell, Aggie, was all this necessary?"

"Yep. Calm down, lover boy. She'll heal. We've got problems. That's why I called you here." Aggie frowned when there was a triple clap of thunder.

"Relax. We've got you Casanova and two more vampires lined up for Wednesday night. Ahead of your deadline. Give it a rest." He pulled up my sweater. "You shifted? Wow, Glory, you must be exhausted. And I need to heal this."

"Watch it, Caine." Valdez moved up next to me and looked at my back. *"Flesh wound. No big deal, so hands off."*

"Quit fighting, you two. So glad the fact that my back's torn open and I'm about to drop is no big deal." I sat up and shoved Valdez out of the way so I could stare at my puke green nemesis. "Hell, Aggie, I'm wet again. Couldn't you have waited until the rain let up for this confab?"

"This rain won't let up, vampies." Aggie snuffled and wiped her slimy green snout. If I didn't know better, I'd say she was crying.

"What do you mean?" Even Valdez was interested now.

"This isn't your ordinary Austin cloudburst. This weather is courtesy of my boss. I'm in deep doo-doo here."

"Circe did this?" I looked at Ray. "I know she threw a little thunder at you before, but—"

"No, you don't get it. I told you. Circe's not my boss. I just made a side deal with her. To try to rescue my lover. This is the work of my real boss, the Storm God, Achelous. He tracked me down here. What you're seeing tonight is Achy kinda pissed." She waved a flipper and lightning lit up the night sky. A wind gust sent a ten foot wave crashing into the dock, almost tearing the boat loose.

"*Man, I'd hate to see him* really *pissed.*" Valdez backed away when water ran over the deck and covered our feet.

"That's when you get typhoons and Category Five hurricanes." Aggie shuddered. "Anyway, we've got to move everything up."

"Up?" I grabbed on to Ray before I went for her throat. "You know how hard we've worked to get you—"

"Not interested in hearing it. Already heard it actually. But now Wednesday won't cut it. Tomorrow night. Tuesday. Got to seal the deal with Circe Tuesday night or it's Glory, Ray and Will goin' bye-bye. I'm already skating close to the edge of extinction myself. Achy wants this cleared up yesterday, if you know what I mean. Was up to him, I'd toss you three down below right now and be stuck lookin' like the Jolly Green Giant gone bad forever." Aggie sniffled again.

Hey, I was right there with her, ready to cry buckets that would make the waters lapping my ankles come up to my thighs. She had to be kidding. But her drooping snout and redder-than-ever eyes weren't saying anything but serious.

"I don't see how the hell we can do it." Ray's arm tightened around me. "Especially if this weather keeps up."

"Oh, it'll keep up all right. This is Achy venting." Aggie seemed to suck it up. "Get Casanova out here. I want my beautiful Siren form back. And I sure as hell didn't go through all this just to give up a shot at seeing Charlie again. You hear me?"

Hear her? The voice of doom? I put my head down on the table again. Lightning flashed, thunder roared, and I figured I was having a preview of hell and my destiny.

Eighteen

"It's about time you got in here. I was about to try my luck with your Siren." Jerry dragged me into his arms.

"God, Jerry, don't even joke about that." I held on to him, ignoring the fact that I was soaking his dry clothes.

"You do realize what time it is, don't you?" Jerry treated Ray like he was invisible.

"I know. I feel dawn in my bones." I turned to our host. "Ray, can we sack out here?"

Ray, his mouth firm, studied Jerry's possessive hold on me. Finally, he shrugged. "Sure, there are plenty of extra bedrooms and I wouldn't make my worst enemy"—he nodded in Jerry's direction in case he didn't get the reference—"go out in this weather. Sniff out one that doesn't have a mortal in it. I assume Nate and Sienna aren't in the same one."

"Nathan was complaining about that, but apparently Sienna Star sees him as a friend and nothing more." Jerry smiled like he was happy with Ray's hostility and he wasn't about to let go of me.

"Poor Nate." I saw that Brittany had found Valdez and they were having a heated discussion in the doorway to the kitchen. I heard enough to know Brit was worried about my bodyguard. She was in good company. Aggie's new timeline had me in a full-blown anxiety attack.

"Let's go, Jerry. Ray, I'll call Flo, Richard and Damian right now. You've got that direct line to EV headquarters, right?"

Ray frowned. "Sure. But what are the chances Simon will drop everything and come out here tomorrow night instead of Wednesday? Aggie's really screwed things up."

"What's this?" Jerry looked down at me.

"I'll tell you upstairs. Ray, I'm going to stop in your bedroom and grab some clothes."

This perked Ray right up. "Sure, Glory. You know where everything is. You've slept there many times." He grinned at Jerry's glower. "If you need anything at all, babe, you'll know where to find me."

"Right." I grabbed Jerry's hand and hustled him up the stairs. Outside Ray's bedroom door, I stopped. "I'll be right out." I tried to slip inside alone, but of course Jerry had to check out the fact that Ray had a king-size bed.

"You slept with him here."

"Vampire sleep. Unconscious." I said this from the closet, hurrying to grab a T-shirt to put on when I woke in the evening. I figured I'd sleep raw next to Jerry because I needed to feel his strong body close to mine. There was nothing more reassuring to nerves that were frayed almost unbearably thin. I rushed into the room with a pair of Ray's shorts in my hands too.

"You're very familiar with the layout here." Jerry leaned against the bathroom door checking out the large shower and the Jacuzzi tub. "You do like your baths."

I stopped and put my hand on his chest. He wore one of Ray's T-shirts, but it was snug on him. Jerry was bigger than Ray, broader where it counted. I smiled up at him and let him read that thought in my mind.

"Jerry, I'll take a shower with you in the extra bedroom and bath if you'll hurry. The sun's going to be coming up in a little while. I'd hate for us to fall asleep with the water pounding us in a shower stall."

Jerry lifted me into his arms. "No danger of that. I'd have you in bed well before that happened. Point the way."

I laughed and did just that. Foolish of me. I had phone calls to make. But I knew Richard and Flo would get here tomorrow night no matter what. And Damian would be happy to push Casanova and especially Maurice to join the party. Hopefully the council would be on board too. How could they resist with a serial killer and his helper to apprehend? I sure didn't want to meet that creep Maurice without significant backup.

I'd definitely quit laughing by the time Jerry set me down inside the bedroom that was as far away from Ray's master suite as we could get. The storm still raged outside, a good reminder that there was a lot riding on getting everyone to cooperate. So much could go wrong.

Jerry looked down at me and took my face in his hands. "Quit worrying. I'm not so jealous you need to play games with me to keep me pacified. Make your calls now."

"Aggie's moved up our deadline. We've got to get everyone here tomorrow night or Will, Ray and I are hellfire bound."

Jerry kissed my cheeks, my nose, my chin and then my lips. "You will *not* be going to hell. Tomorrow night or ever. Just tell me how I can help."

I leaned against him for a moment. "Thanks, Jerry. I'm really glad I don't have to face this alone. Let me call Flo first, then I'll tell you what you can do." I pushed back. Of course my cell was in my purse locked inside Jerry's car on the other side of the raging river we'd crossed. I mean how do you carry anything when you shape-shift? The more experienced vamps did it all the time, but I'd been so freaked-out, I hadn't been able to organize my thoughts, much less my stuff. I'd even left my "engagement" ring in my purse.

I grabbed the phone by the bed. In this rock-star household, there were four outside lines. I hit one that wasn't lit up and punched in Flo's cell phone number.

"Hello?"

"Flo, it's Glory. Our plans are all shot to hell."

"What do you mean? I talked to my brother. He's got Casanova hot to work his wiles on some beautiful women at Israel's party." Flo muttered something in Italian. "I'm not happy with *mio fratello*. He showed Berto a picture of you, Glory. Are you mad?"

"No! Whatever works." Though it did make my stomach churn a little. Stupid. Like that man could somehow lure me away from Jerry. If Israel Caine couldn't, I figure nobody could, even a notorious lover.

"All right then. And Maurice is happy he will get to meet Simon at last. Even the council members are coming on Wednesday. As soon as all the nasty ones are in Circe's hands we'll have a great celebration. No?"

"No. I mean yes. But not Wednesday. It's all got to happen tomorrow night instead." I sat on the side of the bed and kicked off my wet high heels. Damn. Those new peep-toe pumps would never be the same.

"*Insano.* If I know Berto, it will take him two days to decide which shirt to wear. And have you seen this weather? Maurice hates rain. It rusts his knives."

Wasn't that a happy thought. "Can't be helped, Flo. Aggie's moved things up. Surely Damian can persuade them . . ."

I heard Flo sigh. "If he must. I call. I beg. But I wanted to wear my new leather pants and, if it is raining, I cannot."

"Sorry, Flo, forget leather pants. You'll even have to shape-shift to get here. The road is impassable."

"Did you? Shift?" Flo said something to Richard. "My poor roomie. You were desperate. What did you make yourself? Not a bird in this wind. And I can't see you as a dog. Though something with a curly tail would be cute. Tell me. I must know."

I closed my eyes and counted to three. All I had time for. "Flo, forget it. This is an emergency. All of Austin is going to float away if we don't do something. This weather is the work of Aggie's boss, Achelous, the Storm God. He's letting her know he doesn't like her doing business in Austin behind his back. Aggie seems to think that getting the Circe thing settled will calm him down and she's determined to get her Siren form and her lover back. I figure you can relate to that."

"I would never end up looking like a monster for a man." I heard a squeal and Flo gasped. "Except for my darling Ricardo, of course. Tomorrow night. We won't let you down, Glory. Ricardo wants to talk to you. *Ciao.*"

"It's already pretty bad here, Gloriana." Richard's deep voice came on the line. "The TV is full of stories about local flooding. And the winds have taken out some huge old oaks at the state capitol. Those trees were hundreds of years old."

"See? I told Flo this is no ordinary storm. The sooner we can get this stopped, the better."

"We'll get right on it. It's only a few minutes until dawn. Stay safe."

"Richard! I just had a thought. We don't want any of the good guys to accidentally fry. What if they hear the Siren song and go south?"

"Damn. You're right."

I rubbed my head. Thinking. Then I remembered something I'd seen recently, when I'd been with Ray. "You have some of those noise-canceling headphones? Like techies use when they're on the computer in Mugs and Muffins?"

"Yes, I do. I use them when Flo's watching the DVR of her soap operas. I get it, Glory. The good guys need to wear them. I'll tell Damian and he should tell the council members to use them too. That way even if your Siren is singing when they go over, hopefully they'll be all right."

"I hope it works." I hung up and turned to Jerry. "Did you hear that?"

"Brilliant. And obviously Florence and Richard are making those calls." He smiled and put his hands on my shoulders.

"Yes, they're on it. Thank God for friends."

"You're right. Now look at you, soaked to the skin." Jerry grabbed my sweater and ripped it off over my head.

"Yes, that's happened to me a lot lately." I stood and un-buttoned and unzipped my corduroy jeans. Oh, boy, were they shrinking? I shoved the pants down and they came off easily with Jerry's hands doing most of the work.

Jerry smiled as he studied me in my black lace bikini panties and matching push-up bra. "How much time until dawn?"

"I'm going to wash off the floodwater." I popped open the clasp on my bra and dropped it on the floor. "I know I offered to let you join me, but obviously you already show-ered. I could smell that deliciously clean scent when I came up from the dock." I sauntered to the bathroom, pausing to look back over my shoulder. "I'll hurry."

"I could wash your back." Jerry was right behind me, dropping to his knees as he pulled my panties down my legs so I could step out of them. "I could hurry too."

"Doubt it." I turned and buried my fingers in his hair when he kissed my stomach and breathed against me, mak-ing me shudder.

"So do I. I could spend hours just on this one little part of you." As if to prove it, he used his teeth and tongue to ex-plore me, his hands pushing my legs apart.

I moaned and grabbed the door frame for support. Clos-ing my eyes, I tried to forget that I didn't have time. That there were other things . . .

"Stop!" I stepped back, stumbling on weak knees.

"Why, Glory? Doesn't this please you?" Jerry smiled, knowing good and well it pleased me way too much.

"I hate to say this, but you need to call Lily. To see if she'll agree to bring Drac and the boys here tomorrow night." I backed up to lean against the shower door, even picked up a towel and dragged it around me to show I meant business.

"You're right." Jerry got to his feet, his smile gone. "She may balk. It's one thing to complain about Dracula, another to doom him deliberately. I'll call her while you shower." He rubbed the back of his neck. "My body tells me you have less than fifteen minutes, lass. Make it quick."

"Thanks, Jerry. I know this could harm your relationship with your daughter." I dropped the towel and went to him, resting my head against his chest. "She *is* yours. I feel it when I look at her. The test will only confirm it."

"We should know tomorrow night." Jerry ran his hand down my back and patted my rump. "Thanks, sweetheart. I've had the feeling too, but I'm glad it's not just my imagination or wishful thinking at work. Now go take that shower."

So I got clean, even did a quick shampoo, then staggered out to fall into bed. Jerry barely had time to wrap us both in blankets before we fell into our dead-to-the-world sleep.

I woke up with Jerry's arms around me, his lips on mine and the storms still trying to tear the roof off the house. The storms could wait.

"Mmm. Do that again."

"What?" Jerry nudged my knees apart and rolled on top of me. "The kiss or this?" He slipped his fingers inside me, knowing just where to touch to make me tremble.

"Both." I pulled his head down and kissed him, as wild as the storm to make things right between us. The soul-deep connection was still there, the thing that kept pulling us together when the years and others would keep us apart. Thunder roared, the wind battered the walls outside, but my body screamed for Jerry to come inside. I wrapped my legs around him and held on as we created our own Category 5 on a wide bed with soft sheets and the heat of our inner fires.

Jerry lifted me above him, staring at me for a long moment. It didn't take a mind reader to see he was remembering that I'd spent days and nights in this house with Ray. Had shared a bed with him.

"Quit thinking, Jerry." I ran my hands along his rib cage, touching old warrior's wounds that had been made centuries ago, before he'd been turned. "*You* are filling my body, my head, my heart, Jeremiah Campbell." I leaned down and kissed him. "A newly made vampire is nothing compared to you. Now quit fashing yourself and get on with this. Or do you plan to leave me less than satisfied?"

"Have I ever not satisfied you, wench?" He grinned and rolled me under him.

"Well, now. There was that time in 1777. We were supposed to be helping the British, but you took a liking to the American cause." I yawned. "Spying was all you could think about. Many nights I had to, um, take matters into my own hands."

"Did you now?" Jerry sat back and grinned at me. "I'd like to see how you did that."

I pulled myself up against the cushioned headboard. "Old news. Back then everything was pretty primitive. They didn't have the modern conveniences like they do now. I love progress, don't you? Sex toys. Wow." I ran my hands over my body, lingering over my nipples then trailing one hand through the curls between my legs.

Jerry's eyes followed my every move. "Ye know, lass. I've always been fond of primitive ways." He growled when I slid a finger inside and moved my hips.

"Mmm. True. Primitive can be very, um, satisfying." I added another finger and saw him swallow. "No, this is a new century." I gave him a measuring look and had to call on my acting ability to keep my cool. He lay on his side, gloriously naked, fully aroused and so deliciously male I wanted to taste every inch of him. Instead I smiled and stretched, flaunting my breasts and letting my knees fall open.

"So what does the modern woman do to satisfy herself?" He reached out and ran a rough fingertip along the same path I'd just used—breast, tummy, ah, lower. Then he stopped, waiting.

I grinned, ready to challenge him. "Sorry, Jer, but you'd have to go some to beat the Tickler Turbo with the rechargeable battery."

"I would, would I?" He dove between my legs, grabbing

my ankles and draping them over his shoulders. "Can this tickler thing do this?" He slid his tongue along my folds.

"Of course." I gasped when he went in for a more up close and personal attack. "I direct it, you see. Put it exactly, ah, where I, um, want it. And then it has different speeds."

Jerry raised his head and grinned. "Do you really want me to rush this?" He didn't wait for an answer. "Give me your hands. What's this? They're shaking. Are you upset? Nervous? Or could it be I'm getting to you already?" He put my hands in his hair. "Now direct me. Just like you do your little toy. Where do you want me, Gloriana? Well?"

I threw back my head, already more aroused than I wanted to be. Because he was making me lose control. And making me forget that this was an important night. Where things could go so horribly wrong . . . What the hell? If I didn't survive, wouldn't I want this to be a fine farewell? So I gripped his hair and had a flashback to riding him through rushing water.

His ears! My eyes popped open. Faint pink marks. I should have known he'd have healed. Though I wondered when and where he'd fed. Forget feeding, he was following my directions and taking me into crazy-out-of-my-mind territory, his tongue teasing my pleasure point, circling then drawing the nub inside, between his lips, to suckle it until I bowed off the bed.

He pulled back. "Am I pleasing you, my love? I'm not turbo charged but at least you don't have to worry about my battery."

I couldn't form words so I just pushed him back to where he was proving to be the ultimate sex toy. He gripped my bottom, holding me down while I blew apart in the kind of— Oh. My. God.—orgasm the Tickler had never delivered.

"Jerry!" I pulled him up and practically threw him on the bed to climb on top of him. When he entered me, I came again, so sensitive I almost couldn't stand it. But of course I could and did. I leaned down and kissed him, then licked my way down his body, proving that I could toy with him as well.

I knew every muscle, every hard ridge and smooth expanse as I kissed the length and breadth of him. Why did I never tire of this man? Ray had called it habit. More like addiction. Right now it was enough that Jerry still wanted me, still loved me and thought me the best of lovers after all this time. I sat astride him once more and looked down into a face I knew as well as my own. Better, really, since mirrors didn't work for us. But the thought fled as lust took over, as it always did. I was crazed as I rode him, glad the thunder kept booming because I screamed my pleasure.

Finally we lay side by side, both of us sated beyond speaking. But of course we didn't have the luxury of just lying there. I glanced at the bedside clock. We'd wiled away more time than we could afford. We had a party to go to. Or to be more accurate, a wake.

"Is Lily going to bring Drac and his crew?" I sat up and kicked away the sheet.

"Yes. I assured her they were only a backup plan. That we hoped to send others first. Lily's not crazy about the idea of dealing with Dracula and the guys this way. She still thinks they're salvageable."

There was a knock on the door. "Glory, your company is arriving." Brittany was on the other side.

"We'll be right out. Who's here, Brit?"

"Florence, Richard and Damian. Said they wanted to get here early. Ray's with them in the living room. Sienna and Nathan are down there too." Brit said something quietly. "Valdez is antsy. Wants you both out here where he can keep an eye on you."

"Fine. We're getting dressed now." Jerry rolled out of bed and offered his hand to help me up. Then he held me for a moment. "This is it, then. No matter what happens, Gloriana, promise me you'll not go outside to face that damned Siren."

"I can't promise that, Jerry. She has control over me. I'm

surprised she hasn't called me out already tonight." I kissed him then slipped into my underwear that I'd rinsed out the night before. It was dry and gave me a semblance of respectability under my T-shirt and shorts. My own clothes were too damp and dirty to even consider wearing.

Not exactly how I wanted to look when I met Casanova. Though it would sure do the trick as far as getting him outside. He'd take one look and hit the skies.

I ran a brush I found in a drawer through my hair and wished for my purse and some makeup. I hoped Flo had some things I could borrow once I got downstairs.

"Okay, let's go." I saw that Jerry had dressed in the borrowed clothes he'd worn the night before. Ray's clothes. Black T-shirt, snug jeans that were an inch too short. He still looked all male and all mine. I could barely keep my hands off him. It was going to be a long night. Oh, God. Or a very short one. I blocked my thoughts. No sense in sharing my misery with Jerry. I knew he was already worried enough. I did have to issue another warning, though.

"Jerry, I have to act as Ray's fiancée tonight. Are you going to be able to handle that?"

"What choice do I have?" He frowned and pulled on his shoes, which must have dried.

"Thanks." I sat in his lap and gave him a hug, barefoot because my own shoes were showing an unfortunate tendency to fall apart. I was a lot like my shoes when I thought of all the things that could go wrong tonight. "I know this isn't easy. Just knowing you're here for me gives me courage. If Simon comes . . ." I got up.

"Relax, Glory. I know what to do. How to guard my thoughts. Richard and I had a talk." Jerry opened the bedroom door and we almost tripped over Valdez and a brown overnight bag. "What's this?"

"Brittany sent Glory some makeup and a few other things. Girl stuff. Blade, one of Nathan's shirts is hanging on the doorknob. He's bigger than Caine so it might fit you better." Valdez stood and stretched. *"You guys hurry. We need to get downstairs."*

I grabbed the bag and rushed into the bathroom. Bless Brittany. Not only makeup, but a cute low-cut burgundy top and a black short skirt made of a miracle stretchy material that managed to go around me. Miracle since I was a lot shorter and wider than the statuesque Brittany. When I finally emerged from the bathroom, I felt much better able to face what was to come. Maybe Casanova would even hit on me. I didn't know if that was a good thing or not.

Jerry looked better too in Nate's white shirt over his jeans. I reached up and unbuttoned a button.

"You want me to take it off?" Jerry grinned. "Valdez wants us to hurry."

"No, I just wanted to see more of your chest. You don't want to look stuffy, do you? Compared to a rock star and Lily's edgy friends?"

Jerry grabbed my hand and pulled me to him. "*Am* I stuffy?" He ran his hand down my back to the edge of my short skirt. "Sorry I can't get a tattoo or a piercing for you, but I can take you back in the bedroom and give you a demo—"

"*Hello, audience here.*" Valdez bumped against us. "*You two need to move on down the hall. No, wait. Sienna's down there. Maybe Glory should go down first, Blade a few minutes later. Since Glory's supposed to have slept with Caine.*"

"If Sienna says something, I'll just say I ran into Blade in the hall. Now listen, both of you." I jumped in front of them and gave them a this-is-serious look. "No one kills Ray tonight no matter what he does." That got their attention.

"What the hell does that mean?" Jerry put his hand on my shoulder.

"Just that it's his house. I'm his quote-unquote fiancée, and he's going to want to rub it in your face, Jerry." I reached up and patted his cheek. "Especially after the way you beat the hell out of him at the EV headquarters."

"*Wish I could have seen it.*" Valdez wagged his tail.

"I should have ripped out his throat." Jerry got a fierce look I recognized.

"Then I never would have forgiven you." I stepped away from him and marched on down the hall.

"All right, Gloriana. I'll show restraint tonight." Jerry was right behind me. "Valdez and I will *both* show restraint tonight. Toward Caine anyway. Now I know what will make you feel better." Jerry slipped his arm around my waist and pulled me to a stop. He pressed his lips to my throat. "We need to feed. Caine's friend Nathan is your favorite type."

I pulled away and saw Jerry's smile. "You didn't!"

"What? I had to take care of myself. When you were hanging on my back, monkey girl, you nearly tore my ears off. Nathan was available." Jerry leaned against the banister. "I'm sure he's fully restored by now, and he doesn't remember a thing. Valdez said he's downstairs."

"No way. I've had enough of drinking from mortals. I'm going back on the synthetics. Hunting's dangerous and then you never know what else you might pick up in a mortal's blood." I grabbed Jerry's arm. "And leave Ray's friends alone. Ray has a fridge stocked with premium synthetics. All brands and types. It's in his bar area. I'll tell you where we hide the key."

"It's kept locked?" Jerry grinned. "Why?"

"His band members think it must be an exotic drug and want to try it." I grabbed his arm when we got to the bottom of the stairs. "I mean it, Jerry. While we're here, mortals are off-limits."

"Now surely that doesn't apply to us, Gloriana." Dracula and crew strolled in through the front door accompanied by a frowning Lily. Their black capes were wet, but apparently waterproof. They hung them on a hall tree next to the door where the capes dripped on the tile floor. The men wore black suits, black shirts and black ties. Lily had chosen to wear red, which looked stunning with her dark hair and pale skin.

She gripped a black evening bag that matched Louboutin heels that made my mouth water.

"Lily, you look gorgeous!" I looked down at my borrowed outfit and bare feet. "We got caught in the storm."

"You look fine, Glory." Lily forced a smile. "Drac, you heard our hostess. Synthetics tonight. Please don't embarrass me."

"Darling. Have I ever?" Drac put his arm around her and laughed. "No, don't answer that. Do I see a piano? Boys, let's get the great Israel Caine to sing with us."

"They sing?" I noticed Jerry and Lily staring at each other.

"Oh, yes. Like the angels they resemble. Just wait. They can be the life or death"—Lily grimaced—"of a party." She opened her purse. "This came while we slept today." She held out a certified envelope. "Guess it's our DNA test results."

"You want to open it?" Jerry didn't reach for it.

"Sure." She started to rip open the envelope, then stopped. "Either way, it's been great getting to know you better, Jeremiah. You were Dad's best friend. He thought a lot of you. Now I know why." She took a breath then pulled out the paper and unfolded it. She stared at it for a moment, then handed it to Jerry.

I was about to scream with curiosity. Finally, Jerry handed the paper to me and took Lily in his arms. The print blurred in front of me, but I could tell that at the ripe old age of five hundred plus, Angus Jeremiah Campbell III was now a proud papa. Wow.

"This is awesome!" I pounded Jerry on the back, then took a turn at hugging Lily. "At least I hope you think it's awesome, Lily."

"Yes, I have a father again." Lily wiped her wet cheeks. "We'll have to talk later. I hear Drac getting started in there. And he's not singing. Is there a mortal in the house?"

"At least two that I know of." I glanced toward the living room. Great. Sienna and Nathan had both joined the group gathered around the piano. This was not good. Of course Sienna didn't see it that way. She was hip-deep in hot guys. Damian was an Italian stud and she already knew Drac, Luke and Benny. Nathan was seriously hot in a mortal, not exactly superhero way. Of course there was always Ray, brilliant, talented Ray, who was watching me from across the room. I kept a careful distance between myself and Jerry and gave my fiancé a dazzling smile, acting already.

"We need to get those two mortals upstairs and out of sight before the real action starts." Jerry glanced at the French doors that led to the deck and the usually spectacular view of the lake. Tonight all we could see was driving rain and lightning that lit up the sky at regular intervals accompanied by booming thunder. I guess a day crew had struggled to bring in patio furniture, because the only things blowing around outside were leaves and the occasional tree limb. We stepped into the living room just as thunder boomed loud enough to rattle the French doors.

Flo rushed up and pulled me away from Jerry. "You are supposed to be promised to Israel, my friend, so is not nice to walk in with another man and a flush that says you have just been well loved."

"Flo!" I looked to make sure Sienna hadn't heard her. Not likely. She was at the piano. And then there had been that thunder. As for Drac, Lily and crew . . . Well, they knew I'd spent the night before at Jerry's and in their crowd apparently musical beds were fairly common. I doubted they gave my bed-hopping a second thought.

"Am I wrong?" Flo grinned. "Of course not. Israel's sending mental death threats to Jeremiah. Your lover is strutting around like he's cock of the walk." She giggled. "Why does that sound dirty?"

"Are you forgetting why you're here?" I looked her over. No leather pants, but a cute electric blue sequined minidress and Dior platforms. "You look more ready to party than kick butt."

"Can't I do both?" Flo frowned as another clap of thunder rattled the glass doors. "I don't forget for *un momento* why Ricardo and I are here. No one will send my roomie to hell. But I can look good while I kick butt. *Si?*"

I gave up. No sense in spreading my case of nerves and impending doom around. I flinched when something cold hit my palm. "What's this?"

"New shade of lipstick. What you're wearing? All wrong for you. Put this on. It's called Vampilicious or something like that. It will make Jeremiah drag you into a closet and kiss you until your eyes cross, girlfriend. I think Casanova will like too." Flo nodded toward Lily. "There's another one who will stir Berto's blood." She glanced toward the French doors, which rattled with another wind gust.

"But every woman here, even Brittany, is in danger if Maurice takes a liking to them. Damian told all three of them— Berto, Maurice and his friend—to fly in over the lake. I hope your Siren snatches them before they ever get here." For a moment her eyes glittered with what I swear were tears.

"You and me both, Flo." I put the lipstick on by feel then handed it back to her. "Better?"

"Much. Now I go back to my Ricardo. Not to worry. We have your back." She sniffled, then gave me a quick hug and hurried back to Richard's side.

I headed toward Ray and the piano, determined to play my part as dutiful fiancée. He threw his arm around me when I got there.

He leaned down and whispered in my ear. "Listen to these characters."

"I'm telling you, Sienna. Elton wrote that song about *us*. We were really hot in the late sixties, early seventies." Drac leaned down and tapped Benny on the shoulder. "Play one of *our* songs, Ben."

"Quit teasing me, Drac. You guys are way too young to have been around back then." Sienna sat on the piano bench next to Benny. She was sipping a martini and had on one of the vintage cocktail dresses she'd bought in my shop last night. It was a short lime green and yellow sequined sheath that hit her midthigh. She looked great and knew it. So did the men. If Casanova made it here, he was going to take direct aim at her. Not that he'd have a chance to hit the target. Which reminded me. Where the hell was Damian's famous council?

"We're older than we look. We were living in England

then. Had a little singing group called the Jets. Benny used to stammer when he got excited. He got over it. Elton dug our music. He and Bernie wrote the song about us." Drac grinned and Benny played. The three of them broke into song, not Elton's classic, but a sixties rock tune that did sound familiar to those of us who'd been around back then. The three youngsters in the crowd—Ray, Nate and Sienna—looked confused but were soon tapping their feet to the beat. Flo and Damian laughed and danced around the room.

Danced. I was glad Flo could pretend to enjoy herself. I felt like I was about to scream or fall apart. Ray squeezed my shoulders, kissed my cheek and sent me a mental message.

"Don't worry. Simon promised he'd try to make it."

"Try?" I probably looked horrified because Luke looked at me curiously. I took a breath and plastered a smile on my face. Jerry was across the room, not smiling. Especially when Ray nuzzled my neck. The song finally ended and everyone clapped.

"Okay, I don't know how you did that, but I still say no way." Sienna waved her glass at me. "That song's about the same age as my dress. Right, Glory?"

I nodded. "If it came out in the early seventies it is."

"There you go. Plus in Elton's song Benny is a 'she.' " Sienna polished off her martini and set the glass on the floor. She played and sang part of the tune to make her point.

Drac laughed. "Benjamin here used to swing both ways. Even did some cross-dressing. You should have seen him in those electric boots. Too cute. This decade he's way into women. Right, Ben?"

"Shut up, Drac. No one here's interested in a history lesson." Benny jumped up from the piano. "I want to hear Sienna and Ray sing. The new duet. What do you say, Ray?"

"Be glad to, but later. We're expecting more guests. Maybe when everybody gets here." Ray glanced down at my ringless hand and frowned. "Glory, baby, don't you think Sienna and Nate should . . ." Unspoken was the "get the hell out of here."

"What?" Nathan was all for anything that put him with Sienna. He looked around and was sharp enough to realize there were some seriously creepy characters behind all the big smiles and good music.

"Sienna and I need to go over some lyrics. In the study. And, Glory, maybe Nate could help you bring out some refreshments." Ray nodded toward the kitchen and bar area. "You know what our guests like to drink and Nate can fix Sienna another martini."

"This is a party. Right?" Damian pulled Sienna up and Luke took her place on the piano bench. "Surely you won't take this beautiful lady away now. Study can wait."

Luke started playing a current hit, a love song that made Flo grab Richard and dance him around the piano. I knew what my BFF was doing, trying to forget what might be coming. Damian wanted to keep the bait, I mean Sienna, in the room. She smiled and let Damian dance her around in what looked a lot like foreplay. Someone found the dimmer switch on the lights. What was this, a freakin' night club? Even Lily and Drac started dancing.

"Come on, Nate, help me with the drinks." I dragged him with me to the bar where I found the key in its hiding place and unlocked the special fridge in the pantry. Then I poured goblets of synthetics and set them on a tray while Nate made Sienna what he called a dirty martini. He was hitting the Jack Daniel's pretty hard, even set the bottle on the tray with the martini. Valdez stood guard at the door.

Jerry and Ray had stayed in the living room to keep watch over Sienna and over each other, no doubt. Should I be worried? Since I didn't hear glass breaking or cracking heads, I put their feud out of my mind. I also didn't hear any more guests arriving and it was close to ten. Not good. Where were Damian's guests? Since the storm was going strong, I figured Aggie still hadn't snared any vampires trying to fly in over the lake.

I was about to shove Dracula outside as a token when I realized that not only would it ruin Jerry's relationship with

Lily, but it also wasn't likely to work with Benny and Luke around.

One thing I could do was try to save the mortals we'd dragged into this. I got in Nathan's face.

"All right, Nate. Listen to me. I guess you've figured out by now that this is a party for vampires only. You and Sienna are in grave danger. Do you hear me? Grave danger."

"You mean they could kill us? Not just drink from us?" Nate's voice shook and he swallowed some Jack.

"Exactly. So I need for you to take Sienna upstairs and lock yourselves in one of the bedrooms. I can whammy both of you, but I hate to do that." To hell with bait. I figured this late, Aggie would probably get the bad guys before they ever reached the house. I could hope anyway. If not, I didn't want Nate or Sienna anywhere near the infamous Maurice.

"I hate for you to do that too. Don't know what good a bedroom door will do, though. I've seen you guys in action. You make kung fu fighters look like pansies." Nate sat on a bar stool.

"Well, any vamp who wants you is going to have to go through me, Ray, Jerry and Valdez first. You can count on us."

"I know that, Glory. Thanks." Nate stood, picked up the tray and straightened his shoulders. "I know I can't tell Sienna what's going down, but if I can't lure her away from a bunch of creeps like that, then I'm a loser with a capital *L*."

"Stop right there, Nate." I put my hand on his arm. "Don't think like that. These guys have an unfair advantage. They have an aura and mind control to work with. Besides, danger is seductive for a lot of women. Crazy, I know, but women have always been attracted to bad boys, and there's a room full of them out there. Look at Lily. Beautiful, intelligent, and now we know she's Jerry's daughter. She could have any man she wants and yet she's hung out with the likes of Dracula for over a hundred years. Go figure."

"That *is* crazy." Nate paced around the small room holding the tray like a waiter looking for his customers. "I'll never understand women."

"Of course not. Just don't be surprised if Sienna doesn't want to leave the room with you. Because, despite being handsome and intelligent, you're clearly one of the good guys."

"Never thought I'd be sorry to hear that." Nate glanced at an array of bottles. "Maybe I should fix Sienna a double martini. Try to get her drunk."

"Nope. Doubt it would be you who'd get to take advantage of that situation." I hated the worry I'd put in Nate's eyes. "Listen, friend. One of us, your vamp buddies, may have to coerce her out of the room. Just keep your eyes and ears open and be ready to make a run for it at our signal, okay?"

"Thanks for scaring the shit out of me, Glory." Nate looked grim, but determined.

"You're welcome." I picked up a second tray and walked with Nate to the living room just in time to see the front door blow open again. Didn't anyone knock anymore? But when I saw who it was I didn't care. Simon Destiny, Greg Kaplan and another Energy Vampire were shedding black waterproof capes in the entry.

"Ray, baby, Simon's here." I set my tray on a table and hurried forward. Valdez started growling and I gave him a look that should have silenced him. Instead, he merely got louder.

"Am I going to have to do something to your canine before I even meet your guests?" Simon smiled slightly.

"Of course not." I turned and looked into the living room. "Blade, would you come control this mutt of yours?" I clutched Ray's arm when he joined me in front of Simon. "We're all trying to get along, for the sake of the vampire community, but"—I glanced at Valdez, who'd finally shut up—"it's a work in progress."

"Admirable, I'm sure." Simon cocked his head. "Wonderful music, but then I'd expect no less in the house of Israel Caine."

"Thank you, Simon." Ray nodded. "Come meet some of

our guests. Glory, you need to put up the pets. Drac and his friends are going to drain them dry if we're not careful."

"Sorry, darling." But I saw that I might be too late. Nathan had set his tray on the coffee table and had been cornered by Lily. She was talking to him and giving him looks that could only be described as hungry. Of course she'd promised to lay off mortals here, but Nate's rare blood type was a powerful draw and the fact that she was a beautiful woman didn't make Nathan look exactly reluctant either. So much for putting him on alert.

Sienna sat beside Luke at the piano and they were singing a duet. The music *was* wonderful and amazing considering Luke never looked at the keyboard, only at Sienna's pale neck where she had a small tattoo of a golden key. Oh, yeah. Talk about an invitation. Trying to get either Sienna or Nate out of the room was going to take artillery fire or one of Westwood's arrow barrages.

Just then I heard a croaking sound from outside. Aggie's Siren song. Oh, boy. Now the party was really getting started.

Nineteen

"I think there's something out there." Sienna pointed at the French doors.

Now if those weren't words to freeze me in my tracks. I glanced at Simon. This was it. Could I get him to go outside and check?

"Gloriana, why would I want to go out in that weather when I just got in out of it?"

Damn, I'd forgotten the mind blocking trick. "You're the most powerful person here, Simon. If it's something danger-ous, I figure you're the one best able to handle it." I saw that everyone in the room was moving toward the doors, though my friends were smart enough to realize that this was probably what we'd been planning for. Flo and Richard made room for Drac and Benny at the glass, while Damian practically pushed Greg Kaplan toward the door. I was frantically counting the tiles on the floor near my feet when the door opened.

"It's Will!" I was the only one who ran forward to help the vampire as he staggered inside. Everyone else jumped back when rain blew inside. Damian finally wrestled the door shut for me.

"Who's Will?" Drac brushed raindrops off his suit and

nodded at Benny, who went back to the piano and started playing again.

"He's one of my bodyguards." Ray grabbed Will's arm and helped me drag him toward the hall. "What the hell were you doing outside, man? I never told you to patrol the grounds in this weather." Ray waved at the startled guests. "We'll be right back. Please help yourselves to drinks. Thanks, Ben, for playing. Maybe Sienna and I will sing in a few minutes." This last got everyone back to talking and dancing. Even Simon smiled and introduced himself to Dracula.

Ray and I managed to get Will into a downstairs study where he collapsed on a couch. He wore the same ripped jeans and T-shirt he'd had on when Aggie had captured him days before.

"How did you get away from Aggie?" I ran to the bar and returned with a couple of bottles of synthetic. Will gulped one down, then sighed and looked at Ray, then me.

"Bad news. She sent me here with a message. You got an hour to get Casanova and two others here or she's calling the three of us to her." Will shuddered. "I didn't think she'd do it. I've gotten to know her, and she's not that bad if you look past the creepy exterior."

I put my hand to his head. "Are you sick? Crazy? She just sent you in with a death threat."

"Yeah, yeah, but you see this weather? That's her boss going nuts. The woman's got problems. Achelous is way more powerful than anything *I've* ever seen before. Aggie's in big-time trouble because she dealt with Circe."

"So why don't we call her bluff? Maybe the boss will pull Aggie out of here and she won't be able to give Circe anything." Ray looked back toward the living room. "Frankly, I don't think anyone in there is willingly going outside in this weather. If Aggie can't lure them out with her singing . . ."

"She tried. Didn't you hear her earlier?" Will grimaced, pulled off his wet T-shirt and wiped his face. "She's lost her voice. She can still draw the three of us to her, but that's about all the power she's got left unless someone flies right over the lake. The Storm God zapped her a good one when he saw what she looked like. He takes pride in his beautiful Sirens. Then when he heard it was because she'd been dealing with Circe . . . Man, he really flipped out. He *hates* the goddess."

"Why does he hate her? Did you see him? What's the story?"

"Yeah, I saw him. Yelling at Aggie. He's a big dude. Looks like a statue straight out of one of those museums." Will grabbed another bottle of synthetic and took a swallow. "Man, I'm weak. I just could *not* drink from Aggie. She smelled sorta human, but fishy too." Will made a face. "She offered, believe it or not."

"Come on, Will. Did you find out anything that could help us?" I wanted to shake him when he took another drink.

"Don't know if it'll help, but Achy and Circe used to be an item back in the day. Not clear who did the dumping, but it was an ugly breakup. Then the goddess started throwing lightning bolts and thunder around, getting on Achy's turf. That really pissed him off. Now she's messing with one of his Sirens. The dude's gone ballistic." The house shook with an especially loud boom of thunder to prove the point.

I had an idea. "You think he's stronger than Circe? Maybe if someone talked to him, he could help us get off the hook."

"Are you nuts?" Ray jumped in front of me and put his hands on my shoulders. "You're not going outside and that's final."

"Did I say I was going outside?" I looked at him until he released me. Just in time. Jerry appeared in the doorway, summoned by Valdez no doubt. You didn't think they'd let me out of their sight for long, did you?

"For once, Caine and I agree on something. You sure as hell aren't setting one foot outside." Jerry nodded at Ray. "Your guests are restless. I think you'd better sing, Caine, and keep Ms. Star next to you or she's going to end up with someone's fangs in her neck."

Ray just stood there, not exactly inclined to jump to Jerry's command.

"What about Simon? Is there a chance we can get him near enough to the doors to push him out?" I realized how stupid that sounded the minute the words left my mouth. No one pushed Simon Destiny anywhere.

"I'm going to my room to shower and change. I'll be right down and maybe we can figure out something. I wouldn't lay odds on who's stronger out there." Will stood and stretched. "One good thing. Aggie's so busy juggling the god and the goddess, I think we really got more than the hour. And if she was listening in right now, I figure we'd be getting hit with some serious pain. Either of you feeling it?" Will glanced at us.

Ray and I looked at each other. Not a twinge. It was a freakin' miracle.

"Me either. Okay then. We've still got time. Hours before dawn. I know Aggie's impatient, throwing out ultimatums, but I don't think she'll follow through." He smiled. "Hey, what can I say? I've been working my mojo on her. The lady's crazy about me." He winked and headed for the stairs.

"I so don't want that picture in my head." I looked at Ray.

"No kidding. Will's lost his freakin' mind." Ray shook his head.

"Makes you wonder whose mojo was working, Will's or the slime sister's?" Valdez bumped Ray over so he could stand in front of me. *"You stay away from her, Blondie."*

"I hear you." I looked at Valdez, Ray, then Jerry. "*All* of you. Now we'd better get back out there. Ray, you can sing and I can keep the synthetic coming." I walked up to Jerry. "You'd better remind your daughter of her promise. Lily was looking at Nathan like he was one of the last Cheetos in the bag."

"I noticed." Jerry shrugged. "I'm afraid she's got a lot of her mother in her."

"Yep, Mara's daughter would tend to be all about 'me first,' wouldn't she? You'll have to go some to rein that in." I smiled. "You can do it." I jumped when Ray slid his arm around my waist.

"Let's go, Glory. We have guests."

"Oh, right. Later, Jerry." I hoped my smile took the sting out of the way I let Ray hold on to me.

We headed out to the living room just in time to hear a double volley of thunder that made the electric lights flicker and then go out. Most of us had vamp vision, but I found some matches and lit candles around the room so Nate and Sienna could see. It did add some charm to the setting when Ray sat at the piano, pulling Sienna down beside him.

They sang their hit song just like they'd been practicing it. A love song. Even heartless Simon seemed moved. Not that I could really concentrate on what everyone was doing or feeling. I was easing my way around the room and out to the kitchen. I wanted to get to Aggie. There had to be a way to settle this without sending the good guys, including me, to hell.

I picked up a long hooded slicker from the utility room and shrugged into it then struggled to open the back door against the wind and rain. I immediately heard Aggie's Siren song, if you could call the pathetic croaking a song. The sound was pretty weak, but I felt the pull. It was wasted on me because she was who I was headed for anyway.

Was this stupid? I didn't think so. Circe wasn't interested in a female sacrifice. And Aggie had just let Will go. I saw this last as a sign that the Siren really wanted to wiggle out of making the wrong choice.

"Aggie, where are you?" I held on to the railing and took the stairs down to the dock below. Sure enough, Aggie was huddled under the overhang, trying unsuccessfully to stay out of the blowing rain.

"I'm here. Are you the only one coming? Damn, this is a

disaster." She laid her snout on the deck, a pink tear trickling down her scaly cheek.

"Where's your boss? I'd like to talk to the Storm God."

That got her attention. "Are you freakin' insane? He could blow you to hell before you even got close enough to say hello."

Hmm. Maybe this had been a bad idea. "What? He's not open to a logical discussion?"

Aggie looked around like she figured we were both destined for a lightning bolt. "Shut up. Of course he's open to logic. He's brilliant, charismatic, the best boss a woman could have." She rolled her eyes at me. "And he's a man with a capital *M*, vampy, with a harem of Sirens. Does that tell you anything?"

The deck shook with a tremendous crash of thunder. "Harem?"

A light shimmered in front of us, finally taking shape as a man. Not just an ordinary man, but a Greek god complete with toga and laurel wreath. Great body, of course. I couldn't look away.

"Glory, meet my boss, Achelous, the Storm God." Aggie pulled herself up to a sitting position. "Yes, sir, I consider it a harem. Bunch of women serving one man." She smiled and fluttered her long lashes. "And you know we're willing to serve."

"That would play a lot better, Aggie, if you didn't look like a sea serpent who'd lost a battle with a coral reef." Achelous frowned. "Glory. I understand you've been involved in Aggie's misdeeds here in this backwater."

"Yes. Though involved isn't what I'd call it. We were dragged into it." I had to stifle the absurd desire to flutter my own lashes. I did throw back the hood and fluff my hair, which wasn't reacting well to the blowing rain. "Aggie wants to send me and two of my friends to Circe's hell."

"Maybe you should already be there." Achelous's deep voice made my stomach turn over.

"But, Achy, Circe doesn't—"

"Circe? You dare speak her name to me?" The deck shook with thunder and lightning sizzled close by, taking out a sapling in a neighbor's yard.

I figured this was a good time for me to beat a hasty retreat. Achelous noticed my first step and threw a lightning bolt at me. I felt like my heart was being ripped out of my chest as I turned to stone. No! The world darkened and I knew this was it for me. Jerry!

"You're killing her because you're mad at me? Come on, Achy, ease up." Aggie's voice seemed to come from very far away.

Suddenly I could see again. Aggie had actually saved my life. Why? I still couldn't move, but my heart was beating again, though my chest hurt like hell.

"Let me finish this thing with the, uh, goddess. You don't like Casanova either, do you, Achy?"

"He disrespects women. He deserves hell. So does this Charlie you are such a fool over. You should have come to me with your problem. Never to that bitch Circe." Achelous waved a hand toward the lake and a mini tidal wave headed toward the far shore. I hoped the residents on the other side had flood insurance. "And she stole your beauty. Is that piece of excrement worth it?"

Aggie sniffled. "I don't know. I'm hideous. Please don't look at me. I'm a disgrace to my Siren sisters."

"And to me." The deck shook when he stomped a sandal. My statue self wobbled and I was terrified I was going to be swept into the lake. Water lapped at my knees and I felt something slimy touch my foot. I couldn't even scream.

"I know you and Circe have issues, but she won't let me out of this deal. Glory here's promised this will be settled before dawn. Can you give me this night? Please? Forget Charlie. You're my number one, always have been. But if I'm stuck like this I can't . . ."

I couldn't hear what she said, but Achy smiled so Aggie must have some hidden talents.

"Very well. To show you who is *really* powerful,

Aglaophonos, I will give you your song back. You have until dawn. You're my Siren. Prove it." The Storm God's voice was cool. He narrowed his gaze on me, gestured, and I staggered, almost falling into the water. I was weak and shaky and wasn't sure I could walk, much less make it up the stairs. Suddenly Aggie and I were alone when Achelous shimmered out of sight.

"Okay, Glory, you sure Casanova's on his way?"

"Yes! But I'll have Damian call him again and check. And we've got two more vamps ready to go."

"Get out of here then. Because, you heard him, vampy. Both our fat butts are on the line." Yodeling a warm-up, Aggie turned toward the lake. "My voice! God, I love you, Achy!" she shouted.

I found some strength from somewhere, tossed up my hood and ran for the stairs, bumping into Valdez and Jerry at the top. "Get inside. Now!"

"What's going on?" Jerry grabbed my arm.

"What's that noise?" Valdez tried to go around me.

"Aggie, trolling for vampires. Jerry, cover your ears and get inside, damn it." I shoved him toward the door.

When we got back inside, I shed the slicker and wiped my wet feet off with a towel from the powder room. I still felt like my heart hadn't found its natural rhythm yet. Jerry and Valdez waited for me in the kitchen.

"What the hell was that about?" Jerry tried to brush my hair back from my face. Hopeless.

"Aggie and her boss had a showdown. Bottom line: We've got till dawn to finish this."

"Dumb stunt takin' on Aggie by yourself, Glory." Valdez watched me load another tray with goblets of synthetics. My hands were shaking.

"He's right, Gloriana. Stop that and look at me." Jerry pulled me into his arms. "My God, I might never have seen you again."

I leaned against him for a moment, the truth of what he'd just said hitting me like one of Achy's tidal waves.

"I . . . I . . ." The room spun and I sucked in air, then focused on Jerry's white shirt, now smeared with Flo's pink lipstick. Damn. I pushed back.

"Sorry, Jerry. Temporary meltdown. But I'm together now." I grabbed a dishcloth and wet it. "Look at your shirt. If our guests see this, our cover's blown." I scrubbed at his shirt until he grabbed my hand.

"Let it go, Glory. Start some rumors." He pulled my hand to his lips. "You're going to be breaking it off with Caine soon anyway."

I looked up, mesmerized by the gleam in his eyes. "Come here, then." I pulled his lips down to mine and kissed him, no holds barred, relieved to have survived my temporary insanity in facing Aggie.

"You two want to get caught? Seems like one fight this week ought to be enough for ya, Glory." Valdez sat next to the door, a reluctant lookout.

I pulled back, my cheeks warm and my heart racing. "Valdez is right." I used the cloth to clean off traces of lipstick from Jerry's face. "And you don't need to look so self-satisfied, mister. If Ray grabs me out there, I'll kiss him too."

Jerry cocked an eyebrow at me. "Then I'll make sure he doesn't get that chance." He picked up the tray and pushed open the kitchen door.

Simon watched us reenter the living room. Of course he didn't miss the smear on Jerry's shirt but probably filed that information away to use to his advantage later. The flickering candlelight made it difficult for the two mortals in the room to notice. Flo, as usual, didn't miss anything. She winked at me from across the room.

The Sienna and Ray show was still going on as they played requests. Naturally everyone was focused on the talented duo and their singing. And why not? I wanted to lean against the piano and just lose myself in the music. No such luck when Simon cornered me.

"Gloriana, I still don't see those very important conservative vampires your *fiancé* wanted to impress." Simon's smirk and nod at Ray gave me chills. "Or am I confused about who you're with at the moment? No ring?"

"I'm with Ray. My ring's locked in the car on the other side of a low-water crossing. I had to shift to get here, just like you did, Simon, and I was afraid I'd lose it."

"Really? You shape-shifted? And you hate it so." Simon looked at Ray, then Jerry. "Interesting. Perhaps I underestimated you. Again."

I smiled and let my mind fill with the song Ray was singing. "My guess is the weather has delayed the men Ray wanted you to scare, I mean impress." I looked around the room. "Let me see if Damian has heard from them. They're members of a council he's been working with."

"Ah, yes, I received a letter from this council. Seems they're not very happy that I've taken up residence so close to their precious Austin." Simon smiled and picked up a goblet. "Hypocrites. At least one of them regularly orders Vampire Viagra from my Web site."

"Well, yes, you do make some excellent products. Or at least some people seem to think so." I faked a smile, then hurried over to Damian. "What's going on? Any of your guys coming? What about the council?"

Damian had been staring at Sienna, who'd just started another song. She almost lost the lyrics when Luke leaned down to whisper in her ear.

"Glory! Sorry." He turned to me with his usual charming smile. "Yes, I am taking care of everything. Sent pictures of Lily and Sienna to Casanova with my cell phone. That lit a fire under him, I tell you. He finally decided on a shirt and left ten minutes ago. Then I sent a text to Maurice. Let him know Simon's here. He hit me right back. He should already be here. Don't know what the hell happened to the council. Last I knew they were shopping for headphones. I'll call and check." He pulled out his cell phone. Several calls later and he was frowning. "None of them are answering at home or their cells. I don't know where they are."

There was a sudden silence that was almost as startling as

the thunder had been. We all looked toward the glass doors. The rain had stopped. No thunder, no lightning and, most amazing of all, the moon, a three-quarter one, was actually visible through the clouds.

"That's a relief." Simon walked over to the doors and threw them open. "It will make a much more enjoyable trip back to the compound." He stepped out on the deck and looked at the lake. "Kaplan, come here and check out this view. I think the EVs should buy some lakefront property. It would be a good investment."

I was holding my breath. Waiting. Was he going to be sucked down to hell? Please. Please. Please. I heard singing and someone said there must be another party going on close by, but the song stopped abruptly. Aggie? She did have a beautiful voice. Simon frowned, but he didn't seem inclined to head down the stairs. Surely he wasn't the one vampire immune to a Siren song.

Greg came outside, leaned against the railing and looked out at the lake, really dark with the power outage. "I see what you mean, sir. I'll have one of the shifters call a Realtor in the morning."

"Do that." Simon turned to gaze at the water again. "There. Running lights. Looks like someone's taking a boat out now. It would be a nice change to have a boat for pleasure cruises. Gloriana, do you and Ray enjoy the water?" Simon turned and smiled at me.

Damn. What was going on here? No singing. No storm and Simon making small talk. I remembered my blocking techniques and began a quick count of the buttons open on Greg's shirt. Ray came to my rescue, leaving Sienna at the piano and slinging an arm around my shoulders.

"Glory isn't much for the water, Simon, but I've got a great little cigarette boat with a powerful motor. Right now isn't a good time, with so many guests here, but some night we'll have to go out and take a ride." He leaned down and kissed my lips. "What's up?" He whispered this in my ear.

"Not a clue."

Will walked up behind me with a beautiful blonde on his arm. "Hi, everybody, look who I found stranded down the driveway. This is Aggie."

Ray and I gawked. No way. Long blond hair. Legs!

Simon came forward and his nose twitched. "Charming. I swear I can't quite place . . ." He extended his hand. "Simon Destiny."

"Will's told me about you, Mr. Destiny." Aggie smiled, her bright white teeth perfect. She had on a sparkly blue minidress that matched her eyes. "Sorry, but he warned me not to shake your hand. Hope you're not offended."

"Not at all, my dear. Just proves you're wise as well as beautiful."

Sienna jumped up from the piano. "I swear, Glory, is there no end to the number of hot guys you have around here?" She smiled when Luke threw his arm around her. "Do you think the roads have cleared yet? Luke wants to take me home for a nightcap."

I shuddered, figuring Sienna's juice would be Luke's nightcap of choice. We had to put a stop to this.

"Sienna, the storm was pretty bad." Nathan walked up to her and risked his life by pulling her away from Luke. "I bet it'll be another twenty-four hours before you can drive across that road. You'll have to spend the night here again."

Aggie held on to Will. "He's right. I don't think the water's gone down yet." Her cute little nose quivered and she nodded at Luke. "But your guy there can take you right over it, can't you, fella?"

"What does she mean, Luke?" Sienna looked puzzled.

"Pay no attention to her." Luke's smile had a glacier's warmth when he looked at Aggie.

"But I don't get it. How did all these people get here then?" Sienna looked around the crowded room. "Ray?"

Ray shook his head. "Guess there's no help for it this time, Glory. Who's going to do the honors?"

"Please, let me." Luke looked into Sienna's eyes, and she was instantly very still. "What shall I have her remember?"

"That we had a hell of a party, of course." Ray smiled at me and glanced at Aggie. "And lived to tell about it."

Before I had time to bask in the truth of that statement, there was a loud knocking on the front door. Ah, maybe the council had finally arrived. Though now that Aggie was in human form did that mean Casanova, Maurice and his side-kick were now enjoying Circe's hospitality? I prayed it was true, bitterly disappointed, though, that Simon was back on the outside deck, still talking real estate with Greg.

Since Brittany and Valdez were practically shadowing Simon, Will finally remembered his bodyguard duties and rushed to answer the door. Barry stood there, waving a hand-ful of newspapers.

"Wow. Am I missing a party or what?" He came in and looked around, rushing to give Sienna, who was happily en-joying the party again, an air-kiss. "Ray, Glory, why didn't you tell me you went to the island last weekend? This is the second scoop you let me miss. Ray, I'm your publicist, bud. You've got to keep me in the loop." He threw the papers on the coffee table.

"We didn't go to the island." Ray picked up a paper, then frowned and turned toward the deck. "Damn it, Simon, what the hell is the meaning of this?"

"What is it, Ray?" Simon walked back inside and took the paper from Ray's hand. "Son of a bitch."

I grabbed a paper, then wished I could take the lot and hold them to a candle. Maybe start a fire in the stone fire-place. Drac and Benny shared a copy with the front page in full color. Their glances at me, then at Jerry and Ray were sly, but they were smart enough not to say anything.

"What is it, Glory?" Sienna peered over my shoulder. "Ooo. That doesn't look like the island." She looked over at Jerry. "They fought over you?" She patted my arm. "Wow."

Wow. No, more like ow. There was a picture of Jerry and Ray hitting each other. Rolling in the sand, trying to kill each other. But my favorite was a shot of me topless, pulling myself out of the pool with Ray behind me and Jerry in front of me. Nice. They'd blurred my nipples. Big blurs. 'Course I looked like I was wearing fuzzy pom-poms. Hell.

"Interesting snaps, Glory, Ray." Aggie waved a paper at me. "I can see how *stressed* you were over my little problem."

I ignored her. Easy to do when I got a look at Jerry's face. He didn't bother to pick up a paper. He didn't have to with Aggie and Will holding their copy up just a foot away. Great headline on that one: "Rocky Romance for Rock Star Romeo."

Lily took her newly found father's arm. "Looks like you were getting the best of him in that fight. But then . . ." She studied me, then Ray. "Never mind. I know better than to ask about your love life when mine's a suckfest."

Drac glared at her. "Hey, I heard that. What's wrong with our love life? I treat you right, don't I?"

Lily smiled. "Sure, when we're not dodging mobs with stakes."

This had Barry scratching his head. "I wouldn't mind someone throwing a steak at me. Make mine medium rare. But, hey, if this isn't the island, Ray, where is it?"

"A resort not far from here. Owned by this guy." Ray nodded toward Simon then snatched the paper from him again. "Supposed to have tight security. That's why we went there. Simon? I'm waiting for an explanation." Ray crumpled the paper in his hand.

"I'm sorry, Ray. All I can say is that we have security cameras. Tina must have seen the footage and used some of it to capture some stills and do this." Simon said something to the third EV who'd come with him. That man stepped out into the dark and disappeared. "She will be dealt with."

"Wait." I rushed out to the deck. "You're not going to, uh"—I glanced back at the mortals in the crowd—"you know."

"Why do you care what I do with Tina? Do you see how she's humiliated you, Gloriana? And ignored my—yes, Ray— very tight security requirements." Simon's hands were fisted and he narrowed his gaze on the picture I held in my hand. "I will not tolerate this."

"Wait a damned minute, Destiny. Don't make Tina the fall girl here. What the hell were 'security cameras' doing in the sunlight rooms? You got them in the shower stalls too?" Ray proved he was hero material by getting right in Simon's face. I was scared for him, moving in close and holding on to his arm. I was flanked by Valdez and Brittany, but even then knew we were fighting a losing battle if Simon used some of his Energy Vamp superpowers.

"Ray? Honey?" I tugged on his arm. He needed to give Simon some space.

"No, Glory, I've got to say this. We assumed we were alone. Simon invaded our privacy." Ray threw down his paper. "This really pisses me off. What do you do with the videos you take in there, Simon? Work a little blackmail scam if you catch someone doing something they wouldn't want to go public?"

I held my breath, waiting for Simon to blast Ray with one of his EV special effects. Believe me, he has some bad stuff in his bag of tricks and could blow Ray, me and our backup crew off the deck with a look or a gesture.

Simon looked around the room. What saved us, I guess, is that there were several potential clients inside, including Dracula and his buddies, who he probably didn't want to alienate. I figure he could care less what Jerry, Flo, Richard or I thought. Ray, though, he'd wanted to pull into his EV spiderweb.

"Let's go somewhere else to discuss this, Ray. I can explain." Simon put his hand on Ray's shoulder and tried to capture his gaze. Ray was too smart for him. Even stepped away from his touch, dragging me with him. Believe me, I was happy to go.

"I'm not interested in discussing this right now. Glory and I have other guests. Mortals I need to tend to." He nodded toward Barry, who was gawking at this byplay.

"Glory, who's Tina?" Barry whispered. "What does Ray mean? Mortal?"

I looked at Richard and he stepped in and put Barry under the whammy. Could this get any messier?

"Hopefully another time, then. And I assure you the

person responsible will pay for this." Simon turned toward Greg. "Kaplan, get our capes. We're leaving."

"Simon, don't hurt Tina." I don't know why I was so worried about the twit. Maybe because I have this irrational need to preserve human life. Okay, I'm a softie.

"I'll hold off her punishment until I calm down. Will that satisfy you, Gloriana?" Simon pulled his cape around his shoulders when Greg handed it to him.

"No, I mean, you don't have to be mad to put someone on your demon's energy-sucking machine, do you?" I glanced down at the picture of me topless again. Oh, God, could I look any worse? Sure. Tina could have picked a butt shot as I'd climbed out of the pool. I took a little solace in the fact that those double Ds were perky and that some women paid big bucks for breasts that size.

Another headline caught my eye—"Titty Wars." Flo grinned and winked at me. I would *not* giggle, especially with Tina's fate hanging in the balance.

"You're right, Gloriana. Using Tina's energy would be a fitting punishment. If I take too much? C'est la vie. Thank you for the suggestion." Simon turned as if to leave.

"No, wait!" I darted in front of him. "Don't do it. Just wipe her memories of loving Ray. Make her back into an ordinary woman with the kind of simple existence of someone who goes to a job she hates and lives with her mother. Put her like she was before, except without the Israel Caine obsession. That's the best punishment, Simon. Make her ordinary. Boring. Dull."

Simon shuddered. "I can't imagine anything worse." He looked at Ray, who nodded as if this would work for him too. "Very well. Consider it done. Though I have to admit she was an interesting plaything for a while." Simon swept around me, shifted into a bat and flew into the night.

"Wow!" Nate came up behind me. "That was one scary dude."

"You'd better believe it." Greg Kaplan looked Nate over. "Nice blood type. This one must be your favorite pet,

Glory." He put on his cape. "You handled Simon pretty well. As for the cameras, you had to know he'd be watching you out there, Caine. Sorry about the tabloids, but that was a freak thing. Won't happen again. I'm sure Simon will make it up to you. Free weekend in the sunlight room." He winked at me. "Now how are you going to turn that down? Looked like you two had a pretty good time out there before Blade crashed the party." Greg shifted and flew after his boss.

"Now there was a badass vampire if I ever saw one, but Circe wouldn't have touched him with a ten-foot pole, Glory. Ugly as sin." Aggie had a glass in her hand. "She'd have liked his friend, though."

"About Circe." I couldn't stand it that she'd just strolled in here like she was ready to join the party after what she'd put us through. I wanted an explanation at the very least. And where was the apology? "What—"

"Not now, honey. We're having a party and I've got my body back and Will here to get busy with." She fluttered her eyelashes when he topped off her glass with Jack Daniel's. "I'll fill you in later. Much later. Tend to your mortals."

Sure enough, Luke, who had Sienna under the whammy again, brought her to the door and snapped his fingers.

"Is the party over?" Sienna walked over to Ray.

"Just about. You look tired." Ray smiled. "You were great tonight."

"Hey, Sienna, need a ride to your hotel? I rented a Hummer. That's how I got across the water." Barry had obviously just been snapped out of it too.

"Yes! Thanks, Barry." The singer turned to Luke. "I gave you my number, didn't I?" She rubbed her forehead. "Funny, I guess I'm more tired than I thought. Call me."

Luke leaned down to kiss her cheek. "Definitely."

I shuddered and locked eyes with Lily. If she had any say over Drac's posse, she needed to put a stop to this budding romance. She just shrugged and kept her eyes on Nathan. They called *this* a party? I wanted to take all the mortals and lock them up with Valdez guarding the door. Not that I'd be able to pry him from my side. He bumped against my knee to assure me of that.

"Give me a sec, Sienna." Barry smiled apologetically at Ray. "Sorry to crash the party and bring you down, Ray." He suddenly noticed Jerry. "Whoa, guess you guys settled things between you."

Jerry walked up and stuck out his hand. "I'm Jeremy Blade, the man beating the hell out of Ray in the picture. Glory and I used to date. Obviously I wasn't ready to give her up."

"Can I give out your name? You've got to know the tabloids are screaming at me for details." Barry whipped a notebook out of his back pocket.

"I'd rather you didn't. Glory's made her choice and I made a fool of myself. I won't say the best man won, because I'd be lying." Jerry ignored Ray's grumble. "Anyway, Caine and I have decided to act like adults. I came here tonight to prove we could be in the same room without trying to kill each other."

Barry frowned. "That's good, I guess. But don't be surprised if the paparazzi try to get pics of you with Glory. The reporters for the rags will investigate too. They'll stalk you until they get the details they need for their stories."

Jerry glanced at me. "That's crap."

"True, but that's the way it is. Ray's used to it. And all this press may seem like crap to you, but it's golden to our boy Ray here. Especially right before the Grammys."

"Not this kind of publicity, Barry. Do what you can to put a lid on it." Ray put his arm around me. "Glory's not used to it. And, for the record, I beat the hell out of Blade."

"You know I can't just kill a story like this. But be patient. Some other celeb will be caught with his pants down or her top off." Barry grinned. "Sorry, Glory."

"That's okay. I knew when I started dating Ray that I'd be in the public eye."

"That's my girl." Ray took advantage and gave me a big

kiss. Testing Jerry's temper? I eased away from him, not daring to look at Jerry.

"I'll do what I can, Ray." Barry gave me an approving look. "It would help if you two were seen together in public acting like this. You know. Lovebirds."

Ray grinned. "No problem."

"You about ready to go, Barry?" Sienna tugged on his sleeve. "I'm tired and I'm ready to get back to the hotel and a hot bath."

"I'll go with you. Barry, you don't mind dropping me at my place, do you?" Nathan stayed close to Sienna, obviously trying to keep Luke away from her.

"Not at all. I figure I've done enough here. Sorry, Ray." Barry pulled his car keys from his pocket. "Anyone else need a ride? Got plenty of room in the Hummer."

Everyone else murmured and shook their heads. We watched the three mortals leave, the mood in the room subtly changing as we no longer had to guard what we said or did.

Ray and I turned to Aggie. Jerry was suddenly on my other side and I felt his hand on my elbow. Time for a showdown.

"You've got some nerve, Aggie, showing up here dressed to party and knocking back shots of Ray's booze after what you did to us." I moved in and felt Ray grab my hand. Jerry's hand tightened on my elbow.

Aggie flicked a perfectly manicured nail at me and I felt a jolt from my head down to my toes.

"Relax, vampy, or do you *want* to play statues in front of your guests here?" The blonde, who, except for her long eyelashes, had absolutely no resemblance to the freakish sea monster we'd been dealing with for the past weeks, grinned at us.

"Come on, Aggie, spill. Why'd the storm stop? What happened with Circe?" You knew I couldn't just let this go, didn't you?

"Forget it. Now's not the time to ask me your burning

questions. Will and I are headed to his room to celebrate my return to this gorgeous bod." She ran her hands down Will's chest, and we saw him swallow and nod, obviously more than happy to oblige.

That's when the first flaming arrow hit the coffee table.

Twenty

Whap! *Whap!* *Whap!* More flaming arrows hit pieces of furniture. Which was better than hitting some of the vampires who scattered.

"What the hell?" Lily grabbed Jerry's arm while Drac and his crew grinned and ran to snatch their capes next to the front door. We could hear thuds from there, which meant it was being hit too. No easy exit that way.

Brittany ran out of the kitchen with a fire extinguisher and began futilely spraying the flames that had already consumed the table and were doing a number on the sectional sofa.

"*Mio Dio!* Let's go, *amante.* Glory, you'll shift with us, *sì?*" Flo held on to Richard and beckoned to me from across the open expanse between us that had quickly turned into a wall of flames. It was apparent, though, that anyone trying to go from one side to the other would be toast, no matter what form they shifted to. Ray and I had been stuck on the opposite wall from the others when the arrows had started flying.

"You bet your life she will. But she'll go this way." Ray answered for me, holding me back as I instinctively started forward when it seemed like the arrows had quit coming. Sometimes my instincts suck.

Whap! Whap! Whap! Round two of flaming arrows. The heat was getting intense. Ray dragged me toward the kitchen.

"Glory!" Jerry lunged for me, but Lily had him in a death grip. He too was across the great divide.

"Get out of here, Jerry. I'll meet you at the car." I shouted this above the roar and crackle of fire and the whoosh of Nate's bottle of Jack Daniel's, which went off like an incendiary bomb when the fire reached it on an end table.

"I've got her, Blade. Get the hell out of here with the others." Ray tried to pull me out of the room into the hallway leading to the kitchen but I wasn't about to go yet.

"Glory, keep Valdez with you. Leave!" Jerry's yell was in my head since there was no other way I could have heard him. The heat was almost unbearable.

"Not until you do! Stay safe. I love you." I sent him that message then looked down and realized my furry friend was dogging my steps. Sorry, blame the metaphor on smoke inhalation. I figured I'd better quit breathing. I got a glimpse of the vampires across the room shifting into bats to fly up the fireplace chimney.

"I'm going. Now get the hell out of here. I love you too." Jerry was the last to leave, shifting right after Lily did.

"There goes our girl. Now we're going to kick some hunter ass." Drac grinned at Benny and Luke, their faces glowing in the firelight. The three stood next to the front door.

"What are you waiting for? The fire's getting worse." Why did I even care if these three fried? Couldn't they see the flames licking up the walls and running up the stairs to the top floor? And feel the heat? I wasn't breathing in the heavy smoke, but it made my eyes sting and tears run down my cheeks.

"You coming with us?" I shouted over the roar of the flames. I guess I felt like I owed it to Lily to make the effort.

"We're going after Westwood. I figure this is his work." Drac pulled a mean-looking knife that Jerry would have admired out of his cape. "With any luck, this will be his last chance to take a fang. Right, boys?"

"Right. He messed with the wrong vampires this time." Ben used his ax to break out a front window, the three shifted into bats and took off.

Ray and I barely made it into the study when we heard a crash behind us.

"Valdez!" I turned and could just see dark fur under a huge wooden shelf that had fallen on top of him. "God, V, are you all right?" Books and knickknacks were scattered everywhere.

I reached for him, but the doorway was on fire and Ray jerked me back.

"Are you crazy? You can't run through those flames." Ray wrapped his arms around me.

"I'm okay, Blondie. Just stuck. Can't get a grip on this damned shelf. Listen to Ray. I'll wiggle out of here in a second."

"Don't be stupid. Shift, V. Into whatever you need to save yourself. That's an order."

"Only if you let Ray pull you into the kitchen. Go, Glory, I promise I'll meet you there. Don't want you to see me do it." He coughed and I thought I was going to knock Ray on his ass and take my chances with the flames anyway. *"Not a pretty sight."*

"Damn it, V." I wiped my eyes, almost leveling Ray when he made the mistake of trying to force me. "Be careful where you step. There's broken glass everywhere."

"Go. Before I fry my pretty ass. Just wait till you see."

"Okay. Meet me. Promise." I took one last look through the heavy smoke then ran with Ray to the kitchen.

"He'll be okay, Glory. The shifter's resourceful. He's come out of worse, hasn't he?" Ray was practically dragging me. We heard another crash behind us and I stopped in the kitchen doorway.

"Maybe we should have gone out the front with Drac and

his buds. Then Valdez wouldn't have been hurt." At least so far the flames hadn't made it to the kitchen. Brittany was there, a worried look on her face.

"What? Valdez is hurt?"

"No. I'm right here. And no way I'd take you out front with men shooting arrows out there. See, Glory, told you I'd make it." Valdez was right behind me. At least I guess it was Valdez. A dark-haired, dark-eyed stranger stood there. He was grimy and covered with soot and not much else. At least he'd tied a red towel around his waist. I took inventory. Broad shoulders. Ripped abs. Quick grin with *dimples*?

"Valdez?" I stood rooted to the spot.

"None other. Had to shift twice to get through there, but now you finally know what I look like when I'm not in dog body. Hope you can deal."

"Are you a bodyguard or not, Rafe? Seems we're in the middle of a situation here." Brittany was obviously over the worry and ready to move on. She waited by the back door.

"What ya got, Brit?"

"Seems like they're hitting the front and back. I shifted and did reconnaissance. They've got a boat and three men with crossbows on the water hitting the lake side. Guess they went out as soon as the weather cleared. The land side there's three more men armed the same way working out of a black Hummer. No sign of them here at the side door. Maybe they couldn't get access." She looked Valdez up and down. "You going cowboy again? You could use a bigger towel."

"Boss gave me permission. You find me a bigger one and I'll use it. Now let's hit it. Where're Aggie and Will? I saw them run in here when the fire started." Valdez eased open the door and crept outside a few feet to look around.

"They insisted on going ahead. Since Will didn't smell any mortals, they figured it was okay. Aggie's headed for what she called her little hideaway across the lake, and Will was going along. They shifted into dolphins or something, I guess. Aggie said she'd bring Glory and Ray up to speed later, if they lived through the attack. Her words, not mine."

Brittany grabbed Valdez's shoulder. "I hear something. Get back in here."

"What you hear are sirens, Brit." Valdez looked back and we could all feel the heat and noise from the fire getting worse. "We definitely need to get the hell out of here right now. I figure one of the neighbors called this in. Sirens will send Westwood running. Doubt he wants an arson charge to deal with." He grinned and I swear I saw something of my old pal in his eyes. "Man, do I hope Drac and crew get the jump on him and bring Blade a trophy."

"Yeah, well. If you're sure we've got an all clear, Valdez, let's get downstairs. I can hear whiskey bottles exploding in the bar. That's too damned close. Come on, Glory." Ray grabbed my hand and pulled me along.

Valdez took point, Brittany guarded the rear. I was on autopilot, stuck safely in the middle. I know. Where was my kick-butt attitude? Ray's house was going up in flames behind me. A freak with an arrow could pop up out of nowhere at any moment and yet all I could think about was the man in front of me with a towel flapping in the breeze showing off a buff butt. Yep, he did have bragging rights on that ass. This was crazy. Valdez was my friend. We'd lived together for five freakin' years. This—sorry, but I had to call it like I saw it—*stud* couldn't be *my* Valdez.

We got to the bottom of the stairs and I realized the other three were staring at me.

"What?"

"Don't suppose you'd consider doing the bat thing, Glory?" Ray put his hand on my shoulder.

"No, don't even ask her." Valdez gave Ray a firm look. "She has a hard time shifting back. It stresses her out."

"Thanks, V. Not sure I could shift right now if I wanted to. Achy did something to me . . ." Ray and Valdez stared and I shrugged. "Never mind. I survived, but it took a lot out of me. If it's the only way, I'll give it a go."

Valdez looked back at the burning house. "We've got some time. There are other options."

"What about the boat?" Not my favorite mode of trans-portation, but it was fast.

"Afraid not. Look." Ray pointed and I saw that the Storm God's temper fit had left the boat battered and full of water.

I could hear sirens getting closer. "You think we could flag down a fire truck?" I gasped when windows exploded above us.

"Westwood's guys could still be lurking out there with orders to shoot you on sight. I'm sure they've all been prepped with your picture, Blondie. I'm not willing to take that chance." Valdez was constantly looking around, just like he always did, I guess. It was just more obvious in his human form.

"Right. 'Cause I'm the vampire he *really* hates. Thanks for reminding me, V."

"He hates all vampires, Glory. Don't think this is all about you." Valdez glanced at Ray. "I'm sure he'd love to collect Caine's fangs."

"Not going to happen. Looks like we walk or swim out." I know which option I preferred.

"Forget walking. The high security fence is one reason I rented this place. So the paparazzi couldn't get in. And now we can't get out. There's razor wire and glass on top of those rock fences. The people that own this place had a child kid-napping scare before they moved here." Ray frowned up at the blaze that was so close we were sweating. "Hope they have the place fully insured."

"If they don't, you'll have to make good on it. You can af-ford it." I smiled to take the sting out of that. The heat, the sparks drifting down from above and then the windows that kept exploding now from the second floor, made where we were headed obvious.

"It's going to be a total loss." Ray took my hand. "Okay, Glory. Guess you're going to have to get wet again."

"Of course. That's all I do around you. Since I don't have a life jacket, maybe you'll keep me from drowning." I didn't look for Valdez's reaction. Somehow the human Valdez was a lot tougher to face. The dog version would just growl or show teeth. This guy . . . Well, he'd just have to accept that Ray was a strong swimmer and I . . . wasn't. So we'd be cozy in the water. I glanced at Brittany.

"Brit, would you fly up and see if Westwood's boat is gone first? Please?"

"Sure, Glory. No problem." Brittany shifted into hawk form as casually as I changed from black to brown shoes. Amazing. She was back in less than two minutes while we swatted away burning embers and huddled under the edge of the boat house.

"The boat's gone. No sign of it. Looks like you guys can swim down just a few hundred yards and climb out onto a grassy slope. It should put you not too far from where Rafe said you left Blade's car."

Rafe. Right. Rafael Valdez. At least the first name was his. The last name was the same for all my dogs. Shape-shifters. Not really dogs. I had a knot in the pit of my stomach and it had nothing to do with the fact that I was going to have to jump into Lake Travis for the umpteenth time.

"Okay, so we swim for it, but listen up." I forgot and took a breath, coughing when I inhaled smoke. When I could finally speak, I looked at Valdez. "Sorry, but I do not want to see *this* Valdez come out of the water sans towel. I know it's a lot to ask, bud, but it's back into dog body for you."

"No! Glory, you're kidding, right?" Brittany put her hand on Valdez's really nice bicep. "Give the guy a break."

"I get it, Brit." Valdez grinned, showing me those dimples. "Blondie and I have to live together for another year. She's not comfortable with me like this."

"You got that right." Flames blew out the back door above us with a bang that made me wince. "Kiss Brit goodbye. Come on, Ray. Don't let me drown." I headed down the dock. Okay, I know I was being a bitch, but I was having a hell of a night. And Valdez the hunk was behind me laying a kiss on Brittany that looked to be world-class. Why was that twisting my gut?

"Glory, wait." Ray caught up with me. "Be careful of the rocks. This isn't like the pool or even when you went overboard in the lake before."

"Oh, great. Way to make me feel better, Ray." I looked back at the conflagration, at what had once had been a beautiful home, and tears filled my eyes. "Damn, Westwood! Ray, your piano, everything's being destroyed. This is terrible."

"Hell, it's just stuff." Ray pulled me close. "At least no one was hurt."

"Good attitude, Caine. I'm sure Glory's suitably impressed. Now let's get the hell out of here." Valdez was back in a form I could live with. He woofed and jumped off the end of the dock, landing with a splash that gave me a preview of how cold and wet I was going to be in a moment. Swell.

Ray gave Valdez a go-to-hell look. "For the record, I meant what I just said. Now let's go. Me first. Then, Glory, you come in after me." Ray cursed when sparks suddenly ignited the roof of the boat house. "Now I'm mad as hell. Some stuff I'm pretty attached to. I don't know what Benny was planning with his ax, but if he doesn't get to Westwood first, that bastard's mine." Ray coughed as clouds of smoke billowed out toward the lake. "Brittany?"

"I'm shifting and flying above you guys as lookout. Any problems at the place where you want to come out, I'll dive-bomb Valdez and head you off."

"Good idea." Ray dragged me close to the edge of the dock then reached for my skirt.

"What do you think you're doing?" I swatted at his hand. "This is a stupid time for a pass."

"I'm always up for a pass. But this time I'm trying to keep you from drowning. Your skirt looks stretchy. If it gets caught around your knees, you won't be able to swim. So pull it up." Ray kicked off his shoes.

"Sorry, I get it." I pulled my skirt up until it was little more than a wide belt. "Hey, take off your pants if you need to. Won't embarrass me." Overhead, a hawk shrieked her agreement.

"Not necessary. Here goes." Ray dove off the dock, then appeared beside Valdez. "Come on, Glory, jump."

So I held my nose and threw myself into the water. Damn, but that water was cold. And I swear something slimy crawled up my leg. Then Ray had me, his arm around my waist as he swam us along the shoreline. We saw strobe lights at his house and I realized the fire trucks had finally arrived just in time to watch the second floor collapse in a shower of sparks and with a roar that could probably be heard for miles.

I bet the paparazzi were there snapping pictures, hoping to get Ray and me running naked from the flames. Or, even better, the firemen dragging our charred bodies from the rubble.

"Quit muttering about those damned paparazzi." Ray's arm was rock solid around me. "The firemen will keep them back and we've dodged them."

"It's just wrong that they hope to make news out of a tragedy."

Ray kissed the top of my head. "No tragedy, babe. I'm okay. So are you. Even the boat can be replaced. And, look, we can get out of the water now. You beat Westwood again."

"You're right, Ray. I should be singing."

He laughed as we practically crawled out across the blessedly grassy slope. "No, you promised to spare me. I'll sing for you later. Maybe write a new song about this. After some healing sleep. Right now my throat's raw from that smoke."

"Yeah, mine too." And I was beyond cold. I pulled down my soaked skirt and picked my way through mud and rocks, ignoring Ray's curse when he found a few sharp stones with his bare feet. Valdez walked on my other side and, when Brittany appeared, we were all glad to stop for a breather.

"Blade and Lily are next to his car, just a few hundred yards down the way. You guys okay?" She put her hand on Valdez's shoulder.

"We're cold, wet, Ray's homeless, and his voice is temporarily cooked, but other than that we're great." I heard my own bitterness and sighed. "Sorry, Brittany. What time is it anyway?"

"Time for you to die, vampire."

We all froze for an instant, just long enough to see the man emerge from the shadows, a crossbow in his hand. He had it aimed at my heart of course. Because Brent Westwood had had me on his most-wanted list for a long time.

I sent Ray and Valdez mental messages. *"I'm okay. Don't try to be heroes."*

My answer? Twin growls of rage. I put out my hands to try to physically restrain them. Yeah, like that would work. They did stay put temporarily. Probably trying to figure out a plan of attack that wouldn't get me skewered in the process.

"Westwood. Cool plan tonight. Too bad all you managed to do is start a very expensive bonfire." I kept my chin up and my voice steady. Good for me.

"You telling me not one monster fried?" Westwood sneered. "That's okay. I was just flushing them out anyway. I want my trophies, you know. Let me see your pretty fangs, vampire."

"Don't you know anything, vampire hunter? My fangs only come down when I smell mortal blood. Come closer and I bet they'll slide right down." I snarled for effect.

"What if I peg the dog there? Bet his blood would get you going." He swung his crossbow to aim it at Valdez and I could see his finger tightening on the trigger.

I didn't think, just sprang, leaping the thirty feet between us before Westwood could get off the shot. I didn't have time to savor the look of shock on his face as I jerked the crossbow from his hands and aimed it at his heart.

"Big mistake, Westwood, threatening my friends." I felt Brittany, Ray and Valdez at my back, but none of them touched me. I guess they realized this was my fight.

"You and your friends are dead, vampire." Westwood laughed, obviously a few cans short of a six-pack. "You don't think I was stupid enough to come alone, do you?"

"Maybe you didn't start out alone, but you are now." The voice coming out of the dark was smug. "Sorry, asshole, but your backup guys were easy takedowns. Just like you're gonna be. Take him, Glory."

I didn't think I could do it. Just kill a mortal in cold blood like that. I saw the necklace around Brent Westwood's neck with more than a dozen pairs of fangs. One set had belonged to MacTavish, a man I'd admired. Still I hesitated. Westwood obviously sensed it and suddenly tried to grab my hand. When he screamed, I realized I'd pulled the trigger.

"You got him, Glory!" Drac's cackle of triumph made me shudder.

I handed someone the crossbow and turned my face to Ray's chest. I was glad Westwood was finally dead, but wasn't sticking around for a victory dance. I heard Drac, Benny and Luke talking about the reward Blade had offered.

"Think he'll give it to you, Glory?" Benny wanted to know.

"I'm not interested." Somehow Ray had gotten me a few feet away from the body sprawled on the ground. "If you guys can clean up the, uh, scene, you can have whatever Jerry's offering." Jerry. Yes, I needed to see him. Ray's arms tightened around me and I realized he'd read my thoughts.

"Come on, Glory. It's been a rough night. Let's go. We've got only about an hour until the sun comes up." Ray carefully kept me away from Dracula's celebration. The smell of fresh blood did have my fangs down, but my stomach heaved. I felt Valdez's warm presence beside me and dug my fingers into his fur. Maybe I should be dancing around Westwood's remains. Instead, my legs felt limp and I stumbled. Ray swung me up and into his arms.

"Brittany, can you make sure . . ."

"Yeah, boss, but send Drac's girlfriend if you can. Lily? She'll know what to do about cleaning up this mess. The car's that way, just a hundred yards or so down that hill, then up again. Can't miss it. She's there with Blade."

I closed my eyes, tired to the bone.

"Come on, Glory girl. I think you're in shock. Valdez, you know where we're going. Lead the way." Ray carried me and I was glad to let him. I heard splashing and realized he was wading through water. The low-water crossing. Almost there. I finally opened my eyes and saw the SUV and Jerry standing there. Lily stood beside him.

"You can put me down now, Ray. Thanks. I guess I *was* in shock. That whole thing was pretty intense." I kissed his cheek.

"Anytime you need me, babe. I'm here." Ray eased me to my feet.

I turned and Jerry was right there.

"What happened? You look—"

"Please don't finish that sentence. It'll only make me feel worse." I reached up and patted his cheek, then looked at his daughter. "Lily, Drac and his crew have hit the jackpot. Brittany's with them. Valdez, would you take Lily back to the scene?"

"Sure thing, Blondie." Valdez bumped against me. *"You okay now? You scared the hell out of me."*

"Yep. We're survivors, aren't we? I guess I'd better quit calling you puppy." I smiled and, out of habit, rubbed his ear.

"I don't mind. It grew on me." He wagged his tail and loped off. Lily gave me a searching look, then hurried after him.

It didn't take long to bring Jerry up to speed. He cursed, gathered me into his arms, and I think I even saw his eyes gleam. My Scotsman close to tears? Impossible. Must have been the moonlight. Finally, I could tell he wanted to go see Westwood for himself, but I made it clear that I'd seen enough of that horror show. He wasn't about to leave me— especially alone with Ray.

"Hey, give me the car keys. I'll drive Glory home. You can shift for yourself. Right, Blade?" Ray was all for taking the car and *me* himself. Valdez and Brittany were back, glad to leave clean up duties in Lily's experienced hands.

"Never mind. I'll hear all about it from Dracula tomorrow night." Jerry helped me into the car.

"Ray and Brittany are going to need a safe place to stay tonight, Jerry." I knew it would take a while to get arrangements made. "My place is pretty small."

Ray grinned. "We've slept together before, Glory. No big deal. Right, Blade?"

"Forget it. Come to my house. I have spare rooms. All of you come to my house. Get in the car." Jerry opened the back door. "Glory and I sleep together and it *is* a big deal. Right, Glory?" He winked at me. Yep, *Jerry* winked. Don't you love male competition?

"I'm in shock. So I think I'll just sit here and keep my mouth shut." I picked up my purse from the floorboard and handed Ray my cell phone. "Ray, call Nate and let him know you're okay. Have him call your parents. If they see on the news that your house burned down, they'll worry themselves sick. And get him to call Barry too. To prepare a press release. Just that we got out all right and we're staying with friends."

"Look at you, Glory. Thinking like a rock star's fiancée every minute." Ray reached between the seats and squeezed my shoulder.

"She won't be your fiancée for long, Caine. You're about to be dumped on your rock-star ass." Jerry started the car and backed out of the driveway.

"If she does it right after my house burned down, she'll look like a heartless bitch. The tabloids will have a field day." Ray punched in some numbers. "Hey, Nate. You get Sienna home okay? Good. Listen. Bad news . . ."

I tuned out the rest of the conversation and turned to Jerry as he headed home. "You know Ray's right. I can't break off the engagement right now. It should wait a while. At least until he's set up in a new place."

"And how long will that take?" Jerry frowned and reached over to wipe what was probably mud from my cheek. "I'm stopping at your apartment. You need some dry clothes. But hurry. The sun will be coming up soon."

"Not long. Ray was leasing. Nate found the last place fairly fast. Then he had to get the black-out shades installed in the master bedroom."

"Be quicker to let him sleep in a closet." Jerry took my hand and laid it on his thigh.

"We have to stay together at least until after the Grammys." Ray handed me my cell phone. "You *are* going to the Grammys with me, aren't you, Glory?"

Okay, I admit this was a big deal for me. How cool to go to the biggest music-awards event of the year as Ray's fiancée. And of course Jerry saw my reaction.

"She wants to go. And wear a fancy dress that you'll pay for, Caine."

I looked at Jerry. Yeah, that's why I loved the guy. Sometimes he actually paid attention at the right times.

"Of course." Ray grinned. "We'll have to spend about a week in L.A. That's why I'd given my mortal bodyguards this week off. So they'd be ready for the marathon of that week. Good thing they weren't there tonight." He shook his head. "Hey, good news, though. Now that Westwood's out of the picture, Glory won't need her own bodyguard."

"*Forget it, Caine.*" Valdez spoke from the third seat, which he shared with Brittany. "*Where Glory goes, I go. There are other dangers besides Westwood. L.A.'s full of creeps.*" Valdez managed to slap a paw on Ray's shoulder. "*So's Austin.*" He smiled at me, and for the first time I noticed that even his dog face had dimples.

Blade pulled up in front of my shop. It was close to dawn and he would barely have time to get back to his house. I knew what we should do and made the decision.

"I'm getting out and staying here. Jerry, you take Ray to your house. Brittany, you and Valdez come with me. Jerry, I'll see you and Ray tomorrow night. If we don't hear from Will and Aggie, somebody's going to have to fly to Aggie's cave and find out what happened with the Circe/Storm God deal."

"Glory, wait." Jerry jumped out while Brittany and Valdez were climbing out of the car. Ray didn't bother to argue. I figure he was as tired as the rest of us and knew he could count on clean clothes at Jerry's.

I stopped wearily in front of my shop, for once not even caring that there were a couple of customers inside and that Lacy was making a sale.

"Don't you dare kiss me out here, Jerry. Paparazzi could be hiding in the bushes and I don't need any more bad press." I backed up until I was next to the security code box and punched in numbers. Valdez and Brittany waited until I was safely inside, then came in with me. Jerry pushed in before I could close the door.

"Now can I kiss you?" He smiled down at me.

"You'd better." I reached for him, needing to feel his mouth on mine. It had been one of the longest nights of my life. He smelled like smoke and I'm sure I smelled like that and lake water too. Neither of us cared. I held on to him for a moment and just absorbed his strength because mine seemed to have seeped out on a slope next to the lake when I'd gotten way too familiar with a crossbow.

"Hurry home and don't let the sun catch you." I hugged him, then pushed him out the door. "See you tomorrow. And don't kill Ray between now and then."

"No promises there." He smiled and strutted, yes, strutted to the car. Ray was up front, totally ignoring him. Oh, yes, they made a fine-looking pair. But I knew which one owned my heart.

I headed up the stairs, two shifters waiting for me patiently. They could shower after I slept, so I hurriedly got rid of all my stenches and dropped like a rock into bed.

Twenty-one

"I know you said no more food in your shop, Glory, but these are by way of an apology." Ellen laid the plastic bin on the counter. "I realize those last cookies were horrible. Because I was so worried about Tina."

"Why?" I lifted the lid and inhaled. Blueberry, white chocolate chunk cookies. Heavenly. I slipped one out and surreptitiously dropped it into Valdez's mouth. Because you knew he'd followed Ellen to the counter and parked himself beside me when he'd seen the tub she was carrying.

"Oh, she'd been working out of town. I hadn't heard word one from her for over a week." Ellen sighed. "But she's back now. Got her old job back. She's even dating an accountant at work. It's weird, though." She leaned over. "Stop that! Glory, your dog is trying to bite the lid off the cookie container."

"Oh, bad dog!" I grabbed the carton and stuck it in a drawer. "Well, as long as Tina's happy . . . What's weird about that?" She was lucky to be alive. I was actually surprised Simon had kept his word.

"She's lost all interest in Israel Caine. Won't even help me with your MySpace page." Ellen sighed. "She's boring!"

"Lots of mothers wish they could say that, Ellen." I looked up when the bells over the door signaled a new arrival. Flo hurried inside with two bags from Nordstrom. No one had ever called my best friend boring.

"I guess you're right."

"Glory! You must see these shoes I bought." Flo looked Ellen over. "Latest spring styles. One pair may work for my honeymoon. This will be number twelve with Ricardo I think. We go to an island this time. I love Capri, don't you?" Flo focused on Ellen again and frowned.

"Oh, I'd better go." Ellen had the faintly overwhelmed look mortals sometimes got around Flo. Maybe my BFF was doing a little mind control. She had a bad habit of sending mental messages to mortals. Nothing like the power of suggestion . . .

"Thanks for the cookies." I walked Ellen to the door, then hurried back to Flo. "And thanks for the rescue. I just wanted to know if Tina was alive or dead. After that, forget her."

"I hear you, girlfriend. Now look at these shoes."

"Let's take them in the back, in case a customer comes in." I turned to Bri, who had already pulled out the cookies and was dividing them with Valdez. "Bri, will you handle the front for a while?"

"Sure, Glory. You girls have fun. The V-man and I are busy here." All this was said around a mouthful of cookie.

"I need a drink." I headed for the back and the refrigerator I kept stocked with synthetic.

"Still off the hunting?" Flo pulled a shoebox out of her bag.

"Definitely. I can barely get this down after the other night and what happened with Westwood. I don't think I'm a normal vampire." I took a swig of B positive and wrinkled my nose. "Whatever a normal vampire is supposed to be."

"I cheer you up, *mia amica*. See my Balenciaga gladiator sandals. A new color. The next big thing. *Sì?*" Flo lifted them carefully out of the box. "And look, a new magazine. I finally find the perfect dress for you as maid of honor. I listen. You want slenderizing, no? This is black. *Perfetto!*"

We amused ourselves for the next ten minutes with shoes and wedding plans.

"The new council members will be groomsmen. I'm still working on who else I should ask to be a bridesmaid."

"What do you mean 'new' council members? What happened to the old ones? And why didn't they show up the night of the storm?"

"Pah. Because they were stupid, macho men who cared more about which headphones to buy than about their duties." Flo carefully laid her bridal magazine on the table. "That's why Damie fired them. They spent so long arguing over the best ones to buy in the stereo store that they didn't arrive at Israel's poor house until the fire trucks did. Which reminds me . . ." Flo gave me one of her looks that meant she had an agenda.

"What?" I sat on the oak table while she settled into the chair.

"Spill, Glory. What's it like living with Israel?"

"Hard on Jerry, of course. He has to shift and come in on the roof while Ray's practicing at the studio with Sienna." I finished off my synthetic and headed to the bathroom to rinse out the bottle. "He hates it, but it was the logical thing to do after the fire."

"No house for Israel yet?" Flo admired her new sandals, which she hadn't yet taken off.

"No, and I don't think Nate's really looking. With the Grammys coming up, he's busy with the logistics of getting us out there. Ray's in your old room, and you couldn't blast Valdez off the foot of my bed. He's in serious bodyguard mode."

Flo looked up, her dark eyes gleaming. "And how is that? Now that you've seen our Rafael as a man."

"Strange." I dumped the bottle in the recycle bin and sat

on the table again. "He was really good-looking. And, of course, we're such great friends. I mean he knows *everything* about me. Even more than you do, Flo."

"Now I'm hurt. You confide in him, *mia amica*? Am I not your best friend?"

"Of course. But you didn't live with me for five years when I was a dancer in Las Vegas. Or help me go through some problems there. Never mind."

"You won't tell me?" Flo leaned forward. "You block your thoughts. Was it a man?"

"No, money." I really didn't want to get into this.

"Pah! I won't pry then. Money comes and goes. This I understand. I have had my little emergencies. That's why I keep a stash of good jewelry in a special place in Roma. Not even my Ricardo knows this. I never be poor again, I tell you. That diamond from Israel? Keep it, girlfriend. I don't care if this was a pretend engagement. It's your future. Hide it somewhere safe."

"I couldn't—" I was seeing a hard edge in my friend's eyes I hadn't seen in a while.

"Yes, you could. We have to look out for ourselves, Glory."

"She's right." Suddenly there were three of us in the room. With the same shimmering light trick the Storm God had used, Aggie materialized in front of me. The beautiful, blond Aggie, not Swamp Thing Aggie.

"*Mio Dio!*" Flo leaped up, fangs down. "What the hell are you?"

"Relax, Flo. You guys weren't formally introduced at Ray's party. Meet Aglaophonos, also known as Aggie the Awful. The Siren who almost fed Will, Ray and me to Circe."

Flo snarled. "I should tear out your throat. Right after you tell me where you got those boots."

Aggie laughed. "Little boutique in Capri. I have to do my shopping fairly near water. It's a Siren thing. Good for me Austin is full of lakes, rivers and creeks."

"Your Siren thing almost got me killed." I had to admit her brown leather boots were gorgeous. Hey, her whole outfit, from tan suede jacket to moss green velvet mini looked to be designer fabulous. Didn't hurt that Aggie had one of those perfect bodies—size four or less—and the kind of big blue eyes and long blond hair that probably made men willingly crash on rocks just to get a close-up look.

"Almost doesn't count." Aggie was keeping an eye on Flo. "Hey, relax, lady. I won't hurt your friend now. I came here in peace."

"Say the word, Glory, and we—" Flo was frozen, just like that.

"Uh-oh. Don't think you should have done that, Aggie." I could see Flo's eyes darting around, looking for escape. I knew the feeling. A quick read of her mind was a lesson in Italian profanity.

"She was threatening me, Glory. I had to defend myself." Aggie looked down at her freshly manicured nails.

I was having a hard time matching this woman with the slimy creature in the lake. "Just tell me something. Why did the storm stop the other night?"

"Circe left the area." Aggie grinned. "You guys really came through. First Casanova flies over, all hot to hit your party. Circe said he even had *your* picture on his cell phone, Glory. You dodged a bullet there, vampy."

"I wish I could have at least met the man. With his reputation . . ." I winked at Flo, who was thinking some *really* evil thoughts.

"Better you didn't. Even Circe is having a hard time roasting him. Something about how he's equipped." Aggie looked over her shoulder. "Keep thinking she's going to pop out somewhere and shoot a lightning bolt at me or turn me green, but Achy says she really has left the area, gone back to the Med where she belongs." Aggie looked wistful for a moment.

"Anyway, the goddess is a slut if you ask me. Always after

handsome men. I don't think they're in hell at all. Unless servicing her is part of the fiery package. The other two vamps she nabbed were just as good-looking." Aggie shuddered. "Wouldn't want to meet either of them in a dark alley, though. You should have seen the knives they were carrying. Circe better watch her backside with those two."

"So I've heard." I really hated to see Flo in statue mode. She was almost quivering, her eyes were darting frantically as she tried to break free. I sent her a mental message to give it up, that she was wasting her energy. Not that I expected her to believe me.

"Thanks to you and Ray, Glory, Circe was satisfied, Achy was satisfied and I'm back in business." Aggie flipped her hair back behind her shoulders. "Out of my ugly suit and back to what you see here." She grinned and did a model's strut around the room.

"And Charlie? The lover that started it all?"

"I told Circe to keep that rat bastard. Achy told me he'd been cheating on me with my Siren sisters. I checked it out and it was true. I finally figured out I deserve someone better. A guy like Will." Aggie sighed. "He's such a hottie."

"Great story. Now release my friend. She's going nuts." I put my hand on Flo's shoulder.

"She'd better not go after me again. I can freeze her little butt permanently. You could use her to display clothes in your front window." Aggie picked up a vintage mink hat and pulled it on. "Fun stuff here. I think I'll shop before I leave." She reached for the door.

"Aggie . . ."

"Okay." She waved a hand and Flo collapsed, falling into a chair. "Behave, vampy. Listen to Glory about what I can do. And, sister? I bought those sandals last year. In Italia, vampy." She opened the door, then slammed it behind her.

"*Quella femmina, diavola.*" Flo jumped up, staggered, then fell into the chair again. "What she do to me, I not do to my worst enemy." She looked at her sandals and a big, fat tear ran down her cheeks. "Last season? No, it cannot be."

"She lied. I could see it in her face. Couldn't read her mind, though. The woman's a bitch."

"That's what I said." Flo sat up straight. "Of course she lied. She's a manipulator. I should know. I am the best. That statue trick. We should try to learn it from her. And she is still in our lake. Hah! She's obviously in big trouble with her boss. Sirens should be in the big waters, not in little lakes. This Siren is here to be punished." Flo smiled and reached down to unbuckle the straps on her sandals. "We will use this Aggie person to our advantage, Glory. Not the other way around. Oops. Your cell phone ringing in the other room."

There was a knock on the door and I opened it to find Bri with my cell in her hand. "It's been ringing and now I think you have voice mail. I'm sorry, I would have brought it to you sooner, but I was helping a customer." She waved a hand toward Aggie, who was actually building a nice stack of clothes on the counter. Hmm. I could overlook obnoxious if it could make me a profit.

"Thanks, Bri. I'll check my messages." I turned to Flo, who was heading out the back door. "Wait, are you sure that's safe?"

"No worries. Westwood's taken care of and Richard's in the car waiting for me. Call your man back. I bet it's Jeremiah looking for you. Oh, and when you have your dress for the Grammys, call me. I want to see it. We can pick out the perfect shoes together. This Aggie person. She is pretty. I think I ask her to be bridesmaid. *Ciao*." Flo waved and headed out.

I shook my head, no longer surprised at anything Flo said, then checked my voice mail. Yep, it was Jerry. He was upstairs. Waiting for me. Ray was at the studio. Valdez was to remain in the shop and we had the apartment all to ourselves. Why wasn't I up there with the man who had always appreciated my curves and couldn't wait to get his hands on them? Why not indeed?

But I still had a few issues with the delicious Mr. Blade.

I hit speed dial on my cell and told Jerry to meet me on the roof for a little surprise. Then I loaded my water cannon.

Sorry, but you don't trot out the "My mother was right about you all along" slam and go unpunished, buster. And then, hey, I was tired of being the only one wet around here. Ya know?